SILENCE
IN THE **DARK**

Books by Patricia Bradley

LOGAN POINT

Shadows of the Past
A Promise to Protect
Gone without a Trace
Silence in the Dark

LOGAN POINT ■4

SILENCE
IN THE DARK

A NOVEL

PATRICIA
BRADLEY

Revell

a division of Baker Publishing Group
Grand Rapids, Michigan

© 2016 by Patricia Bradley

Published by Revell
a division of Baker Publishing Group
P.O. Box 6287, Grand Rapids, MI 49516-6287
www.revellbooks.com

Printed in the United States of America

Library of Congress Cataloging-in-Publication Data
Names: Bradley, Patricia (Educator), author.
Title: Silence in the dark : a novel / Patricia Bradley.
Description: Grand Rapids, MI : Published by Revell a division of Baker Publishing
    Group, [2016] | Series: Logan Point ; 4
Identifiers: LCCN 2015047414 | ISBN 9780800724184 (paper)
Subjects: | GSAFD: Christian fiction. | Mystery fiction. | Suspense fiction.
Classification: LCC PS3602.R34275 S55 2016 | DDC 813/.6—dc23
LC record available at http://lccn.loc.gov/2015047414

This book is a work of fiction. Names, characters, places, and incidents are the product of the author's imagination or are used fictitiously.

16 17 18 19 20 21 22   7 6 5 4 3 2 1

The LORD himself goes before you and will be with you;
he will never leave you nor forsake you.

Deuteronomy 31:8

Prologue

Ten-year-old Bailey Adams huddled with the Carver twins on Cassie's bed. They'd given up pretending Cassie and Jem's parents weren't arguing or that their dad wasn't drunk. Bailey avoided their eyes, knowing how embarrassed they were. "Maybe I should just go home."

Jem shook her head. "No, stay. He'll go to sleep soon, and tomorrow it'll be like nothing ever happened."

Cassie threw back the blanket. "I'm going to tell them to stop!"

Jem grabbed at her arm and missed. "You'll just make it worse."

"I don't care. I can't stand it anymore."

She wasn't gone five minutes when it sounded like firecrackers exploding in the living room. And screams.

"No! Don't shoot!"

Another boom.

Silence.

Jem jumped from the bed. "Cassie! I have to go help her!"

"No! He might shoot you."

"My daddy wouldn't hurt me. You climb out the window and go next door to Mr. Arnold's house and call the police." Jem ran out of the room.

Bailey's thumping heart jerked in her chest as she turned and stared at the open window.

Another gunshot bolted her into action as footsteps stomped down the hallway. She climbed through the window and ran for all she was worth to the neighbor's.

■ ■ ■

A week later at the funeral home, Bailey slipped away from the room where three caskets lined the wall. Every time she heard someone say how lucky she was, her insides cringed at how she'd run away. Why did she live and Cassie and Jem and their mother have to die? What if she'd stayed and tried to talk to Mr. Carver? Maybe he would have listened and the twins would still be alive. She should have stayed . . . but sweat ran down her back just thinking about it.

She found the washroom and hunkered down in one of the stalls. She didn't think she could face one more person. The restroom door opened, and Agnes Baker's nasally voice filled the room.

"Such a pity."

Just her luck to be caught in the same room with the worst busybody in Logan Point.

"I know. I heard he started drinking and lost his company and that gorgeous house."

"Really? I hadn't heard that."

"They say he was gambling too. Christine Carver was a saint. And those two beautiful girls. Only ten years old and so sweet and innocent."

Correction. Maude Arnold was the worst busybody. Bailey just hoped they didn't want the stall she was in.

"Well, I've heard that God only takes the best," Agnes said.

"Explains why the Adams girl survived without a scratch."

"Maude, you shouldn't say things like that. And you certainly don't joke about it."

Bailey's cheeks burned as she stared down at her Mary Jane shoes.

"Well, it's true," Maude snapped. "Don't you remember when she hid my keys in Vacation Bible School? And wouldn't tell where they were until I threatened to paddle her? That girl gets into more trouble—"

Bailey flung the stall door open. "Excuse me."

"Bailey! I didn't mean—"

She glared up at Maude. "Yes, you did. You don't think I'm good enough to go to heaven."

She walked out of the washroom, her head held high.

But what if Maude was right?

What if she wasn't good enough?

1

Bailey Adams lifted the 9mm Smith & Wesson and aimed at the water bottle nestled in a bank twenty-five yards away. She squeezed the trigger. The bottle jumped in the air, and she fired again, hitting it once more.

"Bueno!" Elena clapped.

Bailey lifted her eyebrows. "English, please." Her smile took the sting out of the words.

"Very good. How did you get so good?"

She aimed again. "My dad taught me to shoot when I was fifteen."

Too bad he hadn't taught her earlier—maybe Jem and Cassie would still be alive. Her breath hitched. Where did that come from? She hadn't thought of the twins in years. The gun wavered, the weight too heavy to hold up, and she lowered her hand. She tried to lick her lips, but her mouth had turned to cotton.

"Are you all right?"

She glanced down at the gun. Would she have run away if . . . She shook her head as if to break free of the memory. Woulda,

11

coulda, shoulda did nothing but keep the memory alive. "Yeah. Now it's your turn."

Her friend eyed her but took the gun Bailey held out. Once another plastic bottle was in place, Elena quickly shredded it.

"Very good yourself," Bailey said.

Elena tilted her head. "You are a strange missionary. You handle a gun like a pistolero, yet you let Father Horatio run you out of the valley. Why?"

Bailey skittered her gaze away from the question in Elena's eyes. *Because running is what I do.* She holstered the gun. "I think it's time to head back. Miguel is probably ready to leave, and it'll take at least thirty minutes to reach your village if we take the lower trail back."

"Sí. It was kind of Miguel to allow you to come along on his visit to his family."

That's what she liked about Elena. She didn't push subjects Bailey didn't want to discuss. They hiked in silence along the trail, Bailey admiring the emerald mountain vistas when a clearing allowed an occasional view of the river below. The rest of the time, she mentally ran through her litany of excuses for not staying: it just wasn't working out . . . she caused more harm than good . . . she was needed at the church school in Chihuahua. Excuses were something else she was good at.

No excuse covered the fact that she hadn't worked hard enough. If she had, a way would have been found for her to stay. They rounded a bend on the trail, and Bailey caught her breath. Not twenty yards from where she stood, bright flowers dotted a plot of ground. Reds, purples, all colors. Her heart pounded in her throat. Poppies. Mexican opium poppies.

Elena pulled on her arm. "It is not good for us to be here. Come. Quickly."

Bailey nodded. But as she turned to leave, a man stepped from the rows. His eyes widened when he saw her, then narrowed. She stared, transfixed by his intense blue eyes. Elena pulled harder. "Run," she hissed.

He started toward them. "Hey! *Qué haces?*"

Bailey turned and ran the way she'd come. Minutes later, the whine of a four-wheeler split the air. He was coming after them. The trail forked, and she followed Elena on the narrower path.

"This way," Elena said as she branched off again on an even smaller foot trail.

Thank goodness her friend knew this area. They half-ran and half-stumbled on the overgrown path until they reached the edge of the village. Bailey collapsed against a scrub oak. "Do you think he'll find us?"

Elena sank beside her. "I doubt he will look. He probably wasn't even coming after us—there are so many poppy fields around here, if they chased everyone who stumbled across one, they wouldn't have time to do anything else. He probably was going to check on another plot."

"When did the farmers start growing poppies?"

Elena shrugged. "A few years ago. At first it was only one or two farms, but now probably half the farmers in the village have poppy fields."

Bailey had no idea it had gotten that bad in the village. "Did you see the man? He didn't look like a farmer to me."

"No. I was running too hard."

"He was an Anglo."

"You must be mistaken. Gringos do not come to the poppy fields."

A shiver crawled down Bailey's spine. She knew what she saw and would never forget the cold stare he'd fixed on her with eyes the color of blue ice. "I think we should report the field."

Elena's fingers clamped her wrist like a vise. "Do you want to get me killed?"

"Of course not." Bailey struggled for an answer. The villagers never viewed growing marijuana in the light of others being harmed. It was a way to feed their families and that was all that mattered to them, especially when Father Horatio encouraged it. She didn't realize so many had switched from marijuana to opium.

"Then you will say nothing?"

She held Elena's wide-eyed gaze. With a sigh, she said, "Let me think about it."

Bailey would say nothing for now. The poppy field wasn't going anywhere, and it would be a few weeks before the opium could be harvested. When she came back from the States, she would report it anonymously, and no one would be the wiser.

Elena hugged her. "I wish you didn't have to leave so soon."

"Me too. I miss Valle Rojo."

"You had the best tea parties, and I learned so much at the computer classes. I miss your teaching."

"But not me?" Bailey teased.

"Of course, but it is easier when you are not here to . . ." Her friend frowned. *"Tu pincha mi conciencia."*

"English." Their friendship had started when Elena wanted to practice her English, but by the time Bailey left Valle Rojo, Elena was even more than a friend. She helped Bailey organize the tea parties that brought the village women to the church and even taught some of the Bible classes.

Elena pressed her lips together. "Sometimes you were like pretty shoes that are too tight."

"I only wanted you to know your worth." She hated that she hadn't been able to make a difference in the village or help her friend deal with an alcoholic husband.

"I know. You just cannot change overnight what has always been."

So she'd discovered. And as usual, she didn't stand well against attack, preferring to cut and run. Still, it hadn't been her decision to leave but the mission board's, after the so-called priest ramped up his campaign to get rid of her. "Father Horatio could have asked me politely to leave. He didn't have to put the rattlesnakes in my car. I'm surprised he hasn't found me today and demand that I leave."

"He's in Chihuahua this weekend."

So that was why Elena had invited her to visit. She'd known the priest would be away. Not that he was an actual priest. The folk-healer-slash-spiritual-mystic had proclaimed himself one and taken the name Father Horatio. And because he had success in healing, many in the village followed him, especially the men.

She'd run afoul of the man when some of the women came to her tea parties, then came back for the Bible studies and stopped following him.

Her friend ducked her head. "I have not told you, but I have been teaching the Bible studies again. And I've been thinking about asking Pastor Carlos if I can start the tea parties."

Pastor Carlos, bless his heart, believed change took place very slowly, and that had been her problem with Father Horatio—Bailey had moved too quickly. She turned to stare at her friend. "Elena, that is absolutely wonderful."

She lifted her chin. "I got tired of my conscience pinching, and I still had the instructor's book you left."

"I always said you were a natural-born teacher." Bailey smiled at Elena, hoping her friend could see the admiration she felt. To go against Father Horatio took courage. Remembering his vile tactics to get rid of her, Bailey had second thoughts about encouraging Elena. "But would your husband allow it? And Father Horatio—what does he say?"

Elena shrugged. "As long as I'm home to cook his meals and keep his clothes ready, my husband won't care. And I don't care what Father Horatio says. He isn't even a real priest."

Bailey squeezed her hand. "In three days I fly home, but when I come back, I hope you'll come to Chihuahua and visit—you could ride with Miguel sometimes, and I could see to it that you get home. I'd like to show you the school where I teach, maybe give you more material to use with the women here."

Elena broke a stick off the scrub oak tree and scratched the ground with it.

"You will come?" It angered Bailey that for all of Elena's bluster, her husband would be the one who decided.

"I will try. But why do you go home now? Isn't the school in Chihuahua still in session?"

"My sister that I told you about has come back, and—"

"They found her?"

"Yes, and the man who took her has been arrested. I couldn't wait until June to see her. And one of my students needed someone to escort her to visit her grandparents, so I'm killing two birds with one stone." She stood and brushed the seat of her pants. "I better find Miguel and see if he's ready." She took a card from the tote around her waist. "Here's my email address. You can use Pastor Carlos's computer at the church to write me, so I expect to hear from you."

"I will." Elena stood and hugged her. "Be safe. And please do not report what we saw today."

Bailey returned her embrace. "You be safe too."

In the state of Chihuahua, that meant staying under Father Horatio's as well as the drug cartel's radar.

■ ■ ■

Three days later, Bailey savored the rich atmosphere of the small Chihuahua cafe as the sun warmed her face. She would miss this while she was in Logan Point. A guitar played in the background as she cut up an egg and sausage burrito for the kindergarten student she was accompanying to Mississippi. "Did you show your uncle the new bows I brought for your hair?"

Four-year-old Maria pulled the red and white bows from her

tiny purse. "Do you like them, Uncle Joel? We're going to put them in my hair after we eat."

Joel McDermott leaned toward her. "I like them very much, sweetheart. Did you tell Miss Bailey thank you?"

Maria nodded and picked at her food.

The child seemed so much more subdued than at school, but it could be nerves about flying. Or it could be because she was leaving her uncle, who had taken over raising the child after her mother's death. But Bailey figured once she was with her grandparents, she would perk up.

Bailey speared a piece of sausage for herself and lifted the fork to her mouth. Her eyes widened.

No. It couldn't be Danny. Not here in Chihuahua.

She returned the fork to her plate as Danny Maxwell sauntered through the outdoor cafe toward their table, his dark blond hair falling over his forehead. The pounding of her heart drowned out the soft guitar music.

He stopped at her table, and she tipped her head up to look at all six feet of him. "Not lost, are you?"

Sea-blue eyes lazily slid from Bailey to her companions, then back to her. "I'd say you were the one lost since I'm a regular to the area. Last I heard, you were in some small town near Mexico City doing your missionary work, not in one of the most dangerous states in Mexico."

She twisted the napkin in her lap. So he hadn't heard she'd fled rural Mexico for the city. She took in a breath to steady herself, but he spoke again before she could explain.

"I had no idea that you knew Joel." He nodded to her companion, then, not waiting for her answer, he shifted his attention to the child. "Hello, Maria. You are looking as pretty as ever."

She beamed at him. "Hi, Mr. Danny. Do you know my teacher, Miss Bailey?"

"Indeed I do."

"Did you know she's taking me to see my grandparents?"

"I didn't."

Danny shot Bailey a look she couldn't read. Surprise, maybe. If so, then they were even. She shifted her gaze from him to her companions. Joel McDermott stared at her, puzzlement in his pale blue eyes, while excitement lit Maria Montoya's darker blue ones.

Joel pointed first at Bailey then at Danny. "You two know each other?"

"We were engaged once."

Bailey drilled him with her gaze. "Since I said no to your proposal, we weren't engaged."

"You first said yes, then a day later changed your mind. Close enough." Danny offered his hand to Joel. "Good to see you, man. Just called your secretary for an appointment this afternoon, and she put me off until tomorrow. I understand why now."

"Wrong conclusion, unfortunately. I'm dropping Bailey and Maria off at the airport and then going back to the office." Joel took a sip of coffee and then pointed at the chair next to Bailey. "But since you two are friends, why don't you join us?"

Danny scratched the space above his lip. To hide a grin, she was sure.

"Only until my food arrives."

He took the chair next to her, and Bailey wanted to disappear. She'd dreaded running into him when she returned home, and now here he was. Why was he being so nice? They hadn't parted as friends—he'd made it plain that friendship wasn't what he wanted.

A flutter in her chest made her catch her breath. And why did her heart have to go nuts on her right now? She shook the fog from her brain and addressed Joel. "So how do you and Maria know Danny?"

Danny answered for him. "The company he works for produces the porcelain dinnerware for Maxwell Industries. I met Maria at the office last year."

The somberness in his eyes made her think it was after Maria's mother had died. In the weeks after the funeral, the child had missed school on numerous occasions, and Bailey discovered later that she'd spent the time in the care of one or more of the secretaries in Joel's office.

"And he took me to get an ice cream." Maria's eyes danced.

It was clear she had succumbed to Danny's charm. That she remembered him surprised Bailey. But he was a hard one to forget—she ought to know.

"Do you live close to Miss Bailey? Maybe I can come see you too."

Danny shot her a quick look. "You're coming to Logan Point as well?"

Bailey nodded. "While Maria is spending a couple of weeks with her grandparents, I'll stop off in Logan Point. Robyn's home and I want to see her." She'd asked for a leave as soon as she learned Robyn was home, and then Joel had asked if she would take Maria with her.

"What Robyn did was amazing. And I've never seen anyone change as much as she has," Danny said.

"You've seen her?"

"Yeah. In town at Molly's Diner with her daughter and husband." He chewed his bottom lip. "So you planned on slipping in and then leaving, hoping I wouldn't find out."

"I didn't say that." She was not discussing their past in front of Joel. She checked her watch. Their flight wasn't until two thirty. Four more hours. She wished it was sooner so they would have an excuse to leave. She glanced at Maria's half-eaten food. "Finish your meal, sweetie. We have a plane to catch."

"If you let me know," Danny said, "I could have flown you home in my plane and saved you the hassle of flying commercially."

"That would have been super." Joel raked his fingers through his short-cropped red hair. "We could still—"

"No." She had no intention of flying home with Danny. Being

19

that close to him for however long it took to fly home would not work. Especially with him in that black cashmere turtleneck that hugged his lean body and showed he'd been working out. "We've already made plans to leave today, and besides, your parents are expecting us tonight."

Danny pricked her heart with his slow smile that always made her feel like she was the only one in the world who mattered.

"I had a friend who flew out of Chihuahua a while back. Plane had mechanical problems, and he sat in the airport for ten hours before boarding. How about I program my Mexico number into your phone. That way if there is a delay, you can call me. I'm sure her grandparents would rather wait a day than to have Maria all exhausted."

"Great idea," Joel said. He waited for Bailey to hand her phone over.

She fumbled in her purse and finally dragged out the smartphone Joel had given her and handed it to him. "Thank you for being so thoughtful, although I bet your friend wasn't flying a premier airline." Neither of them even seemed to notice the saccharine in her voice.

Danny held his phone out. "I don't have your number for Mexico. Why don't you put it in?"

She took the phone and punched in her number, purposefully transposing the last two digits. She did not want him calling her. When he leaned over to exchange phones again, his woodsy aftershave brought back memories she wanted to forget.

"Good. Glad we got that settled." Joel turned to Danny. "Now, what did you want to discuss?"

"I'll catch you tomorrow. I'm sure you and Bailey have things you need to talk about before you take them to the airport."

Bailey jumped on the opportunity. "Joel, we do have a few things to go over."

"And my food has arrived, so I'll take my leave." Danny stood and flipped his gaze over her once more. "Be sure and call when you get to Logan Point."

"Oh, I will." As soon as he left, the frozen smile slid from her lips. She slipped the phone back into her purse. Like she'd ever call him.

2

"Gracias," Danny said when the waitress offered to refill his coffee.

"My pleasure," she replied.

He smiled up at her. "Your English is very good. Do you have American friends?"

"No, family in Arizona. I only just returned from there last week."

He pushed his plate back. He was sure the egg-topped enchiladas were delicious, but seeing Bailey with Joel had taken his appetite. Besides, there was something different about Bailey. Nothing he could put his finger on, maybe a dampening of her boldness . . . a hesitancy.

Or maybe he just imagined it. After all, she was in Chihuahua, one of the most dangerous places in all of Mexico, especially for an American woman alone. She couldn't afford to come across too bold. When he returned home, he would enlist her family to help convince her to stay in Logan Point.

Not that it would likely do any good. She believed her God had called her to Mexico, and that was it as far as she was concerned. Well, he didn't believe God called her to have dealings with Joel McDermott.

Danny had flown to Mexico determined to find the Blue Dog

Company and the man behind it. This same man was the one who had bought stolen Maxwell AR-15 rifles from Geoffrey Franks, former chief financial officer of Maxwell Industries. McDermott was on his list of possible suspects.

"Leave it alone, Danny. Let the ATF handle it—they'll get the information from Geoffrey." His cousin's words rang in his head, but Danny brushed them aside. Ian didn't understand, and while a full investigation last year had cleared Maxwell Industries of any wrongdoing, Geoffrey Franks had tainted the company's image.

The way Danny saw it, the only way to prove that none of the owners were involved was to find the person Geoffrey had done business with. He couldn't believe a judge had granted Geoffrey bail. The man steadfastly refused to give up his contact in Mexico and probably thought he'd beat the rap.

Danny glanced toward Bailey's table again. He hadn't expected to find her in the company of a possible suspect. Not that he came to that conclusion easily.

He'd known Joel for years, ever since he went to work for Montoya Ceramics . . . probably eight or nine years ago. And the man had already had enough trouble for one lifetime with his sister dying last year, leaving him with a four-year-old niece to care for. But, until Danny ruled him out, Joel McDermott would remain on his suspect list.

Danny took another sip of coffee and took note once more of a man sitting a couple of tables away from him. Light coloring but definitely Latino. Earlier he'd been staring at Bailey. That wasn't unusual. Even though she didn't have the sultry beauty of Mexican women, she had a way of attracting attention, especially in Mexico with her fair skin and ashe blonde hair that she'd pulled up in a ponytail.

No, her beauty came from within. Like a fountain, it bubbled up and spilled out of her as almost childlike innocence and joy. And those eyes that saw only good in people, good even in him. Even

23

though he'd dated a lot of women, he'd never met one with eyes as beautiful as Bailey's. Rich blue-green framed a gold starburst in the center. Unfortunately those eyes would never look at him filled with love again.

With a sigh, he picked at his breakfast, keeping a wary eye on Bailey as well as the man watching her.

■ ■ ■

"I can't get over that you two know each other." Joel seemed mildly amused.

"I certainly didn't expect to run into him in Mexico." Bailey had known somewhere in the back of her mind that Maxwell Industries contracted for their ceramic production somewhere in Mexico. If Danny was a frequent visitor to Chihuahua, it was a wonder she hadn't run into him before. Or that Joel hadn't mentioned him.

After all, how many people did Joel know from Logan Point? But then, Bailey's involvement with Joel was mostly from their contact at the school and with Maria.

"Why did you break the engagement?"

Why indeed?

"We want different things from life. I should have realized that before I accepted his ring." She grabbed her cup and drained it. That was only half true. The problem hadn't been with Danny. It had been with her. Keeping the ring and marrying him would have been a disaster, something she'd been able to see after wrestling with it all night. After she'd returned the ring, she'd run away to Mexico a week later. *Coward.*

Bailey cast a covert glance at Danny. The waitress tilted her head as he spoke, and part of her wondered what he'd said to bring such a warm smile to her face. How many times had her heart ached for one of his smiles?

"I won't say I'm sorry," Joel said and covered her hand with his own.

Her heart stilled. So she hadn't been imagining the long looks he'd been giving her. She swallowed. How could she tell him she couldn't commit to him any more than she could to Danny? She pulled a smile out of her bag of tricks. "I think it's time to discuss Maria's medicine and whatever last-minute instructions you have for me."

His eyes twinkled as he reluctantly moved his hand and took papers from his briefcase. Handing them to her, he said, "I printed your flight information out last night, as well as info about Maria's headache medicine. You have my cell phone number so you can get in touch with me whenever you need to, and I have yours. Do you have any questions before I go over the info about Maria's medicine?"

Before she could answer, the waitress appeared at his side. "Coffee?"

"No, and I'll let you know when I do," Joel snapped in his perfect Spanish.

The waitress froze. "Excuse, please."

Bailey flinched and noticed Maria did as well. "I'll take more." She moved her cup closer to the edge of the table and gave the waitress an encouraging smile.

She'd noticed earlier that Joel made the girl nervous. The poor thing couldn't be more than twenty, and Bailey figured the pronounced limp she walked with did nothing to boost her confidence. Bailey glanced down. The girl wore some sort of orthopedic boot or cast.

The waitress's eyes reflected her gratitude. Her hand shook as she poured the coffee, sloshing a little on the table.

"Stop. You're making a mess." Joel waved her away before turning to Bailey. "Now, about Maria's headache medicine. I've given her the morning medication, and there will be another dose due at noon."

Her attention was on the nervous waitress, and a little of the old Bailey stirred. "She didn't spill the coffee on purpose."

She didn't know if it was her tone or her pointedly raised eyebrows, but the scowl on Joel's face softened. He called the waitress back. "I didn't mean to take my frustrations out on you," he said, his voice much softer. "How about if I let you know if we need anything else."

"Sí." With one last, questioning glance at Bailey, the waitress limped away.

He gave her an "Is that better?" look, then took out a notebook. "Give me your cell phone number so I can write it down."

"It's in your phone."

"I know that, but something could happen to my phone, and although I have your number memorized at the moment, I may forget. I've learned to never rely on my memory—messed up too many things in the past when I did. Now I write *everything* down."

"So I noticed," she said and pulled out another sheaf of papers he'd given her when he picked her up. "I have the letter giving me medical power of attorney as well as one for your parents, Maria's passport and visa, the headache medicine, and *three* pages of instructions and phone numbers. I am to drive Maria straight to your parents' house after renting a car at the airport."

"Good. The number, please?"

She gave it to him, managing to keep laughter from her voice—he totally did not hear her emphasis on the three pages.

He closed the notebook and put it in his jacket. "My parents have arranged to take Maria to our family doctor so he will be familiar with her health issues, just in case something comes up. You should have their contact information in those papers, along with a photo of them."

"Yes." The photo, showing an older couple, was tucked in her black bag, and she had an extra copy of the numbers and the medication in her purse. According to the nurse at the school where Bailey taught and Maria was a kindergartener, the child had only been on medication since her mother died eleven months ago, and the nurse believed it had resolved her headaches. She glanced at Maria, who had picked up a crayon and was coloring the place mat.

Though small for her size, Maria made up for it in personality. Other than having blue eyes, she didn't favor her uncle at all, with his fair skin and red hair. Perhaps Maria looked like her father, Angel Montoya.

Maria never mentioned him, making Bailey wonder if the child even remembered him. When Bailey questioned the other teachers, they didn't seem to know anything about him other than he'd died two years ago, which would have made Maria about two at the time. So it was possible she had no memory of him. After Angel died, Joel brought his sister and niece to live with him and became the primary male figure in Maria's life.

The girl was being unusually quiet, and Bailey wondered if she was nervous about flying. Or meeting the McDermotts. "You say she's never seen your parents?"

"No."

He offered no explanation, and she couldn't think of a way to ask why not, not with Maria sitting across from her, listening to every word they spoke as she colored.

"My dad's health is not good, and when Claire—"

"They couldn't come," Maria said matter-of-factly. She looked up at Bailey with an expression that gave nothing away. "But it was all right. Mama was in heaven, anyway."

Joel's lips pressed together. "You know you're not supposed to interrupt when grown-ups are talking."

Bailey flinched, and judging by the way the brightness in Maria's eyes dimmed, Bailey suspected this wasn't the first time her uncle had hurt her feelings. She softened her lips into a smile for the girl. "It's quite all right. I'm sure you're a little nervous, with it being your first plane trip and all."

Maria darted her eyes to Joel, then she lifted a small shoulder. "Yes, ma'am."

"There are no other grandparents?" She didn't want to come right out and ask about Maria's father.

"No. They've both passed away."

Maria dropped her crayon, and when she stood to retrieve it, she bumped the chair with Joel's briefcase on it, knocking it to the floor. The child froze, and Bailey threw her a quick smile. "Looks like you've been around me too much," she said and bent over to retrieve the objects that had fallen from the opened briefcase.

Joel reached at the same time. "I'll take care of it."

Her fingers closed around a beautifully wrapped box, and she set it on the table. It had the child's name on it. "Oh, you bought Maria a going-away present."

"What?" He jerked his head around and stared at her, then at the box, a frozen expression in his eyes.

She could tell she'd said the wrong thing. The gift was probably a surprise. "I . . . I'm sorry. I thought—"

Joel held up his hand. "No, it's fine."

It wasn't fine. His tight voice gave him away. Her stomach roiled as he picked up the box and handed it to Maria.

"I, ah, planned to give this to you at the airport, but now is fine."

Maria's eyes lit up. "A present for me? Can I open it?"

"Of course."

She reached for the box, then hesitated. "Do you have one for Miss Bailey?"

"Maria!" Bailey was mortified.

"Actually, I do." He pulled an identical small box from the brief-case.

"I can't—"

"Yes, you can. Now let's allow Maria to open her gift, then you can open yours."

Joel had already given Bailey an expensive phone so he could keep in touch, not trusting her three-year-old model. She didn't care what he said, she was not accepting another gift from him, especially when he didn't seem at all happy about it.

Once again she thought about the long glances he'd given her when they met to discuss the trip. She could no longer tell herself he was only interested in getting Maria to the States. She focused her attention on the child as Maria carefully untied the bow and without tearing the paper opened the box. She gasped and lifted a dainty locket with an *M* on the front. "Isn't it so pretty," she whispered.

"Let me open the locket for you," Joel said and flipped it open. Maria peered inside. "Mama's picture?"

"Yes. Now she's with you wherever you go, so never, ever leave this anywhere."

"I won't, I promise." Maria threw her arms around Joel, and Bailey blinked away the stinging in her eyes. Maybe she misread his reaction.

"Let me put it around your neck," he said. Maria stood and lifted her long hair so he could fasten the necklace.

The child fingered the locket and then pointed to Bailey's unopened gift. "Miss Bailey, open yours."

Bailey picked up the small box. As happy as Maria was, she couldn't refuse, but somehow she would return the gift to Joel. The box yielded an identical gold locket minus the initial and photo. "It's beautiful, but I—"

"Let it go." Joel lifted a hand. "It makes Maria happy that you have a locket like hers. It was a closeout, and I can't return it. Here, let me help you with yours."

"That's fine, I can do it myself." She slipped the dainty locket around her neck and fastened the clasp. At least he no longer seemed angry.

"Miss Bailey, it looks so pretty on you."

Bailey fingered the heart-shaped locket, troubled that Joel would give her such a nice piece of jewelry that was no closeout. And she wasn't buying for one minute that it was because of Maria. When a man gave a woman an expensive piece of jewelry, it meant something more than friendship.

That's not a bad thing, Bailey. She raised her eyes to find his pale blue eyes studying her and instantly snapped her gaze to Maria. "Would you like to go to the ladies' room and see how your necklace looks around your neck?"

"Yes, ma'am!"

She smiled at Joel. "If you will excuse us, we'll be right back." Her fingers found the necklace again. "And thank you, but you really shouldn't have."

"Indulge me." He cleared his throat. "And before you go, I realize I've been a little grouchy today, but I hope you'll chalk it up to my type A personality, plus it's stressful letting Maria leave. When you two get back to Mexico, I'd like to take you out to dinner and make amends for my bad mood."

"Why, ah, sure, that would be nice."

She helped Maria out of the chair and led her inside to the restroom. Joel and her dating? Briefly the thought intrigued her. From what she knew about him, he'd worked his way through college, doing first one odd job then another, unlike Danny, who'd never worked hard at anything. Joel did seem like a good man under his sometimes grumpy exterior—after all, he was raising his sister's child. *It's a dead end.* She sighed. Why fight it? If nothing else, the experience with Danny taught her she wasn't relationship material.

Bailey turned to glance back at Joel and froze. *Father Horatio?* It couldn't be, but then his eyes met hers, and it was like staring into the eyes of a rattlesnake. He lifted an eyebrow, then shifted his gaze away from her.

She pulled Maria into the restroom and gulped air, trying to keep her breakfast down. *What is he doing here?*

"Miss Bailey." Maria tugged on her hand. "Are you sick?"

Bailey swallowed hard and shook off her fear. It was only a

coincidence. Elena had said he was in Chihuahua. And this was a popular restaurant. "I'm fine, sweetie. Let's look at your necklace again."

Maria turned first one way then another as she admired the locket in the mirror. "It's so pretty. I guess Uncle Joel does like me."

Bailey winced at the child's words. Raising a child alone was a tough job, particularly a child who wasn't your own. And of course there was that driven personality. "Of course he does. I'm sure sometimes he misses your mother quite a bit, and that makes him grumpy." Bailey smiled at Maria. "Are you ready to go to the airport?"

Maria nodded slowly.

"Are you just a tiny bit afraid?"

Again the nod.

"Well, it's very safe and feels like riding in a big car." Not at all like Danny's single prop plane.

"Really?"

"Yes, really. I've flown bunches, and it's really cool, looking out the window at the clouds. They almost look like cotton candy." She tried to make the trip sound exciting.

"Really?" Maria smoothed back a strand of hair that had fallen across her face.

"Really. Would you like for me to put your hair up in a ponytail?"

"Yes, I would appreciate that."

Maria's vocabulary was far advanced for a four-year-old, and sometimes talking to her was like conversing with a tiny adult. More than anything, Bailey wanted to put a little fun in the child's life.

Yes. This trip was going to be a good thing for Maria. And it would put her far away from Father Horatio.

3

Danny had long finished eating but couldn't make himself leave or take his attention off Bailey. If ever there was an exercise in futility . . . With a sigh, he placed his napkin on the plate.

They were perfect for each other in so many ways. Bailey had a way of making him feel as though he could do anything.

"Maxwell Industries is your dad's passion, and Ian's," she'd told him once, "but not yours. Think about it—you're the last to arrive and the first to leave. So what's your passion, Danny Maxwell?"

"You," he'd said.

She'd laughed at him and told him he couldn't make a career out of being passionate about her. But she never stopped believing that he was capable of great things.

Sometimes he wondered if his lack of focus was as big an obstacle to their relationship as . . . what? One night she accepted his ring, and a day later she gave it back with a rambling explanation about how she just couldn't do it and had to answer her "calling." The next thing he knew, she was in Mexico.

He didn't understand why he continued to sit here, watching Bailey make eyes at Joel. When she accepted a small box from him, Danny'd had enough—time to leave. He asked for his check and once again noticed that the man who had been watching Bailey earlier continued to observe her.

However, when Bailey and Maria left the table, the man's gaze didn't follow them. It stayed at the table, on Joel. Something about the man seemed familiar. Abruptly the man stood and threw a handful of bills on the table.

Danny hesitated, torn between wanting to follow the stranger and staying where he could watch Bailey. For what, torture? His gut said to go after the man, and he usually followed his hunches. Placing enough money on the table to cover his bill and a generous tip, he stood and hurried to the street in time to see the man look away as a stocky Mexican climbed out of a car and stared at him. Danny followed as he strode purposefully toward a blue Jeep Cherokee parked half a block away.

"Hey, wait up," he called in Spanish, but the man kept walking, and Danny jogged after him. "Can I—"

Gunshots rang out behind him.

Danny whirled in tandem with the stranger. Three men carried a slumped Joel from the restaurant while two more stood guard. *Bailey!*

He sprinted toward them as Joel was thrown in the backseat of a waiting car, and two of the men hopped into the front seat. Tires squealed, and the car shot down the street. The other men dashed toward the restaurant, and Danny changed direction, going after them.

One of the men shouted a command: "Find the girl!"

They want Maria. Bailey wouldn't let her go without a fight. To the death.

"Out of my way!"

He had forgotten the stranger who now shoved past him into the restaurant. Danny followed on his heels.

The room was empty. No waitress. No men. No Maria.

No Bailey.

■ ■ ■

Gunfire froze Bailey as she and Maria left the restroom. The shots were close. Too close.

"Miss Bailey, I'm scared."

"We'll be all right." She tried to sound strong, but her feet refused to move. What if it was Father Horatio? And he was looking for her?

Men shouting. "Find the señorita!"

If they were after her, then it was Father Horatio. *But why?*

The waitress materialized in the hallway. "Follow me."

With her heart jackhammering in her ears, Bailey almost missed the whispered words. The waitress motioned toward another hallway, and Bailey scooped the wide-eyed child up in her arms. "Shh, it's going to be all right." But was it? The back door was straight ahead, not the way the waitress led them.

What if she was leading them to the men? No. The waitress had been too kind.

Maria whimpered against her shoulder. Bailey hesitated, and the waitress motioned again. Something crashed to the floor in the dining room, spurring her forward into another hallway, then through a doorway.

They entered the kitchen, and the waitress whispered something to the cook. He jerked up a woven rug, revealing a trapdoor. While he lifted the door, she motioned them into the cellar. "Hurry!"

Bailey winced as Maria's fingers dug into her shoulder.

"Now! Hurry!" The Spanish words were more urgent.

She handed Maria to the waitress and scrambled down the steps. "What happened to my friend?" she asked, lifting her arms for the child. The pity in the woman's eyes told her all she needed to know.

"They took him. Kidnapping, I think. Or they would have shot him dead on the spot. And now they're searching for you two."

Bailey's throat tightened as she pulled Maria close.

The waitress put her finger to her lips before the cook closed the trapdoor over their heads, sealing them in the cool room. A

34

cellar where they kept root vegetables from the smell of onions and garlic that permeated the air.

With her chest heaving in the pitch dark, Bailey felt for the wall beside the steps. They needed to get deeper into the room. Not for the first time, she wished she had her gun. But she'd left it in her apartment. She held Maria tight against her and used the wall to guide her farther away from the steps.

If the waitress was right, the men were after Maria for money. Kidnapping was so common in Mexico that wealthy people took out insurance in case they had to pay a ransom, but she never thought it would happen to one of her students . . . or her, especially since she had neither insurance nor money.

"Shh," Bailey crooned as Maria whimpered, then pressed her lips against the girl's ear and whispered, "Remember the school lesson last week? How Daniel survived the lions' den?" In the darkness, she felt Maria nod. "God will take care of us, but we must be quiet."

Why couldn't she hold on to that truth? Why had her gun, and not God, been her first thought? She tried to focus on her breathing and slow her heart rate down, but waiting in the dark to be discovered made that impossible.

She held Maria tighter and struggled to release the tension that constricted every breath. Footsteps shook the boards overhead. *Please let her stay quiet.* A small cry escaped Maria's lips. Adrenaline shot through Bailey. The door was thick. Maybe they wouldn't hear her. She stroked the child's arms, straining to hear the muffled words spoken, automatically translating them into English.

"Where are the woman and girl?" They wanted her and Maria.

She tightened her hold on the child. They would get Maria over her dead body.

Somehow she doubted that would be a problem for the men.

■ ■ ■

Danny pushed open the door to the kitchen. The waitress who had brought his food earlier stared at him with huge brown eyes. "The woman and girl, where are they?"

She stared blankly at him. The stranger who had followed him repeated the question in Spanish and received a torrent of words too fast for Danny to understand as she pointed toward the back door. The man jerked open the door.

"Hey, wait." Danny followed close on his heels, almost bowling the guy over when he halted in the alley.

The narrow street was filled with delivery trucks backed up to doorways and people milling about. Danny caught a glimpse of one of the men he had chased into the restaurant a couple of blocks away, and he started after him.

"No. You do not wish to follow." The stranger spoke in English.

Danny whirled around. "Who are you? And why not?"

"Angel Guerrera. And you do not wish to follow these men, Danny Maxwell, because they belong to one of our drug cartels."

"How do you know?"

"They are the only ones who kidnap people."

Danny eyed the lean Hispanic who stood shoulder to shoulder with him. While Danny might outweigh him, he would not want to tangle with the rock-solid Angel Guerrera. Something about him rang a bell. "I remember the name Angel from when I was a kid. Do I know you?"

"There are many named Angel in Mexico, but we met once, years ago when my father still lived. I recognized you—you look like *your* father the last time I saw him." Angel's mouth quirked. "And your Spanish still has a Mississippi accent."

Fragments of memories came together. A trip to Mexico with his dad when he was twelve or thirteen. His dad to talk business with the owner of a ceramics factory, Danny to experience the country and speak the language his father had made him learn. A boy his own age named Angel—the son of one of the employees, he thought. But he couldn't come up with anything else. "You have a good memory."

"It was not often back then that I met an American my age."

"You speak excellent English." Like someone who grew up in the States but more formal.

"I spent some time in a Texas hospital not long ago, so I've had practice, thanks to the Calatrava."

"So getting even with the Calatrava is your stake in this?"

"Sí."

A weight lodged in the pit of Danny's stomach. And now they wanted Bailey and the child in her care. Headstrong and stubborn described the woman he'd once thought he would marry, but this? What had she gotten herself into?

"Bailey and Maria could have ducked into one of the stores along the street. They could be anywhere," Angel said. "Let's go talk to the waitress."

"How do you know them?"

Without answering, Angel turned and walked back into the restaurant. With one last glance down the street, Danny turned and followed him. "How will we find Bailey?"

"I saw you put something in her phone—your number, I assume. Once her head clears, she will call you."

Wait, Danny had Bailey's number. He jerked his phone out and scrolled to her name.

Angel grabbed his hand. "What if she's hiding and her phone rings?"

Slowly Danny moved his finger away from the number. "How did you know I put my number in Bailey's phone? Why were you watching us?"

A shrug was the only answer he received as Angel turned and called to the waitress they'd questioned minutes ago. She appeared almost instantly, and when Angel peppered her with questions, she shook her head. He spoke so quickly, Danny had trouble following his words. He didn't have any trouble seeing that the waitress didn't intend to tell them anything. "Did you call the police?"

"No. It would do no good. The men will not be arrested. Your friend is probably no longer alive."

The finality of her words expressed a futility he knew nothing about. He glanced at Angel. "But we should."

Angel shook his head. "You do not want to involve the police. It is possible they are on the payroll of the Calatrava. Instead, let's go to your hotel and wait for her to call you."

Waiting was the last thing he wanted to do. But Angel had already turned and walked out of the kitchen.

Danny turned back to the waitress. She knew more than she was telling. He just didn't know how to get it out of her. "She was my fiancée," he blurted.

For a second, hesitation wavered in her eyes, then the waitress shook her head. *"Lo siento."*

He was sorry too. Danny took a card from his billfold. "What's your name?" he asked in Spanish.

She hesitated, then pointed to the name on her shirt. "Solana."

"Okay, Solana, if Bailey comes back, or if you decide to help me, call this number." He circled his cell number on the business card before putting it in the girl's hand. Maybe she wouldn't trash it as soon as he was out of sight.

When he caught up to Angel outside the restaurant, Danny said, "She knows where Bailey is."

"Probably, but she doesn't trust you, and you will get nothing from her. If she thinks we are leaving, maybe we will discover something. Where's your car?"

"Around the corner."

"Then that's where we want to go."

No, that wasn't where Danny wanted to go. He wanted to return to that kitchen and cajole the waitress into telling him Bailey's whereabouts. But Angel was right. Danny had seen the suspicion in her eyes. "Do you think Bailey is still in the restaurant?"

"No. She is probably in one of the businesses along the street."

"Then we should—"

"What? Go knocking on doors? Do you think there's a merchant on that street who will tell a gringo anything?" The look Angel gave him said more than the sarcastic tone in his voice.

Danny pinched the bridge of his nose. He had to do something. His fingers automatically went to his phone again.

"Like I said before, if I had strange men after me, I think I would turn my phone off so it wouldn't ring at a bad time."

Danny ground his back molars. Angel was beginning to get on his nerves. "We need to report her missing. And Joel—we need to contact the police."

"It will do no good, but if it will make you happy, there is a police station nearby. We can walk."

Half an hour later, they exited the police building, and Danny shot Angel a "don't say it" look. He said it anyway.

"I told you they would do nothing."

"What's with the police here?"

Angel sighed. "It's like I told you, Calatrava pockets run deep, and the Federals who aren't on the take . . . well, it takes a brave man to go against the cartel."

Danny's cell phone rang, and he jerked it from his pocket. "Hello?"

"Danny Maxwell?"

He held his phone out but didn't recognize the number. "Who is this?"

"Solana."

His heart ratcheted up a notch. "Have you heard from Bailey?"

"No." She said something else, but he couldn't follow her Spanish.

"You're speaking too fast for me. Slow down, or speak in English."

"Your friend, she left a bag with medicine. Come to the cafe."

"I'm a couple of blocks away. I'll be right there." He turned to Angel. "Let's go back to the restaurant."

"What's going on?"

"Maybe Solana is ready to talk to me." In less than five minutes, Danny rounded the corner to the restaurant and continued around to the back alley. At the door he knocked, and a beefy Mexican opened it. "I'm looking for Solana," Danny said.

The big man nodded and stepped out of the way.

"Thank you, Juan." The slight waitress limped toward him. She held a small black bag in her hand. "Your friend may need this when you find her. I heard the man say it contains medicine for the little one."

Angel snatched the bag and rifled through it. When he pulled out a medicine bottle, his face paled. "Depakote? Maria has seizures?" He grabbed Solana's shoulders. "Do you know where they went?"

The beefy Mexican grabbed Angel's wrist in a vise until he released Solana. "Do not touch her," he spat in Spanish.

"*Siento.*" Angel stepped back, his hands held up. He glanced at Danny. "We must find them, now."

"Depakote is used for illnesses other than seizures." Danny slid his phone from his pocket. "But now maybe you'll think calling Bailey is a good idea?"

Angel gave him a sour nod, and Danny found the number she'd put in his phone. It rang twice, then went to a message that the number did not work. Oh great. She'd given him a false number.

"I took them to the store around the corner."

They both turned to stare at Juan.

"They could not stay here. La Calatrava will return when they don't find her. But she didn't stay there. I saw her leave. Just the two of them."

Danny raked his hands through his hair. Bailey and the child could be anywhere. The cartel might even have her by now. "Wait.

I should have thought of this earlier. Bailey and Maria were flying to the States today. Maybe she'll try to make it to the airport."

"Do you know which flight?"

"No, but I know someone who can find out. I'll call her on the way to the airport."

4

Stay here until I know the Calatrava are gone, and then I'll be back for you," Juan had said as he led them into a small grocery. "And whatever you do, stay away from the police!"

Then he'd been out the door, leaving Bailey and Maria on their own. She had at least discovered the names of their protectors once they were out of the cellar. Juan and Solana. And that their pursuers belonged to the Calatrava gang, a small-time Chihuahua drug cartel that had grown in power over the last year.

Her heart pounded in her chest as she glanced around the store filled with noonday shoppers. "Do you want something to drink?" she asked Maria.

The child shook her head. "My tummy hurts."

Bailey knew how she felt. Her stomach ached just from thinking about Joel. If it was the Calatrava, they probably had already killed him, and she and Maria might as well be dead if they stayed in Mexico. And Danny. What if he had been caught in the gunfire? Her mouth was so dry, she couldn't swallow.

Her mouth got even dryer when the door opened and a stocky Mexican entered, glancing first one way then another. She ducked behind a display of canned peaches and searched for an exit.

"Miss Bailey—"

"Shh." She placed her finger to Maria's lips.

When the man walked in the opposite direction, she pulled Maria toward a side door. Once on the sidewalk, she scooped Maria up in her arms and hurried away from the store.

Bailey's mind reeled as they walked the sidewalk. As a gringa with a Mexican child, she stood out. And she didn't know this part of town that well. Where could she go if she couldn't trust the police?

Her familiarity with Chihuahua was limited to the areas around the school and Joel's house. The cartel might even know she was a teacher and where. The problems swept over her like a tsunami.

She had to find somewhere to think. A children's clothing store caught her eye, and she pulled Maria into the small shop. Mindlessly she sorted through the racks of girls' dresses.

Stop it. She fought for control of her jumbled thoughts. *Breathe. Relax. Formulate a plan.* She could go back to Elena's village. But what if the man she saw in the poppy field was behind this, and those men were after her and not Maria? But that would mean Elena had told them where to find her, and she wouldn't do that.

She took out her new smartphone and emailed the pastor at the small church in Valle Rojo, asking if Elena was okay and if anyone had been looking for her. Then she stared at her phone. Had only an hour passed since they'd escaped from the restaurant? It seemed like a year. They still had three hours to make the flight.

Miguel. Maybe the driver who took her to Elena's village would come get them and take them to the airport. She scrolled to his number. After the sixth ring, it went to voicemail, and she left Miguel a message to call her, then dropped the phone into her purse.

At least she still had her cell . . . and the plane tickets. If they could get to the airport, they would be safe. She startled when Maria tugged on her arm.

"Miss Bailey, I'm tired. I want to find my uncle and go home."

"I know, honey, but I'm afraid we can't do that." She rubbed her temples. They had to get to the airport, and if Miguel didn't return her call, she had no idea what she would do. She feared going to the police. She'd heard too many stories of the Calatrava infiltrating their ranks. And many of those who weren't part of the gang were on the take. Numbness fogged her brain so she couldn't think.

"Can we call Mr. Danny?"

Bailey stared at Maria. Danny? He could get them to the States in his plane. Why hadn't she already thought of him? Maybe because she didn't want to ask him for anything after the way she'd dumped him.

Seriously? Here I am, running from a drug cartel with a small child, and I don't want to ask the only person in Mexico I trust for help?

Her cell phone rang, and she fished it out again. The caller ID read Miguel, and she almost dropped the phone in relief. Now she wouldn't have to call Danny. "Miguel, thank goodness you called me back. Where are you?"

"What's the matter, mi pequeña?"

Tears burned her eyes. Miguel always called her his little girl. "I'm in trouble. Can you come get me and take me to the airport here in Chihuahua?"

"Oh, mi pequeña, I am so sorry. I am at my sister's near Monterrey."

Bailey's shoulders drooped, then she turned her head as she realized someone was speaking to her. The salesclerk.

"May I help you find something? Perhaps a pair of shorts for your daughter?"

She frowned, then forced a smile to her lips as she spoke to Miguel. "Hang on a second."

She grabbed a white organdy A-line dress with embroidered roses on it. "I think we'll see if this dress will fit. Where are the dressing rooms?"

Maria pulled against her. "But I don't like that."

The clerk crossed her arms. "Señora, I'm not sure—"

"I'm sure she'll like it just fine once she tries it on."

"Then you might want to get a smaller size. Like this."

Bailey groaned. She'd picked a dress two sizes too large. "Thank you. Now, the dressing room?"

Once inside the tiny room, she sank to the bench and pressed her finger to her lips. Maria stared at her, her eyes rimmed with tears ready to spill. If Bailey looked in the mirror, she'd see the same thing. "*Un momento, niña.* I need to talk on the phone. Okay?"

Maria barely nodded, and Bailey spoke to Miguel again. "Are you still there?"

"Sí. I've been thinking. My cousin Clemente lives in Chihuahua. I will call him, and he will come and take you."

The band around her chest loosened even as sirens wailed somewhere in the city. "Oh, Miguel. Gracias. Muchas gracias."

"I will call him and call you right back. But first this trouble. What is it?"

"It's nothing that leaving Chihuahua won't fix."

"Bueno."

After hanging up, Bailey leaned against the wall. Now for just a moment to collect herself.

"How did the dress fit the little one?" The clerk's voice penetrated the door.

She glanced at the dress still on the hanger. Maria made a face. Bailey stood and grabbed the dress as she opened the door. "I don't think it's for her. Is there a place to get a cup of coffee around here?"

The clerk wore a just-as-I-expected expression. "Down the street. It is on the left."

"Thank you." This time Bailey found a real smile deep inside her. "Thank you. You have been very kind," she said in Spanish.

As they exited the store, Maria twisted to look back inside the shop. "That lady is looking at us funny."

"I just hope she doesn't call the police," Bailey muttered. But it wasn't only the police she feared. She scanned the street, not sure what she expected to see. She hadn't seen the men after them, but surely they would look suspicious. Seeing nothing out of the ordinary, she led Maria to the small outdoor cafe and chose a table behind a potted plant.

"What's that smell?" Maria wrinkled her nose.

Bailey sniffed the air. An acrid scent burned her nose. Something was on fire, but she couldn't tell which direction the smell came from. When the waitress came, Bailey ordered herself a coffee and Maria chocolate milk, then asked about the odor.

The waitress shrugged. "Someone said a business caught on fire."

Bailey placed her phone on the table. Why didn't Miguel call?

Maria fingered the locket Joel had given her. "Miss Bailey, why don't we call Mr. Danny?" Her tiny voice cracked. "He would help us, I know he would."

She glanced at the small girl. She was right, and Bailey was being silly. Danny would help, and if he knew the cartel had taken Joel, he would be frantic when he couldn't find them. He'd probably already called the false number she programmed into his phone.

She hesitated with her finger on the keyboard. Did she really want to hear him say "I told you so"? *Yes.* She didn't care what he said. She wanted him to come and get her and take care of everything. Her hand shook as she scrolled to his number and called. It went immediately to voicemail. *No!* Tears scalded her eyes. "C-call me."

Another call beeped in, and she answered. Miguel. He had his cousin on hold. After she told him where she was, he checked with the cousin and told her Clemente would pick her up in ten minutes in a maroon van. She waited until it was almost time, then picked up Maria and carried her on her hip to the sidewalk, watching for Clemente's van.

What if Miguel is part of the cartel? Or Clemente? What if they were in cahoots with Father Horatio? She tried to shake the thought off as a lime green Volkswagen Beetle whipped around the corner. It had a taxi symbol on the side.

On impulse she flagged the car down. "Can you take us to the airport?"

"Sí." The wiry Mexican old enough to be Bailey's father hopped out and opened the back door. His grin widened. "For the beautiful señorita," he said in broken English. His smile dimmed at Maria's head drooped on Bailey's shoulder. "And the little one, she is tired."

"Sí. And gracias for taking us." She put Maria in the backseat and looked for a seat belt. There wasn't one, so she slid in and cradled Maria in her arms. A photo ID hanging from the mirror identified the driver as Tito Alaniz.

"What terminal?" he asked over his shoulder as he put the car in gear.

"US Airways."

Maria blinked her eyes open. "My head hurts."

Bailey's heart stilled. She'd left the black bag with Maria's medicine and prescription at the restaurant. The Depakote was the only thing that would ward off one of Maria's migraines. She leaned forward in the car. "Can we go to . . ." What was the name of the restaurant? She pressed her hand to her forehead. "Something about bread . . . they only served breakfast."

"La Casa del Pan?"

"Yes. That was it. I think we only walked a few blocks."

"Not to worry. I know this place."

The car lurched forward, sending Bailey against the back of the seat. After several turns, they rounded a corner, and a policeman stopped them a block from the restaurant.

"What's wrong?" She peered through the windshield. Fire trucks blocked the street ahead, and smoke billowed into the air.

Tito pulled beside the policeman. "What happened?" he asked in Spanish.

"A fire at the restaurant. Maybe from a faulty gas valve. The restaurant is destroyed."

Bailey didn't believe it was an accident for one second. The Calatrava thugs must have come back, looking for her and Maria. "Ask if anyone was hurt."

The police heard her and answered. "One body has been found."

Chills swept over her. Solana or Juan? They had helped her escape, and now one of them was dead. She swallowed the nausea that rose up in her throat. These people didn't care who they killed.

But why did they want Maria so badly?

5

Bailey slumped against the backseat of the VW. Solana or Juan dead. Maria's medicine and prescriptions gone. They had no clothes—their bags were in Joel's car.

Joel's car. They had parked in a lot and walked a couple of blocks. It had to still be there—Joel had placed some of the Depakote in Maria's bag. She leaned forward. "Tito, our bags are in a car, and I need to get them. It's in a lot somewhere near the restaurant."

"Señora, I think we should go straight to the airport."

"But I need medicine that's in one of them."

Tito turned at the next corner and inched down the street.

"There!" She pointed to a parking lot across from them. "And there's the car." He hung a left and pulled into the lot. "Someone's been here already."

The car had been stripped, and the trunk popped open. She'd heard that thieves could strip a car in fifteen minutes in broad daylight.

"We need to not be here!" The cab shot forward. "What time is your flight?"

She checked her watch. "Two hours."

He nodded. "I will get you and the little one to the airport. Eh?"

"Gracias." Joel had chosen this restaurant because it was less

49

than five miles from the airport. Once they were inside the airport, they would be safe. Even a drug cartel would think twice about attacking them with Mexican TSA agents hanging about. At least she hoped that was true.

Surely the Lord is my salvation. I will trust and not be afraid.

She repeated the verses over and over as Tito wound through the streets to the airport, yet she felt no peace. He kept looking in his rearview mirror and turning down side streets. "Is anyone following us?" she asked.

"One never knows. You seem to be in trouble, so I'm taking the long way to the airport, just in case. We will arrive in un momento."

"I don't know how to thank you," she said. "I didn't mean to put you in danger."

"I face robbers every night, so this is nothing."

If Tito intended to make her feel better, he fell short. But if she and Maria could get inside the airport, she wouldn't have to put anyone else in danger. Like Danny. Especially Danny.

Why hadn't he called back? Had he seen her number and hadn't wanted to be bothered? But he had no way to know it was her—she'd given him the wrong number. Maybe it was just as well. She'd managed so far, and she really didn't need to be indebted to him.

When he'd appeared at the restaurant earlier today, she realized she was nowhere near over him. Even now, the ache to feel his arms around her threatened to overthrow her good judgment. *No.* Nothing had changed. She read that in his swagger and teasing tone. Danny Maxwell believed he could do as he pleased and apologize if he was caught, like an apology would smooth everything over.

She stared out the window at the people on the sidewalk. Her eyes widened. A woman with raven hair and a pronounced limp. In black pants and a white waitress shirt. "Pull over!"

"What?"

She pointed toward Solana. "I need to talk to her." When the VW rolled to a stop, she hopped out of the car. "Solana!"

The woman turned, and her eyes grew round. "No! Go away!"

Bailey hurried to her. "Come with us. You'll be safe at the airport."

Solana hesitated. "Juan is dead."

"I know."

"They came back after you left. I hid in a closet, but they beat Juan, trying to find out where you two were . . ." She faltered.

"Come with me, and I'll buy you a ticket to the States. You can stay there. Oh, wait. You would need your passport and visa, but maybe we can get around that."

She'd read somewhere about a Mexican cameraman who outed a drug cartel and received asylum in the United States.

"I have them both with me, but why would you do that for me?"

"It's the least I can do. You saved our lives." She pulled Solana toward the Volkswagen. When Bailey had time, she'd ask Solana why she carried her papers with her. "We have another passenger, Tito," Bailey said as she opened the front passenger door.

As soon as Solana was in, Bailey hopped in the backseat, and Tito gunned the VW away from the curb. She pulled Maria toward her and smoothed her hair back. "You must stay close to me when we get to the airport. Okay?"

"Will you carry me?"

Since she had only her purse with their tickets and identification, carrying the child would be no problem. "Sure, honey."

Tito pulled the VW into the long line of cars dropping off passengers at the US Airways terminal. An airport guard motioned them over to the curb a hundred feet from the sliding doors, but Tito ignored him and inched closer. He parked, and she paid him. "Thank you."

Sweat ran down her face as she opened the door and climbed out with Maria, scanning the drop-off lane to see if anyone was following them. As soon as they were out of the car, Tito pulled away from the curb, and she hurried toward the sliding glass doors with Solana on her heels.

Tires screeched behind them. Bailey turned as men scrambled from a nearby car. She gasped. One of them looked like the man in the grocery store they'd hidden in earlier.

■ ■ ■

Danny checked his watch as he paced outside the US Airways departure terminal. He'd been so sure Bailey would be at the airport, but he and Angel had been hanging around where passengers unloaded for forty minutes with no sign of either her or Maria. A phone call to the receptionist at Maxwell Industries had gotten him Bailey's flight number. Boarding started in ninety minutes.

Angel approached from the doorway where he'd been scanning the crowd in line to get boarding passes. "Do you think they've already gone through security?"

"I hope. But I'm going to hang around until the flight leaves." Danny scanned the area once more. A green Volkswagen Beetle ignored the guard directing traffic and inched closer to the front of the US Airways line. "You don't have to stay—I can get a taxi back to my car."

"No. I'll stay."

"Why? You don't have a dog in this hunt."

Angel's eyebrows pinched together, then a look of understanding lit his eyes. He shook his head. "You Americans say crazy things. But I'm staying."

Tires screeched, and Danny jerked his head toward the sound. He lasered in on the green VW pulling away from the curb. Was that Solana, the waitress from the cafe? His gaze shifted. That was definitely Bailey with Maria in her arms, her eyes on a car that was barreling toward the curb. He shot forward, running toward them with Angel on his heels.

"I'll take care of the women," Danny shouted. "You get Maria."

Bailey stumbled, and Angel scooped Maria from her hands as Danny caught Bailey before she hit the pavement. She tried to jerk away.

"Stay with me!" he hissed as he steadied her. Beside her Solana froze, and he jerked his head toward the door. "Go!"

Solana stood as though she were chained to the concrete. He grabbed the waitress's hand and pulled. "Come on!"

Danny hustled them toward the doors to the terminal. He looked back and saw men exit the car that had pulled up to the curb. He recognized two of them from the restaurant earlier. The doors slid silently open. Angel darted through with Maria, and they followed. Danny jerked his head toward the escalator. "Over there!"

Solana limped toward it, but Bailey pulled away from him. "No! We're safe now. They won't try anything in here with all the security. Where's Maria?"

He glanced around as Angel ran down the moving steps two at a time with the girl. "Too late. Let's go!"

Danny pulled a reluctant Bailey toward the escalator as he scanned the area behind them. The men no longer searched the cars but marched toward the terminal. "They're coming, and they don't look too afraid of security."

She jerked her head toward the door and gasped. He grabbed her hand. "Quit being so stubborn and come on!"

This time, she joined him, and they raced down the escalator, slipping past the people already on it. At the bottom, he searched for Angel and saw him exit the baggage claim area with Maria. He pulled Bailey toward the door.

She balked. "Wait! Where's Solana?"

He swiveled his head, looking. "There, by the other exit."

They bolted for the small woman. "This way," Bailey said when they reached her.

"No, I'll just slow you down." She pointed to the cast on her right foot. "I can't run anymore."

Danny swept her into his arms. "Then I'll carry you. We're not leaving you behind."

He carried her through the door and searched for Angel and Maria.

"There they are, at the taxi stand." Bailey threw him a wild look. "Is he leaving us?" She broke into a run. "Wait!"

"I want Miss Bailey!" Maria's plaintive cry carried over the noise of the traffic.

Danny checked the inside of the terminal. The men who were looking for Maria and Bailey bounded from the escalator, but so far he didn't believe they had seen them. He was on Bailey's heels when she reached Angel and grabbed Maria from his arms.

"Get in," Angel said.

Bailey hesitated.

Angel palmed his hands. "I was not going to leave you."

Without a word, Bailey slid into the backseat of the taxi with Maria.

Danny wasn't so sure that his new friend was telling the truth. He set Solana on the ground, and she scrambled into the front seat beside the driver. "Weren't you?"

"We don't have time to argue. The men are coming." Angel turned and handed the driver money. "Casa Grande?"

"Sí!"

He turned to Danny. "I've made arrangements at the hotel. I'll meet you there later, after I get my car."

Danny nodded, his mind whirling. He'd forgotten Angel's SUV. "How will you find us?"

"Don't worry." Angel pressed a card into his hand, then looked over his shoulder. "Go!"

"Be careful." Danny hopped into the backseat with Maria and Bailey. As soon as he slammed the door, the taxi shot forward.

At least the car had darkly tinted windows, blocking passengers from view.

"Miss Bailey, I want to go home." Maria sobbed into Bailey's shoulder.

The poor kid had to be terrified. But she'd been a trouper, for sure. Not only Maria, but Bailey as well. Danny patted the girl's arm. "It's going to be okay, honey. When we get to the hotel, I'll get you an ice cream. Okay?"

She stared at Danny with tears falling from her huge blue eyes. "Will you find my uncle?"

■ ■ ■

Light encroached the darkness, but with it pain. Unbearable pain. The forlorn whistle of a train raked his ears, bringing with it the memory of being carried. Kidnapped. Then the questions and the blows. This was all wrong. He couldn't give them what they wanted, and he no longer knew what he'd said and what he hadn't.

"He's coming around."

The words were spoken in Spanish, but not by the ones who had beaten him earlier. The second string must have been sent in. Someone shook him, reeling his senses. Maybe if they thought he had other information, he could bargain. Stiffening his backbone, Joel raised his head, sending pain through his arms bound behind him. He struggled to look the men in the eye, but his left eyelid refused to budge. He cracked the right one even though it was almost swollen shut. It appeared they were in a warehouse of some kind.

"The woman and child?"

He bared his teeth. "I don't know what you're talking about."

Talking cost him strength. Strength he had to save for thinking. And for trying to get untied. He wiggled his hands, feeling the rope that bound him give.

"Your niece. And the woman with her. Where are they?"

A shred of relief spread through him. If they didn't have Maria, she and the necklace were safely on their way to the States. Now all he had to do was stay alive long enough to get to her. "How would I know? The last time I saw them was at the restaurant."

The man questioning him swore. Joel closed his eye and braced for another blow to his head. When it didn't come, he risked another look. The man stood, his arms folded.

"They went to the airport. What's their destination?"

He wasn't stupid. If he gave up the information, he would be of no further use to them. "Why do you—"

"No questions. You owe—"

A door burst open, and a flash of light followed by an explosion rocked his head.

"Police! Put your guns down!"

Gunfire rang out. Joel rocked the chair, managing to tip himself over, and crashed onto the floor. He lay unmoving until the shooting stopped. Then someone lifted him, and rough hands jerked the ropes loose. He inched his stiff arms forward, and a wave of pain tore through him. He groaned.

"Are you all right?"

"Do I look all right?" Joel eyed the wiry Mexican who knelt beside him.

"Sorry. I'm Sergeant Quinten Chavez—with the PFM. And you are?"

Police of the Federal Ministry. The big guns. "Joel McDermott. I work for Montoya Cerámica." He worked his shoulders, and circulation returned to his arms. "How did you know—"

"Lucky for you, someone saw them bring you into the warehouse and reported it. We knew this was a Calatrava operations building, and we jumped on it."

"So it was the Calatrava?" But why? It hadn't been the cartel he'd lost money to.

"*Was* is correct." The inspector jerked his head toward two bodies on the floor. "At least for these two. They won't be hurting anyone else. Do you know why the drug cartel took you?"

Joel rubbed his arms. There was not a muscle in his body that didn't hurt. "No."

Chavez lifted his eyebrows.

"If I knew, I would tell you."

A beep on the sergeant's phone interrupted whatever he intended to say. Chavez read the message. "Your niece. Where is she?"

Joel's heart stilled. Chavez already knew about Maria? "On her way to the States with her teacher."

"I'm afraid not."

"What do you mean?"

"According to the message I just received, Bailey Adams and Maria Montoya were no-shows on the plane."

Joel's heart sank. This could not be happening. "The cartel doesn't have them. That was the information they wanted from me—their whereabouts. If they're not on the plane, then I don't have a clue."

"What would the Calatrava drug cartel want with your niece, Mr. McDermott?"

"You have to ask? How about ransom? Her great-uncle Edward Montoya is quite wealthy, and it's common knowledge wealthy people in Mexico carry insurance."

Chavez nodded. "And you yourself have such insurance."

"Yeah. So?" He leveled his gaze at the detective. "You seem to know a lot about me."

Chavez ignored his inference. "Can you call Miss Adams?"

He felt for his phone. Gone. He swore. He needed that phone. He nodded to the men on the floor. "They must've taken my cell."

Chavez took out his phone. "Give me her number, and I'll call."

Joel closed his eyes and tried to recall Bailey's number. He gave the sergeant what he thought the number might be.

Chavez dialed it, then disconnected. "That's not the number."

"That's why I need my phone. I can never trust my memory." He tried once more to visualize Bailey's number, but it was no use. Joel shook his head. "I'm sorry. If you find my cell phone, it'll be in it."

"Let's see." Chavez rifled through the pockets of the dead men, producing two black smartphones and a wallet. First he flipped the wallet open, then handed it to Joel. "Yours, I believe." Then he held the phones up. "And one of these, maybe?"

Joel took the first one he handed him and turned it on. "Not this one."

The detective powered up the one he held, and it showed a photo of Claire and Maria on the beach. "I assume this is a photo of your wife?"

"My sister." Joel reached for the phone. He was pretty sure Chavez already knew that.

Chavez moved it out of his reach. "I also assume you have Miss Adams's cell number in your contacts, so first let's see if she will answer."

What was the man's problem? "Hey, I'm not the bad guy here."

"I never said you were." The detective's hooded gaze said otherwise. He scrolled through Joel's contacts and pressed Bailey's number. The call went immediately to voicemail. "She doesn't seem to be available." Chavez tossed the phone to him. "Maybe you have another number where you can reach her?"

"Look, Detective—"

"Sergeant."

Joel took a deep breath. He knew that many of the federal police supplemented their meager salary by extortion. Pretend that a victim was actually the perpetrator, and for a price, the harassment could end. "Sergeant Chavez, let's stop playing games. I don't know why they kidnapped me or why they want my niece. If you know, please tell me."

"If I knew, you would probably be under arrest. The drug cartel doesn't beat up innocent citizens—they only demand money from them."

"Well, this time, they did." He waited for the extortion demand.

"We'll see. How much insurance do you carry on your niece?"

"I carry five million on both of us. Not sure how much her great-uncle carries." Joel couldn't wrap his mind around the sergeant's strategy, and he didn't have the time or brain cells to figure it out. He stood, and dizziness threatened to put him back on the floor. "I have to find Maria. With or without your help."

"You are unable to drive in your condition."

His car. He'd forgotten he left it in a parking lot near the cafe. Joel felt his pockets. "They took my keys." Which probably meant the Mercedes was long gone by now. Or stripped.

"Was your house key on the ring?"

Joel nodded. His day had just gotten a whole lot worse. No. Even if they got into his house, he'd locked the safe before he left. Without the combination, it'd take dynamite to get the door off . . . or a plastic explosive.

Chavez's mouth settled in a firm line. "I'll take you to get your car, then follow you to your house. Direct me to where you left it."

Talk was minimal as the sergeant drove. As they turned the corner where Casa del Pan was located, Joel caught his breath. Smoke hovered over what was left of the cafe. He turned to Chavez, and the intensity of his gaze made him flinch. The sergeant had purposefully not told him of the fire to see his reaction. "When did this happen?"

"Not long after you were taken."

"Maria?"

"No *child's* body was found."

But a body had been found. "Who? Why?"

A slight shrug lifted Chavez's shoulders. "That seems to be the question of the day. But for your first question, the size of the body indicates it was the cook."

The image of the small woman who waited on them flitted in his mind. "How about the waitress?"

"She seems to have escaped. I want to know why someone would kidnap you, burn down a cafe, and commit murder to find your niece."

"I'm telling you, I don't know." Joel forced himself to not look away from the dark eyes that bore through him, but he couldn't do anything about the sweat that trickled down his back.

Chavez cocked his head. "Where did you park your car?"

Joel's shoulders relaxed. "Around the block."

Chavez drove to the lot. The car wasn't gone, but it might as well be. Only the shell remained. Everything else was stripped away.

Chavez's cell phone rang, and he answered. "I see. We'll be there in ten minutes." After he hung up, he turned to Joel, his expression unreadable.

"Maria?" Joel fisted his hands, waiting for the bad news.

The detective shook his head. "Your house has been ransacked."

6

Danny kept his eye on the traffic behind them, but so far it didn't seem that anyone was following them from the airport.

"Will you find my uncle?" Maria asked again.

Danny knew he shouldn't make that sort of promise, but the look in the child's eyes made him want to try. "I'll do my best," he said. He wished Bailey would look at him the way Maria did. So far, they might as well be strangers. No. With a stranger, at least he had a chance. With Bailey there was no hope.

Maria climbed out of Bailey's lap and into his and hugged him. "You can find him, I know you can."

"I'd rather you sit with me," Bailey said. "I wish the taxi had a car seat for her." She tugged the child back into her lap and frowned at Danny like it was his fault there was no safety seat and that the car reeked of stale cigarette smoke. "Why didn't you call me back?"

"When did you call?"

"I don't know. Before we went to the airport."

Danny took out his phone and checked his missed calls. He frowned. How did he miss her call? It was right below the call to his secretary at the plant. No wonder she was angry. "I must have been talking to Tiffany."

Her shoulders stiffened.

"I called her to get your flight number." Was she still upset about what had happened with Tiffany? Or rather what didn't happen. But even if something had happened, after she broke the engagement, she shouldn't have cared what he did. Unless . . .

Maria wiggled free. "I want to sit in Mr. Danny's lap."

Bailey sighed but let her stay with him. Maria leaned against his chest, and he wrapped his arms around her. An emotion he wasn't familiar with filled his chest. Who would've thought a little girl could wrap her fingers around his heart so fast?

Maria raised her head to look up at him. "Who was that man? The one who carried me."

"I'd like to know that as well," Bailey said.

Before Danny could answer, Solana turned where she could face them. "His name is Angel, and he's a good man."

Admiration for Angel rang in her voice, but a question nagged at Danny. Everyone else in the restaurant had run when the shooting started. But Angel had rushed to rescue them. Why? Danny had a few questions for Angel Guerrera when they reached the hotel.

"Do you know his last name?" Bailey asked.

"It's Guerrera," Danny said and shifted his gaze to Solana. "How do you know Angel?"

"All the small businesses know him. We call him the Angel of the Streets because he and his friends patrol our businesses. They are fighting a war against the Calatrava. His men were there, trying to put the fire out at the cafe today, but they could not save Juan."

He jerked his head toward her. "What fire?"

"The cartel. They came back after you left, and they beat up Juan, trying to find out where . . ." Solana faltered and glanced at Maria. "Then they set fire to the cafe and left. I tried to put it out, but it was too big. Angel's men came, but it was too big for them too. They helped me escape."

Bailey pressed her hand to her mouth. "Did Angel's men say why . . ."

Solana shook her head. "The cartel doesn't have to have a reason."

"He was a nice man," Maria said. "Will we see him again?"

"Yes. He's coming to the hotel." Danny chewed the inside of his cheek. The cartel had gone to too much trouble for their actions to be random kidnappings. Maybe Angel would have answers. He leaned as the taxi made a sharp right turn.

"Casa Grande." The taxi driver pointed toward the hotel on their left.

■ ■ ■

Half an hour later, Danny opened the connecting door between the two rooms. Solana lay on the bed beside Maria as the two of them napped, but Bailey stood at the window, staring out. She turned, dejection showing in her slumped shoulders.

Quietly he walked across the room and took her in his arms. She leaned against his chest. "Thank you for coming after me," she said. "I . . ."

"I was so scared when I couldn't find you in the cafe," he murmured against her hair. What he wouldn't give to hold her like this all the time. "Are you okay?"

She stepped away from him, and some of the sass returned to her eyes. "Let's see. Joel's been kidnapped, I've hidden in a cellar, and you know how I hate being in dark, dank places. I called you and you didn't answer. I've been chased. Twice. I missed our flight and have no idea how I'm going to get this child to her grandparents. I lost Maria's medication for her headaches, and I understand when she has one, it's very painful. The medicine was in a bag with her prescription and contact information for the grandparents that I left at the cafe. And last of all, I'm holed up here with you." She folded her arms across her chest, but a tiny smile played at her lips. "What's not to be okay about?"

His heart swelled with pride. Bailey had more courage than anyone he knew. She might get knocked down, but she always bounced back up. He held up his hands. "Hey, I'm just trying to help."

"I know. I'm sorry."

"And maybe the medicine isn't lost."

"What do you mean?"

He nodded toward the bed. "Solana found a bag you left behind and gave it to me. It's in Angel's car."

"Really?"

For a second, he thought she was going to throw her arms around his neck. Then she caught herself and stepped back.

"What if he loses it?"

"He won't. And he'll be here soon. Let me text him to bring it to the room when he gets here." Danny quickly sent Angel a text and received an acknowledgment. "He'll bring it, but he's not sure how long before he'll get here."

"That would be one worry gone—Maria's already mentioned her head hurts. If we just hadn't missed the flight." She massaged the back of her neck, then loosened the clasp holding her golden hair in a ponytail and shook her hair out, sending it tumbling around her shoulders.

He wanted to smooth her hair back, to feel the silky strands in his fingers once more. There had to be a way to make her see that they could work things out. "I'll fly you home," he said softly. "Then go with you to take Maria to her grandparents."

"You will?" Her eyes widened, then she shook her head. "Thanks, but I really think I should go to the police. It's what I should have done first."

"I've already tried that. It won't do any good."

Maria cried out in her sleep, and Bailey rushed to the bed, but Solana soothed her with soft Spanish words.

Bailey waited until Maria settled into a deeper sleep, then motioned him to the connecting door. "We don't need to talk where she can hear us." Once they were in the other room, she turned to him. "What do you mean, you've already tried the police?"

"I went there after I didn't find you in the alley. Angel warned me it would do no good, and it didn't. Once they found out the Calatrava was involved, it was like . . ." He struggled to find the right word. "There was nothing they could do about it."

"Solana and Juan warned me as well." She rubbed her arms. "In the restaurant today, I saw a man from the village where I served as a missionary. When I first heard the gunshots, I thought he was after me, but then I didn't see him again and they wanted Maria. I'm still not sure he isn't part of this."

"Why do you think he—"

"It's a long story." She tilted her head. "You seem to know this Angel pretty well. Just who is he?"

"I don't really know him. I met him once when we were kids, but he just showed up today."

Maria cried out again, and Bailey walked through the doorway and peeked into the other room, then returned. "I'm so afraid she'll wake up—"

"And you want to be there for her. Solana will let you know."

Bailey swallowed and looked everywhere but at him. When her chin quivered, he pulled her to him again. "It's going to be okay."

At first she resisted, then as he stroked her back, he felt the tenseness ebb. "We'll keep her safe."

She stiffened and pulled away. "Maria is not your responsibility."

He gave her a crooked grin. "She is now. Solana too." He had to convince her to give up this idea of the police. "When we get to Logan Point, we'll turn all of this over to Ben."

Her eyes widened. "Are you talking about Sheriff Ben Logan? I thought you two—"

"Were like oil and water?" He chuckled. "I discovered he wasn't such a bad guy. He'll know what to do."

A soft knock at the door stilled his heart. Angel? He turned to Bailey. "Go in the other room and lock the door."

As soon as Bailey closed the connecting door, he looked through the peephole. It *was* Angel. Danny jerked the door open. "You scared me to death. You could've texted."

Danny's phone whistled, and Angel grinned. "That's probably my text."

"Did you bring the bag?"

"It's in the car."

"I told you to bring it to the hotel. Bailey's worried because Maria has the beginnings of a headache."

"So she doesn't have seizures?" The frown lines in Angel's face smoothed out.

"No, but there's something else—we have to talk Bailey out of going to the police."

"That could be a fatal mistake. I will convince her." He started for the door.

"Wait. I have another question first. I'm not sure you should continue to be a part of getting them back to the States."

Angel's eyes narrowed. "If you want to get to your plane, you will need me, amigo."

"Then tell me how you knew those men would be there today."

"I don't know what you are talking about."

"Don't play dumb with me. I saw you watching Joel this morning at the cafe. Then I saw you look away as one of the men who took Joel stared at you. What's your stake in this?" Had his overactive imagination read Angel wrong?

"I don't know what you are talking about."

Angel tried to brush past him, but Danny blocked his way, then stood in front of the door with his arms folded. "You're not going in there until I get some answers."

For a minute, he believed Angel would bulldoze past him, and he wasn't sure he could take the Mexican. In fact, he was pretty sure he couldn't. Then like mercury, Angel changed. His stance relaxed, and he slapped Danny on the back.

"I like you. You stand for what you believe."

Danny stared him down. "Answers."

Angel shrugged. "The man who stared at me was a minion of the Calatrava. I did not want him to recognize me. But he probably did."

"Okay," Danny said. "Why the interest in Maria?"

"A long time ago and not so long ago, I knew Maria's mother. I told her I would always protect her and the child. Unfortunately, I failed to protect Claire."

"How did she die?"

Something flashed in Angel's eyes. "A reaction to an antidepressant that she wouldn't have been on if . . ." He cocked his head. "Now I have a question for you. Why are you here?"

"What do you mean?"

"You said earlier today that I didn't have a dog in this hunt. What interest do you have?"

Danny squared his shoulders. "Bailey was my fiancée once."

Sympathy filled Angel's eyes. Finally the Mexican nodded. "If she was my woman, I would fight for her too."

"She's not *my* woman. We were engaged once, and I still care about her. That's all."

"Sure. And if you are through asking questions, let's go make plans to get out of Chihuahua. We should've been gone five minutes ago."

Danny turned the knob on the connecting door. "I told her to lock it."

He rapped twice and waited. Seconds passed. He knocked again. Why didn't she open the door?

"Do you have a key to her room?"

"Somewhere." He felt his pockets, then checked the dresser. There it was. He grabbed it and hurried through the exterior door to their room that Angel held open. The Mexican yanked the key from his hand and opened Bailey's door.

The room was empty.

■ ■ ■

Joel moved the ice bag he'd put on his left eye to the right one and stared at the open wall safe. It was supposed to be foolproof and could only be opened with the combination. He should know by now that nothing was foolproof.

Behind him, Sergeant Chavez cleared his throat. "I hope you didn't have any nice jewelry in there."

"No." He didn't feel the need to explain that what jewelry Claire had owned was in a lockbox for Maria when she was older.

"I have to say, whoever did this knew what they were doing."

"Yeah." Or had the combination that was stored in an encrypted file on his now-gone computer. Which just went to show he'd been right in believing any computer could be hacked. Not that it mattered, anyway. The machine could be replaced and the files restored. But it would take time. What if whoever did this recognized the number encrypted in one of the files? Or the file he needed failed to back up?

Then he'd have to use the backup to the backup. And it was where no one would think to look. Unfortunately, after this morning, it'd be hard for him to get to, and without that number, the millions of dollars in the account would do him no good.

Chavez closed the safe. "I'd like to have an itemized list of what was in the safe."

"There was nothing there but insurance papers and my work computer."

The sergeant took out a pen and pad. "Is it backed up?"

"On the company server." He didn't trust Chavez. The man was looking for something to pin on him, and Joel didn't have a clue why. "If you want a look at my hard drive, you'll have to talk to Edward Montoya." He'd be surprised if his boss gave Chavez the time of day. "Are your men through with my house? I'd like to put it back together."

Not that he cared about his house—he just wanted Chavez and his men gone. Then he could start looking for Maria. At least Claire's car hadn't been bothered, so he'd have wheels.

"If not, they will be finished soon. The safe seems to have suffered the most scrutiny." Chavez turned to leave. "Oh, don't leave Chihuahua anytime soon."

"What do you suspect me of?"

"Should I suspect you of something?"

"No, of course not." Joel hated this cat-and-mouse game. Why didn't Chavez just spit out what he wanted? It had to be money, because there was no way the sergeant could actually suspect him of anything—he'd never even had a parking ticket. And if it was money, he wished Chavez would just give him an amount. He was tempted to name a price, but if he was wrong, the sergeant would probably arrest Joel for trying to bribe him.

Chavez hung around for a few minutes longer, then called his men off. "If you hear from your niece, let me know."

Joel nodded. In a pig's eye he would. As soon as Chavez was out the door, Joel scrolled through his contacts for Bailey's number. He'd give it one more try. This time the call didn't go straight to voicemail.

"Joel?" Bailey's voice sounded hesitant. "I was afraid you were dead."

"Not quite, but thank goodness you're all right," he said. "Is Maria okay?"

"Yes. How did you escape?"

He rubbed his ribs that shot pain through him every time he breathed. At least the ice had brought the swelling in his eyes down enough for him to see. "It's a long story, and I'll explain when we're together. Where are you?"

She hesitated.

"Never mind. Meet me . . ." He tried to think of a safe place.

She answered before he came up with a plan. "There are men after Maria, maybe the same ones who took you. I don't think I should bring her to you. I'm taking her to the States, and you can meet up with us at your parents'."

"She's my niece. Do you think I'd put her in danger?"

"I don't know, Joel. I don't know anything anymore, other than I want to keep her safe."

"She's my sister's child. No one will keep her as safe as I will. Where are you? I'll come and get her."

"No. I have to hang up."

He stared at the dead phone. Then clicked on an app he'd put on Bailey's phone. Her location popped up. Casa Grande.

7

Bailey slipped her phone into her pocket. She was not handing Maria over to Joel. Not until they were safe in the States. Where was Danny? She'd carried his instructions to lock the door a step further and herded Maria and Solana into the bathroom.

"Bailey! Where are you?"

She opened the door. "In here."

He whirled around, scowling. "What are you doing in the bathroom?"

"It seemed like a good idea. I thought if someone broke in, they would think the room was empty."

The lines in his face relaxed. "Good thinking."

Once they were out of the bathroom, Bailey realized Angel had joined them. Like before, he carried himself with the assurance of someone used to being in charge.

"Mr. Angel, you came back!" Maria wiggled from her arms onto the floor, and Angel bent over and picked her up.

"Yes, little one, I came back. And now we must leave."

When he straightened, Bailey held out her hand. "We haven't been introduced. I'm Bailey, and you must be Angel. Did you bring Maria's medicine?"

He shook her hand, bowing slightly. "Yes, I am Angel, and no,

I did not bring the medicine. It is in the car, but we need to leave right away—every minute we stay in Mexico is dangerous."

Since she'd decided against going to the authorities, Bailey agreed with him. "We're ready. What's the plan?"

"My plane," Danny said. "That's our next destination. We'll go down the stairs and out the back. Angel will go in front, and I'll be behind you three."

Sounded like a plan to her. "I'll carry Maria."

"If you get tired, I can help," Solana said.

In the hallway, a couple strolled by, giving them a curious stare. Bailey turned to Danny. "Joel called. He wanted Maria."

"What? You didn't tell him where you were, did you?"

"No. I told him he'd have to come to the States to get her."

"Good."

Angel opened the door to the stairwell, and they trooped down the stairs. By the time they reached the lobby, she felt a little silly with the cloak-and-dagger when no one seemed to pay any attention to them. Maybe everything was going to be okay. They rounded a corner, and she gasped. "There's Joel."

He stood outside the doorway, trying to get in. She faltered. His face looked as though it had been used as a punching bag, and both of his eyes were swollen and bruised. In her peripheral vision, she glimpsed a man running toward her.

Angel grabbed Maria from her arms. "Follow me!"

She half turned. "Where's Danny?"

"Behind you. He'll make it. You help Solana." Angel shot out the exit door, and she grabbed Solana's hand and together they ran after Angel.

Once outside, Angel raced toward a dark blue SUV. "You two, get in the backseat." He handed a wide-eyed Maria to Bailey before he hopped into the driver's seat and started the motor. She barely had her seat belt fastened before he shot forward.

"We can't leave Danny!"

"There he is." Angel pointed toward the door they'd exited.

Danny ran toward them, and as the car slowed to a stop, he hopped in. "Go!" he shouted. "He has friends."

"Where's your plane?"

"At Chico's Airfield outside of Chihuahua."

"I know where it is." Angel made a hard right turn.

Bailey held Maria tight as they barreled out of the hotel parking lot.

"Joel must have brought the Calatrava to the hotel, but how did he find us?" Danny turned to look at her. "Did you tell him?"

The accusation in his voice burned her, and she gritted her teeth. "I told you I didn't. I don't know how he knew."

"You have to know."

In her lap, Maria started to cry, and Bailey narrowed her eyes at Danny. "This is not the time to discuss the matter."

His gaze skittered to Maria. "But we will discuss it later."

"Fine." With the lump in her throat threatening to choke her, she sank against the seat beside Solana. Tears stung her eyes, but she would not cry. Danny acted like she'd brought the men after them.

Maria burrowed against her chest. "Is Mr. Danny mad at me?"

"No, honey."

"Why are the bad men chasing us again?"

"I don't know, Maria." Bailey stared out the window as Angel made another turn. How did Joel know where they were? Did he lead those men to her? She couldn't believe he would do something like that, and if he had, she was the worst judge of men ever.

Her cell phone dinged, and she slid it from her pocket. "It's Joel. He wants to know where we are."

Angel looked in the rearview mirror, his eyes wide. "Do not answer him. He'll lead the cartel to us again."

Danny reached from the front seat for her phone. She moved it out of his reach. "I'm not totally stupid. I didn't text him back."

Her phone chimed again, and she read the text, then hugged Maria. "And he said to tell you he loves you."

"Will we see him again?" Tears rimmed Maria's eyes.

"I'm sure we will." Bailey shifted her gaze to the front and caught Angel staring at her from the mirror with a cell phone pressed to his ear. Why was he helping them? She tilted her head. "Who are the Calatrava? Who runs the cartel?"

Angel glanced in the mirror again. "No one knows," he replied. "The only name I've heard on the streets is El Jefe."

"The Boss," Danny said. "Somebody has to know his real name."

"No. He is like a ghost, and no one breathes it. Some say there is more than one in control."

"Like a governing board?" Danny asked.

"I've never heard of it in Mexico before, but maybe."

"But even a board usually has one person with more power."

"El Jefe." Angel shrugged. "I'm just repeating what I've heard."

"Why do you think they want . . ." She let her gaze drop to the top of Maria's head.

"Ransom," the Mexican replied.

"But Joel doesn't have the kind of money the drug cartels demand when they snatch someone."

"I'm sure he carries kidnap and ransom insurance." Bitterness laced Angel's voice. "It's also possible they want her in order to have control over someone."

That someone could only be Joel. But what did he have that the cartel wanted? He was a purchasing agent for a ceramics company. An image of his battered face popped into her mind, and she winced. He'd really taken a beating. She would like to know how he escaped from the men who took him.

The SUV turned, then a couple of blocks later turned again. Bailey raised up and looked out the back window. Did Angel think someone was following them? They had left Chihuahua and were headed south into the countryside. "Where are we?"

"Near my plane," Danny said.

"I don't feel good," Maria said, her fingers rubbing the necklace. "My head hurts."

Bailey felt the child's head. No fever.

Danny leaned over the backseat. "What's wrong?"

"Her headache is worse. Where's her medicine?" Danny had said Angel had it. "She hasn't had any since early this morning, and that may be what's wrong."

"Look on the floorboard," Angel said.

She pinched her brows together. "What?"

"Her medicine bag is on the floor."

Relief washed over her when she saw the small bag she'd left in the chair at the restaurant. She pulled it on the seat next to her and sorted through it for the bottle of Depakote. "I guess it's too much to hope there's bottled water in the car."

Angel glanced at her from the rearview mirror again. "Look in the area behind your seat. Should be water and even food."

The look on her face must have shown surprise because Angel laughed. "I always make sure there is food and water stashed in my car. Never know when you might have to go on the run."

As Solana looked for the water, Bailey stared at Angel. "Who are you?"

He grinned. "You Americans ask so many questions, and we are at the airport now. Maybe there will be time later for answers."

Solana handed her a bottle of water, and Bailey quickly uncapped it and gave Maria a pill. Water dribbled from her lips as the SUV made a sharp turn, jostling them. Bailey braced against the door and wiped Maria's mouth. "Did you take it?"

The child nodded as the car made another sharp turn and they swayed against the door. Bailey glanced through the window and saw a white single-prop plane. Cars in the distance caught her eye, and in the front seat, alarm flashed across Danny's face.

"They found us!"

Bailey's heart crashed against her ribs. There were two more cars behind the first one. Her phone dinged again. She glanced down and caught her breath.

"What is it?" Danny asked.

"Could Joel have put a way to track me on my phone?"

"Of course. No wonder he knew where we were. Give me your phone!" Danny held out his hand.

A lightbulb clicked on in her head. The men probably had Joel's phone and were using the app to locate them. She handed him the phone, and he threw it on the floor and stomped it. "Wait! All you had to do was take the SIM card out."

Danny lowered his window and tossed her shattered phone through it. "Not taking any chances. I'll buy you a new one when we get home."

Home. Bailey glanced out the window at his plane. She feared they would never get off the ground.

■ ■ ■

Joel drove aimlessly through the streets of Chihuahua. No one seemed to be following him. The kidnappers were probably hot on Bailey and Maria's trail. There'd been no answer to his last text. He tried to access her location only to receive a message telling him it was unavailable.

If he could have gotten in the side door at the hotel, they would be with him instead of Danny Maxwell. Joel had only seen the back of the man with Danny, but something about him seemed very familiar.

He stared at his cell phone on the console. If the Calatrava weren't following him, there was a reason for that. Of course. While they had his phone, they must've installed a tracking program on it. They knew where he was every second.

He pulled into the parking area of a small mom-and-pop grocery and grabbed the phone. A quick scan of the programs found nothing unusual, then he checked for hidden programs running in the background. TrackGenie. His stomach soured. He'd read about this particular spying software a month ago in a trade magazine. It would not only track the phone it was programmed on but also the point of origin of arriving messages. The men who kidnapped him must have put it on his phone. Or Chavez.

If it was the cartel, it meant they knew where Bailey was when she answered his text. He closed his eyes. Not good. Could he ping her phone now and get a reading on her location? He wasn't sure how the software worked, but before he removed it, tracking her current location was worth a try.

He opened the app, and her message appeared with a location. When he'd texted her, it had gone to a location near the outskirts of Chihuahua. He tapped the location, then tapped it again. A spinning wheel appeared, and he waited. *Location unavailable.* Either she'd turned off her phone or . . . A number of possibilities crossed his mind. She'd lost the phone or she'd discovered the program or the cartel had them . . . That option wasn't one he wanted to consider. He had to believe Danny Maxwell had outsmarted the cartel and that Bailey and Maria were safe.

So where would he take them? No-brainer—the States. Joel disabled the app rather than deleting it—it might come in handy later. Then he clicked the internet search engine on his phone to find the next flight to Memphis, Tennessee. His heart sank. No, he wouldn't. He no longer had a passport—his had been in the safe.

He leaned his head against the seat and pressed the heels of his hands to his eyes. It might take weeks to get a passport. Abruptly, Joel sat up straight. Edward Montoya. His boss should have been his first thought, not his last. The man could get anything done. Joel dialed his number.

"Did you send my girl off safely?" While there was no hint of a Spanish accent in Edward's voice, he spoke more precisely than most Americans.

Joel hesitated. Since before Claire's death, his boss had taken a special interest in his great-niece. He would not be happy about today's events. "Not exactly. I have to see you. I need a passport."

"What do you mean, not exactly?"

"I don't want to get into it on the phone. I'd rather talk to you in person."

"I was just going back to the office, but I'll wait for you here at the house. Why do you need a passport? What happened to yours?"

"I lost it, and I need to go to the States."

"I suppose that's something else you want to wait until you arrive to explain."

"Yes."

Twenty minutes later, the security gates swung open, and he drove to the front of the two-story mansion that once belonged to Edward's brother. Joel's hand froze on the steering wheel. The man who had seemed vaguely familiar. *Angel Montoya.* No. Joel's brother-in-law was dead, had been for two years.

But what if he was alive? Joel's breath came in short bursts. He didn't know which would be worse—if the cartel had Maria or if Angel was alive and had his daughter.

■ ■ ■

Danny judged the distance of the cars following them. It'd take five minutes at least to get his plane down the runway. It would be close. At least he'd refueled when he landed, and the plane was ready to take off.

"Do you have a gun?"

Danny stared at the Glock in Angel's hand. He wished he hadn't left his automatic in the plane. "Not on me. It's in the cockpit."

"I'll cover you." Angel jerked his head toward Bailey and Maria. "Get them on board and get that plane in the air."

"I don't want to leave you behind."

"Don't worry about me." Angel barreled through the gate and skidded to a stop. "Go!"

"Come on!" Danny flung open his door and jumped out. He motioned to Solana and Bailey to get out.

Solana scrambled out the backseat first, followed by Bailey with Maria in her arms. Danny grabbed the girl and sprinted for the plane. Tires screeched behind him. He shot a glance over his shoulder. Angel had wheeled the SUV around, blocking the entrance to the runway. He caught sight of someone in his peripheral vision. The airport manager.

"Hey! You can't do that!"

Danny didn't break stride. "Calatrava men," he shouted over his shoulder.

The man turned and ran back into the terminal. Danny didn't blame him. At the plane, he hopped up on the wing and unlocked the door. "Get in," he said, handing Maria to Bailey. "Buckle up."

White-faced, Bailey took the child and fumbled for the seat belt. Gunfire erupted as he scrambled into the pilot seat and started the engine. More gunshots and he jerked his head toward the road. One of the cars veered off the pavement and flipped over. One down, two to go. Wait. There were two more cars turning off the highway. But they were shooting at the Calatrava. Angel fired, then he turned and ran to the plane.

"Get this bird off the ground," he yelled as he slammed the cockpit door.

Danny gave him a thumbs-up and taxied to the runway. "Your men?"

Angel nodded, but his gaze went beyond the cockpit.

Danny glanced back. The Calatrava had breached the SUV. They were still close enough that a bullet could hit the plane. A quick check of the wind sock indicated the wind was out of the south. Good. He was on the northern end of the runway and only had to taxi a short distance to take off into the wind.

Just as he turned the plane to the runway, gunshots popped like firecrackers, and a hole appeared in the wing on Danny's left. *Not now.* They were so close to taking off. He checked his gauges. Fuel holding steady. Hydraulic system the same. Maybe they'd literally dodged a bullet.

"Will that affect the plane?"

Evidently Angel had seen the bullet hole. Danny shoved a headset into his hands. He didn't want Bailey to know they'd been hit. As soon as they both donned the earphones, he said, "I don't think it hit anything vital. The holes might make it a little harder to control. If that happens, once we get across the border in Texas, I'll land and check it out."

Danny taxied into position and ran the engine up to 75 percent of power, then seconds later he pushed the throttle against the fire wall to full power. As the plane raced down the runway, he checked his gauges again. Everything showed green. When he passed sixty-four knots, he pulled back on the yoke and felt the Cessna lift off the ground.

As the Cessna lifted higher, he glanced below. A man stood on the runway, a gun in his raised hand. They were sitting ducks. Three of Angel's men ran toward the man, and he whirled, firing in their direction. Angel's men returned fire, and the man crumpled to the ground. Danny wiped sweat from his face with the back of his hand. He never wanted to be that close to a man with a gun pointed at him again.

He swung the plane toward home. Didn't seem as though the bullet hole would be a problem. Bailey punched his shoulder, and he looked back. Her mouth was moving, but he couldn't hear her over the noise in the cabin. He handed her three headsets, and she put hers on after handing the other two off to Solana.

"The bullet hole—are we okay?"

Her anxiety transmitted through the microphone loud and clear. He checked his gauges again. "We're fine." He glanced at the small girl with her face plastered against the window. "How's Maria?"

"Better than I am. She seems to think we're in a TV program."

Danny laughed. "Someone needs to monitor what she watches."

She gave him a tiny smile back, then her expression sobered. "The plane is really okay?"

He looked around again. More than anything, he wanted to erase the worry in her eyes. To be her hero again. "Yes. And there's nothing standing in our way of landing at the Logan Point airfield in about six hours."

The warmth in her eyes gave him hope that just maybe he'd redeemed himself a little in her books.

Angel's voice cut into their conversation. "What do you plan to do about Maria?"

Danny figured he was talking to Bailey, so he waited for her to answer.

"I still want to take her to her grandparents—oh no!" She leaned forward. "They'll be looking for us tonight. I was supposed to call them when we got off the plane in Memphis. When I don't, they'll be worried. I have to let them know where we are."

"No!" Angel's sharp retort startled him.

"Why not? They're her grandparents."

Even over the microphone, Danny heard the stubbornness in her voice. He glanced at Angel. For once, Bailey may have run up against someone as stubborn as she was.

Her eyes widened, and she shook her head. "How about if I tell them we won't be there tonight."

Angel nodded. "As long as you don't try to take her to them. Her grandparents are old and won't know how to protect her if the Calatrava show up."

Danny glanced at the backseat. Bailey leaned back and at least seemed to be considering what Angel said. "He's right," Danny said. "None of us know how far these men will go to get Maria."

"Do you really think they'll follow us to Mississippi?"

He shrugged, but Angel didn't respond. It was evident he knew more than he was sharing, and when they landed to refuel, Danny intended to find out just what he knew. But first he had to alert the Border Protection Agency that they were crossing from Mexico into the States.

He frowned as Angel nodded toward Bailey and handed him a note that said to turn off her headphones.

8

Joel paced his boss's den. What if it was Angel he saw? He stopped when Edward Montoya asked him the same question for the second time. "If I knew why those men kidnapped me, I'd tell you. I don't have a clue about that or why they want Maria other than a ransom demand. What did you find out about my passport?"

"I contacted the correct authorities. You will need to go to the American Embassy when you leave here and pick up a temporary one. Now, sit down, you're making me nervous." Edward Montoya selected a cigar from the humidor and cut the tip off.

Joel sank into the leather wingback chair farthest from the fireplace. The ever-present fire in the den had made him shed his jacket five minutes after he arrived. At least he'd have his passport for flying commercially to the States in the morning.

"Do you owe the cartel money?"

"No. I don't deal with the cartel for anything. Besides, if I needed money, I would have come to you." He could never let Edward know about the money he'd lost at the casinos. At the time, he hadn't realized the person he was getting in debt to was connected to the cartel.

"You have no gambling debts?"

"Nothing I can't pay." Except last night, he'd added to his debt instead of reducing it. As soon as he could access the offshore account, he'd pay it off. But when he did, he had to be prepared to disappear for good, unless . . . he was brazen enough to steal the money and sit tight. It was something to consider, and if he could pull it off, at least he wouldn't be looking over his shoulder the rest of his life.

"And these men said nothing? Gave you no indication of what they wanted?"

"No. They just kept hammering away about where Bailey and Maria were." Montoya's interest in Maria puzzled him. While she was his great-niece, he'd never been sentimental about family.

Joel studied his boss. Edward Montoya had the Spanish name but not much else that marked him as Mexican. His father had immigrated to Mexico from Spain by way of Sweden before the Second World War, where he met and married a beautiful blonde. The marriage produced two sons who bore little resemblance to each other. Jorge, who died with his wife when a bomb blew up his car, resembled his father, receiving the Hispanic coloring and dark hair and eyes that he had passed on to his son, Angel, while Edward's lighter hair and coloring and eyes came from his Swedish mother, along with her height. Both Edward and Angel's six-foot statures stood out in a country where the average male stood five eight.

"Cigar?"

Joel shook his head. He'd never acquired a taste for the Cuban cigars Edward had shipped from Havana.

Montoya used a double-flamed lighter to fire up his cigar. "Where is Maria?"

"I don't know. Last I saw, she was in the lobby of the Casa Grande. Men were after her and Bailey, and I couldn't get in the door—it was locked, and I didn't have a key. By the time I got inside, she was gone."

Edward drew deeply on the cigar, and after a minute he took it out of his mouth and stared at the glowing red tip. "I still find it difficult to understand why you were sending Maria to the States."

Joel rubbed the back of his neck. He'd explained this to his boss once before. "Because my parents wanted to see her before either of them passed on. They're not young or well. And Maria has been asking why she couldn't see her grandparents like the other kids at school. Besides, she was only supposed to be there two weeks."

"What if your parents want her to stay? They no longer have a daughter."

"They won't do that. Besides, Bailey has full authorization to legally take charge of Maria if that happens."

"You trust this Bailey Adams?"

"I have no reason not to." He did more than trust her. The beautiful teacher intrigued him, and at some point, he intended for her to be more than a friend. But that was not something Edward needed to know.

Edward puffed on the cigar. "So by the time you got inside the hotel, Bailey and Maria were gone. Do you think the men took them, or did they magically evade them?"

He flinched at the sarcasm. "Danny Maxwell was with them. I saw them speeding away in a dark-blue SUV."

"Why did you not say this in the first place? Instead you raise my blood pressure." Edward nodded. "Danny is a good man, but could he evade Calatrava men by himself?"

Now, he hesitated. It was not good to be the bearer of bad news to Edward Montoya.

His boss stared at him, his pale blue eyes cold. "Spit it out, Joel—whatever it is that you do not wish to tell me."

Joel averted his gaze. "There was another man with him."

"Must I drag it out of you? Who?"

"I'm not sure. Maybe your nephew, Angel."

Edward rocked back in the chair. "Impossible. Angel is dead."

"I'm just telling you what I saw. I certainly don't want it to be Angel."

"You saw wrong. I would know if he was alive." Montoya flicked the ash on his cigar in the crystal ashtray. His cell phone rang, and he glanced at it before answering in Spanish. After a few minutes, he disconnected and leveled his gaze at Joel. "It seems you may not have seen wrong. That was Sergeant Chavez of the Federal Police. There was a shootout at a small airfield, and two men were killed. The survivors swear the man who did one of the killings was my nephew."

Angel. Alive. Joel's blood turned to ice. "Where has he been for the past two years?"

Montoya leveled his gaze at him, not looking any happier about the news than Joel. "That's a good question. Just hope you don't get close enough to him to ask."

"What happened was not my fault." Joel paced the room.

"I doubt my nephew feels the same way. One other thing. You were right that the men were Calatrava."

If Edward intended to make him feel better, his news did just the opposite. It was looking more and more like the man he'd borrowed money from was Calatrava. If Edward found out . . . He licked his parched lips.

"They probably want Maria so they can extort money from me." Edward ground the cigar in the ashtray. "Back to my nephew. Evidently Angel has learned patience, but he is not the only one who knows how to wait. Chavez indicated Danny Maxwell's plane was at that particular airport this morning, and now it's gone. If Miss Adams and Maria were with Maxwell at the hotel, it's safe to assume Maria left on that plane. Where would he take her?"

Focused on his own problems, Joel barely caught the last of his boss's question. "Probably to his hometown—Logan Point. That's where Bailey is from as well, and my parents live within a hundred miles."

"And Angel is with them." Edward steepled his fingers. "He is sadly mistaken if he thinks he can whisk Maria away from us. He lives too dangerously to be a part of her life. We must go after her. Do you have an address for Miss Adams's home in Mississippi? We will go and get my niece and bring her back to Mexico."

"No, but I can get one. We've been in contact by phone. Maybe she'll answer my call." He dialed her number, wishing he'd known Angel was with them. He could have warned her that the man was dangerous. The call went straight to voicemail. "Something must be wrong with her phone."

"They're in the air—she has no service." Edward waved his hand. "Never mind. Logan Point is small, and Bailey Adams shouldn't be too hard to find." He drummed his fingers on the table. "I'd like to leave right now, but I have a few things I need to tidy up this afternoon. I'll contact Phillip Maxwell to move our meeting scheduled for later this month to the present. We'll leave first thing in the morning for Mississippi."

That would give Joel time to visit the jeweler and get a duplicate necklace . . . and also to get a temporary passport. "Thank you for everything you're doing."

"We must get Maria back."

The intensity in Edward's voice took him aback. He'd known Edward had grown fond of Maria, just not to the extent of disrupting his schedule to go after her. He just hoped they didn't encounter Angel Montoya.

The man hated his guts. With reason.

■ ■ ■

"We're approaching McKinney Airport just north of Dallas and will be landing in a few minutes."

Danny's voice startled Bailey, and she glanced out the window, impressed that he was putting the plane down in darkness. He'd impressed her a lot today, the last time being when she listened through the earphones as he persuaded the Customs and Border Protection Agency to let them reenter the States.

After a lengthy conversation, he provided the documentation needed and convinced them they were not illegally trying to cross the border. He gave a thumbs-up when the person gave him a time that a customs agent would meet them.

Bailey had never seen Danny so . . . in charge and commanding. She had to keep reminding herself why she'd returned his ring. It would be easier to remember once she was home and he wasn't around.

With a bump, the plane touched down on the runway and taxied to the terminal building.

"Sit tight until customs gives us the go-ahead."

Finally they were given the okay, and she waited while Danny and Angel climbed out, then Solana. A cold March wind sent shivers through Bailey as she climbed out on the wing and handed Maria to Danny. She wished for their coats that had been in the suitcases. Danny handed Maria off to Angel before he turned back to help her down.

An overhead light bathed him in a soft glow as his lopsided grin speared her heart. For a second, the question of why she broke up with him resurfaced. What had sent her running to Mexico? Oh yeah. Fear. Plain and simple. Fear that he would wake up one day and leave. Fear that she couldn't depend on him. Fear that he would turn into someone she didn't know.

She wanted to believe none of that could happen. Desperately wanted to, but wanting to didn't make it so, didn't change that she couldn't trust him. And he deserved better than that.

Bailey conjured a smile for Danny and held out her hand. After she was on the ground, she asked to borrow his phone.

"For . . . ?"

"To call Maria's grandparents and let them know I won't be bringing Maria to their house tonight."

He pressed his lips together, and a frown creased his brow. "Angel and I were talking, and we think you shouldn't contact them. What if the wrong people got the grandparents' phone and discovered my number? They could track us wherever we are."

She hadn't heard him and Angel talking. "Did you turn my headset off?"

At least he had the decency to look embarrassed. "It was Angel's idea."

She glanced toward the terminal. Solana stood beside the man in question. He'd placed Maria on his shoulders, and the little girl was laughing for the first time since all of this started. Even Solana smiled. Bailey chewed the inside of her cheek. Angel was an enigma. Something about him was off-kilter. "Why is he here? And why should his opinion matter?"

"Bailey, he saved our lives. What's your problem?"

"How well do you know him?"

"I don't really know him, so I'm keeping my eye on him. But my gut instinct says he's a good guy."

"Are you sure? Maybe he has his own agenda." Shivering, she folded her arms across her chest and rubbed her arms. "I'm going inside."

As she hurried to the terminal, Danny caught up with her. She tilted her head at him. "How did you meet Angel, anyway?"

"He was at the restaurant this morning. When you disappeared, he helped me search for you and Maria."

Danny pushed the door open, and warm air wrapped around her. But her mind was still on Angel. "See? That alone should make you suspicious of him. What was he doing at the restaurant? How do you know he's not part of those men at the hotel or the airport?"

"Even if he has his own agenda, he's done nothing but help us." He shook his head. "Besides, why would he shoot one of his own men? Maybe he just likes excitement. Solana acts like he's some sort of hero."

Solana did seem to know him. And admire him. But Bailey still wasn't comfortable. "Once we're in the air and Maria can't hear us, I want to ask him a few questions," she said, keeping her voice low. "And don't you dare turn off my headset again."

"I won't. Just don't take his head off. Okay?"

She rolled her eyes at him. "All right. But I don't agree that I shouldn't let the McDermotts know we won't be coming tonight. They'll worry."

"Let's see if we can find a pay phone."

"Are you serious? No one has pay phones anymore. I don't understand the problem with me calling her grandparents."

"There are plenty of pay phones still around. It's not about calling them, it's about calling them from a number that can be traced back to you. And when you do call, don't tell them where you are or where you'll be."

Her shoulders slumped. Sometimes she didn't grasp what a deep mess they were in, and he was right. If those goons showed up at the McDermott house, it would be better if the grandparents didn't know where they were. "Do you really think those people will follow us? Or if they do, they'll know who Maria's grandparents are?"

"Do you think they'll give up just because we're no longer in Mexico? If they follow us, trust me, they will know who the McDermotts are and where to find them."

She massaged the back of her neck. Since eleven o'clock this morning, getting back to the States meant safety, but evidently that might not be true. "At least let me call my mom and let her know I'll be arriving early."

"Tell her you'll be staying somewhere other than the bed-and-breakfast."

"You don't think—"

"Do you want to take a chance? It's your family that would be endangered if someone comes after Maria."

"Where will we go?"

"My cabin."

It was clear he'd given this thought. She chewed her bottom lip. A person would definitely have to know where they were going to find Danny's cabin on the lake. "I don't like it that there's only one way in and one way out. And unless you've done some work on it, that road into your cabin is narrow and the woods are dense. Anyone could be hiding in them, and you wouldn't know."

"I've put in security cameras where you turn off the main road, as well as around the cabin. If anyone comes my way, I'll know it."

"Isn't your cabin in Duncan County?"

"Well, yeah."

"That's out of Ben Logan's jurisdiction. I don't even know the sheriff over there."

"I'm telling you, my cabin would be the safest place. And I know the sheriff in Duncan County. Maybe not as well as Ben, but he's a good guy."

"And I'm telling you, I don't think it is. I think we'd be safer in Logan Point with Ben."

The muscles in his jaw twitched, and his lips pressed together. "Do you think your mom has extra rooms available?"

"For?" Surely he didn't intend to stay at her mother's bed-and-breakfast.

"Me . . . Solana and Angel. Where else will they stay?"

He definitely intended to stick close to her. She'd nixed going to his cabin and had hoped once they were in Logan Point and under Ben's protection, Danny would simply fade away. She needed him to fade away. Today's events brought back all the reasons she'd fallen in love with him in the first place. He'd been her knight since she was ten years old and he'd come to her rescue when a Doberman had her cornered on the school playground. She tried one more time.

"Really, Danny, there's no need for you to stay. If Ben thinks there's danger, he'll put a deputy at the house."

He crossed his arms. "Ben doesn't have that kind of manpower. I'm staying. Inside the house or outside, but I'm hoping it'll be inside."

She held up her hands. "Okay, I'll ask. It's the middle of the slow season, so she probably has room."

His shoulders relaxed. "If she does, we'll try it your way, but the first sign of danger and we're going to my cabin."

"Agreed. Now, can I use your phone to call my mom?" He handed it over, and she dialed her mother's number, smiling when "Bailey's home phone" showed up in his contacts list. So he hadn't taken it out of his phone. When the call went to the answering machine, Bailey left a message asking her mother to call back.

"Satisfied?" she asked as she handed Danny his phone.

"Yep. In the morning, I'll pick you up a phone, but I need your account password."

She eyed him. "I can get my own phone."

"I want to do this. I'm the one who destroyed your other one, and it's one less thing you'll have to do tomorrow."

She hesitated. He was right, as usual. She gave him the password, then she walked toward the counter near the front of the terminal.

"Where are you going?" Danny called.

"To find a pay phone."

"I'll go with you—I need to buy fuel." He followed her to the front.

He probably didn't trust her not to tell the McDermotts where she was and wanted to listen to the conversation. *Men.* She waited while he wrote out an order for fuel and handed it to the man behind the counter. The name "Greg" was stitched over the pocket of his shirt.

"Be about ten minutes before I can get to it," Greg said. "I'll let you know."

"Thanks."

Danny moved, and she stepped closer to the counter. "So Greg, do you have a pay phone?"

"A what?"

She gave Danny an I-told-you-so look. "I lost my cell phone and need to make a call."

He pointed to the phone on the counter. "Use that one."

It surprised her that he didn't think it a strange request. If it'd been her, she would have wondered why one of the people with her wouldn't loan her a phone. "It's long distance."

"No matter."

Bailey found the card Joel had given her with his parents' number on it and dialed. After several rings, she finally disconnected. Evidently they didn't have an answering machine. She checked the time. Where could they be? It seemed strange that they wouldn't be home, given it was close to the time she should have been arriving with Maria.

"Happy now?" Danny asked.

"Not really. I think that was their home number, and they weren't there. I should have their cell number." She scanned the information Joel had given her. He hadn't listed another number. Maybe there was a number on one of the other papers in the bag with the prescriptions. "I need to go back to the plane to get Maria's bag."

"I'll get it." He jogged back to the plane.

When he returned with the bag, she rummaged through it. No number. Maybe they didn't have a cell phone. She'd try their number again after she reached her parents' house. If she didn't get through to them tonight, she would have to figure out something in the morning. Right now she was too tired to think it through. She started to zip the bag closed and noticed the photo of his parents that Joel had included. She'd barely glanced at the photo when he'd given her the bag, but now she took time to really look at it. She sensed Danny behind her rather than saw him.

"That's the grandparents?"

"Yep."

"I don't know, Bailey . . ."

His tone of voice echoed her own feelings. She hated it when he was right. White haired and plump, the McDermotts looked to be a good ten years older than Bailey's own parents, who were in their sixties. No match for the men who had chased them today. But maybe the men wouldn't chase Maria all the way to the States.

Maria. She'd been with Angel and Solana when she saw her last. Bailey whirled around, her heart in her throat as she searched the terminal for the girl.

How could she let the child out of her sight?

9

Why did Solana have her passport with her? The question had nagged Angel ever since she'd handed it to Danny so he could give the information to the customs agent. Could she be a mule? One of those who ran drugs over the border? He hated being so cynical and suspecting her of such a thing. *No.* He thrust the idea from his mind. There had to be a logical explanation.

"Want one?" Maria held up a cracker.

"No, you better eat it." Angel brushed crumbs from her cheek. The vending machine's choices ranged more to the sugary snacks except for one offering of peanut butter and crackers. He turned to Solana. "Are you sure you don't want something?"

"No. The soda is fine," she answered in her soft voice.

"Are we going to stay here?" Maria asked, looking up at him with Claire's blue eyes.

Part of him was glad she did not favor him—so far no one had connected that he was her father. But every time she looked at him with those eyes, he longed for his wife. If he had not gone to that meeting with the Federals that day . . .

"Are we?" She tugged on his pants leg.

"No, we'll be flying again soon." He bent down to her level and pointed to her necklace. "This is pretty."

"Uncle Joel gave it to me. It has my mommy's picture in it. Do you want to see?"

His heart almost stopped. Joel had given her a locket with Claire's photo? Just when he had it settled in his mind that Joel was a sleazeball, he did something nice. "Could I?"

She fumbled with the locket.

"Here, let me." Angel's fingers shook as he opened it and stared at the photo. A thousand memories bombarded him as he blinked back tears. He cleared his throat. "She's very pretty. You look like her."

"I do?"

Solana limped to stand beside them. "May I see?"

Angel tilted the locket.

"Yes, you will be just like her when you are grown, only with a tan."

Maria giggled and Angel closed the locket. Solana leaned against the wall and rubbed her hip.

"Does your leg hurt?" he asked.

She nodded.

Angel pointed to the cast on Solana's foot. "How did you hurt your foot? Did you break it?"

She waved his concern off. "No, the tendon pulled away from the bone. I'm supposed to have this thing removed next week."

Maria looked up at him. "What's a tendon?"

He shot Solana a plea for help. He had no idea how to explain what a tendon was.

Solana tilted her head. "It's like a rope that holds your foot to your leg, and mine came loose."

"Oh. Okay." Maria turned back to her crackers as Solana limped to the table and sat down.

Good answer. He had to figure out a way to get Solana back to Mexico. Not that she'd complained once about being uprooted. In fact, the raven-haired waitress had not complained about anything. He was certain the ankle pained her with the running they'd had

96

to do. She sat at the table with her eyes closed. "You should prop your leg up to keep the foot from swelling more."

She opened her eyes, and he noticed how thick her dark lashes were.

"Later maybe," she said.

Solana's dark eyes continued to hold his gaze, and his heart missed a beat. "What?"

"You. I see you rub your chest sometimes and make a face. An old injury?"

Now it was his turn to shrug off concern. "Depends on how long 'old' is. I hurt my shoulder a couple of years ago."

She took a long sip of the drink. "Why do you fight the cartel? Are you wishing to begin your own? That's what some of the merchants say."

"What do you think?" He held his breath, waiting for her answer, not sure why it mattered.

"I think you are a good man."

Her words sent a warm shiver through him. A different time . . . Until Maria was safe, he couldn't consider what he wanted. "Why do you fight the cartel?"

She rubbed her arms and looked away. "They ensnared my fiancé with their talk of money and good living."

"Is he still with them?"

"He's dead."

■ ■ ■

Danny grabbed Bailey's arm to keep her from bolting. "What's wrong?"

"I don't see Maria."

"She's fine. Solana went with her to the restroom, then she and Angel took her to a break room while you were on the phone."

Bailey pressed her hand to her forehead. "I was afraid . . ."

"It's been a hard day." He lifted her face, and she looked at him with such trust. His heart twisted, unleashing the yearning he'd suppressed for two years.

When she'd left him for Mexico, it'd been easy to tell himself that Bailey Adams would never get the opportunity to hurt him again. But staring into those incredible eyes made him feel alive again. Made him want to do anything to erase the worry lining her face, to protect her. "Maybe you need to freshen up a bit while I check on Maria and see what's in the vending machines."

The grateful smile she threw him as she turned and walked to the restrooms sealed his fate. *Don't get stupid. She'll only leave you again.* Maybe not. Maybe this time . . . He sighed and took his phone out and dialed Ben Logan's number.

Ben answered on the third ring. "Logan."

"Ben, Danny Maxwell. I have a little problem." By the time he disconnected, he'd given the sheriff an overview of what had happened and asked for his help when they landed. Ben had assured him he'd be at the airfield waiting for them. Then Danny went looking for Maria and for something for Bailey to eat when she returned.

In the break room, Angel stood by the window, holding a sleeping Maria on his shoulder. Danny told him about Bailey's decision to stay at her parents' house. "It's a bed-and-breakfast, so there may be room for you."

"I hope so. I'd hate to camp out in their backyard."

"Yeah, I know. Maybe her mom will—"

"My mom will what?"

He turned. "Call you back so we can find out if there's room at the inn," he said with a grin.

Bailey ignored his play on words and turned to Angel with a question on her face. "Why do you want to stay there? Or even in Logan Point?"

Angel rubbed the sleeping girl's back. "I want to stay near Maria."

"Why?"

Danny was interested in that answer as well, but unlike Bailey, he understood why Angel wanted to protect her. Danny wanted to protect the child too. But even though the Mexican helped save Bailey today, it had occurred to Danny that Angel could have been buying guns from Geoffrey Franks. Might even be Geoffrey's contact. To fight a war against the Calatrava, Angel needed guns. And he'd been evasive when Danny had questioned him earlier.

"I told you before that I made a promise to Maria's mother to protect her."

Maria stirred in his arms, and Bailey stepped toward him to take the child.

"No. She's fine where she is."

Danny could tell from the expression on Bailey's face that she was going to take the child anyway. He put his hand on her arm. "Let her sleep."

She hesitated, then stepped back. "Why did you make her mother a promise like that? How did you know her?"

Angel's jaw shot out. "It happened so long ago, it doesn't matter now."

"It might."

He shook his head. "It's a long story and not one I want to discuss here."

Danny's cell phone rang, and he unhooked it from his belt. "It's your mom," he said to Bailey.

When she took his phone and walked to a far corner of the room, he glanced around the small break area. Angel had moved from the window to the doorway, and Solana sat in a chair at the table, twisting a napkin in her fingers as her gaze followed Angel. Exhaustion lined her face, and he realized she was older than he thought. Not a teenager as he'd supposed but a young woman, probably in her midtwenties.

She still wore the black pants and white shirt with her name stitched in black. It dawned on him that the waitress uniform was all she had, and he imagined she was overwhelmed by the turn her life had taken. All because she'd tried to help someone. He sat in the chair beside her. "It's going to be okay. We'll find a way to make things all right."

Solana gave him a small nod.

"How did you happen to have your passport with you?"

She looked around at Angel's question. Danny had wondered the same thing.

"My sister's husband is gravely ill. I expected a phone call anytime. It just made sense to keep the papers with me." She spoke English slowly. "But I should not have come. I should have stayed behind and helped Juan's family."

Angel's eyes softened. "No, Solana, you could not stay behind." His voice was low but urgent. Then he continued in Spanish. "You cannot return until the Calatrava is destroyed. I'll take care of you. Understand?"

Tears filled her eyes. "Why? You don't know me."

A gentle smile teased Angel's lips. "But I do. You are Solana Lopez y de la Fuente and an excellent waitress." Then his voice dropped. "And you have helped many more than these two you helped today. Like Raúl Barra Monje."

Her eyes widened, then she dropped her gaze. "We are in a war for our country."

Danny's admiration for Solana grew, and he squeezed her arm. "You're very brave."

"No. I just do what I must."

Bailey rejoined them at the table. "There are no guests at the bed-and-breakfast, so there's room enough for all of us." She eyed Angel. "Maybe we can finish our conversation once we get settled."

Danny figured getting information out of Angel Guerrera would be next to impossible. "I didn't tell you, but Ben Logan is meeting us at the airport in Logan Point."

"That's wonderful, Danny. You might be useful for something after all." She bumped him with her shoulder.

That was high praise from Bailey Adams, and he knew his face was red from the heat in his cheeks.

Bailey turned to Angel. "Maria must be getting heavy. Why don't we lay her on the couch where she can stretch out."

"She's not heavy. We'll be leaving soon, sí?"

The last was directed at Danny. "As soon as the plane is refueled and I do the preflight. Probably fifteen, twenty minutes—I'll check again in a minute to see if the airport manager can get to me."

"Maria will be more comfortable on the couch." Bailey used that stubborn tone he knew so well.

Danny watched to see who would win, and struggled to hide his grin when Angel finally nodded. Already he saw a control issue developing between Bailey and Angel, and his money was riding on his former fiancée.

Maria barely stirred as Angel stretched her out on the sofa beside Bailey. Angel shifted his gaze to Danny. "Who is this Ben Logan?"

"The sheriff," Danny said. "He's our friend, and he'll figure something out."

"Sheriff? No!" A torrent of Spanish flew from Solana's mouth.

He caught only a few of the words that Angel shot back at her. He didn't know if it was what Angel said or that the tall Latino pulled the trembling woman in his arms, but she quieted down. Danny had no idea mentioning Ben would upset her so. He held up his hands. "It'll be okay. I promise. Ben's a good guy—he'll help us."

She looked doubtful but nodded.

Bailey stood and walked to her side. "Ben isn't like the police in Mexico. I promise."

"Me too," Danny added. After his experience with the Federals this morning, he understood her fear.

■ ■ ■

El Jefe looked each man in the eye until they broke contact. Except one. Defiance emanated from him. This one—Enrico— would bear watching. "I wanted the missionary dead. Can you not do one simple thing?"

"Angel Montoya was her protector. He's like a ghost, coming and going as he pleases."

"You fool. Because you didn't do your job two years ago, we must now make him an ally." Making Montoya an ally had not been his idea but the decision of the board.

The defiant one lifted his chin. "He will never align himself with the Calatrava."

"I have a plan, and when I'm finished, he will do whatever I say." He cocked his head. "Why did you kidnap McDermott?"

A sly grin spread across Enrico's face. "A little fun."

"Your little fun cost us two men."

Enrico shrugged. "They were stupid. Stupid people die." His eyes narrowed. "What is your plan?"

Heat flushed through El Jefe's body. If Enrico were not the son of a board member . . . "You will know in due time."

While their mission to kill the woman had failed today, it had given him an idea. And once he had Angel Montoya where he wanted him, he would deal with the insolent Enrico.

10

Bailey Adams asked too many questions. Questions Angel couldn't answer yet. Her loyalties lay with Joel, and Joel's loyalty belonged to Edward Montoya. The American would not understand or approve of Angel's plans. He glanced at the back of the cabin, where Maria dozed on Bailey's lap. Neither would she approve his plans for his sleeping daughter.

He fingered the gold cross around his neck. His mother's. He gazed out the window into the starlit night. A full moon hung heavy in the sky. Just the kind of night his mother had loved. He sighed. She would understand.

Danny's voice in his headset drew him back to the present. "Logan Point Tower, Cessna F3851Charlie five miles northwest, at 1800 feet, landing Logan Point airport."

He and the tower control talked back and forth like old friends. Which they probably were. Angel missed his flying mentor—they'd had an almost father-son relationship. Soon the lights of the runway came into sight and the plane nosed down to the ground, the wheels touching the tarmac smoothly. Danny was a good pilot, almost as good as Angel. But that was another thing he'd keep to himself.

He glanced toward the backseat passengers. Bailey had removed her headset and was waking Maria, but Solana sat stiff, a pallor to her skin as she stared out the window. The answer about her papers seemed all right on the surface, but he still had questions for her, and now wasn't the time to ask. Not with others around and while she seemed so fragile.

Her dark hair framed a worried face as her fingers gripped the black pants of the waitress uniform. In the morning he would buy her something to wear, and it wouldn't be black or have her name on the pocket. Something colorful. Something that would make her smile. Angel touched her knee, and she jumped. He smiled and motioned to the headset hanging around her neck.

When she'd put the headset on again, he spoke to her in Spanish. "Where is your courage, little one? And that fiery temper I've seen at the restaurant that you use to put admirers in their place? You faced much worse this morning."

She gave him a weak smile. "But I was in my own country. Here I don't know what to expect. What if my papers are not in order and I'm arrested as illegal?"

"You won't be arrested. I promise that. Do you believe me?"

Although she nodded, her dark eyes told a different story. He would have to change that.

"Ready?" Danny asked as he killed the engine.

Angel took Maria while Danny helped Bailey to the ground. Once Bailey was off the plane, she immediately took Maria from his arms. The American did not trust him.

Angel lifted Solana off the wing, surprised at how light she was. Briefly their eyes locked, and his heart responded, kicking into high gear. He jerked his gaze away. He didn't have time for distractions. "Ready?" he asked.

"Sí."

They hurried to the terminal to escape the biting north wind. Inside, Danny and Bailey talked with a guy in jeans and a plaid shirt under his leather jacket. Angel noted the way the man stood, relaxed but alert. His dark eyes seemed to be taking Angel's measure.

"Oh, here you are," Danny said. "Angel, Solana, this is Ben Logan."

Ben stuck his hand out and Angel shook it, liking the firm handshake. Then the sheriff turned to Solana and took her hand. "Danny tells me that you helped Bailey escape today."

Solana nodded stiffly. "Sí," she answered quietly, and it hurt Angel to see how tense she was.

"Thank you. You don't have any reason to fear me," Ben said. "And Danny said you had your visa and passport, so everything is good."

Angel felt her physically relax, and he wanted to shake the sheriff's hand again.

"I do not intend to remain in the US—it was a mistake coming. I must return to Chihuahua."

A band tightened around Angel's chest. "Why, Solana?"

Bailey echoed his question. "You can't go back. Those men will . . ." She glanced down at Maria and shook her head. "You know what I mean."

"I must. And for the same reason Angel will not remain here—if all the law-abiding citizens leave, the drug cartels will win."

Her fiery spirit had returned, but still the band constricted his breathing. "No. You will stay here where it's safe."

Solana fisted her hands on her hips. "Do not treat me like I am Maria. I will return to Chihuahua when you do." She tossed her hair back, and he read the determination in her face.

"We'll discuss this later."

"There is nothing to discuss, and I'm tired. Can we not go somewhere to rest?"

"That's a good idea," Bailey said. She turned her attention to Danny. "Are you in that little red convertible of yours, or something more sensible?"

He shrugged. "Neither. I flew out from the airstrip at Ian's cabin, so I'm afoot."

"I'm in my Highlander," Ben said. "I'll be glad to drop you off at Kate's, and on the way, why don't you call this Joel McDermott you were telling me about from my cell phone?"

"Who is Kate?" Angel asked.

"My mother," Bailey explained. "Like I said earlier, she runs the bed-and-breakfast."

Once they were in the SUV, Ben handed Bailey his cell phone, and she dialed. Sitting beside her, Angel memorized the number.

"It goes straight to voicemail."

"Put him in my contacts, and I'll keep trying and call you in the morning with a report on what he says."

Fifteen minutes later they pulled into the circle drive of a two-story gabled house. Even though the area around the house was well lit, Angel didn't like the long drive lined with trees. Anyone could drive up to the house without being seen. "I suppose it's too much to hope your mother has a security system," he said to Bailey.

"Actually, she does. She had it installed a few years ago because she can't hear customers when they arrive if she's in the house or working in the back of her pottery workshop."

That made him feel better, but he would still talk with the sheriff about having a deputy patrol the area. Once everyone was out of the SUV, he turned to him. "Are you coming in, Sheriff Logan?"

"Call me Ben, and no, I have to get home to my family."

Ben's apparent happiness sent an arrow into Angel's soul. He'd had a wife and family once. If only he hadn't been shot . . . He shook the thought off. He could not change the past. He and Danny hung back as the others climbed the steps to the house. Shivering against the cold, Angel stuck his hands in his pockets.

"Sorry about the cold," Ben said. "It's usually warmer than this in late March, although we've actually had snow on the first day of spring."

"Maria would probably love that," Angel said. "Could I speak with you a moment about security before you leave?"

Ben nodded toward Danny. "He told me the men who tried to kidnap the child might follow you to Logan Point, so I've already assigned a deputy to drive by here at different times through the night. I wish I could do more, but we're understaffed."

His respect for the sheriff grew. "Gracias."

"Do you think they will follow you? Or do you know why they want her so badly?"

"I think they will." As for why . . . he wasn't ready to share that information.

■■■

Home. With Maria's hand in her own, Bailey climbed the porch steps with Solana trailing behind. Earlier today she hadn't been sure she'd ever see it again. But home had its own problems. Especially now, with Danny determined to stick to her like glue. Surely she could talk him out of hanging around.

The door flew open, and her mother wrapped her in an embrace. "Welcome home, baby." Tears glistened in her eyes as she held her at arm's length. "Don't they feed you anything in Mexico? You're skinnier than Robyn."

Bailey laughed. From the reports she'd heard about her little sister, that wasn't possible. She turned and hugged her dad waiting in the background, then put her hands on the child's shoulders. "This is Maria. And this is Solana," she said, nodding toward her friend.

Her mom knelt. She cupped the child's face in her hands, and again Bailey noticed tears threatening. "Bailey has told me so much about you. Do you speak English? I know this much Spanish"—she held her thumb and forefinger close together—"*un poco*."

Maria giggled.

Kate rose and took Solana's hands. "*La . . . bienvenida a . . . mi casa*. Bailey and Charlie"—she nodded toward her husband—"they taught me that much, but I'm afraid I don't practice. I hope I said it right."

Her mom's eyes became even wetter. What was with the tears? Kate Adams was not a crier, but in spite of her concern, Bailey grinned at the Southern-accented Spanish. She wasn't sure Solana understood that her mom was welcoming her into her home until the young woman's face lit up and a smile graced her lips.

"Gracias. I do speak some English and understand more, so do not strain yourself."

"*Si necesita un intérprete, puedo ayudar.*" Her dad's eyes crinkled as he smiled, waiting.

"Ah . . . your Spanish . . . it's *mucho mejor*—I mean, much better than Bailey's," Solana said with a laugh. "But I don't think I need an interpreter."

"I *should* be more fluent," Charlie said. "Most of the men I sailed with were Spanish speaking. It was learn it or talk only to myself."

"He was a merchant seaman," Kate said.

A familiar voice spoke behind Bailey. "Well, don't I get a hug?"

Robyn? Bailey whirled around and squealed. "Oh, I didn't think I'd see you before morning! I thought you'd be home with Abby."

"I was so worried, I couldn't wait."

Bailey looked from Robyn to her mother. They knew?

"Ben told us what happened," her mom said and picked up Maria.

So that was the reason for the tears.

Maria's stomach growled.

"Are you hungry?" Kate asked. "I have potato soup and can make you a grilled cheese sandwich."

Maria glanced toward Bailey, and her expression almost seemed to be asking permission.

"You can answer."

"Uncle Joel said I shouldn't ask for food when we go visit."

"But you didn't ask," Bailey said.

"My stomach did."

The front door opened, and Angel and Danny entered, bringing cold air with them.

"You're just in time for some of Mom's famous potato soup," she said after introducing Angel all around. From the looks on the men's faces, the vending machine snacks were long gone. Bailey followed the others to the kitchen, her mind replaying Maria's words. Sometimes she seemed afraid of Joel. Bailey shook the thought off. They were all tired. It was probably something as simple as Joel's authoritarian parenting style, which was understandable considering he'd never been married. She certainly admired him for taking care of his sister's child. He just needed to loosen up a bit.

Her mom ladled soup into bowls and handed Angel and Solana each a bowl. "There's plenty of room at the table." Then she turned to Danny. "It's good to see you around here. I've missed you," she said.

"Not nearly as much as I've missed being here." He directed his gaze to Bailey.

Heat rose up her neck as she took her soup and sat beside Robyn. Her mom had always liked Danny, even after they broke up.

With a start, she realized Robyn had asked her something. "What?"

"Did you know Livy resigned from the Memphis Police Department?"

Her cousin wasn't a cop anymore? "No. What's she doing?"

"You won't believe it—private investigator. With Alex, this really hunky guy. He's the one who helped her find me, and now she's gone to Texas to meet his folks."

Bailey realized her mouth had dropped open, and she snapped it shut. Livy must really be serious about this Alex. Her cousin had been her ally after Bailey broke off the engagement with Danny. "We'll be two old maids with fifty cats," Livy had said. A sigh settled in her heart. Now it looked like one old maid. She fingered the locket Joel had given her this morning.

"That's a beautiful necklace," Robyn said.

Her face flushed. "Maria's uncle gave it to me this morning." She nodded toward Maria. "She has one just like it, only with her initial on it." Bailey dropped her hand. "I'm glad for her."

"Glad for who?" Danny said as he sat across the table from her.

"Our cousin Livy."

"Oh yeah. I met Alex, and he's okay." He grinned at her. "Let's see . . . Taylor, Robyn, there's even Ben, and now Livy. Looks like that'll just leave you the only one not married."

"There are worse things than not being married," she said, making a face at him.

"Name one."

"Being married to the wrong person."

When the color drained from his face, she wished she could snatch the words back. Instead they hung in the room like a bad odor.

"At least you didn't make that mistake."

She didn't know what to say. Denying it might give him false hope, but neither did she want to hurt his feelings. "I didn't mean it that way."

"Yeah, you did. But that's okay—it's completely understandable that you might view being married to me as a bad thing."

"What I said about being married to the wrong person had nothing to do with you."

He lifted the locket and examined it, his nearness sending a shiver down her spine. "Joel has good taste."

With the mood Danny was in, it would do no good to tell him there was nothing going on with Joel.

Then his blue eyes swept over her. "Just don't forget, like it or not, you're stuck with me for as long as it takes to know you'll be safe."

She yanked her gaze away, searching for Maria, and found her snuggled in her mom's lap, completely engrossed in the song Kate

110

quietly sang to her. "You don't have to hang around. It's not that I'm not thankful you were there in Chihuahua today. I am, but I believe we are completely safe in Logan Point. Besides, Angel is here."

"Sorry, but you're stuck with *me*. When I thought those men had taken you . . ." He shook his head. "I want to be here if anyone tries something like that again."

Danny's sincerity touched her heart. And that was something she had to guard against.

11

Weariness seeped into Bailey's bones, and between the warm kitchen and a full stomach, she could barely keep her eyes open. A glance around the room confirmed she wasn't the only one ready for bed. Maria had fallen asleep in her mother's lap, and Solana's sagging shoulders reflected her own weariness. "Why don't we all go to bed?" She looked at her mother. "Where are you putting everyone?"

"You and Maria are in your old room, and Solana is in Robyn's room." Her mom glanced at Danny. "Are you staying?"

"Yes, ma'am."

Bailey sighed. From Danny's tone, she knew there would be no dissuading him.

"Then you and Angel decide who gets the third bedroom and who gets the study with the daybed, although there are bedrooms downstairs."

Danny shrugged. "Other than remaining upstairs, it makes no difference to me."

"Or me," Angel said. "You take the bedroom. If I can't sleep on the daybed, tomorrow night we'll switch."

Tomorrow night? Reality sank into Bailey's mind. This nightmare would not be over in the morning. Maybe not for weeks. And what if those men had recaptured Joel? What if he was dead?

What would become of Maria? She didn't care what Danny said, tomorrow she had to try to contact Joel. And Maria's grandparents. Oh, wait . . . Ben said he would call Joel. There was still so much to do. What would it hurt to let Danny be here in case she needed him? She sighed.

"What's the matter?" Danny asked.

Concern deepened his blue eyes. She'd put him through a lot today. "I bet you didn't expect to sign on as my bodyguard when you got up this morning."

A slow grin spread across his face. "I didn't even expect to see you. But I'll take whatever I can get, even if I have to run for my life. But what were you sighing about?"

"I'm not sure where I should start in the morning." She shivered as he brushed a strand of hair from her cheek. How easy it would be to just let him take care of her and her problems. She threw the idea off and straightened her shoulders. She wasn't some fragile china doll that needed to be encased in a glass box. And that's what Danny would do if she didn't watch it.

He tilted his head. "Why don't you let it rest tonight? After breakfast we'll talk about it."

"Sounds like a plan." Problem was, she doubted Danny or Angel would like what she planned to do. She reached for Maria, but Angel picked her up first.

"I'll take her. You show me where you'll be sleeping."

Robyn stood and spoke to Solana. "Come on, and I'll show you to your room. I think I can find a pair of Bailey's pajamas for you to sleep in." She turned to Bailey. "And then I'll go up into the attic and see if I can find a pair of Abby's pjs from when she was Maria's age."

A little later Bailey helped Maria up into her high bed. She tucked the quilt under the child's chin. Abby's pajamas were a little big, but they would do until they could go shopping. Another item to add to tomorrow's list.

Maria snuggled under the quilt. "Miss Bailey, would you tell me a story, like you do at school?"

Bailey sat on the side of the bed and smoothed the child's dark hair away from her face. She searched her memory for a story. "How about Snow White?"

The child's eyes brightened. "Oh, good! I like the prince in it and the dwarfs, especially Bashful."

The door opened, and Robyn slipped into the room. "Solana is all settled, and Mom sent me up to get your clothes. She's going to put them in the wash so you both will have something to wear in the morning."

She glanced down at the clothes she'd put on this morning. "Maria's are in the bathroom, but mine can wait. I'll wear something I left in the closet, but you're not leaving right away, are you?"

"I'll be here a little longer, but right now I'm going to take the clothes downstairs."

"Wait until I tell Maria a story, and I'll go down with you."

"Sure. I haven't heard one of your bedtime stories since Abby was her age."

Bailey turned her attention to Maria. "Once upon a time . . ." She softened her voice and quietly began the story, hoping to quickly lull Maria to sleep. When she came to the part about the wicked queen giving Snow White the poisoned apple, Maria interrupted her.

"That's not nice. It will make her sick, like Mommy."

In all the times Bailey had told the children in her classroom the story of Snow White, Maria had never once mentioned her mother. "Why do you think that?"

"Because everyone brought Mommy food, and she got sick and went to heaven. Tio and Uncle Joel brought her candy too."

"Oh, honey, that wasn't the same thing. They just wanted to make her feel better."

Maria's eyes held her gaze until finally she sighed. "Okay. Do you think Mommy and Daddy are in heaven together?"

Bailey faltered. Maria was full of surprises tonight. "I'm sure they are." She hesitated. "Do you remember your daddy?"

Maria grew quieter. Her fingers rubbed the edge of the quilt. Finally she shook her head. "But sometimes when I'm asleep, I hear him say, *"Te amo, niña.*"

I love you, baby girl. Bailey took in a shaky breath. "I'm sure he loved you very much."

"That's what Cook says." Maria smiled. "Finish telling me about Snow White."

When she saw Joel again, Bailey would ask him about Maria's dad. *If* she saw him again. She tucked the sheet under the girl's chin. "Okay where were we?"

"The wicked queen was giving her the apples."

A text beeped on Robyn's phone. "That's Mom wanting the clothes. I'll see you in a little bit," Robyn said and left for the bathroom.

As Bailey returned to the story, Maria settled deeper in the bed and touched her neck. Her eyes popped open. "My necklace. It's gone!"

Bailey lifted the blanket and sheet and shook them. No necklace. "Maybe it's in your jumper." She hurried to catch her sister. "Maria's lost her necklace."

Robyn paused at the top of the stairs. "Maybe it got caught in her top." She shook first the pullover, then the jumper Maria had worn over the shirt. The necklace tumbled onto the floor.

"Thank goodness!" Bailey stooped to pick it up. "Looks like the clasp is broken. She'll be so disappointed."

"Mr. Stevens at Logan Point Jewelers can mend it," Robyn said. "I can take it in for you tomorrow and drop it off when I take Abby to school."

"That would be great. I might not have time. I'm going to talk to Danny and Angel again about contacting Maria's grandparents in the morning. I'd like to go see them."

"Do you plan to take her with you?"

She hadn't thought about what she'd do with Maria. Certainly not take her, not until she knew exactly what was going on with the grandparents. "Maybe I can get Danny to stay here."

Robyn eyed her with amusement. "Yeah, right. Why don't you let her stay with Mom? I'll come over and help. How about Angel and Solana—are they going with you?"

"I don't know." She hadn't even thought about them and what they would do, but now that she had, she knew Angel wouldn't leave Maria. What if he was the one trying to kidnap her? No, because if that were the case, he wouldn't have helped them get out of Mexico.

Her mind went round and round with possible answers, none of them satisfying. The one thing she knew—Angel would not let anything happen to Maria while she was gone. And given the way he seemed to feel about the child, she didn't believe he would do anything like whisking her away. Maria had been traumatized enough in the past twenty-four hours.

"If you can come over, it would be great. I probably won't be gone over a couple of hours." She hesitated. "We haven't talked about what happened, but I'm so glad you're home safe."

Robyn hugged her. "Me too."

"How did you do it? I mean, mentally. I've read the papers, so I know the physical things that happened, but what kept you going?"

"God, plain and simple. But you know all about that. You're the missionary."

"Yeah, you're right." What would Robyn say if she told her she didn't know all about it? That she'd lost her grasp of who God was. If she'd ever had it. "You have so much peace. Let's find time to talk soon."

Robyn tilted her head. "Anything going on I should know about? Danny, maybe?"

Her mixed feelings about Danny surfaced. Robyn had always liked him, so Bailey didn't know if she was the right person to talk to. "Nothing that can't wait."

■ ■ ■

Later after Robyn left and Maria had fallen asleep, Bailey stood by the window, searching the skies. When she was a child, the stars had shone like diamonds from her window, but now only one or two managed to peek through the bright security lights. The urge to recapture that time before days like today propelled her to the closet for a coat and the fur-lined boots she'd left behind. She checked Maria, and, satisfied that she was sleeping soundly, Bailey eased her door open and tiptoed down the hallway to the stairs.

She skipped the squeaky second step and soon sat on a stump beyond the lights, on the other side of the barn. Facing north, she scanned the velvet sky for the Little Dipper, then followed the handle to the North Star. Polaris, her dad always called it. The one star that did not rise or set and that could be seen even with a full moon like tonight. After she found it, tension eased from her body. Even though everything else in her world had crashed and burned, Polaris remained.

The mask slipped from her heart, and at this moment, Polaris seemed more real than God. How many times had the sight before her filled her heart with the nearness of him? Under these very stars, she'd preached God's love to Danny. Her cheeks burned in spite of the cold air. What a fraud she was. At the first sign of trouble, her faith had deserted her like a rat fleeing a raging fire.

Today hadn't been the first trouble. No, today was just meringue on the pie. Doubt had started the first day in Copper Canyon when the self-proclaimed priest Father Horatio took one look at the new missionary and decided she was trouble. Later, he pointed out the starburst pattern in Bailey's eyes and had declared her a witch. Then when she encouraged the village women to question his authority, his campaign to get rid of her began in earnest and culminated on the day of her most successful tea party . . .

It had been a beautiful day, so she'd moved the tea party from inside the church to under the trees. The air had been filled with laughing women excited about the purses sent by the church she'd partnered with back in Mississippi.

"I don't know which is the bigger hit—the purses or the New Testament," she said to Elena.

"I think the little white Bible is," her friend replied. "But do you see Father Horatio? He's standing across the road."

Bailey looked up and gasped as he stepped out of the shadows of the abandoned building across from them. The look of anger and hatred he shot at her sent chills down her back. Abruptly, he turned and disappeared around the corner of the building.

She thought by now he would realize no matter how many dead roosters or other things he left in the seat of her van, she wasn't leaving. Not when she was finally reaching the women after eight long months.

She checked her watch. It was time to end their party. "Okay, ladies, all good things must come to a close . . . until next week. We start our Bible studies next Monday. If you need me to pick you up, just let me know. And those riding with me today, load up. Don't want your husbands upset because their supper isn't on the table."

The last thing she needed was an angry husband. As the women dispersed, six of them slowly walked to the van. Except for Elena, these were her older women who had a hard time walking the mile to the church. She hurried to get the stool for them to climb into the back of the van. Once everyone was in, she hurried around to the driver's side and hopped in.

A slight rustling, and Bailey cocked her head, listening. Nothing. Maybe she imagined the sound. She reached for the ignition.

Chi chi chi chi chi.

Her fingers froze on the key. Ice water raced through her veins. She hadn't imagined that sound. Rattler. Under her seat.

Very slowly, she took her hand off the key in the ignition. Another *chi chi chi chi chi.* Further over this time.

"Ladies . . ." Her voice trembled. "Very quietly, get out of the van."

"What's wrong?" Elena asked from the backseat.

"I . . . I'll explain in a minute." If she mentioned the rattler, they would panic. "Just get out."

Elena must have realized something was very wrong. She urged the women to ease from the vehicle. As soon as they were all out, Bailey opened the driver's door and scrambled out . . .

There had been not one but three rattlers under the front seat. Even now, Bailey's heart pounded in her chest. Horatio had endangered not only her but all the women, and her mission board had pulled her out of the village two days later.

She looked up at the sky again. *Why are you letting all these bad things happen?* She waited as her breath floated up in white streams.

A twig snapped, and Bailey jerked her head toward the noise. "Who's there?"

Oh, how stupid could she get! She jumped up, ready to run.

"Bailey?"

"Danny?"

"What are you doing out here?" he said, moving where she could see him.

"Looking for the North Star." The adrenaline dump turned her knees to water, and she sank back on the stump. "You just took ten years off my life."

"What do you think you did to me? Why are you out here?" he repeated.

She pulled her jacket tighter. "I couldn't sleep. Is that why you're here?"

"No, I wanted to walk the perimeter, familiarize myself with the property again."

She swallowed, her gratitude for Danny's concern overwhelming her. After the way she'd treated him, she wouldn't have blamed him for running in the opposite direction. "I don't know how to thank—"

"There's nothing to thank me for."

"I want to anyway. And I want you to think about something."

He raised his eyebrows, waiting.

"I want to call and talk to Joel's parents in Corning. Maybe even go to see them. They're anxious to see Maria—she's their only grandchild. You could take me there tomorrow, and we could check out the situation . . ."

He pressed his lips together and at least seemed to be considering her request.

"So will you take me?"

He shrugged. "If I don't, I'll never hear the end of it."

Tension eased from Bailey's shoulders. It had really worried her that she hadn't called the McDermotts yet. "Thanks."

Her heart thudded in her chest as he studied her.

"The North Star," he said. "Did you find it?"

"Yes," she said, pointing northward. "See the Little Dipper? Follow the handle and you'll see it."

He moved closer to her and looked in the direction she pointed. The musky scent of his cologne reminded her of other nights when he had been this close and had taken her in his arms and kissed her.

"Yeah, I see it. And it never moves?"

Savoring his nearness, she couldn't bring herself to move away from him. "That's right."

He turned and gazed into her eyes. "Care if I sit with you?"

She scooted over, and he sat beside her on the stump barely

big enough for the two of them. With their shoulders and legs almost touching, she willed herself to move so he wouldn't sense her treacherous heart thumping against her ribs. Instead she found herself leaning into him. "Why did you do it? Risk your life today to help me?"

"How could I not? I . . . I still love you, Bailey, even if you don't love me."

His words pierced her heart and opened a floodgate of emotions. Unable to speak, she stared down at the ground. A minute ticked by as he apparently waited for her response.

"Why did you go to Mexico?" The question dropped into the still night.

A tentative smile curved her lips. "Because they needed me, and I wanted to help, especially the women and children. Ever since I was eighteen, I've gone to Creel to work in summer missions. The poverty is so overwhelming, but the people are so joyful even though they have nothing."

"Couldn't you have just kept going in the summer?" His voice was low, sad.

She'd felt the pull to go into missions full time for several years, but it had taken running from his proposal to get her there. "I could have, but summer missions wouldn't get me away from you. I was afraid if I stayed, you would change my mind."

"And that would have been bad?"

"Yes. I couldn't be the wife you need."

"So you ran away."

"Yeah." She hugged her arms to her body. "I'm good at that."

■ ■ ■

Angel pulled the frilly spread back on the daybed and pressed his fingers into the mattress, testing it. Firm, just the way he liked it. A quick scan of the room indicated guests didn't usually occupy the study. Mrs. Adams—no, Kate—had already refused payment, saying she would not take money from someone who had helped her daughter.

The older woman had not said much tonight, but her keen eyes seemed to take in everything. He wouldn't be surprised if she had figured out he was Maria's father. Which posed a dilemma. Right now, he needed Danny's trust in case the cartel came after Maria in the States. If Danny discovered Angel had lied by omission, that trust would be eroded, even if Danny understood the reason behind the secrecy.

For six months, he or one of his men had kept a watch on his daughter from afar, following her as she went back and forth to school or anywhere else. He'd feared if the cartel discovered he was alive, Maria would be in danger. Either they had found out or it was simply a random kidnapping so prevalent in Mexico. Anyone who was wealthy had become a target.

He cocked his head as footsteps padded down the hallway. Since they were coming toward him, it couldn't be Bailey returning. He'd seen her go down a short time ago, dressed for the outside. Easing the door open, he glimpsed the top of Solana's raven head. Eleven o'clock here, but only ten in Chihuahua. Like Bailey, Solana probably couldn't sleep, either.

Questions about the gentle waitress nagged him. The story of why she had her passport seemed plausible, and he hoped it was true. Otherwise, it raised possibilities he didn't want to consider. He hated the suspicion that crept into everything, but he'd long ago learned not to take anyone or anything at face value. Now might be a good time to learn more about this mystery woman. And if she was everything she claimed to be, then that also opened the door to other possibilities. Instantly, he shut the door to that thought.

Solana looked up when he entered the kitchen, wariness stamped in her big brown eyes. His heart hitched at how the T-shirt swallowed her, making her look like a little girl playing grown-up.

Tomorrow he would buy her clothes that fit. Across the table from her, Kate gave him a warm smile.

"Couldn't sleep either?" Kate asked.

"No."

"We're having chamomile tea. Interested?"

Laughing, he shook his head. "I haven't acquired a taste for that yet. No, I think another bowl of that potato soup will do the trick for me. But I'll fix it myself," he said as she started to rise. He'd noticed where the bowls were kept and opened the cabinet door, taking out one. "I saw Bailey come downstairs . . ."

"She's probably out looking at the stars." Kate stood. "My body says it's my bedtime, so if I can't help you with the soup, I'll bid you a good night."

"Good night," Angel and Solana said in unison as Angel took the pot from the refrigerator. Silence filled the kitchen as he ladled soup in the bowl, then warmed it in the microwave.

He sat across from Solana at the table and began eating. A light jasmine fragrance floated from her direction. "How is your room?"

She looked up, and her eyes had not lost their wariness. "Beautiful. Kate told me the vases in it were some she'd made. Tomorrow I want to see her studio."

"So do you think you would like to be a potter?"

Some of the caution left her face, replaced by a faraway look. "My grandfather was a potter, and I always wanted to try it, but when he was alive, I was too small to kick the wheel. And now . . ."

The yearning in her face matched the yearning in his heart for things that could not be. He pushed the half-eaten bowl of soup away. "Why not now?"

She fluttered her hand. "So many reasons." She swallowed. "When will we return to Mexico?"

"I don't know yet. Do you have business that needs your attention?"

123

The wariness returned, and she lifted her shoulder in a shrug. "Nothing that can't wait."

"How about your family? Do you need to contact them?"

"I only have my sister in Arizona, and she probably won't try to call me since I was just there."

"Which is why you had your passport and visa with you."

She stiffened, and her gaze pinned him to the wall. "Why do you think I had those things with me?"

Uh-oh. His voice had given him away, and he was seeing some of the temper he'd observed at the cafe. Her reaction showed either she was very good at lying or she was telling the truth. He hoped for the latter. "In my line of work, coincidence rarely happens, but in this case, I think it has."

Her lifted eyebrow indicated she hadn't bought his answer. "And it was just a coincidence that you were at the cafe this morning?" she said.

Heat rose up his neck. "I have to eat."

"Sure." She stood. "I'm going to bed."

"No, don't go." With a start, he realized he really didn't want her to leave.

"Why not? It's obvious you don't trust me."

He dropped his gaze. "It's hard for me to trust anyone."

She hesitated, and for a minute, he thought she would stay. "I understand that, but I'm tired. We will talk more tomorrow."

"Yes." After she left, Angel sat in the empty kitchen with the lingering scent of jasmine mocking him.

12

The sensation of falling jerked Danny out of his sleep. He checked the time. Four thirty. Still fully dressed except for his shoes, he eased from the bed and padded to the window. His room faced the circle drive, and he checked to make sure no one lurked about. Security lights outlined the oaks that lined the drive, their branches reaching into the night sky like silent witnesses. Nothing moved. He turned as boards creaked in the room across the hall. Angel was also up. Probably hadn't slept.

Danny wasn't ready to communicate with anyone just yet and returned to the bed. He stared up at the ceiling with his hands clasped behind his head. He'd intended to sort out his thoughts last night, especially after he blurted out his declaration of love to Bailey, but sleep found him faster than he'd expected. He stared at the ceiling as though it would give him the answers he sought.

He'd exorcised her from his life, or so he thought. It didn't take a rocket scientist to tell him he'd risked his life yesterday and almost destroyed his plane, all because he was still in love with her.

What had he been thinking when he told her that he still loved her? That she would say she felt the same way? The words had come out of his mouth before he could stop them, and she had said nothing. Now, the logic that ruled his life demanded that he process the way he felt toward Bailey, starting with everything else that happened yesterday.

When he saw her sitting with Joel, looking at *him* the way she used to look at Danny with those incredible eyes, jealousy ripped through him. Then when he thought those men had taken her . . . His stomach clenched and a vise squeezed his chest, just as it had yesterday. What a crock of lies he'd fed himself for the past two years.

He closed his eyes. Thinking about his non-relationship with Bailey was futile. He needed to focus on a plan of action. But first he had to know Angel and Solana's plans. Bailey's, he knew—contact the grandparents. She'd mentioned last night she wanted to meet with them in person, today hopefully. If she did, he'd take her—she would not get out of his or Angel's sight until this was over. She wouldn't like it, but she might as well get over it.

First thing on his list for today was to get someone to run him over to his house to pick up his SUV and some clothes. He relaxed as he did what he did best—plan. Even when he flew by the seat of his pants like yesterday, his mind jumped ahead, planning the next move.

The plane. He had to get the wing repaired. Two inches to the right and the bullet would have hit the fuel tank. Pure luck that it hadn't. Bailey would have said it was God. He shook the thought off as he relaxed into the mattress. He'd rather believe in luck.

Pipes rattled, and his eyes flew open. Danny glanced at the clock. Almost six thirty. He'd dozed off. Maybe Kate was up and he could get a cup of coffee. He slipped on his shoes and stepped out into the hallway. Angel's room was quiet again, and no one else seemed awake yet so he tried not to clomp as he walked to the stairs and then down them. The rich aroma of coffee met him at the foot of the stairs. Kate was a woman after his own heart.

She looked up from the end of the table and closed her Bible as he came into the kitchen. "Good morning. You're up early. Couldn't sleep?"

He shrugged and made a beeline for the coffee. "There's a lot to do today. Do you think Charlie can run me over to my house?" He picked up an earth-toned cup.

"I'm sure he can. He's at the barn right now." She took the cup from him and handed him another mug. "That's Bailey's favorite. This one's bigger anyway."

"If it's her favorite, it'd be my luck to drop and break it."

They both laughed, then Kate folded her arms. "Can we talk? I want to know what's going on. When I asked Bailey, she skirted my questions."

He scratched his jaw, his beard stubby to his fingers, then took his coffee to the table. "Not sure how much I can help you."

Kate poured herself a cup and joined him. "But you were there, so tell me what happened."

Danny sipped the hot liquid. Anything less than the complete story and Kate would find the holes. "I ran into Bailey at an outdoor cafe yesterday morning. She was with Maria and Joel, the girl's uncle. Joel took Maria in to raise after his sister died. The father died two years ago."

He'd been surprised when he learned Joel had legal custody of the girl. He didn't seem the type.

"What happened to her mother?"

"According to Angel, Claire died from a reaction to melatonin and an antidepressant drug she was taking because of her husband's death. She was under the care of a doctor, but she failed to tell him about the melatonin."

"There were no grandparents to take the child?"

"Only one set, and they're the ones Bailey was bringing Maria to see. When I ran into Bailey yesterday morning, she and Joel and Maria had stopped to eat on their way to the airport. Joel was kidnapped after I left the cafe, and whoever took him wanted Maria as well."

"Bailey wouldn't let that happen."

Kate was already ahead of him. "No. They went on the run with help from Solana, made it to the airport just ahead of the men looking for Maria. That's where Angel and I stepped in, rescued the three of them and took them to a nearby hotel."

After another sip of the coffee, Danny raised his gaze to Kate. "The men followed us there along with Joel, but we made it to the plane and here we are."

Kate held his gaze. "Sounds like you've skipped over a few of the details. Do you think the uncle was in some way involved?"

"I don't know." He chewed the inside ridge in his mouth. "Probably not. He had been beaten up pretty badly. I'm not certain how he escaped his kidnappers."

"How did they find you at the hotel? Did the uncle lead them there?"

"Possibly. Or they may have put a tracking device on his phone and let him go, knowing he'd lead them to Bailey and Maria."

"Why do they want Maria?"

"Angel says for ransom."

"But you don't think that."

"No. I think if it had been for ransom, after they botched it, they would have moved on to an easier target."

She nodded. "Who is this Angel?"

"All I know is his name and that if it hadn't been for him, Bailey and Maria would more than likely be in the hands of the kidnappers."

"Doesn't mean you should completely trust him."

He didn't. But he owed him. "I know."

She squeezed his hand. "Thanks for being there for Bailey. I think God put you at the right place at the right time."

Danny shook his head. "Nah. God wouldn't use me for anything."

An amused smile lit Kate's lips. "You don't really believe that."

Oh, but he did. He stared down at the dark liquid that had

grown cold. God couldn't use him when he was to blame for his mother wrapping her car around a bridge abutment. If he'd only gone to the store when she'd asked him, she wouldn't have driven herself on icy roads. He shoved back from the table and dumped the coffee in the sink.

She pushed her Bible toward him. "Ever read this?"

He turned around. "Some of it." When he was a kid, his mom had read it to him and taken him to church. Then, he'd tried to read it again when Bailey made it plain she wouldn't date him if he didn't.

"What did you think?"

"What I understood sounded good, some of it even like a fairy tale, but I just can't buy into it."

"One day, Danny, you'll discover the Bible is true. That God's forgiveness covers everything."

He started to protest, but the look in Kate's eyes stopped him. It was the same look his mother had given him when he'd disappointed her. "You don't understand. I wanted to believe it because it means so much to Bailey. Jesus healing all those people and preaching about love and raising that guy from the dead. Talking about forgiveness. I'm sorry, but I believe some of the things I've done are unforgivable."

"Like your mother's death? You were just a kid, Danny, and you made a mistake."

"How did—"

"Bailey told me a long time ago what happened." Her eyes softened. "Do you think your mother would forgive you if she had the chance?"

His throat tightened, making it hard to swallow. "She did—in ICU before she died."

"Do you think she'd want you to still carry that burden?"

She wouldn't, but that didn't make it any easier to let it go. "Why did she have to die so young?"

"Christians aren't promised a long life or one without problems." She refilled her cup and held the pot up. "Would you like more?"

"No, I've had enough."

She tapped the worn book on the table. "I have to start breakfast in a minute, but first I want to ask you to do something for me."

Whenever his mom had said those words, he'd known he wasn't going to like what came next. He tilted his head to one side. "And what's that?"

"Read the Gospels."

His heart sank. "I don't know if I can wade through all those thees and thous again."

"Hold on a minute." She left the table and in a minute came back with a book in her hand. "Try this one. It's written in today's language and in the order it happened. Might be a little easier for you to understand."

She held it out, and he took it and flipped through the pages. He would read it, but he wasn't promising anything.

■ ■ ■

At eight, Danny pulled into the Maxwell Industries parking lot and waved at one of the employees as he shut his car door.

"Aren't you going to lock that?" Ian asked from behind him. "And why aren't you in Mexico?"

He turned. Mr. Bright and Early was dressed in a Hickey Freeman suit and probably a two hundred dollar tie. He ignored his cousin's questions. "Do you know where Dad is?"

"He's in the boardroom, waiting for us to join him. Edward Montoya is arriving midmorning, and I assume you'll be here to meet him since I've never met the man."

"You assume wrong. I have something I need to do."

"But we're starting negotiations on the contract this afternoon."

"Sorry. You can handle it without me. You're better at negotiations than I am, anyway."

"Does it have to do with Geoffrey Franks? Because if it does, you need to let it go. You've spent entirely too much time on this Mexico connection. The lawyer called yesterday, said you were at Franks's place last week."

"So? I never saw or talked to him."

Ian sighed. "He saw you, and you know you're not supposed to go around him."

Danny keyed in the door code, then opened the door and let Ian go first. "My business has nothing to do with Franks, but I still can't stay. Bailey needs me to take her to Corning."

"Bailey's home?" Ian's expression added the question he didn't ask. *And she's talking to you?* "When?"

"She flew back with me yesterday along with a couple of friends."

"Why does she need *you* to take her?"

He shrugged. "Why not?"

"I thought—"

He grinned. "That's your trouble, cuz, you think too much. And be prepared to conduct the negotiations 'cause I'm out of here in five minutes."

■ ■ ■

Bailey burrowed deeper under the quilt, not quite ready to get up yet. Maybe it wasn't even time. She lifted her left arm to check her watch. *Ten o'clock? No!* She was late for school. She threw back the fleecy blanket and sat up.

Wait. She rubbed her eyes as her pounding heart slowed. She wasn't in Mexico. Yesterday's events came flooding back. Beside her Maria stirred and reached for the blanket. "I'm cold," she said in Spanish.

Funny how even with an American mother, the child defaulted to Spanish. Bailey tucked the blanket around her and slipped out of bed. There was so much to do today, and she hated that she'd overslept. Coffee. That's what she needed. Slipping on a terry cloth robe she'd found in her closet last night, she padded downstairs in her bare feet.

Her mother stood at the sink. "Good morning, sleepyhead."

"I wish I'd told you to get me up by eight. Now I'm way behind."

"It's just barely eight now." Her mom pointed at the kitchen clock. "And I put your favorite mug out."

Bailey stared at her watch. She'd somehow managed to move her watch forward three hours instead of just the one that Chihuahua was behind Logan Point. She poured coffee in the earth-toned mug and opened the refrigerator. "Any cream?"

"Half-and-half is in the back."

She'd been hoping for something hazelnut. Or French vanilla. Another item to put on her list to pick up. "Is anyone else up?"

"Danny came down earlier. We had a nice talk."

Uh-oh. "About?"

"Oh, he sort of filled me in on what's been happening."

Double uh-oh. Bailey stirred her coffee, hoping her mom would drop the subject.

"What are your plans?"

She took a sip of coffee. "First, I have to shop for more clothes for Maria and Solana. I'm sure Danny told you we didn't bring anything other than what we had on."

Her mom nodded. "And those are on the dryer, ready for them."

"Thanks. I really appreciate that you washed them."

"What do you plan to do about Maria?"

Bailey rubbed the back of her neck. "First thing I'm going to do is call Ben and see if he got in touch with Joel. Then I'll try the grandparents again. I don't understand why they're not home. If they still don't answer and we have no word from Joel, I have the directions to their house in Corning. It's only an hour and a half away—I'll leave Maria here, and Danny and I will drive over to see what's going on."

"And if you find the grandparents, are you going to take Maria to them?"

"I don't know. I'm hoping they've heard from their son." Bailey sipped her coffee. Not quite strong enough to walk but strong enough, just like she liked it. Cupping the mug in her hands, she walked to the double windows that looked out over the pasture. Frost blanketed the field where she and her friends had ridden horses. That seemed so long ago.

Her mom joined her at the window. "I've missed you."

Bailey leaned into her.

"You've been through a lot since you left."

Tears sprung to her eyes. Her mother didn't know the half of it. "I'm okay."

"Are you? I know that first year was bad."

Bailey stepped back. The eight months she spent in Copper Canyon haunted her, but the way she ran from the problem haunted her even more. "How—"

"Your letters."

"But I didn't say anything."

"I know—it's what you didn't say. Anytime you want to talk, you know I'll listen."

"I know, but not right now. I better go check on Maria." Bailey didn't want to confront yet another of her failures just yet or how she'd let Father Horatio intimidate her. She stopped at the hall door. "Is Danny still here?"

"Charlie took him to get his SUV. Angel's upstairs, though."

Bailey stepped back into the kitchen. "What do you think of Angel?"

"He's very intense."

"I know, and he's so protective of Maria. Solana too, for that matter. But I think Danny trusts him."

"He must," her mother said. "He left Angel here to go get his SUV."

It didn't surprise Bailey that Danny wanted someone here to protect them. Her heart fluttered. Yesterday she'd seen a different side to him. Just thinking about how he risked his life for her . . . Why couldn't things be different? Why couldn't she give him what he wanted? And why did he have to tell her last night that he still loved her?

Because that was Danny. Honest. Plainspoken. She ought to be more like him. She pushed the thought away and grabbed the clothes on the dryer. "I'll take these upstairs."

A moment later, she tapped softly on Solana's door, and in less than a minute it opened. "Yes?"

"Mom washed your clothes. Later today we'll go shopping."

"Gracias, but I have no money."

"Don't worry about it."

Solana lifted her chin. "But I do. I want to pay my own way. And I want to return to Mexico."

Bailey didn't know how to answer her. In her place, Bailey would feel the same way. "Let's just take one day at a time. And I don't know how safe it would be for you to go back."

"Then I will go to my sister's."

"You'll have to talk to Angel and Danny about that."

When Bailey came back downstairs half an hour later with Maria, Danny had returned, and he and Angel and Solana were in the kitchen, eating breakfast. "Hey, leave something for us," she said, then turned to Maria. "Would you like biscuits and eggs or cereal?"

Maria pointed to Angel. "What's he eating?"

"I'm eating the best biscuits in the world," Angel said. "Would you like to taste?"

She nodded and ran to him, surprising Bailey. The two had bonded from the start. Something that had taken her a good week to accomplish with Maria.

"Can I sit on your lap?"

"Most definitely." He pulled her up. "This biscuit has butter. You want?"

Maria glanced at Bailey, a question in her eyes.

"You don't have to ask," Bailey said. "Eat all you want." She had to have a talk with Joel. Maria was not a small adult, she was a child and needed to be treated like one. An arrow struck her heart. What if he was dead? No. She wouldn't think about that. "Has Ben Logan called this morning?"

"A few minutes ago. Joel still doesn't answer, but Ben left him a voicemail."

She walked to the phone mounted on the wall and dialed the grandparents' number from memory. After more rings than she could count, she hung up. "They still don't answer."

"What time do you want me to drive you to Corning?" Danny asked. "Angel and Solana can stay here with Maria."

"In thirty minutes?"

"Sure, but aren't you going to eat?" Danny asked.

"Cereal." She poured little squares of frosted shredded wheat in a bowl and cut up a banana. "Robyn said she'd help out with Maria and should be here before we leave."

"She doesn't have to bother," Angel said.

But Bailey wanted her here. Angel's secretiveness disturbed her. Even though he'd helped save their lives yesterday and he'd totally captivated Maria, she felt he was hiding something behind those dark eyes. "It won't be a bother for her."

Forty-five minutes later, she and Danny had left Logan Point behind and traveled eastward in his luxurious black Escalade.

"There's something for you on the backseat. It's in the white bag," he said.

"For me?" She twisted around and found the package he was talking about. "What is it?"

"A new phone. The rep said she was able to retrieve your contacts and set up your email from the cloud."

"Yes!" Bailey hated to admit she'd been lost without her phone. She opened the package and gasped. "This is the latest version!" If he wasn't driving, she'd plant a kiss on his cheek.

"It has all the bells and whistles."

"I don't know what to say, except thank you." She turned the phone on and scrolled through the emails that showed on the screen. One was from the school where she taught, and she started to open it when she saw one from Elena that came yesterday. Pastor Carlos must have helped her get an email account. Bailey slid her finger across the screen, opening the email, and grinned at the greeting.

My first email!

Her grin faded as she read on.

I hope everything is good. I am continuing the Bible classes at the church, and many of the women come. Father Horatio is very angry. So angry I think maybe his blood will boil. But the women are so happy to be here. I will need more material when you return. Email me when you come back to Mexico!

Love, Elena

P.S. Please do not report what we saw.

"Bad news?" Danny asked.

"Sort of. My friend Elena has angered the village priest, and he can be very nasty. She says she's made his blood boil."

"What kind of priest is this?"

She frowned. "He's not really a priest, more of a shaman. He's the man I saw in the restaurant."

"Do you think he'll harm her?"

"I don't know. He's involved with the Calatrava, so he'd have the means. But Elena's husband has some standing in the village, and I don't think he will let Horatio hurt her." Unlike the woman who accused the priest of fathering her child. She'd been beaten so badly she was permanently crippled, not that it could be proven that Father Horatio did it.

She reread the email. "She's asking me not to report a poppy field we stumbled on when I was there."

"Poppies? As in opium?"

"Yes. It's a poor village, and the farmers there are growing them so they can take care of their families."

"But don't they know what that stuff does?"

"They do. But I think they justify it when they see their babies' bellies swollen from not having enough food to eat."

"That's sad too."

"Yes, it is. I've learned some hard things in Mexico. But I did mean to report the field when I got back to the States, not that it would do any good. I need to talk to Ben about it. Let me answer this, and I'll put my phone away."

"No hurry. We still have at least an hour."

It hit Bailey just how much Danny had altered his schedule to accommodate her. "I just realized I haven't thanked you for driving me to Corning."

"It was better than the alternative."

"Alternative?"

"You coming by yourself."

She rolled her eyes at him, but at the same time part of her bristled that he thought she couldn't take care of herself. She'd seen this protectiveness earlier, and she understood where he was coming from, that he was scared for her. But she was thirty-one years old. He wasn't her father, and he couldn't tell her what to do . . . or not do. Not that her dad ever had any luck with that, anyway.

With a sigh she responded to Elena's email and put her phone away. As soon as they returned, she needed to report the poppy field to Ben. He'd know the right authorities to contact in Mexico.

Without the phone to distract her, silence settled between them, a silence that became increasingly uncomfortable. All she could think about was Danny's declaration last night. *"I still love you, Bailey, even if you don't love me."*

"Do you mind if I turn the radio on?" she asked.

"No."

At least the music drowned out the silence or rather it and Danny's fingers tapping on the steering wheel.

She couldn't stand it any longer. "About last—"

"Bailey—"

Silence again. "You first," she said.

"No, ladies first."

He would pull that card. She sucked in a deep breath. "It's . . . not that I don't love you." There. She'd said it. Admitted to herself as well that she still loved him.

"But we don't share the same values." He finished her sentence.

She smoothed a wrinkle from the pants she'd found in her closet. The shape her faith was in, it wasn't even that. "I can't . . ." She moistened her lips.

He turned his head toward her. "You can't what?"

"Some things happened that first year I was in Mexico. I—"

"Did someone hurt you?"

She shook her head. "Not physically."

"I don't understand."

That made two of them. "It's not something I want to discuss. I just want you to know, you're not the problem. It's me. I just don't know who I am anymore."

13

Joel sank into the leather seat of the corporate jet. He'd slept little last night and hoped to catch a nap. Across from him, Edward worked on his tablet. The man never let up, and Joel was certain his passion to succeed was one of the reasons the man had never married. A relationship took an investment of time, and Edward Montoya only had time for making money.

Joel cleared his throat. "Can you tell me why my password didn't work when I tried to access my backed-up files?"

"There was an attempt to hack into the system. When we return, you'll get a new password."

"What if I need my files before then?"

"Why would you need them? You won't be working while we're in the States."

Joel dug his fingers into the armrest. When Montoya was like this, it did no good to try and change his mind. Even if Joel's whole world was crumbling before him. He settled back in the seat and closed his eyes and tried not to think about his problems.

"Did you reach Bailey Adams?"

Joel jerked away from the edge of sleep. "No. My calls still go straight to voicemail."

"How about Danny Maxwell. Did you try him?"

"He doesn't answer, either, although the phone rings several times before it's routed to a message center." Danny may have figured out the men after Bailey and Maria were able to track them through Bailey's phone. If that was the case, her phone was probably in a ditch somewhere. He just hoped she wasn't with it.

"How about your parents? Have you heard from them?"

"Finally. Unfortunately, my dad was taken to the hospital late yesterday afternoon. Suspected heart attack. My mother called me on a cell phone."

It surprised him that they had a cell phone. They didn't have an answering machine on their home phone because neither of them wanted to learn how to program it, and from the way she shouted into the cell phone, his mother hadn't quite gotten the hang of how to use it. She'd called because she wanted Joel to let "that nice lady bringing Maria" know they weren't home.

When Montoya returned to his iPad, Joel closed his eyes, but thoughts swirled through his brain. He didn't understand why his boss was coming along on this trip, why he didn't just send him to get Maria. Sure, Montoya was fond of the girl, but emotional attachments were not high on his list of priorities. "I could have handled this," Joel said abruptly.

Edward glanced up from his iPad. "I know that, but Maria is family. I would be very upset if anything happened to her and I hadn't done everything in my power to protect her. Besides, I had a visit to Logan Point scheduled later in the month to discuss the new contract anyway, and it was no problem to move it up."

That sounded more like the Montoya that Joel knew.

"What do you hear about Geoffrey Franks?"

Joel uncapped the bottle of water in the cup holder on his seat and took a long draw of water. "I understand his trial is coming up soon but that he's currently out on bail. Do you know who received the guns he shipped?"

Montoya shrugged. "I thought it might be someone with the Calatrava cartel, but after I had another chat with Chavez, I learned someone has been waging war with the cartel and helping the local businesses to stand up to them. That person would have an interest in obtaining rifles."

"Do you know who it is?"

"Chavez didn't have a name, only that some of the businesses called him and his men the Angels of the Streets."

"You think it might be your nephew?"

Montoya nodded. "He's always seen himself as some sort of Robin Hood, and the description from one of the businessmen I contacted yesterday matches him. If it is Angel and the cartel knows it, the attempt to kidnap Maria could be tied to him instead of me. Of course, the kidnappers could be looking at a two-for-one—control Angel and at the same time jack me up for a ransom." He paused and glanced at Joel. "We need a cover story for your bruises, like perhaps an automobile accident."

Joel gingerly touched his cheek. Shaving this morning had been an ordeal. "Why?"

"This meeting with Phillip Maxwell is to convince him to continue the partnership with Montoya Ceramics. He was not happy with the notoriety from the Franks mess. If he suspects trouble between my company and the drug cartel, he might decide to pull the contract."

"Car wreck it is, then."

■ ■ ■

Four hours later, Joel shook hands with Phillip Maxwell.

"Looks like you were on the wrong end of a punching bag," Maxwell said.

"No, unfortunately I drove a little too close to another car, and it stopped suddenly. I didn't know an air bag could give you black eyes."

"They can be quite vicious."

It had been several years since Joel had seen the owner of

Maxwell Industries. He was an older version of Danny and just as fit. The door opened, and Joel turned as a man entered the paneled office. This had to be the nephew, Ian, whom he'd never met. The family resemblance continued except he appeared more businesslike in a navy suit and white dress shirt. Joel couldn't imagine Danny in anything other than the jeans and pullover he'd always seen him wear.

"Ian, meet Edward Montoya and his assistant, Joel McDermott. They're here to discuss the new contract, and I wanted you in on the discussions since Danny couldn't be here."

An easy smile appeared as Ian extended his hand, first to Edward, then to Joel. "My pleasure. Run into someone's fist?"

Joel went through his explanation once more, then asked about Danny. "I thought he might be here."

"He was here earlier." Ian tilted his head toward Joel. "I'm a little confused. I thought he flew to Mexico to see you yesterday, and yet he was here at the plant earlier. Then he left, saying he had to do something for Bailey. Do you know why he came back so soon from Mexico?"

Evidently Danny had not yet told them what had transpired. He shook his head. "I saw him briefly yesterday, and then I learned he had returned to Logan Point with my niece and Bailey Adams. Unfortunately, my cell phone isn't working properly, so I haven't been able to contact him or Bailey."

"Let me try him on my phone." Ian dialed a number and waited. "Danny. Where are you?" He nodded. "I see. Are you coming home anytime soon? Edward Montoya and Joel McDermott are here, and Joel is inquiring of you." A frown furrowed Ian's brow. "He seems to be fine."

Ian listened for a minute longer, then glanced toward Joel. "Danny's out of town right now," he said, moving the phone away from his mouth. "He said he would call you when he gets back."

"May I speak with him?" Joel had been right that Danny was ignoring his calls. If he didn't talk with him now, Joel wouldn't hear from Danny—he'd bet money on it.

"Hold on, Joel wants a word with you," Ian said and handed Joel the phone.

"Danny, I have a little problem I think you can help me with." He walked to a corner of the office, away from the others, and lowered his voice. "I've tried to call Bailey, but her phone must not be working. Are they all right?"

"She and Maria are fine. From what Ian said, I assume you are as well. When I get back to Logan Point, I'll contact you, and we'll meet."

"You're not going to tell me where they are?"

"Not over the phone."

"Then give Bailey a message for me. Tell her my father has had a heart attack and is in the Corning hospital. They won't be able to take Maria now. I'll pick my niece up this afternoon and take her back to Mexico with me."

There was silence on the other end, then murmuring. Danny wasn't by himself. "If Bailey's with you, may I speak with her?"

"Which hospital?"

His question confused Joel briefly. "Community Hospital—it's the only one. But why?"

"I'll let her know. Where can I contact you later?"

It was evident Danny wasn't going to let him speak to Bailey. "Just call my phone."

"Is it working? Sheriff Ben Logan has been trying to reach you, said no one answered."

Joel took his phone out of his pocket and checked it for missed messages. There were three from a number he didn't recognize. "I never heard my phone ring," he said.

"I'd rather not call you on that phone, anyway. Do you have another number?"

Joel thought for a minute and then gave him Edward's number. "I'll be waiting for your call."

He rejoined the group and handed Ian's phone back to him. "Thanks. Do you know where Bailey might be if she was in Logan Point? My niece is with her, and I'd like to pick her up."

"Why don't you just call her?" Ian's eyes held suspicion. "You can use my phone again."

"I don't think it's my phone but hers. I'll try, though." He dialed the number. Nobody answered. "It went straight to voicemail, like it has every time I've tried to call her."

Phillip Maxwell spoke up. "Bailey would more than likely be at her mother's bed-and-breakfast."

Yes!

Before he could inquire about the location, Ian said, "Why is your niece with her?"

"Maria has never met my parents since they aren't well and couldn't come to Mexico. They couldn't even make my sister's funeral. Bailey is her teacher, and since she planned to return home for a short visit—something about her sister coming home—I thought it'd be a good way for my parents to meet their granddaughter."

"It's more complicated than that," Edward said. "There is much turmoil in Mexico. We thought it best for her to visit her grandparents at this time."

"We?" Phillip looked from Joel to Edward.

Joel nodded. "Edward is Maria's great-uncle. His nephew Angel Montoya Guerrera is Maria's father, and not to be trusted. That's why I want to get in touch with Bailey. We believe he is with them."

■ ■ ■

Bailey rubbed her forehead. Joel was in Logan Point. "So he's okay?"

"Sounded like it. Said he intended to pick Maria up this afternoon and return to Mexico with her."

"This afternoon? What about his parents? Isn't he going to take her to see them? Or at least see his father who's had a heart attack?"

He shrugged. "Do you still want to find them? I think I know where the hospital is."

Why would Joel want to take Maria back to Mexico? Nothing made sense. She realized Danny had asked her another question. "What?"

"Well, do you?"

"Do I what?"

"Do you want to look the grandparents up at the hospital? Find out what happened?"

"Yes. I was just trying to figure out why he'd take her back to Mexico. That's where someone wants to kidnap her."

"Yeah, I know. The turn we need to make to the hospital is up ahead. What do you want to do?"

"Go to the hospital."

Once they arrived at the hospital, they went to the Information Center, where Bailey inquired about what room Joe McDermott was in.

"Surgical ICU. Only family is allowed in to see him."

"I see. Where is the waiting room?" They followed the directions the volunteer gave them, and when Bailey inquired if anyone with the McDermott family was in the waiting room, the receptionist spoke into the intercom.

"Would someone with the McDermott family come to the desk, please."

Shortly, a petite wisp of a woman approached the front. "I'm Sue McDermott. Is something wrong?"

"These folks want to see you."

She glanced toward them, puzzlement on her face. "Hello. I'm Sue. Can I help you?"

Bailey stepped toward her. "Mrs. McDermott, I'm Bailey Adams.

I'm the teacher who brought Maria from Mexico. We were supposed to be at your house last night?"

Sue McDermott raised her hand to her lips. "Oh, dear. You didn't get my message? Never mind. Thank goodness you're here." She looked past Bailey. "Where's Maria?"

"I didn't bring her; she's with my mother. I didn't want to bring her to the hospital until I knew more about what's going on. How is your husband?"

Tears pooled in her blue eyes. "Not good. The doctors say he needs an operation, but the stubborn old coot doesn't want to do it. And now he's using Maria as an excuse, says he won't have it until he sees her. She's our only grandchild, you know. When can you bring her?"

Bailey didn't know what to tell her. "Have you heard from Joel?"

"Late last night. He can't come. Something about business. He's never really had time for his father. They don't get on well, you know."

No, she didn't know. But at least now she understood why he didn't mention seeing his father.

"Claire and her father were close, at least until she married that Mexican man. Angel Montoya."

Could the man Sue McDermott mentioned be their Angel Guerrera? She looked over Sue's head and met Danny's gaze. The expression on his face indicated he had the same thought she did.

The older woman grabbed Bailey's hand. "You will bring her this afternoon, won't you?"

She patted Sue's hand. "I'll see what I can do, but it may be tomorrow."

"Thank you. He'll die without the operation, and he's just stubborn enough to not have it unless you bring the girl. Or wait until it's too late and has another heart attack."

As soon as they were out of Sue's hearing range, Bailey turned to Danny, but he held his hand up. "It can't be him—he was killed two years ago. Besides, there are a lot of men with that name in Mexico, something Angel pointed out when we first met."

She cast a sidelong glance at him. "Why would he do that?"

"Because I mentioned meeting a kid named Angel on my first trip to Mexico when I was twelve years old. Maybe the boy I met was Edward Montoya's nephew."

"Claire's husband and Maria's father," Bailey said.

"Yeah." He held the door open for her.

"Angel Guerrera definitely has an interest in Maria. Another coincidence, and I'm not a big believer in coincidences."

"Me either, but if Angel is Maria's dad, why didn't he come forward after her mother died? Why would he let Joel have custody of her?"

Bailey shrugged. "Maybe he couldn't. Maybe he was in jail."

"Or injured."

He said it with such finality that she shot him a curious look. "You've remembered something else."

"Yep. I commented on how well he spoke English, and he said he'd had practice in an American hospital recently."

As soon as they were in his SUV, she said, "What if he was just waiting for the right time to take Maria? Maybe even Solana is in on it."

"Come on, Bailey. You're letting your imagination run wild. Solana is a victim."

"You're probably right about that, but I need to call and check on Maria."

Before Bailey could call, Danny's cell rang. "Ian" flashed on the console ID. "Let me catch this first. Won't take long." He pressed a button on the steering wheel, and the call went to his speakers. "What do you need, Ian?"

"I don't need anything. But I just left a meeting with Montoya. Those friends you mentioned that came back with you from Mexico. One of them wouldn't happen to be Angel Montoya, would he?"

Bailey's breath hitched in her chest. Danny held up a warning hand. "Why do you think that?"

"Can't you just answer a yes or no?" Ian snapped back.

"He hasn't told us he's Angel Montoya," Danny said.

"A word of warning then—Edward Montoya emphasized he's not to be trusted. Just wanted to let you know."

"Thanks. We'll be careful with him. Is McDermott still there?"

"No, he left about an hour ago."

"Thanks." Danny ended the call and glanced at her.

"So our hunch was right." She rubbed her thumb against her palm. "Why didn't he tell us?"

He tapped his fingers on the steering wheel. "I don't know. He doesn't trust anyone . . . Maybe he plans to tell us when we get back."

She gave him a sour look and took out her new phone. "I need to see where they are." As she waited for the call to go through, she said, "I noticed yesterday you hadn't taken me out of your address book."

"Hope springs eternal."

Her cheeks grew hot from the wicked grin he shot her.

Kate answered on the first ring. "Where are you? I've been trying to reach you."

"Sorry, we've been busy," Bailey said and put the call on speakerphone. "Where's Maria?"

"She's with Robyn, and they've gone shopping for clothes. But the reason I called—Joel McDermott just left. He was looking for you and Maria. I told him you wouldn't be home until later this afternoon. He said he would come back."

"Was Angel there?"

"No, he had already left with Robyn."

"Good. We should be home in another hour." She wanted to get there before Angel discovered Joel was in Logan Point. When Angel found out, he might take Maria and disappear. "By the way, Mom, we think Angel is Maria's dad."

"Are you just now figuring that out?"

Bailey exchanged glances with Danny. "How did you know?"

"If you'd ever paid attention to the way he looks at her, you would have known. But you've had so much else on your mind."

"One of us should have realized it," Bailey muttered and hung up.

14

At a traffic light, Angel glanced back at Maria in a booster seat in Robyn's Camry, and contentment filled his heart, if only for a moment. Buying his daughter new clothes was only the start of what he wanted to do.

"Look, Angel, a park! Can we stop?" Maria entreated him with her big blue eyes.

"Miss Robyn might not have time." Angel queried Bailey's sister with raised eyebrows.

She glanced up at the traffic light, then checked her watch. "My stomach agrees with my watch that it's time to eat. If you don't think it's too cold, why don't we stop and pick up something for lunch and have a picnic?"

The sun had warmed the day up, and even if it was a little chilly, Maria now had a down jacket, as did Solana. He turned to her. "How does that sound to you?"

Solana's eyes danced. She seemed to have forgiven him for his questions last night. "It is a beautiful day. We should not waste it."

At the next block, Robyn wheeled her Camry into a small grocery. "They have really good sandwich meat here. I'll pick up what we need. You can wait here in the car."

Maria unbuckled herself and threw her arms around Angel. "Thank you."

"Thank Miss Robyn too."

His heart warmed once again as Maria thanked her and threw kisses at Robyn. Claire had done well with Maria before she died. The thought of his wife twisted the knife in his heart, shredding his contentment. He had failed her. He must not fail his daughter.

A few minutes later, the driver's door opened, and Robyn handed him a sack. "How does cheese and bologna on crackers sound?"

"What is this baloney?" he asked.

Robyn laughed. "It's a Southern delicacy, but I won't tell you what's in it. You have to get hooked on it first. Like I did. When I was a kid and Daddy took me to town, we always stopped here. But I had to promise not to tell Mama, so it was like our own special secret. I did pick up a jar of peanut butter and jelly for Maria. And a few slices of turkey." She pulled out of the parking lot and drove toward the park.

Angel wasn't certain he wanted to try this Southern delicacy. He glanced back at Solana, but she was off in a world of her own. He really wanted to erase the haunted look in her eyes. The new clothes had helped some, even though he'd had to argue with her about buying them. He'd also won out over the plain white sweater she picked out. The lavender brought a little color back to her face.

"Bailey called while I was inside. It'll be at least an hour and probably longer before she gets back."

"I wonder if she saw the grandparents." Angel had never met Claire's parents, and from the way she had described her father, he wasn't sure he wanted to.

"The grandmother. The grandfather is in ICU. Something about a heart attack." She parked the car.

Angel climbed out of the car and scanned the area. While the park wasn't teeming with people, there were several adults walking the trail, along with a couple of mothers with strollers. He opened Maria's door.

"Can we swing before we eat?" Maria asked as he helped her out of the car seat.

Robyn shooed them toward the swings. "Solana and I will prepare lunch, and we'll call you when it's ready."

At the swings, he helped Maria into the canvas seat.

"Will you push me high?" she asked.

"We'll see." He gave her a small push, sending the swing gently forward.

"Higher!" she squealed.

"This is high enough." Surely God would not give him a daughter like himself. One who craved excitement.

"No! Higher." She wiggled her feet, trying to increase the height.

"Hold on, then." He shoved harder and she laughed. How many times had he longed for this moment? If only Claire . . . He shook the thought off. But what was he going to do? If the Calatrava wanted Maria now, they would want her even more when they discovered he was alive. They would rightfully believe they could control him with her. But why did they want her *now*? The answer came swiftly. The Calatrava already knew he was alive.

He allowed the swing to slow, receiving Maria's displeasure. "It's time to eat, I think."

"Can we come back when we're done?"

"Probably so."

She hopped out of the swing and ran to the picnic table where Robyn and Solana waited.

"Did you have fun, little one?" Solana asked her.

Maria's eyes danced. "Yes. Will you swing me next time? Angel says we can do it again after we eat."

Solana picked Maria up and set her on the concrete seat. "Sí."

Maria glanced down at Solana's feet. "Can you push me with that on your foot?"

Solana touched Maria on the nose. "The cast has not stopped me from doing anything I set my mind to. And you must never let anything stop you, little one."

If they remained in Logan Point, Angel would ask Bailey where to take Solana to get the ankle x-rayed.

"Perhaps we will even try the slide," Solana said.

"Can we?" Maria turned to Angel. "Will you take me up to the top of the slide?"

He laughed. "Thanks, Solana. She hadn't seen the slide yet, and I was hoping she wouldn't."

When Solana's shoulders drooped, he regretted his words. "I was only teasing. She would have found it. What do you say we try this Southern delicacy Robyn has for us?"

He examined the crackers that had some type of meat and a slice of cheese between them. "You are certain it is good?"

"Try it," Robyn said.

He bit into the crackers. The taste was similar to a hot dog with a bit more garlic. "This is good."

Robyn held her thumb up, then turned to Solana, who shrugged.

"Not bad, but I think I will try the peanut butter and jelly with Maria."

After they finished, Maria looked like she had more jelly on her face than in her stomach. "I'll take her to the washroom," Robyn said.

Angel scanned the area again. No suspicious people lurked about, and he nodded. He kept his eye on them until they disappeared into the building.

"When are you going to tell her?" Solana asked.

He jerked his head around. "Tell her what?"

"That you are her father."

He opened his mouth and closed it. "How did you know?"

She replied in Spanish. "She looks like you around the eyes. Once I questioned that she was your daughter, I put two and two together and came up with Angel Montoya and not Angel Guerrera."

He closed his eyes. He hadn't thought anyone would notice any other similarities.

"So, when?"

"I don't know. It's not that simple."

"Why did you let people believe Angel Montoya was dead?"

He raked his fingers through his hair. "I had no choice. Joel walked me into a trap. I should have been dead from the gunshot wound. My men carried me out of the building before it could be discovered I was still alive. By the time I got out of a Texas hospital, Claire was dead and Joel had custody of Maria."

She touched his arm. "I am so sorry."

He looked up and lost himself in the warmth of her dark chocolate eyes. Since yesterday he'd wanted to take her in his arms, but once again he pushed the desire away. He would not make someone else a target for the Calatrava. He stood. "Thank you. I wish things were different."

She stood and cupped the side of his face with her hand. "But they are not, and we have to live each day as if it might be our last. You are a good man, Angel Montoya. God will protect Maria. Tell her who you are."

"Soon, maybe." He turned as Maria called his name.

"Angel! Can we swing again?"

"I'm coming," he said and gave Solana a lingering gaze. Maybe it would be possible to live a normal life someday.

■ ■ ■

Car tires crunched on the drive, and Bailey parted the drapes as Joel climbed out of a light blue hatchback. She hadn't been sure she'd ever see him again. Sunglasses covered his eyes, but from what she could see, he looked slightly better today than when she last glimpsed him at the hotel. She wanted a few answers from him before Angel arrived with Maria, and then she wanted answers from Angel. She met him at the door. "Come in."

Inside the house, he removed the sunglasses, and she gasped. The tissue around both eyes was swollen and bruised. "Do you know who did this to you or why?"

He shrugged. "The drug cartel, and I have no idea why other than they wanted information about where you and Maria were. Where is she?"

"With my sister. They're on their way, but we need to talk before they get here."

"They?" Joel asked.

"Angel and the waitress from the cafe. Solana."

Joel showed no reaction other than a twitch of his mouth. "So the report is true. Angel Montoya is alive."

"Evidently, although the man with us doesn't go by Montoya, and since I don't know what your brother-in-law looks like, I'm not sure. But if it is him, you didn't know?" she asked.

"No. We all thought he was dead, including my sister. Does Maria remember him?"

"No, but let's discuss this in the kitchen with Danny. We both have a lot of questions." She turned and led the way down the hall. In the kitchen, Danny waited, his arms crossed.

Joel held out his hand. "Thanks for getting Maria here safely."

Danny eyed him, then accepted his hand. "How did you get away? I saw you being carried to a car, then the next thing I know, you're delivering the cartel to our door."

"The Federals raided the warehouse where the men took me. Then at the hotel the cartel was more interested in you than me. At least the Federals killed the two who did this." He touched his cheek, then turned to Bailey. "Do you know why the drug cartel is interested in you?"

"Me?" Her breath caught in her chest. "I assumed they were after Maria for ransom."

Danny leaned toward Joel. "Why do you think they're after Bailey?"

Joel shrugged and looked at her. "The men who took me seemed as interested in you as Maria. Of course, that could be because she was in your care."

That had to be it, but the uneasiness stayed with her. "Did the cartel follow you to the hotel?"

"Yeah," Danny said. "*Did* you lead the cartel to the hotel?"

"Good grief, no! Why would I do that?" He turned to Bailey. "I only wanted to protect you and Maria. I thought you'd be safer with me, but evidently, they put a tracking device on my phone and it pinged your location when I phoned you. I didn't find the device until after you escaped the hotel. You have to believe me, I wouldn't do anything to hurt either one of you."

She wanted to believe him, but at this point, she wasn't sure who she could trust, except for Danny.

"I want to warn you about Angel too. He's a dangerous man."

"He saved our lives," Bailey said. "Without his help, we'd probably be in the hands of the Calatrava."

Joel's face turned the color of blood. "You can't trust him, and when Maria gets here, I want to get her away from him. I'll take her with me."

"Maria stays here," Danny said. "You're just one person, and you have no way of protecting her."

"Edward Montoya is with me. He has the resources to keep her safe."

"Why isn't he here?" Danny asked.

"He's discussing business with your father, but he sent me here to collect Maria. I plan to take her to see my parents before we go back to Mexico."

"No!" Bailey didn't intend to allow Maria to go anywhere,

especially Mexico. "I mean, taking her to see your parents is fine, but why do you want to take her back to Mexico?"

"That's our home. I'll hire armed guards to keep her safe."

"You can't take her back," Bailey said. She searched for other ways to convince Joel he couldn't snatch Maria up and return to the place where someone wanted to kidnap the child. "She's been through a lot this week and needs to stay here to recover from being chased by those men. She has stability here."

Joel folded his arms across his chest. "I'm her legal guardian."

"You will not be her guardian for long, and she will not be leaving here." Angel spoke from the doorway, the words dropping into the silence like a bomb.

Bailey whirled around. She hadn't heard him come in. "Where's Maria?"

"Solana took her out to where your mother is working. And your sister had an errand to run." Angel turned to Joel. "You will take my daughter nowhere and especially not around my uncle."

At least they agreed that Maria needed to stay here. Bailey pinned her gaze on him. "Why didn't you tell us you were Maria's father? Why did you give us a false name?"

"But I didn't. My name is Angel de Montoya y Guerrera—Guerrera is my mother's last name, and I simply dropped my father's name after this one tried to have me killed." He pointed to Joel. "I trusted you. You were family, my wife's brother."

"I had nothing to do with what happened in the warehouse. I didn't know we were walking into a trap."

Angel snorted. "You lie so easily. Somehow you miraculously walked away without a scratch while I took a bullet in my chest. Or did you hide and watch?"

"I'm telling you," Joel said, "all I did was set up a meeting with a Federal officer to help you work out your problems. Problems caused because you went off the grid with your vigilante methods.

Buying illegal guns is what made you a target, not me. I had nothing to do with what happened that day."

"Then why were the Calatrava there if you did not tell them?"

"I don't know how they found out about the meeting. Maybe the cop was on their payroll. But since he was killed in the shootout, we'll never know, will we?"

"And yet you were not harmed." Angel shook his head. "And I have *never* bought illegal guns."

Bailey tilted her head. It seemed Joel had a knack for escaping dangerous situations. Or . . . perhaps he was the instigator.

Joel's hands clenched into fists. "If you want to hate me for not sticking around, fine. But don't blame me for what happened. You're the one who went after the Calatrava and broke the law doing it."

Bailey cleared her throat. "All of this is interesting, but it doesn't address the issue of Maria."

Angel stood taller, his shoulders straight. "There is no issue. When she comes from seeing your mother, I will tell her who I am, and we will leave for a safe place."

"Don't you think that's a little sudden?" Bailey said. "She doesn't know you, and she's already had too many changes in her short life. Don't add to her stress."

Danny cocked his head. "How do you propose to leave? You have no transportation, especially since I agree with Bailey."

"So you will not help me?"

"I didn't say that, but I think you need to slow down a little. The Calatrava have you in their sights, and maybe you're the reason Maria is there as well. I mean, if the Calatrava know you're alive, it's possible that's the reason they went after her."

"Listen to him," Bailey said. "Plans need to be made and that takes time. A few more days here won't hurt."

"If you stay, I'd like you to consider allowing Maria to go see her grandparents," Joel said.

"No! She does not leave my sight."

Joel shrugged. "You could go as well." The two men squared off, neither giving an inch until Joel cocked his head slightly. "Wouldn't Claire want her daughter to meet them?"

His soft words sent pain across Angel's face, and Bailey winced. The man had almost lost his life, had lost his wife, and his daughter wasn't safe. She could almost see Angel's thought process.

Finally he nodded. "We'll see. I am not a man who would deprive grandparents from seeing their grandchild. Does my uncle know you plan to take Maria to see your parents?"

"What is it with you and Edward?" Joel asked.

"He killed my parents and stole their company."

The chilling words hung in the room, broken only by the back door flying open.

"Miss Bailey!" Maria ran into the kitchen. "I'm thirs—Uncle Joel!" She flew across the room and threw herself in his arms. "You came. Did you know the bad men were after us and Angel saved us? And I didn't get to see my grandparents yet. Are you going to take me? And can I wear the dress Angel bought me today?"

Joel glanced at Angel. "I don't know, honey. Maybe."

Maria turned her head. "Angel, will you go with us?"

"We'll see."

The doorbell chimed, and Bailey jumped. "I'll see who it is."

Glad to be out of the tension in the kitchen, she hurried down the hallway. Two men stood outside the glass door, their features blurred by the pattern in the glass. She looked through the clear side panel. Ben and some man she didn't recognize. She unlocked the door and opened it. "What's going on, Ben?"

He nodded to the man with him. "This is Sergeant Chavez from Chihuahua, Mexico. He wants to talk to Angel."

The man stood only a few inches taller than Bailey, and he appraised her with serious dark brown eyes set in a face pitted with acne scars. "Is he here?"

She swallowed. Whatever this Sergeant Chavez wanted was not good. She opened the door wider for them to enter. "Take him to the library, Ben," she said. "I'll get Angel."

She hurried back to the kitchen. "There's a man to see you, Angel. I told him to wait in the library."

Angel narrowed his eyes. "To see me? Who is it?"

She glanced toward the others before turning back to him. "A Sergeant Chavez."

"Chavez is here?" Joel said.

Angel's lips thinned as he pressed them together, alarming Bailey. He was also familiar with the Mexican policeman.

Angel glanced at Maria, then Solana. "Keep her in the kitchen. I'll be back in a few minutes."

Bailey followed him as he strode down the hallway and into the library.

"Sergeant Chavez," Angel said. "What are you doing in Mississippi?"

"I've come to question you."

He folded his arms across his chest. "About?"

"Gunrunning and being an accomplice in the murder of Federal Agent Juan Chavez."

15

Danny stepped into the library behind Bailey in time to hear the policeman's declaration. Murder? Gunrunning? Angel? Could he be Geoffrey's Mexican contact? Danny didn't want to believe it, but . . . His eye caught Joel's as he entered the room and leaned against the wall. It hadn't been two days ago that Danny believed Joel was the contact, and of the two, the American was still high on his list. He checked to see Angel's reaction.

He seemed genuinely puzzled. "Who is Juan Chavez?"

"My brother. He was in the warehouse the day you were shot."

Angel flinched at Sergeant Chavez's words, then he shook his head. "I'm sorry about your brother, but I don't know what you're talking about. What guns I have in my possession have been bought legally. I have documentation for every gun I own. I was at the meeting to discuss the Federals providing my men with tactical rifles so we could fight the cartel together."

Chavez stood taller, but even so, he didn't come to Angel's chin. "Your troops—all are armed. Their rifles came from someone. Perhaps the man who worked for Maxwell Industries? Geoffrey Franks."

"I never met or talk with Franks. And did you not hear me say that my men have no tactical weapons, only pistols? I have *never* bought a gun illegally." Angel lifted his hand in a frustrated gesture. "How do you call less than a hundred men *troops*?"

Danny's pulse ratcheted at the mention of his company. Evidently, Chavez believed Angel was Franks's contact. *Is it possible?* Angel needed rifles. Rifles that Franks was providing to someone. Could he be the face of the Blue Dog Company?

Danny studied the man. Brows almost pinched together, a question in his eyes—either he was a great actor or was truly puzzled. The events of the past week flashed through Danny's mind. Events that showed Angel to be a man of honor . . . except he lied about his identity. Danny shifted his gaze to Joel, who registered no reaction at all, then back to the Mexican policeman.

Chavez's lip curled. "Pardon me if I don't believe you."

"That is your privilege." Angel cocked his head. "I have a question for you, though. If you were at the warehouse that day, perhaps you can tell me how the Calatrava knew I would be there."

"I wasn't there. If I had been, my brother would still be alive."

Angel glanced toward Joel. "I think you would do well to discover who tipped the cartel off about the meeting. That is the person who is responsible for your brother's death. And since you do not have handcuffs out, I assume you have no warrant for my arrest. I have other matters to attend to." He bowed curtly before he turned on his heel and walked out the door.

Chavez shifted his gaze to Ben Logan, who like the others in the room, had been silently watching and listening. "You're going to let him just walk away?"

"I'm sorry," Ben said. "But he's right. Like I told you at the jail, you don't have a warrant, and I have nothing to arrest him for. That was okay with you since you said you were on a fishing expedition. I'd like to know just what you were fishing for."

So would Danny, and he noticed that Joel seemed interested as well.

Bailey nudged Danny. "I'm going back to the kitchen to check on Maria," she said.

He nodded. Like Danny, she'd been quietly listening. He refocused on Chavez.

The policeman pressed his lips into a thin line. "You are right that I'm not here officially." He touched his chest. "In my heart, I believe Angel Montoya knows who killed my brother. I came from Mexico to worm the information from him, and I will not rest until I know who killed Juan."

Danny stepped forward. "How much do you know about the Blue Dog Company? Where is it located?"

For the first time, Chavez seemed to notice Danny. "What's your interest in this?"

"I'm part owner of Maxwell Industries. We make the Maxwell 270 hunting rifle and AR15s for the military. Last year, AR15s were stolen from our company and shipped to Mexico as glaze in shipments to Montoya Cerámica."

"But the guns were dropped before the shipment ever reached us," Joel said.

Chavez shifted and stared at Joel. "I see you made it to the States, looking a little better than the last time we met."

Joel returned Chavez's cold stare with one of his own.

Chavez shifted his gaze to Ben. "The man on this end, has he been caught?"

"There were two," Ben said. "And their trial is next month—if it goes to trial. I heard today that the DA's office had authorization from ATF to offer Franks a deal. Give them his Mexico contact, and he can go free."

"Do you think he'll take it?" Danny asked. His stomach churned at the thought of Franks walking away with no consequences.

"I don't know," Ben said. "Probably, since the attempted murder charges would be dropped as well."

Danny could tell from the grimness in Ben's face, that option didn't sit well with him. It didn't with Danny either. But if Franks was willing to tell the ATF, perhaps he'd talk with Danny now as well—he wanted the satisfaction of hearing from Franks's own lips who his contact was.

"Your government would do this?" Chavez asked.

"Franks was a little cog in a big wheel, but what he knows might get some of the higher-ups."

"Would it be possible for me to speak with Franks and the other man?"

"Possible?" Ben said. "Maybe. They're both out on bond, but I'm pretty sure neither of them will welcome you with open arms."

The sergeant raised his eyebrows. "Bond? How is that possible?"

"Slick lawyers and a lenient judge." Ben's disgust was evident in his voice. "And now they'll probably walk, Franks anyway."

"If you go see Franks, I'd like to go with you," Danny said.

Chavez shook his head. "If you're along, he won't tell me anything."

Danny saw his point, but it didn't keep him from being disappointed. "At least tell me where the company is located."

"The run-down warehouse you found is the correct address, but it was just a rendezvous point. I would advise against visiting there again. The building is under surveillance even though there has been no recent activity." He turned to Ben. "Where can I get the addresses of the men involved?"

"I have them at the jail. I'll give them to you when I take you back to your rental car." Ben's cell phone rang, and he glanced at it. "I have to take this, but it shouldn't take long," he said to Chavez.

"And I have to report back to my boss, then find a place to stay," Joel said. "Edward said there were no rooms available at the hotel where he was staying. Something about some kind of COGIC conference."

Danny remembered hearing on the news earlier about all the hotel rooms in Memphis being sold out because of a Church of God in Christ annual meeting. "You'll be lucky to find a place within twenty miles."

"I hope you're wrong about that." Joel glanced around the room. "I'll be back later this afternoon to discuss Maria and how we'll handle telling her about Angel," he said.

Good luck with that. Danny shook his head as Joel disappeared into the hall, then he turned to Chavez, who had walked to the window and stood staring out. He had one more question to ask the Mexican sergeant. "You blamed your brother's death on Angel," Danny said. "How did it happen?"

Chavez turned from the window. "Like I said, my brother was one of the agents in the warehouse the day Angel came to negotiate a deal. The—"

"What kind of deal?"

"Montoya and his men were going to join forces with the local police. The Calatrava showed up and gunfire erupted. The bullet that killed my brother has been traced to one of Montoya's men who was also killed."

"But not to Angel?"

"You are responsible for your men. He must answer for them."

Danny tried to understand where the man was coming from. If Angel didn't pull the trigger, he wasn't to blame for the death of Chavez's brother. "Did you really expect Ben to arrest him without proof?"

Chavez shrugged. "No. It was my hope Montoya would answer my questions voluntarily."

■ ■ ■

"Why did you not stay in the library?" Angel asked.

"Danny's there. He'll tell me what's said." Bailey had been tempted to stay but had been uneasy leaving Maria alone any longer with Angel and Solana. She halfway expected Angel to take off with Maria, maybe even somehow take her back to Mexico. She handed the child a cookie.

"Thank you. Is Uncle Joel coming back?"

"Later," she said.

Maria tilted her head. "Are you going to take me to see my grandma and grandpa?"

Bailey held her breath as a look passed between Solana and Angel. "I don't know. What do you think, Angel?" Might as well put the monkey on his back.

"I think maybe tomorrow? Would you like that, Maria?"

She nodded. "Uncle Joel says I'm to call them Nana Sue and Papa Joe. Do you think they'll like me?"

"They will love you!"

She beamed, then said the names again, rolling them around her tongue.

"I think you like saying those names." Angel smiled at her. "Did you know you were named for your daddy's mother?"

"You knew my daddy?" Maria's eyes grew round. "And my grandmother's name is Maria?"

"Yes."

Bailey poured more milk in Maria's glass. She knew where Angel was leading.

"Mama and Uncle Joel never told me about her. Can I go see her?"

"I'm afraid she's in heaven with your mama."

A frown crossed her face. "Where is your mother?"

He sighed. "In heaven."

"So you don't have a mama, either."

"Nope. And my daddy is in heaven too."

"You're like me! I don't have a daddy."

"But you do have a daddy."

Bailey froze. "Do you think—"

"Yes." He shot her a fierce look. "It's time she knew." He picked Maria up and set her on the counter where they were eye level. "When you were very little, your daddy was hurt. It took him a long time to get better, and when he came back to Chihuahua, he discovered your mama was in heaven and you believed he was there as well. But he's not."

Maria's eyes widened, and Bailey pressed her lips together as tears sprang to her eyes.

"Are you my daddy?" Maria whispered.

"Yes. And I'm going to take care of you from now on. Okay?"

Maria threw her arms around Angel's neck. "I kept wanting to call you daddy, but I was afraid you would laugh."

"I would never laugh at you, precious one." He wrapped his arms around his daughter.

Bailey wiped tears from her face, then sensing the two needed time alone, she slipped out the back door. There was no need to worry that Angel would take off with the girl back to Mexico. He would do nothing to harm her, and they all knew returning to their home country right now wasn't safe. Angel would make a great father.

So would Danny. Sudden longing to marry Danny and have his child caught her by surprise. Her mind's eye captured a picture of the three of them together. All she had to do was say yes. He loved her, she loved him, so why couldn't she do it? Because he deserved someone who wasn't damaged, someone who could love him wholly. And she couldn't do that yet.

She entered the pottery shop through the gallery and looked around. The range of her mother's pieces amazed her. Pit-fired porcelain vases and bowls, sets of dishes and mugs, artistic pieces— the delicate translucent vases with intricate carving. Some of these she hadn't seen before.

Bailey stepped through the doorway into the workshop, and her mom looked up from the wheel. "Come on in, and I'll put you to work. Otherwise I'll be bad company. This order is due in two weeks, and I'm not where I need to be with it."

She held her breath as her mom made another pull on a large bowl, then flattened the rim. "Is that a salad bowl?"

"Yep. Goes with a twelve-piece set of dishes. You know, plates, saucers, cups—the whole nine yards. It's a wedding gift." Kate smoothed the inside of the bowl, then ran a wire under the footing.

"I'll be glad to help."

Her mom pointed toward a mug on the drying rack. "Think you could throw a few of those?"

"I can give it a try. I do teach a pottery class at the school." After Bailey tied an apron around her waist, she picked up the leather-hard mug. She ran her fingers inside, feeling the curve, then measured the height and width. "Five hundred grams?"

"Yep. Clay's in the bucket there." Kate pointed to a five-gallon pail with several rolls of pugged clay in it.

Bailey cut a lump of clay from one of the sticks and weighed it. Five hundred and two grams. Not a bad guess. Then she sat behind one of her mother's extra wheels and tossed the clay in the center. "Daddy still digging your clay for you?"

"Sometimes. I've found a really nice porcelain for the art pieces, though. Comes from Australia. What's going on inside the house?"

"Angel just broke the news to Maria that he's her father."

"Good."

For a few minutes Bailey concentrated on the clay, loving the way it responded to her coaxing. One of the first things she'd learned was not to bully the clay but to coax it into submission. It was easy to forget everything when she worked on the wheel. After she made the last pull on the mug and compressed the lip, she loosened the bat and placed the mug beside the one on the drying shelf. "What do you think?"

Her mom looked up. "Perfect. I'll attach the handle in the morning."

She worked alongside her mother and soon had five mugs on the shelf.

"I see you haven't lost your touch. Of all the family, you have the most talent, and with work, you could be even better than I am."

Warmth radiated through Bailey's chest. For her mom to say that . . . She swallowed down the lump in her throat. "Thanks. Maybe one day." She cleaned the wheel with a rib. "I'll make a couple more and then go check on Maria."

"Let them have time together. I want to talk to you."

Bailey jerked her head up. "About?"

"You and Danny."

"I don't want—"

"I know you don't, but that's what mothers are for—to make you do things you don't want to do."

Her mom was good at getting her to do what she didn't want to do, but the words were said with a smile to soften their truth. Perhaps if she focused on the mug, her mom would let it go. She threw another ball of clay on the wheel and concentrated on centering it and forming a cylinder.

"Danny's matured in the last two years."

Bailey held a measuring stick to check the height of the mug. Not quite there.

"What happened with you two?"

Her hand bobbled, and the cylinder collapsed. She stared at the mess on her wheel, and tears scalded her eyes. Abruptly she yanked the ruined mug off the wheel and squeezed the clay in her hands.

Silently Kate moved from behind her wheel and took the clay. "Let's wash up and sit at the worktable."

A few minutes later, Bailey rubbed the smooth ash lumber where her mother fashioned her hand-built pieces. Kate sat across from Bailey, waiting. When Bailey didn't meet her gaze, she said, "Did Danny hurt you that badly?"

Bailey's eyes teared up again. Fatigue. It was nothing but fatigue and stress. She shook her head. "Our breakup wasn't Danny's fault."

"Do you want to talk about it?

She'd never told her mother why she'd given Danny his ring back, and bless her, until now she'd never asked.

"I know he loves you, but do you love him?"

Startled, Bailey looked up. "How can you be so sure he does?"

"Honey, he risked his life for you, and even now, he won't leave your side. If he didn't love you, he would've handed you over to Ben once you returned. You can trust Danny."

She bit her lip. "Can I? Can you trust any man? Every time I think I can, I think about Mr. Carver." There. It was out. Bailey stared at the dried clay on her hands in the dead silence that followed.

"I thought you had moved past that."

The pain in her mother's voice drew Bailey's gaze. She shook her head, not trusting herself to speak. After a minute of deep breathing, she said, "Just when I think I'm over it and ready to move on with my life, the nightmares start again. I'm in the twins' bedroom, and he's coming for me. I want to stop him, but instead I run and run until I wake up. I'm so tired of being afraid."

Kate hurried to her side and wrapped arms around her. "Have you given it to God?"

Bailey stiffened. That was always her mother's first thought. "Of course I have. But evidently I pick it right back up." She dropped her head. "God must get tired of keeping up with my mistakes."

"God doesn't keep score." Her mother's touch was gentle as she smoothed Bailey's hair.

"I know it's not rational, and I should be able to let it go. You wanted to know what happened to Danny and me. Well, when he asked me to marry him, I thought I could do it. But that night I couldn't sleep. I fixated on Mr. Carver and the way he killed his family. He was a model husband and father. And I kept thinking if he could go bad . . ."

She pulled away from her mother and used the back of her wrist to wipe away the tears that streamed down her face. "By morning I was a basket case. And I knew I couldn't marry Danny. It wouldn't be fair to him. He didn't need a wife who jumped every time he touched her."

Her mom sat in the chair next to her. "I'm so sorry, honey. I had no idea. You seemed so brave, going to Mexico, working in that village—"

"I was running away, Mom. The danger in Mexico was better than staying here and hurting Danny, or . . ."

Kate squared her shoulders and turned Bailey to face her. "I'm going to say something you won't like."

"What's new?" A wry smile pulled at her lips. It didn't matter what her mother said, it wouldn't change anything.

"You've given this fear control and power over you. Shh . . ." She held her finger up when Bailey started to protest. "Hear me out. You're holding on to it so tightly you can't see anything else."

"Mom—"

"I'm not through. God saved you that day, but all you can see is your fear. Over and over he tells us to fear not, that he is with us. The way I see it, you can keep holding on to it and nothing changes. Or you can turn it over to him, trusting he will give you peace. It's your choice."

"But why did he let it happen in the first place? Why didn't he save the twins?"

"Two hard questions I don't have answers for." Conflicting emotions crossed her mom's face. "I wish I did. But for those times I don't understand, I trust who he is. I look at what he's done in the past—the blessings he's poured out on us and all the troubles he's brought us through."

"I wish I could do that. Sometimes I feel so guilty questioning God . . ."

"It's okay to do that. Job did, and in the end, God poured out more blessings than ever. I read Job sometimes when I have questions."

"I've read it. Over and over." She'd even memorized some of the passages, for all the good it had done.

Her mom squeezed her hand. "Read Job 39 and pay attention to what it says about God's power."

■ ■ ■

Danny cornered Angel after Solana took Maria upstairs for a nap. "Do you want to take a ride with me?"

Angel's eyebrows raised. "Depends on what kind of ride you're talking about and who's going along."

"Just me and you. We're going to go talk to Geoffrey Franks." Angel didn't bat an eye at Franks's name.

Angel shrugged. "And you want backup?"

The guy was cool. Danny would have to give him that. Or he'd been telling the truth and didn't know anything about the Blue Dog Company. "Something like that."

After they got in the car and turned to the right out of the drive, Danny glanced at his passenger. "Tell me something . . ."

Angel laughed. "When someone starts a sentence with those words, the other person's guard goes up."

"Is yours up?"

"Not yet. Which do you want to know about? Edward or Joel?"

Danny doubted he'd ever be able to use the element of surprise with Angel. "Both, but right this minute, I'm interested to know why you accused your uncle of killing your parents."

"It's not an accusation. It's true. Edward has always taken the easier road. He wanted what my father had, but he didn't want to do the hard work to get it. He may not have planted the bomb under their car that killed them when I was fifteen, but he was involved. He took over the business, their house, and put me on the streets."

"How? Didn't your father leave a will?"

"I'm certain he did, but I couldn't find it, and there was no record of it at the lawyer's office. Father's old solicitor had died, and many of his papers were missing. Like the contract where my father had bought Edward out." Angel grimaced. "My uncle produced his father's original will, leaving the company to both sons with the provision if one died, his share of the company went to the survivor. Without Father's will and the contract, I didn't have a case."

Angel's voice, devoid of emotion, sent chills through Danny. "What proof do you have that he was responsible for their deaths?"

"None. People like my uncle do not leave evidence behind."

"Then how can you be so sure he did it?"

"My father told me."

"How?"

"He left a letter with a friend to give to me and my mother if anything happened to him. I don't think he ever believed my mother would be killed with him." He drummed the console with his fingers. "If I had not had ball practice that afternoon, I would've been with them as well."

"What did the letter say?"

"For me to make sure Edward didn't get away with his murder. To look at his business associates."

"Did you?"

"Yes, but it is impossible to know everyone he associates with, and like I said before, men like my uncle don't leave evidence lying about. I will exact my own justice."

Passion drove Angel, allowing him to justify breaking the law to get justice. But would that extend to buying illegal guns?

He parked in the drive and climbed out of his SUV. The garage door was down and the blinds pulled. Not surprising.

"You think this guy is home?"

"One way to find out. Coming with me?"

"Why are you doing this?"

Danny jerked his head toward Angel. "What?"

"Coming out here to question this man. Do you really think he'll give you any answers?"

A slow flush crept up Danny's neck. "Won't know until I ask."

He stuck his Glock in his belt, and together they walked to the front door and rang the doorbell. Finally, the wooden door swung open.

Franks kept the screen door between them and shifted his gaze from Danny to Angel, then back to Danny. Franks didn't seem to recognize Angel. "What do you want?"

"Ben Logan said you were cutting a deal with the DA."

"That's none of your business. Get off my property." He opened the screen door, revealing a .38 revolver in his hand.

Angel and Danny stepped back. "Whoa!" Danny said. "I just wanted to ask you a couple of questions."

Franks glowered at him, then his gaze slid past him to Angel. "You and your bodyguard there better beat it. I've called my lawyer. The next time you step on my property, you'll be breaking a court order, and I have a right to protect myself."

"Is that a threat?"

Franks cocked the revolver.

Danny held up his hands. "Okay, we're going."

He didn't think his former employee would shoot him in the back, but nevertheless, he didn't relax until he'd driven away from the house.

"That was a pretty stupid trick you just pulled," Angel said once they were safely back in the SUV. "But if you figured out that I didn't know him and he didn't know me, then I'm glad you were stupid."

Danny's face burned. "I didn't think he had it in him to threaten me with a gun."

"I learned a long time ago, a cornered rat will do almost anything. Tell me more about this Blue Dog Company and the evidence you have on Franks."

A twinge of guilt for not completely trusting Angel pinged his conscience. "Okay, the operation went like this—Franks stole rifle parts, and either he or the other person charged with the crime put the rifles together, and then the rifles were added to shipments that went to Montoya Ceramics and labeled as glaze. They were then off-loaded at the Blue Dog Company before the rest of the shipment was delivered to your uncle. Earlier this week I went to the address on the invoices, but it was no more than an empty building. Chavez indicated there was another building, a warehouse, but he wouldn't give me the address."

"Wasn't Franks afraid the guns would be traced back to Maxwell Industries?"

"He stole the receivers before they were stamped, so they couldn't be traced to any company. If his partner hadn't been on a vendetta against Ben Logan, they probably would have gotten away with their little operation for years. As it was, they'd been stealing the parts and selling them for a couple of years."

"You say he was caught last summer?"

Danny nodded.

"So that means the operation was going while I was in a Texas hospital."

That's what had been nagging at the back of his mind. Angel couldn't be Franks's Mexico contact if he'd been in the hospital. He shot a quick look at Angel. The man had read his mind. "Okay, so I'm a slow learner."

"You could have asked."

"Why didn't you tell anyone where you were?"

A sigh escaped Angel's lips. "That's a question I've asked myself over and over. If I had, Claire might still be alive. But . . ." He shifted his gaze out the window. "The doctors did not hold out much hope that I would live to my friends who got me to the hospital. They feared the cartel would find me and finish the job, so they told everyone I was dead. By the time I was able to correct the lie, six months had passed. I was in a wheelchair, unable to walk, and almost wished I was dead. I couldn't let anyone see me until I was whole again. By that time, Claire had accidentally mixed the two medicines . . . Maria seemed happy enough, and I put off revealing myself to her."

"It would have been hard to know who to trust," Danny said.

"Yes, like you with this Blue Dog Company."

Danny shot him a wry grin. "You do have a good reason to want rifles, especially ones like the AR15 that Franks was selling. You and Chavez said the subject of rifles was one of the things to be discussed at the meeting where you were ambushed. And Joel made it sound like you had been buying illegal guns. I just didn't put the timing together."

"I understand, and Chavez was correct as far as he knew. Joel supposedly set up the meeting to discuss an alliance between me and my men and the Federal police in Chihuahua, and we were going to discuss arming my men. But I believe he set it up to get rid of me and was acting under my uncle's orders. I am a thorn in Edward Montoya's side. Unfortunately, I cannot prove it yet, but when I return to Mexico, I will find a way to corroborate it."

"Do you plan to take Maria back with you?"

"If I can find a way to keep her safe, yes."

Danny drove the next few miles silently, absorbing the information he'd learned. What Joel said versus what he knew about Angel. The man had risked his life for Maria and Bailey, and that put him way ahead of Joel, but what if Angel had an agenda Danny knew nothing about? Still . . .

"Are there any other rooms available at the bed-and-breakfast?"

"I don't know. You're not thinking . . . ?"

"If there are rooms available and Joel hasn't found a place to stay, I would like for him to stay there."

"And your reasoning is?"

"I remember a saying from one of your old movies—keep your friends close but your enemies closer."

Danny grinned. "Michael Corleone said that in the second *Godfather* movie."

"I have discovered it is valuable advice."

16

Bailey didn't really think God kept score of her mistakes. Or did she?

She'd continued to sit in the pottery shop long after her mother left, mulling over her words.

Peace and joy were possible—sometimes she even possessed both. But when something went wrong, like Father Horatio or the cartel, fear and anxiety took over her life. She quit trusting God.

She wasn't sure how she'd go about really trusting God, but recognizing the problem was the first step. The next step was to focus on what God *had* done, like keeping them safe this week.

The security buzzer rang, and she glanced up at the security TV. Joel, in the driveway. Good—she had a few questions for him. She hurried inside the house, speaking to her mom and Maria in the kitchen as she slipped on her jacket.

"We're making apple dumplings," her mom said.

Maria waved a small rolling pin. "I'm rolling out the biscuits."

"Can't wait," Bailey said. The doorbell rang, and she hurried down the hallway to let Joel in.

"I didn't expect you back so soon, but I'm glad you are," she said. "We haven't had a chance to talk at all."

"I know. Where's Maria?" He looked past her.

"Mom has her busy. Why don't we take a walk?"

"Sure."

The air was invigorating, but a cold front had dropped the temperature from earlier in the day, and Bailey pulled her coat tight against the wind as they walked down the drive. "Angel told Maria he was her father, so you may have questions to answer."

He nodded. "Leave it to Angel to make my life harder."

She laughed. "You're surprised he told her?"

"No, I assumed he would, just not so soon."

Sunlight filtered through the oak trees that lined the drive. They were beginning to bud, a sure sign winter was over.

Joel cleared his throat. "I've noticed Maria isn't wearing her necklace, so I'd like to take it back for safekeeping. It's quite expensive, you know."

She glanced sharply at him. "Maybe you'd like the one you gave me back as well."

He paled. "Of course not. Forget I said anything."

She would. Especially since she'd rather not tell him the necklace broke, since he was so preoccupied about the price. Hopefully, she'd have it back before Joel asked about it again. They walked in silence for a few minutes.

"What's that?" Joel pointed to a green clump.

"Daffodils." She smiled. "They're the first ones I've seen this year."

"I thought maybe that's what they were. My mother had some when I was growing up."

"She doesn't anymore?"

"I doubt it. My father always griped about having to mow around all her flowers. One day he just cut them down."

"I think Daddy fusses too, but he'd never do that. Mom would have his head. Oh, there's crocus." She pointed to another green clump, then gave him a sideways glance. "Have you spoken to your parents today? They didn't mention you being in the States."

"They don't know. I talked with my mother early this morning while she was in the ICU waiting room. Talking to her on a cell phone isn't the easiest thing in the world, and getting her to call when she's in the room with my father is next to impossible. She was worried about you and Maria, though, and I reassured her you were all right."

"She seems really nice." Dried leaves crunched under their feet. "Tell me about your relationship with Angel," Bailey said. "I'm visual, so I've been trying to see what's going on as a big picture— like a jigsaw puzzle—but I'm having trouble fitting all the pieces together."

"It's because Angel isn't someone you can put in a nice neat package. He's too unpredictable, and he will lie to you. If you listen to him, there's no way you'll ever have all the pieces."

"He accused you of leading him into a trap."

"But I didn't. I was just trying to help my sister's husband get straight with the law. Angel believes the end justifies the means. At first he stayed under the radar of the Federal police, and I turned my head the other way. But when he started using Claire to procure rifles—I had to stop him."

"She told you she was helping him?"

"No. I was at their house babysitting Maria one night and found invoices in her handwriting. I confronted Angel, told him if he wanted to join forces with the Federal police and work against the Calatrava, I had a contact there."

"Why were you going through his papers?"

"I wasn't." He kicked at an acorn on the drive. "They were on the desk in the living room. He agreed to a meeting."

"The one where he was shot."

"Yes, as well as my contact. I didn't know he was Sergeant Chavez's brother." Joel fell silent for a minute. "I don't know what went wrong that day. While the Federals wanted to rein Angel in, the Calatrava had a contract on his head. Someone informed them that Angel was meeting with the Federals."

"So all this time, you believed he was dead?"

"Yes. I don't know why he didn't get word to us that he was alive. If he had, Claire might still . . ." He kicked at another acorn. "As it was, she just gave up."

"I don't think he could contact you. He almost died in the gun battle and spent months in a Texas hospital."

"He could have if he'd wanted to." They'd reached the hand-carved signs that advertised her mother's pottery shop and bed-and-breakfast, and Joel nodded toward the road. "Go back or keep walking?"

Cold had seeped through her coat, sending a shiver through her. "Let's go back to the house. I'm sure you want to spend time with Maria."

Twice she'd glanced up and found him looking at her the same way Danny did. She looked up, and he was doing it again. And like before, he quickly averted his gaze.

"Those signs," he said. "Who made them? They're quite unique."

"My dad. He's quite good with a carving knife, almost as good as my mom is with her pottery."

"Claire loved working with clay. She was very talented. Sometime I'd like to see your mother's work."

"I'll tell her. She'd be pleased to show you." Bailey jammed her cold hands into her coat pocket. "I've never known for sure how Claire died."

"A drug reaction. Her doctor gave her an antidepressant, but she was also taking an herbal concoction that increased her serotonin level, causing what the doctors called serotonin syndrome. By the time they diagnosed her problem, she'd slipped into a coma. Then it was too late."

"That is so sad."

"Yes." He put his hand on her arm. "I want to thank you for everything you've done for Maria. I don't know how to repay you."

"Nothing to repay me for. Maria is such a sweetheart."

"Yes, she is. And I'm glad for the opportunity to get to know you better. After all that's happened, will you return to Mexico?"

"I have to finish my contract, but after that . . ." She shrugged. "I'm not sure what I'm going to do."

"I don't blame you for that."

"I've been thinking about something Solana said—that if all the law-abiding citizens leave Mexico, the drug cartels will win. I'd like to think when this is all over, I'll want to go back and try to make a difference."

"That's a noble sentiment, but it's not our fight. Waging war on the drug cartels is futile and foolish. It's best to just mind your own business."

Joel's declaration added to her confusion. "Someone has to stop them."

"The Mexican people are the ones who have to stand up to them, not foreigners."

"Like Angel?" They had reached the house and climbed the steps to the front door.

"No, not some vigilante but someone who will work within the framework of the government." He opened the door, and a tantalizing aroma met them. "What do I smell?" he asked.

"Apple dumplings. Maria was helping my mom bake them. Let's go see if they're done."

When they pushed the swinging door open, Maria was standing on a chair at the sink, wearing an oversized apron. "Uncle Joel, I'm washing dishes. Miss Kate said when we cook, we have to clean up."

"Good for you, Mrs. Adams."

"We don't stand on formalities around here. The name is Kate."

"Yes, ma'am."

She dried her hands on a paper towel. "I need to check the kiln. Help yourself to an apple dumpling."

"Thanks."

Bailey helped Maria take off the apron. The child tilted her head toward Joel. "Did Tio come with you?"

"No, he's busy with work. Perhaps some evening you can go with me to the hotel to see him." Joel patted her on the head. "But a little bird told me you did a good job cooking."

"Mm-huh. We're having a . . . a cel—" Maria cut her eyes to Bailey. "What are we having?"

"A celebration," she said and left it at that. Joel wouldn't consider Angel and Maria's reunion something to celebrate.

"Oh." He cupped Maria's chin in his hand. "I don't see your necklace."

Maria looked at the floor and shook her head. "It broke last night."

"What?" he said sharply. "You broke your necklace?"

"I'm afraid it was my fault, and I should have told you earlier," Bailey said. "I think it caught in her jumper and the clasp broke when I put her pajamas on. My sister took it to be repaired."

He waved his hand. "No big deal. Tell me where it is and I'll pick it up."

"Unfortunately, the jeweler can't get to it until tomorrow."

Anger flashed across his face, then just as fast disappeared. "No problem." He looked at Maria. "I didn't mean to snap at you, but that necklace cost a lot of money."

Bailey lifted her brows. If he kept harping on the price . . . "Maybe you should have waited until she was older to buy something that expensive."

"You're right. In fact, I have a cheaper one in my bag at the hotel. Why don't I bring it tomorrow? Then, when you get the other one back from the jeweler, I'll put it away for her."

"That's an excellent idea."

"Will you put Mommy's picture in it?"

"I sure will." Joel glanced Bailey's way. "You haven't lost yours, have you?"

"No, it's in my jewelry box." She helped Maria out of the chair. "Angel is agreeable to take Maria to see your parents tomorrow."

"Really. That's a surprise. Did he say what time?"

"Probably around ten."

"I'll let Edward know I won't be available tomorrow." He rubbed the back of his neck. "Boy, Danny was right when he said I might have a problem getting a room anywhere decent. I've had to settle for a room at a motel here in Logan Point."

She could tell by the tone of his voice that he wasn't happy with the room. She glanced up as Angel and Danny entered the kitchen.

"Then perhaps you would like to stay here."

Joel turned and looked as though he hadn't understood his brother-in-law. "Did you say stay here?"

"Sure." He wasn't looking at Joel but at his daughter.

"Angel!" Maria ran to him. "Can . . ." She hesitated, looking to Joel then back to Angel. "Can I call you Daddy?"

"Of course you can." Angel picked her up and swung her up on his shoulders. "Why don't we go for a walk?"

Joel cleared his throat. "Maria, don't forget to put a coat on. It's quite windy out there."

"Yes, Uncle Joel."

Angel stopped at the door. "And Joel, think about asking Kate if she has room to put you up."

"Wait up for me on the porch," Danny said. "I think I'll go with you." He turned to Bailey, asking with his eyes if she wanted to join him.

"Give me a couple of minutes."

After they left, Joel's shoulders sagged.

Bailey touched his arm. "I know this is hard and that Maria means a lot to you."

"He might be Maria's natural father, but he hasn't raised her for the past two years," he said through his teeth. "Where was he when Claire died? Or when Maria had an earache and

184

screamed all night? *Daddy*." Joel spit the word out. "He doesn't have a clue."

She didn't know how to respond to his outburst.

He turned to her, and his face softened. "I'm sorry. I shouldn't have lost my temper."

"I'm glad you held it in until Maria was gone."

"Do you think your mother would rent me a room?"

"You'd want to stay here? Why?"

"Maybe for the same reason that Angel suggested I stay here—he wants to keep an eye on me. But that works both ways."

■ ■ ■

A blast of heat welcomed Joel as he walked through the door to the reception area at Maxwell Industries. He'd faced the icy north wind as he walked across the parking lot, which chilled him to the bone and increased his foul mood. He wanted nothing more than to wipe the satisfied smirk from Angel's face.

This trip had been a disaster from the start. After he left Bailey, all he'd wanted to do was pick Edward up at Maxwell Industries and get him to drop him off at the auto rental to pick up his own car instead of using Edward's, retrieve his clothes, and get settled in the B&B. Instead, Edward insisted he come up to Phillip Maxwell's office.

"May I help you?"

The question startled him. How did he miss the pretty blonde behind the desk? "Yes. Edward Montoya is with Mr. Maxwell, and I'm to join them."

"Oh, you must be Joel McDermott. They're in the office at the top of the stairs on the right. Just knock and go on in—they're expecting you."

"Thanks." He did as she instructed. When he stepped inside the office, the decor surprised him. While the boardroom they'd been in earlier spoke quality, this room went a step further. Rich walnut paneling and thick carpet along with expensive-looking oil paintings. Phillip Maxwell had good taste.

Edward and Phillip glanced up, and Ian turned from the window with a phone to his ear.

Phillip nodded. "How's your dad?"

"So-so. I'm going to the hospital first thing in the morning to see if I can talk him into the surgery. My mother is beside herself, thinking he's going to die any minute." Not that he would. He was too ornery to die.

"Perhaps he will listen to you," Edward said.

Joel doubted it. He never had. Ian pocketed his phone and took a seat at the table.

"Trouble?" Phillip asked.

"One of the employees had a package stolen from their car. Unlocked, of course." Ian shook his head. "I've warned everyone they should lock their cars, but when one of their own employers argues with me about it in front of them, what can you expect?"

"What are you talking about?" Phillip said.

"Danny and I exchanged words this morning because he never locks his car, and everyone knows he keeps a gun in the console. This very employee was present during the argument."

"Perhaps this will teach him a lesson," Montoya said.

"Perhaps." Ian turned to Joel. "How are things with Bailey?"

"Okay." Joel hesitated. "Is your cousin involved with her?"

"Danny?" Ian laughed. "He'd like to be, but I doubt anything will ever come of it."

"Why not?" He'd like to know what Danny was doing wrong. "I mean, most women would find the Maxwell money intriguing, if nothing else."

"Not Bailey. Money doesn't impress her, and she's always been gun-shy around men. To get her, a man will have to be patient, and Danny is very short on patience."

Joel tucked that piece of information into the corner of his

186

mind. If he got out of this mess and had a normal life, he'd like to have Bailey in it. But she would have to be wooed with kindness and small gestures. Not extravagant gifts like the necklace. He'd have to work on that. When Phillip asked him a question about shipments, Joel turned his attention to the conversation about production schedules.

■ ■ ■

ACCESS DENIED. Joel stared at the computer screen, his jaw clenched so tight pain shot down his neck. Wrong again. He'd had to try one more time—it had become an obsession. Why couldn't he remember the stupid number? Maybe it was because he was tired. He'd slept little last night, and then the meeting with the Maxwells went on and on.

He stared at the numbers he'd penciled on the sheet, willing them to change to the right order. Instead they ran together. It wasn't that he had trouble memorizing numbers, it was remembering them in the right order. He had to be transposing them. But which ones? He had two more attempts before the site locked him out.

Foolproof. The plan should have been foolproof. Engrave the account number in a locket for Maria, put Claire's photo over it, and then place the small, expensively wrapped box with Maria's name on it in the briefcase that went everywhere with him. If anyone found the present, he could easily explain he hadn't gotten around to giving it to her. Just a locket an uncle planned to give his niece.

Then Bailey had to go and find the pretty package, and he'd had to actually give it to the child.

His cell rang, and he pushed away from the computer to answer it. "Hello?"

"Are you with Maria?" Edward Montoya's flat voice sent dread through his body.

"No, I haven't made it to the bed-and-breakfast yet. And I didn't tell you earlier, but she knows Angel is her father." There had been no opportunity to talk about his brother-in-law with Edward, and his boss would not have been pleased to have Angel discussed in front of the Maxwells.

"So the reports were true. He's alive."

"Very much so."

"Did you learn where he's been all this time?"

"A Texas hospital. I think he almost died." When Montoya didn't respond, Joel said, "Angel suggested I move into the bed-and-breakfast, and I plan to. Actually I'm packing up now. And he's going to allow me to take Maria to see my parents. You'll have to carry on tomorrow at Maxwell Industries without me."

"Don't be taken in by his charm. He wants something from you."

"I'm sure he does. Oh, Maria was asking about you. She would really like it if you came to see her at the bed-and-breakfast."

"I won't have time. Perhaps you can bring her to the Peabody."

"I doubt either Bailey or Angel will allow that. They don't let Maria out of their sight."

"Has there been another attempt to kidnap her?"

"Not to my knowledge."

Joel took a small 9mm pistol from his bag and slipped it into his front pocket. "I'll call you after I talk with Angel about bringing her to see you."

He had no more than hung up before his phone rang again, and he glanced at the phone. The number wasn't one he recognized, but it was possible Bailey had gotten a new phone. He answered it before it went to his voicemail.

"Do you have the money you owe?"

Joel almost dropped the phone. "How did you get this number?"

"That doesn't matter. You owe 150,000 dollars today. Tomorrow it will be 200,000."

"That's crazy."

"No, it's the price you pay for losing when you can't afford it."

Dead silence. Disconnected. He quickly tapped the number, and it immediately went to a message saying voicemail hadn't been set up. A burner phone, probably.

He paced the motel room. Money. He had to have money, and the only place he could get that amount was from Edward's offshore account. If he could ever get into it. He halted his pacing to stare at the Grand Cayman bank's website on the computer screen.

It'd been pure luck, a gift, that he had the account number in the first place. Joel had been in an employee meeting with Edward and the production foremen when his boss sent Joel after a needed file. When he picked up the folder, a scrap of paper with letters and numbers fluttered to the floor. On a hunch, he'd photocopied the scrap and then became obsessed with knowing what the letters and numbers meant. It'd been easy to figure out the long number belonged to some sort of account and the shorter one a password and that the letters stood for a bank. But which one?

It'd taken him less than a week to find a bank to fit the letters. He'd accessed the account and transferred a nominal amount and then waited. Evidently Edward never noticed, because the next time Joel tried, he gained access. But he'd been afraid to transfer more money or to even keep the paper he copied, so he embedded the account number in three different files on his laptop.

Then he'd had the number engraved on the necklace and destroyed the paper. He couldn't think of any place safe enough to keep it, although he had considered putting it in the safe. He shuddered to think how *that* would have played out if whoever had broken into his house had gotten their hands on the account number.

The necklace was only supposed to be his backup, one he never should have needed. Not with the account number encrypted on his computer and his computer backed up to an off-site server. But now the laptop was gone, and he couldn't access the backup, and the locket was at some jeweler's. It was like he had subscribed to Murphy's Law.

Somehow he had to get the number to that account and transfer the two hundred grand he owed the casino. He pressed his hands to the side of his face. No, that wouldn't be enough. At the rate he was going, it'd be twice that by the time he got into the account. If almost half a mil went missing from Edward Montoya's offshore account, his boss would notice.

Or maybe not. Edward had millions. Surely he wouldn't miss—

Joel shook his head. Had he totally lost his mind? Edward Montoya was sure to have some sort of alert if that kind of money was moved from the account.

But he'd have no way of knowing who moved it. All Joel had to do was transfer the money, pay the gambling debt, then sit tight. No changes in his lifestyle, no extravagant purchases. Since he'd had time to think about it, disappearing was the worst thing he could do. If he up and disappeared, Edward would know he stole the money, and Joel would always be looking over his shoulder.

What he needed was something to divert Edward's attention when he discovered the missing funds. His boss tended to focus on one thing at a time—it was one of the reasons for his success.

Joel would simply have to come up with a problem bigger than missing money.

■ ■ ■

One more person and Danny believed the bed-and-breakfast would explode. He hadn't really thought Angel was serious when he suggested Joel take a room. The fact that Joel took him up on the suggestion surprised him even more. The undercurrent of tension between the two men vibrated through the house.

He checked his watch. Almost eleven and sleep evaded him. Maybe he would walk the perimeter of the yard—it had helped last night. He shrugged into his down coat and eased down the stairs. Cold air greeted him, and he zipped the coat up to his chin. It wasn't usually this cold in March, and he would be glad for spring, even the hot temperatures of summer.

Danny scanned the parking lot. Funny. He hadn't heard anyone leave, but Joel's car was gone, and so was his Escalade. He didn't mind Angel using the SUV, but he thought Angel would let him know first. He'd ask him about it in the morning.

A waning moon guided him as he walked by the barn, telling himself Bailey wouldn't be at the stump. When his prediction proved true, disappointment shot through him. No use denying that he'd hoped she couldn't sleep either.

Then he turned toward the front of the property, soon leaving the light of the house and barn behind. The quiet wrapped around him, broken only by the soft hoot of a barn owl and dried leaves under his feet.

His thoughts went back to the conversation with Kate. Could she be right that God could use him? Out here under the vast expanse of sky, it seemed possible. He looked up. Was it just last night that Bailey pointed out the North Star? In the crisp atmosphere, stars stood out against the velvet sky, stirring a sense of yearning in his heart. The heavens held him in its grip until he became unaware of time or his surroundings.

And in the beginning God created the heavens and the earth . . . The words formed in his head, and this time, they didn't remind him of a fairy tale.

Could he forgive himself for not going to the store when his mother asked him to? He could have handled the ice patch that killed her.

"Danny, there's nothing you can do that will separate you from God's love. Jesus died for every bad thing you've ever done, ever will do. Don't ever forget that." Words his mother had told him long ago. He'd believed then. But after the wreck, he'd let guilt drive him away. Maybe it was time to let go of the past.

"Danny?"

Bailey's voice brought him back to earth, and he turned. She stood a short distance away with a flashlight in her hand. "You shouldn't be out here," he said, but he was so glad she was.

"You are." She flicked the flashlight off, and the overhead barn light illuminated her silhouette.

"I couldn't sleep. Do you know where Joel and Angel went? His rental and my SUV are missing."

"No. I heard a car leave right after I went upstairs, but I didn't know who it was. I didn't hear a second car. Why couldn't you sleep?"

"I started thinking about last night, and I wanted to see if I could find the Little Dipper and the North Star again."

"Did you?"

He'd gotten so caught up in the beauty of the sky, he'd forgotten to look. "No. Which way do I look for the Little Dipper?"

Bailey came closer and slipped one arm through his and turned him slightly. She raised her right hand. "Follow where I'm pointing. See, there's the pan."

He followed the movement of her finger as she traced the four stars that made the bottom of the dipper. "Oh, wait. I see it. There's the handle."

"And at the end of it is the North Star."

"Polaris. I see it." He turned to her, glad for the moonlight so he could see her face, her incredible eyes. These last two days of being around her and not being able to hold her in his arms had been killing him. "I've missed you."

She pressed her lips together and looked down. He tipped her face back up with his hand. "Have you missed me?"

Bailey licked her lips. "Yes."

His heart filled his chest, pounding so hard he could barely breathe. He lowered his head until his lips found hers, sending a shiver through him. Slowly, relishing her nearness, he kissed her lips, then moved to her closed eyes. He pulled her against his chest. "I've never stopped loving you." He whispered the words against her hair.

She pulled away and looked up at him. "Heaven help me, but I've never quit loving you either."

His heart soared as he held her gaze in the dim light, trailing his finger down her cheek. He cupped her face in his hands and captured her lips, kissing her again, gently at first. She slipped her hands up behind his head and pulled him closer until he lost himself in her arms.

When they broke apart, she rested her head on his shoulder.

"Are you cold?" he asked.

She tilted her head back. "Are you kidding?"

He wrapped his arms around her, just in case. "I still want to marry you."

"I know." She stepped back and took his hand. "Let's go to the barn where we can sit and talk."

At least she hadn't run off screaming. But neither did she say yes. That would have been expecting too much too soon. They walked to the barn in silence, their breath making white puffs in the cold air. They probably should return to the house. But he was afraid if they did, the magic of the night would end, and he wasn't ready for that to happen. He didn't think Bailey was either.

Hay stacked to the ceiling made it not quite as cold inside the barn, and they sat on one of the bales. "Oh, by the way, your mom gave me a Bible, and I was reading it before I came outside."

Her eyes widened. "That's wonderful."

He shrugged. "I don't know how wonderful it is—it's a little hard to understand."

"Try asking God to help you." She squared her shoulders and took his hand. "There's something I need to tell you."

His body tensed. "Then do it."

She bit her bottom lip. "I want to apologize for the way I broke our engagement and then ran off to Mexico."

His muscles relaxed. He'd been afraid she was going to tell him to get lost. "Apology accepted."

"Like I said before, I do that a lot."

"What? Break engagements?"

"No, run away."

"When? Besides when you gave me the ring back."

She dropped her gaze to the barn floor, and he waited.

"I've been thinking about my life a lot these past few days. I think the running away started when I was a kid, and Mr. Carver killed Jem and Cassie—"

"But you were just a kid yourself."

Bailey grew quiet. "God was supposed to protect us that night." The soft words fell like bricks in the void. "I remember thinking the three of us had just been baptized and nothing bad could happen to us. And then they died."

For a minute Danny didn't know what to say. He turned to Bailey. She leaned back against one of the barn posts, her eyes closed.

After a minute of silence, she continued. "I said something to my Sunday school teacher, and she said I wasn't supposed to question God, and I wasn't supposed to get angry at God. I don't know how she knew that I was mad, but I decided I must be a bad person. I thought if I worked really hard and did everything I was supposed to do, God would love me more, and he wouldn't let bad things happen to me."

"Does it work that way?" he asked.

"No, and I know that, but knowing and believing are two different things." She took a deep breath and blew it out. "I can't stop thinking that I gave up everything—you, my family, my teaching job here in Logan Point that I loved—to go to Mexico. Even that didn't please God."

"What happened in Copper Canyon?"

She sighed. "As soon as I arrived, the local priest took an instant dislike to me because the women and children were drawn to me.

He got really upset when the women came to my tea parties for purses and makeup and then came back because I talked about a God who loved them." She smiled. "It was amazing to see them transform right before my eyes as they discovered who our amazing God is. That's when the priest began a campaign to run me off. Said I was a witch because of my eyes."

"But they're beautiful, and they always see good in everything, even me."

"You'd have to admit they're unusual. Not many people have a gold starburst." She shivered. "I found *things* in my car on a regular basis, and the last was rattlesnakes. That's when I left, actually when Global Missions moved me to Chihuahua to teach at their school."

"I wouldn't have stayed after it happened the first time," he said.

She smiled. "You would if you thought God called you there. Evidently I was wrong about that, and now I'm wondering if I've been wrong about everything I believe. How could God love me and allow so many bad things to happen in my life? When I was hiding in the basement from those men after Joel had been kidnapped, even as I quoted Scripture, I wondered where God was. Why he didn't help us."

Danny's breath stilled. Bailey's belief in God was what defined who she was. With everything else around him in flux, he'd always known he could count on one thing and one person who was always the same, who always had the same answer to problems—give it to God. Just knowing that comforted him, even if he didn't agree with her. Bailey had always been like a rock. When she broke their engagement, he'd thought it was because of her deep commitment to God.

"But Bailey, he did help you—he sent me to rescue you."

Her eyes widened, and Danny caught his breath, as surprised as Bailey. The words had popped out of his mouth, but could they be true? Danny pulled her close, and she snuggled against his body.

"I'll always be here for you," he whispered against her hair.

■■■

"Even if we take his daughter, Angel Montoya will never join his men with the Calatrava."

El Jefe pinched the bridge of his nose. The board had given him a week to bring Montoya in line, and he didn't need resistance from Enrico. "If we have his daughter, he will."

"But he and Danny Maxwell watch her like a hawk."

"Then be like the barn swallow that chases the hawk away. I don't care how you do it, just get her."

"Why is Montoya so important to you? Why not just kill him?"

El Jefe ground his molars. He didn't like his orders being questioned by subordinates. "Can you see nothing? Because that would make him a martyr. His death would only serve to unite the people who are loyal to him. Already the Angel of the Streets inspires them to the extent they are willing to die rather than pay for insurance. But if we bring him under our control, they will not have the heart to oppose us. Do I need to get someone else to take care of this job?"

"No. It will be done. How much ransom will we ask?"

He pressed his fingers to his temple. "Do you understand nothing? We are not taking her for money."

"No money at all? That is foolish." Disapproval sounded through the phone. "And the missionary?"

"Kill her."

17

Danny whistled as he lathered his face. For the first time since Bailey had returned his ring, he had hope they could work things out. He regretted now that he didn't go after her that morning and make her tell him why. The things she'd gone through in Mexico could have been avoided. They could have even had a little Bailey or Danny running around. He stopped with the razor halfway to his face.

Tonight he would ask her to marry him again. And this time he would put his mother's engagement ring on her finger. Which meant he'd have to talk to his dad first. What if she turned him down? That wasn't happening. They loved each other.

As soon as he was dressed, Danny hurried down to the kitchen, hoping Bailey needed coffee as badly as he did. He pushed through the swinging door and stopped when she turned from the coffee-maker. The smile she flashed warmed him all the way to his toes.

"Good morning," Bailey said. "On your way to the plant?"

"Yep. Dad insisted that I attend this morning's meetings." He checked his watch. "I hope we can leave by ten. I'll call you when I know."

She handed him a cup of coffee, but what he wanted was to steal a kiss from her. He set the cup on the counter and took her in his arms.

"What are you doing?"

"This." He bent down and kissed her lightly on the lips.

She pulled back, looking over his shoulder. "What if someone comes in?"

"What does that have to do with the price of eggs in Russia?"

A grin teased her kissable lips, and he felt her relax in his arms. "You're crazy. You know that, don't you?"

"Crazy in love," he said. He trailed his fingers down her cheek, stopping at her lips. Then he bent down and kissed her again. His heart leaped when her lips responded. When they broke apart, he put his forehead to hers.

Marry me. He caught the words before they spilled from his mouth. Later tonight he wouldn't stop them.

Footsteps in the hallway made them both jump back. He grabbed his coffee and Bailey turned to pour hers as Angel came into the kitchen.

"Good, coffee is made," he said.

Danny moved away from Bailey to the table, and Angel joined him. "Where did you go last night?"

Angel lifted his shoulder in a half shrug. "To see Chavez at his motel. I knocked on your door, but you didn't answer."

"About?"

"What happened in Mexico two years ago." He took the coffee Bailey handed him. "Do you know a doctor I can take Solana to and get that cast taken off?"

Angel didn't look away as Danny studied his face. Evidently that was all Angel was telling. Maybe later when they were alone, Danny would get more out of him. "I play handball with an orthopedic doctor. Maybe I can get her in to see him."

He searched his contacts for the doctor's cell phone number and called. A few minutes later he disconnected and smiled. "He said to bring her in by nine."

"Great. But I better let her know. That's only an hour away."

"And I have to get to the plant," Danny said. He turned to Bailey. "I'll be back as soon as I can."

Fifteen minutes later, Danny unlocked his office as Ian rounded the corner. "Have you seen Dad?" Danny asked him.

"He's in the boardroom, waiting for you to join him and Montoya."

Edward Montoya was early. That also meant Danny wouldn't get a chance to talk privately with his dad. "Why can't you handle this? You're better at it than I am."

"We decided you need to come to work for a while." Ian followed him into his office.

"You mean you told Dad I needed to be here."

"You've spent too much time on this Mexico connection. The DA called this morning, said you'd been back out to the Franks place."

"So?" Danny opened his desk drawer and rummaged for a notepad.

Ian sighed. "The DA asked you not to go around Franks. If he makes a deal with the Feds, you'll find out then."

"What have you heard about that?"

He shrugged. "Just that the DA made him an offer."

"You could have told me."

His cousin braced his arms on the back of a chair. "You haven't been around long enough for me to tell you anything. If you spent half as much time doing your job as chasing down this gun buyer, the company would be better off."

Danny eyed his cousin. "What's up with you? Why don't you want to catch this guy? He and Franks and Gresham almost ruined our company's reputation. And now Franks won't serve a day for what he did."

Ian held his palms up. "It's over. Get past it. Besides, we were cleared of any wrongdoing. It's time to focus on the tasks at hand. Like this contract with Montoya."

Danny walked to the window and stared out at the parking lot. He didn't want to be like Ian. Get up, come to work day after day. There had to be more to life than that. Ever since his mom died, he'd wanted to make a difference. He just didn't know how.

He blew out a deep breath. But until then, he really should do what he was being paid for. He was part owner, he should want to make the company grow. He turned around. "Okay. As soon as I'm certain Bailey will be safe, I'll return to work. But today I'm escorting her to Corning."

"You'll have to tell your father that yourself. He made it clear he wanted you in on the negotiations."

"No problem." Hopefully they wouldn't drag on all morning. He also hoped he got the opportunity to ask his dad about the ring.

A few minutes later, Danny knocked on the boardroom door and entered.

"Well, Son, glad you can join us." Phillip Maxwell's voice held no sarcasm.

Danny nodded and took his seat at the conference table as Ian joined them, and for the next hour he mostly listened and occasionally added his input as his father and Ian negotiated with Montoya. When Montoya received a phone call and stepped out of the room, Ian left as well, leaving Danny with his father.

His dad tented his fingers. "What do you think?"

"I think Montoya is coming out ahead. His costs haven't increased significantly while our fuel costs for transporting the raw materials have."

"Good point. You should have brought it up."

"I was going to when he received the phone call."

"How's it going with Bailey?"

Danny jerked his head up. "How did you know?"

"Son, you brought her back from Mexico, you're staying at the B&B, and you're itching to leave this meeting, I presume to be with her. So, answer my question."

Danny squared his shoulders. "I'm going to ask her to marry me again, and I'd like to give her Mom's ring, with your permission, of course." He swallowed and waited.

A slow smile spread across his dad's face. "Do you think she'll have you this time?"

Tension eased from his shoulders. "I hope so. We'll know tonight."

Phillip frowned. "You two haven't been near each other in two years. Don't rush it. Give her a little time, a little space."

Resistance welled up in him. "We've wasted enough time."

"One more thing—have you considered she might not want to give up her mission work?"

"We'll work that out."

He held his father's steady gaze, and finally he smiled. "Well, you have my blessing. Of course you can have the ring."

Yes! Danny restrained from pumping his fist in the air.

"I would appreciate your help with the negotiations today," his dad added.

That meant he wouldn't get away anytime soon. "I'll stay, and thank you, sir. Now, if you don't mind, I'm going to give Bailey a call."

"Not at all. Just be back by the time Montoya finishes his business."

Danny took out his phone as he exited the boardroom, his elation tempered by a question his dad raised. What if Bailey didn't want to give up her mission work?

■ ■ ■

Bailey caught a glimpse of herself as she brushed her hair. She had to do something about the dark circles under her eyes.

Maria looked up at Bailey in the mirror. "Don't you feel good, Miss Bailey?"

She yawned and turned the brush on Maria's hair. "I'm fine,

just a little tired." Fatigue caused by another round of dreams, except last night, the man in the nightmares wasn't Mr. Carver. The man who chased her had ghostly blue eyes. Not sky blue like Maria's but pale like Joel's. With a start, she realized it had been the man in the poppy field in Mexico. Maybe she should talk to Ben about what happened.

Maria patted Bailey's hand to get her attention. "Are we really going to see my grandma and grandpa today?"

Bailey finished tying the ribbon in the girl's dark hair and smiled. "Yes, ma'am. As soon as Angel and Solana get back from the clinic."

"Is Mr. Danny going?"

"I think so." Danny. Bailey touched her lips, remembering his kisses last night and her response. So why did her heart ache? Because her admission gave him the wrong impression as evidenced in the kitchen earlier. He thought they were on the same page. And why weren't they?

"Can I wear my necklace today?"

Bailey glanced at the locket that Robyn had brought from the jeweler last night. "If you will be very careful. Like your uncle Joel said, this is a very expensive necklace."

"I'll be careful. I want to show it to my grandmother."

She fastened the locket around the child's neck. "You look very pretty, but remember—"

"I know. Be very careful with it." She mimicked Bailey's words. "Is it time to go yet?"

Bailey laughed, remembering how hard waiting was for a child. "No, not yet."

Bailey hoped everyone would be back from their various appointments in time for them to leave at ten thirty, but she'd heard Joel go out earlier, and he hadn't said when he would return. And she hadn't heard from Danny either.

"Is Tio coming?"

"I don't know." She'd never met Maria's great-uncle and would like to. "Do you have a picture of him?"

Maria shook her head. "I don't think he likes it when someone takes his picture. Am I going to fly to see my grandparents?"

"You are."

If the cartel had followed them to Logan Point and was waiting for an opportunity to grab Maria, the drive to Corning afforded them the perfect time since parts of the highway weren't well traveled. Maria would fly with Danny and Bailey to the little airport outside of Corning, while Angel and Solana drove the Escalade and picked them up. She assumed Joel would drive himself.

Maria tugged at her arm. "Can I put on the dress that my daddy bought?"

"Let's eat breakfast first, little chatterbox."

Maria nodded. "So I don't spill anything on it."

"That's right."

"Where did my daddy go?"

The child couldn't seem to get enough of calling Angel daddy. "He took Solana to get that cast off her foot."

Her eyes widened. "Do you think he'll marry Solana and make her my mommy?"

"Where did you get such an idea?" She'd seen how protective Angel was of Solana but hadn't dreamed Maria had noticed.

Maria hunched her shoulders in a shrug. "He's always smiling at her. Will I live with him when we go home?"

"I'm sure you will." Bailey couldn't imagine any other scenario even though she hadn't heard Angel discuss the subject. How would Joel feel about losing Maria? Her chest tightened. Joel wasn't the only one losing the child. Bailey had grown close to her in the last year, and this week had cemented that bond.

Remembering the sad child she'd first met and seeing her now warmed Bailey's heart. She'd made a difference in Maria's life. That made the trip to Mexico worth all the bad that happened.

Maria tilted her head. "Are you coming home with us too?"

"I don't know." Bailey bit her lip. She hadn't decided if she wanted to return to Mexico other than to finish out the school year. The school expected her to teach next year, but she wasn't sure she could. She shook her head, dispelling the memory of fear, of running away. "How about we go downstairs?" she asked. "I think I smell bacon and cinnamon rolls."

"And then I can put my new dress on?"

"Yes, ma'am."

When they entered the kitchen, Bailey spoke to her mom before helping Maria into a chair. Her cell phone rang and she slid the phone out of her pocket. "Hello?"

"Hey, bad news," Danny said.

"What?"

"Dad's insisting that I sit in on the contract negotiations with Edward Montoya, and Angel called. The doctor who was supposed to see Solana was called out for an emergency. She has to go back to the clinic this afternoon—they're on their way back to the B&B now. Looks like we'll have to reschedule the Corning trip for tomorrow."

Bailey didn't relish telling Maria or Joel that news. "Looks that way, doesn't it. Do you know when you'll be back?"

"Depends on how well the negotiations go." His voice turned husky. "I was looking forward to being with you on the flight over."

A shiver raced through her. "Me too."

"See you soon."

Joel entered the kitchen from the back door as she disconnected from the call, and Maria scrambled from her chair and ran to him. "Uncle Joel!"

He picked her up. "I see you're wearing your necklace."

A grin spread across Maria's face. "Are you going with us in the plane?"

"No, sweetheart. I'll be driving to Corning in case I need to stay behind." He shook his head. "You wouldn't believe the trouble I had getting a rental car yesterday so that I didn't have to use Edward's. How long does that convention go on?"

"Through the weekend," Kate said. She took a breakfast casserole from the oven. "Is everyone ready for something hot?"

"That looks good, Kate." Joel set Maria in the chair Bailey pulled out. "So tell me, how do you have rooms available when no one else does, other than the fleabag I vacated."

Kate poured him a cup of coffee. "My bed-and-breakfast was omitted from the list that went out to attendees. By the time I found out, it was too late to change it." She glanced at Maria. "And now I'm glad it worked out that way."

Bailey was too. She turned to Joel. "I hope you slept well."

"I did. And whatever your mother just took out of the oven smells wonderful."

"It is." Bailey dished out three servings of the casserole, then took a cup from the cabinet. "I'm afraid our plans have changed from last night. Neither Danny nor Angel can go today or at least not this morning."

Joel jerked his head toward her. "You're kidding."

"Not unless something changes." She explained the problem to Joel and her mother.

"I may be able to help with Solana," Kate said.

Joel turned to Maria and took a small box from his pocket. "I have something for you. You don't have to worry about losing this one—it's not that expensive."

Bailey smiled as Maria's eyes grew round as he opened the box and took out a necklace. "She wants to show it to her grandmother."

"Well, this one is just like it."

"Does it have Mommy's picture?"

Joel seemed to stop breathing. "Ah, I'm afraid not. But we can transfer the picture from the other one."

"Let me take a look at it," Bailey said and opened the locket Joel held. She winced. There was no frame to slide a picture into like in the original. "I don't think your sister's photo will fit."

Maria's bottom lip poked out, and she placed her hand over the locket she wore. "I want to wear this one. I want to show Nana Sue my mommy's picture." She raised her tear-filled eyes. "I'll be careful, Uncle Joel. I won't lose it, I promise."

"I'll try to make sure she doesn't lose it, but if something happens to it, I'll pay you for it," Bailey said. She hoped the child didn't lose it since the necklace obviously cost a pretty chunk of money, but Maria had been through so much in her short life, it seemed a shame to deny her wearing the necklace with Claire's picture in it. Besides, Joel should have known how much having the photo meant to Maria. *Men.* They knew nothing about females, even very small ones.

Joel's lips twitched, then he nodded. "I suppose one more day won't hurt. But be *very* careful."

Maria's eyes lit up, and she threw her arms around his neck. "Thank you, Uncle Joel. I'll be careful, I promise."

"You better," he said as Maria climbed back into her chair. He took a sip of coffee. "I'm still making the trip, and there's no reason why Maria can't go with me."

"I doubt Angel would go for that."

The back door opened, and Angel and Solana came in just in time to catch what Bailey said.

"Go for what?" he asked.

"Daddy!" Maria squealed. "Are you ready to take me to see Nana Sue and Papa Joe?"

Angel swept her up. "I think we will wait until tomorrow. Will that be okay with you?"

Her face fell. "Can we go back to that park, then?"

"Maybe." He turned to Bailey. "What is it I won't go for?"

Joel squared his shoulders. "I talked with my mother, and the doctors have scheduled my father's surgery for tomorrow morning. I'm going to see him today, and I want to take Maria with me."

"On Saturday?"

"Evidently the doctor operates on weekends."

Angel folded his arms across his chest. "No."

"Why not? He's facing a risky operation and may die, and I'd really like for him to see Maria. I'm sure Bailey would be glad to accompany me, and it's what Claire would want."

Memories of Wednesday in Mexico sent shivers down Bailey's back. Although there'd been no indication that they'd been followed to Logan Point, she wasn't certain she wanted to risk the trip without Danny and Angel along.

"Please, Daddy, I want to wear my new dress you bought me and go with Uncle Joel."

■ ■ ■

The tendons in Angel's neck throbbed as he ground his molars. If Joel thought he'd use Claire to play on his sympathy, he'd learn quickly it wouldn't work. Maria was going nowhere without him.

"Angel," Solana spoke quietly. "Why don't we reschedule my appointment?"

He directed his gaze to her. "Because you've worn that cast long enough."

"But what if he . . . it would make me feel terrible if she couldn't go because of me."

Kate cleared her throat. "Excuse me," she said. "There'll be no need to reschedule or for Angel to stay behind to take Solana. I can take her to the clinic this afternoon. That is, if Angel wants to work it out that way."

It was a solution. But he didn't like it that Maria would be traveling by car. "Let me call Danny. Perhaps he will be finished by noon—there would still be time to go."

He stepped out of the kitchen and walked to his bedroom to call. Danny answered on the first ring. "Angel? Is everything okay?"

"There's a problem with waiting until tomorrow to go to Corning. Claire's father is having surgery tomorrow, and there's some question as to whether he'll make it through the surgery. I'm trying to work out a way to take Maria to see him today. I'd really prefer her to fly rather than travel by car. Less chance of something going wrong. Do you think you'll be finished by noon?"

"We're waiting on Edward to start the meeting now—he stepped out for a few minutes, so I don't know how long this will take."

"Would you consider letting me fly your plane?"

"What? Are you telling me you can pilot a plane?"

"I guess I am."

"What else have you not told me?"

Danny wouldn't want to know all of his secrets. "That's it. I didn't think my piloting skills were relevant."

"You have a valid license?"

"Of course."

"Let me think about it. If I see I won't get through here by noon, I'll call you."

"Sure. Do you mind if I check out your plane? Maybe take care of refueling it?"

"That's a good idea."

Angel pocketed his phone and walked back to the kitchen. Joel's voice stopped him just outside the door. From where he stood, Angel could see and hear his brother-in-law. Joel was doing what he did best—charming the people around him. The man thrived on attention.

Even though he'd wanted Joel at the bed-and-breakfast, being under the same roof gnawed at his insides. And when Maria climbed in his lap, as she was now, his desire to kill the man intensified. But Joel's death would not bring back Claire, and if Angel wanted justice for what happened in the warehouse that day, he needed to keep Joel alive. There was always a chance his brother-in-law would make a slip, and Angel would have the evidence to turn him over to the Mexican authorities for collaborating with the Calatrava.

Angel stepped back into the room. "Danny said it would depend on Edward as to whether or not he could fly Maria to Corning. Can you influence my uncle into wrapping up the negotiations by noon? Do that, and now that Kate has offered to take Solana to the doctor, we should be able to fly Maria to see your father before he has surgery."

Joel's eyes narrowed, then with a blink, a smile appeared on his lips. But Angel knew from the rigid jaw and tense shoulders, anger at not being in control smoldered just below the surface.

"You can't drive her?" Joel asked.

"I'd rather not, just in case . . ." He cast his gaze toward Maria.

"I'll see what I can do." He took his phone out and walked away from them. When he finished his call, he turned and nodded. "Edward promised to wrap up today's negotiations within the hour."

"Good." Angel winked at Maria. "And now you get to wear your new dress today, after all."

Joel checked his watch. "What time do you think you'll arrive?"

"If everything stays on schedule, around two."

Joel nodded and knelt to hug Maria. "You be good today, okay?"

She kissed him on the cheek. "I will. I wish you could fly with us."

"Me too, honey. But I need to go early and visit with my dad." He gave her one last hug and straightened up. "Don't let anything happen to her."

Angel couldn't reconcile the man he knew with the one embracing Maria. At first Angel thought it was an act, but just as he'd seen unbridled anger in his eyes, he now saw real love.

Joel stopped at the door. "Are you really going to bring her, or is this all an act just to get rid of me?"

"You have my word that I will bring her."

His brother-in-law lifted his eyebrows, then turned and shut the door behind him. With Joel gone, tension eased from Angel's body.

Solana squeezed his arm. "You made a good decision."

"I hope so." He ignored the way his heart raced at her touch, but he couldn't look away from the adoration in her eyes. If she knew the blackness that filled his heart, she would run as hard and fast as she could from him.

Solana turned to Kate. "And thank you that I'm not the reason to keep Maria from going."

Kate hugged her. "Glad to do it. Until then, I'll be in my pottery shop."

Angel said, "And I'm going to the airport to get Danny's plane ready."

Two hours later, he returned to the house. Regardless of who flew the plane, it was ready to take off. Maria met him at the foot of the stairs. His heart warmed at the sight of the only good thing in his life.

All the time he had lain in the Texas hospital, thoughts of Maria and Claire had given him the will to live. Three bullets had lodged in his body that day at the warehouse, one near his spine. For a while the doctors thought he'd never walk again, but as the swelling and inflammation subsided, feeling returned to his legs. Now the only residual effect of the bullets was in his mind.

"Daddy, you didn't answer me!"

He brought his attention back to Maria. "Sorry, baby. What did you say?"

She put her fists on her waist. "I asked how I looked."

Oh, shades of Claire. He laughed and picked Maria up. "You're beautiful, like your mommy."

"Really? Uncle Joel says the picture is so I won't forget what she looks like." She gazed into his eyes. "I feel bad sometimes when I can't remember. I think that's why Uncle Joel gave it to me. Can you open it for me?"

"Let me set you down." His fingers shook as he held the small heart-shaped locket and stared at the photo of Claire from their wedding. His stomach lurched.

Why couldn't Joel stay one-dimensional? When he did something nice like this, it made Angel doubt his assessment of his brother-in-law. What if he was wrong about Joel? What if he wasn't the one who tipped off the Calatrava? But if not Joel, who?

18

Bailey stopped at the top of the stairs and blinked back tears at the sight of Angel holding Maria. To see the child so happy lifted her heart. And when Angel was with Maria, the haunted look in his eyes disappeared. But the child didn't change just him—she changed everyone who came into contact with her. Even Danny had succumbed to her charm. *Danny.* Bailey was seeing a different side of him. Gentler, yet with strength in the gentleness.

Maybe when this was all over, they could . . . do what? Did she dare to hope they might have a future? She'd told Danny last night she loved him. And he loved her. It shouldn't be complicated. But it was. Even though she'd resolved to release her fear and trust God, that resolve hadn't been tested.

But that wasn't the only obstacle. She and Danny didn't want the same things out of life. She'd been the happiest she'd ever been when she first arrived in Mexico, giving the tea parties and teaching the women in the village. What if Danny didn't want her to return to Mexico?

Did she even know anymore what she wanted to do with her life? This week had changed everything. She had another two months on her contract. But after that, what? It was something she had to sort out. But right now she needed to focus on the trip to Corning. "Have you heard from Danny?" she asked.

Angel glanced up and waved. "Not yet."

Footsteps stomped on the porch. "Maybe that's him now."

The door opened, and Danny hurried in. He caught her eye as she came down the stairs and smiled, making her heart flutter in her chest.

"You made it," Angel said. "I've already refueled and checked the plane out."

Danny pulled his gaze away from Bailey. "We haven't seen anyone lurking about, but if the cartel is here and they know where we're going, they probably will expect us to use the plane and land in Corning. There's a small airport in Collegedale, the town just before you get to Corning. I'll land there, and you can pick us up. I programmed the airport into the Escalade's GPS."

"Good thinking. I'll leave now."

"We'll leave in an hour—flight time to Collegedale is twenty-five minutes, so we should arrive at the same time."

"It's been three days," Bailey said. "Is it possible they've moved on to another target?"

"They may have," Danny replied, "but there's no need to take any chances."

The front door opened again, and Kate and Solana came in.

"It's off!" Solana raised her foot that was encased in a purple tennis shoe instead of a cast. "The doctor said it had healed nicely but that I should wear something with support, like these shoes you bought me. And now I can go with you to take Maria to see her grandparents."

Bailey hugged her. "I'm so glad."

Danny frowned. "But I thought your appointment wasn't until later this afternoon."

Kate patted him on the shoulder. "It looks as though my influence is a little better than yours. I made one phone call and got another doctor to take a look at her foot. They said to bring her right away, and so I did, and now we're back. Oh, and I made sandwiches for your trip. Let me get them."

Her mom thought of everything.

In ten minutes, Angel and Solana were ready to leave.

"Watch to see if anyone is following you," Danny said.

"I will. Do you have your . . ." Angel dropped his gaze to Maria.

Danny nodded. "It's in my car. I need to get it before you leave."

"And I'll borrow Daddy's .38," Bailey said.

"Do you know how to use it?" Angel asked.

"She's passable," Danny said with a laugh.

Bailey nudged him with her elbow. "I beat you the last time we target practiced."

"I was kidding." He eyed Angel. "You don't want to compete against her."

Danny walked out with Angel and Solana. When he returned, Bailey was setting out their sandwiches. "Where's Maria?"

"Upstairs with Mom." She cocked her head. "Why was your gun in the Escalade?"

"I had it yesterday when I went out to Geoffrey Franks's house."

"You went to Geoffrey's house? By yourself and with a gun?" Her mom had mailed her newspaper clippings of Geoffrey Franks's arrest last summer. She couldn't believe Danny had gone to see him.

"No, I took Angel with me. Franks ran us off with a semi-automatic."

She stared at him. "What were you going to do? Scare him into confessing who his contact in Mexico was? What if he'd shot you? Or what if you'd shot him?"

"Well, he didn't and I didn't. And I've already caught enough flak from Ian about this, so could you lay off?" He caught her hand. "I'd much rather talk about you, especially since you're all I've thought about this morning."

"Really?" She tilted her head. "I thought you were negotiating a contract with Edward Montoya."

"Nah. My heart wasn't in it." He pulled her close. "I kept thinking about this."

"Miss Bailey! Where are you?" Maria's footsteps tapped toward the kitchen. "I'm hungry."

Laughing, she pulled away. "Business first, Mr. Maxwell." She turned toward the door. "We're in the kitchen, Maria."

■ ■ ■

At the last minute, Bailey decided to leave her dad's revolver behind. She didn't have a license to have a concealed weapon. When they reached the airport, Danny carried Maria inside the terminal.

"Morning, Sam," he said, handing her off to Bailey. "Anyone new fly in lately?"

The airport manager scratched his head. "Couple of ladies from South Mississippi flew in yesterday."

"Anyone from Mexico?" Danny asked.

"No." Sam raised his eyebrows. "You want me to let you know if anyone arrives from Mexico?"

"I'd appreciate it."

"If someone followed us here, don't you think they'd fly commercially?" Bailey said as they walked to Danny's plane.

He shook his head. "I think they'd come in a small plane and probably land in Memphis, like Edward Montoya. If I were looking for you and Maria and didn't know where to start, I'd follow Joel and Edward's trail."

"What's Maria's uncle like?"

"You've never met him?"

"No." He had never come to the school with Joel.

"He seems nice enough."

"Tio is my favorite uncle," Maria said.

"More than your uncle Joel?" Bailey asked.

Maria placed her finger against her chin. "Maybe."

Bailey hugged her. "That wasn't a fair question. Are you excited about flying again?"

"No, ma'am. I wanted to go with my daddy."

"Daddy wanted you to fly with us, and this will be much faster. It will be fine, you'll see."

Danny climbed up on the wing and took Maria from her. "Why don't you sit in the backseat with Maria? We can talk through the headsets. I'll leave hers turned off."

Bailey climbed into the back and settled Maria in her seat, then adjusted a pair of headsets to fit the child's head. "If you need anything, I'll be right beside you." Bailey gave her a reassuring smile. Once they were in the air, Maria would be fine. At least that's the way it had worked the last time. As Danny started the engine, Bailey put her headset on and spoke into the mic. "We're ready."

Danny gave her a thumbs-up and taxied down the runway. Just as she'd predicted, once they were in the air, Maria relaxed, and before Bailey thought possible, Danny was radioing the small airport in Collegedale. As they came in for the landing, she peered out the window to see if she could see Angel. He and Solana stood just outside the small terminal building. Evidently they'd had no trouble.

Once they'd taxied to the terminal and killed the engine, Angel chocked the wheels, then took Maria from Bailey. "Did you like flying?"

She shook her head. "Can I go back with you?"

"We'll see. Maybe Danny will let me fly his plane. Would you like to fly with me?"

A grin spread across Maria's face.

"Any problems?" Danny asked.

"No. As far as I could tell, no one followed us. At least no one exited behind us at Collegedale."

"Maybe they're not even around," Solana said.

Bailey tended to agree with her.

"What if they're waiting for us to let our guard down?" Danny said grimly.

■ ■ ■

Joel walked to the refreshment center in the hospital ICU waiting room and poured a cup of coffee. Even though it had just been made, it was bitter. His phone rang, and he almost dropped the Styrofoam cup. He didn't recognize the number, but it looked similar to the one last night. His finger shook as he pressed Answer. "McDermott."

"Ah, Mr. McDermott. I looked this morning and did not see a money transfer from you."

Joel stood and walked to the window. People walked back and forth to the hospital as an ambulance roared into the emergency entrance. Life and death playing out before him. "I'm having trouble accessing the money."

"I see."

Silence filled his ear, and he checked to see if the call had been disconnected. No. It was still live.

"Look, I'll get you the money by tonight."

"Actually, your debt is no longer important. We have decided to make an example of you for others who do not pay."

Joel swallowed as his knees turned to water, and he leaned against the window frame. "I'll do anything, pay twice what I owe. Just give me until tonight."

"Anything? What if I come up with an alternative way for you to clear your debt?"

Joel caught his breath. He'd do anything short of murder, and maybe even that, to get these people off his back. "How?"

"I want Maria Montoya and Bailey Adams. Their lives for yours. I'll be in touch."

His mother touched his arm, and he jumped. "Joel, is everything okay? You're white as a ghost."

"Yes." He managed to get the word out as his heart pounded against his rib cage. He checked his phone to make sure the call

217

had ended. Joel pressed his lips together. If he could just get access to Edward's offshore account and pay off his debt, he wouldn't have to do what the caller asked.

"Are you certain Claire's little girl is coming?"

"What?"

"They aren't here yet. Are you sure they're coming?"

He shook his head to clear it. "Yes, Mother. Angel promised he'd bring her. Now go sit down."

"Come with me."

His life was falling apart, and his mother wanted him to keep her company? His mind reeled as he walked with her to their seating area.

"Tell me again what happened to your face."

She was driving him crazy with her questions. He'd answered this same question at least three times already. Maybe he'd inherited from her the memory problems that were causing him so much trouble.

"Joel?"

"I was in a little accident, nothing serious." He leaned his head against the back of the chair. *"I want Maria Montoya and Bailey Adams. Their lives for yours."* The caller's words echoed in his head.

He couldn't do it. Somehow, he had to get the necklace back and transfer enough money out of the account to pay off this debt—if he could convince them to take the money. The drug cartel after him was bad enough, but if he was the cause of something happening to Maria and Angel found out . . . he didn't want to think about that.

He had to get the necklace.

He'd tried unsuccessfully to access the bank account again last night and had even thought about searching Bailey's room for Maria's necklace after he learned it had been returned. In the end, he'd feared getting caught and let it go. How could he know his niece would insist on having her mother's picture in the new one? He'd thought his heart would stop when Bailey opened the locket to take Claire's photo out.

The elevator dinged, and he looked toward it as the doors opened, and Angel and Solana got off with Maria. Bailey and Danny followed. He zeroed in on the locket around Maria's neck.

"Uncle Joel!" Maria ran to him, and he swung her up in his arms. His heart skipped a beat when the locket brushed his hand. So close to be so far.

"Thanks for bringing her," he said to Angel, then turned toward his mother. "Would you like to meet your grandmother?"

Suddenly shy, Maria barely nodded, then ducked her head. Joel set her down. "Mom, this is Maria."

His mother seemed overcome as well. Tears glistened in her eyes. She knelt down until she was eye level. "I'm so very glad to meet you."

"It's nice to meet you, Nana Sue," Maria said softly.

His mother lifted Maria's chin. "Oh, Joel she looks like Claire when she was this age."

"She acts like her sometimes too," Joel said as Angel stepped forward. "Mom, this is Angel Montoya, Claire's husband. Angel, my mother, Sue McDermott."

Angel bowed. "It's a pleasure to meet you, Mrs. McDermott."

She rose with an uncertain smile on her lips. "It's good to finally meet you. I'm sorry we never met while Claire was alive, but Joseph has been ill for some time. I couldn't leave him."

Joel didn't understand why his mother made excuses for his father. Even if he had been well, he wouldn't have gone to Mexico. In the three hours Joel had been here, his father had done nothing but complain and gripe and bully everyone who came into the room. Joel couldn't wait to get away.

But first the necklace. "Are you ready to meet your grandfather?"

"I want to show Nana Sue my necklace." Maria opened the locket and held it up for his mother to see. "Uncle Joel gave it to me."

"Why don't we take it off so she can see it better?" Joel asked. Maybe this was his chance.

"I can see it just fine." His mother stared at the photo, then patted Maria's cheek. "You're such a sweet child. Run see your grandfather, now."

Joel took her by the hand, and they walked to the double doors, where he pressed the intercom button. He'd already made the necessary arrangements for Maria to accompany him into the ICU, and after he identified himself, the doors clicked open. They were halfway through when he realized Angel was with them. "Only two are allowed in his room."

"If Maria goes, I go."

"I'm sorry, but you can't go in there." If Angel was in the room, how would he get the locket?

Angel took Maria's hand. "If you want your father to see her, it has to be with me."

His brother-in-law wasn't backing down. Joel clenched his fists, then forced them open.

A nurse sat at a desk between his father's room and the next patient's. "He's sleeping, but go on in. He may wake up."

Joel stepped inside the room, where a monitor beeped over his father's bed. Maria stared warily at the bed, then wrapped her arms around Angel's leg. "Would you like me to hold you?" Joel asked.

She shook her head and clung tighter to Angel. "What's that noise?" she whispered.

"It's a machine that counts how many times his heart beats."

His father opened his eyes, and he stared at Angel, then shifted to Joel. Recognition flashed. "Is she here?"

"Yes, sir," he replied. He bent down to pick up Maria.

"No," she said, twisting away from him.

"Let me hold her." Angel swung her into his arms and whis-

220

pered something in her ear. Maria nodded, and he stepped closer to the bed.

"Hello, Papa Joe," she said, her voice quivering.

His father stared at her, then his expression softened. "So this is Claire's child. You the husband?" he asked, shifting his gaze to Angel.

"Yes. Joel tells me you need an operation."

"That's what they say. Wanted to see the kid first, though. Thank you for bringing her."

Joel almost choked. He'd never heard his father thank anyone. "Maria, can we show Papa Joe your locket?"

She nodded. "It has my mommy's picture in it."

Joel moved to unclasp the necklace.

"I'll do it." Angel put Maria down and unfastened the chain. He opened the locket. "You want to show it to him, Maria?"

Smiling, Maria took the locket to the bed. A frown crossed her face. "I can't see you. Can I sit on the bed?"

"I don't see why not." He nodded to Angel. "Put her up here."

His plan was falling apart. Joel gripped the foot of the bed as Maria showed his father Claire's photo.

The nurse entered the room. "I'm sorry, but your time is up. Mr. McDermott needs rest."

His father grimaced. "She's a drill sergeant. I'm afraid you'll have to leave, but would you bring Maria back to see me?"

"As soon as you're up to it," Angel said.

"I hope you get better soon," Maria said, planting a kiss on her grandfather's cheek.

His mind numb, Joel walked to the door in a daze, searching for some way to get the necklace away from Maria. "Would you like to leave your locket with Papa Joe until he's better?"

He held his breath while a struggle played out on her face. Finally she turned around and went back into the room. "Papa Joe, would you like to keep my locket with Mommy's picture in it?"

"What a sweetheart you are, Maria." He flashed her a smile. "But you better keep it. I might lose it."

At that second, Joel had never wanted to kill anyone as bad as he did his father. But he didn't know why he was surprised. His father had stood in his way any time Joel wanted something. Why should this be any different?

19

A bottleneck slowed traffic on the bypass around Corning to thirty-five miles per hour. Only ten miles and Maria would be safely on the plane. Danny glanced in his side mirror. Nothing stood out. If they were being followed, it was at a distance. Maybe they weren't being followed at all. He glanced toward Angel in the passenger seat. "See anything unusual?"

"No."

Danny glanced at the passengers in the backseat. Maria dozed in Solana's lap, and Bailey seemed lost in thought. He shifted his gaze back to the road. "You know, we haven't seen any evidence that the Calatrava followed us out of Mexico. Don't you think they would have made a move by now, if they were here?"

"It's too soon to tell. My gut says they're just waiting."

"So you'd prefer for Maria to fly to Logan Point?"

"Yeah. I'm not ready to relax my guard."

Once they were past the jackknifed semi that had narrowed the highway to one lane, Danny gunned the SUV to sixty-five. "You said something about piloting the plane. How long have you been flying?"

"Fifteen years, since I was eighteen."

"Ever fly a Cessna 172?"

Angel grinned. "Cut my teeth on one—my flying teeth, that is."

"So how did you get into flying?"

His grin faded. "When my uncle kicked me out of the house, a friend of my dad's took me in. The same friend my father entrusted the letter to. He provided private chartered flights for wealthy tourists around Mexico, and he taught me how to fly."

"Is it possible you're wrong about your uncle?"

"Don't let him fool you. He's like a chameleon—you only see what he wants you to see."

The exit to Collegedale appeared, and Danny checked the traffic behind him again. Everything looked normal. It'd be interesting to see if anyone exited with them. He slowed for the ramp, then turned left at the light. No one followed them, and he breathed a little easier.

"I'm hungry," Maria said.

"I am too," Bailey chimed in. "Those sandwiches are long gone."

He wished they had taken Kate up on her offer to make sandwiches for them to have on the drive home. "I don't see anywhere we can get food."

"There's a place," Bailey said.

The "place" was a hole-in-the-wall diner beside a truck stop, and he pulled in. Thirty minutes later when they pulled out, he *really* wished they'd brought the sandwiches. The restaurant had been a true greasy spoon. They'd all be lucky if they didn't get sick. Ten minutes later he turned in to the small airport.

The wind sock flew straight out from a cold north wind as Danny removed the chocks around the wheels, then climbed up on the wing and unlocked the cabin door. Back on the ground, he tossed Angel the keys. "Enjoy the flight. The keys to the convertible are under the mat. I'll call the airport manager and let him know you'll be picking it up."

A grin spread across Angel's face. "Thanks, amigo."

After he and Angel went over the preflight, Angel helped Maria up on the wing, then Solana before climbing up himself. "See you in Logan Point."

Danny waved, then hooked his arm in Bailey's. "Looks like it's just you and me, kid."

She laughed and leaned into him. "So it does."

With Bailey on his arm, he waited until the plane took off, then they walked through the terminal to the SUV. Once back on the highway, Danny turned the radio on low, and classical music played softly in the background.

"I think today went well." Bailey rested her head against the back of the seat.

"Yeah, and Joel didn't act like such a stuffed shirt. Did he ever tell you where he went last night?"

"I didn't ask him, and he's not a stuffed shirt. He's a good guy."

"Whatever." For communicating, driving was much better than flying, and he didn't want to waste time talking about Joel. He glanced her way and saw she had her eyes closed. "Tired?"

"Some."

"Late date last night?"

A smile tugged at the corner of her mouth.

"Did you mean what you said at the barn?"

Bailey's eyes flew open. He thought that would get her attention. "What do you mean?"

"You said some pretty serious stuff, like you love me, among other things."

She sighed, and his heart took a nosedive. It wasn't the kind of sigh he wanted to hear. "I do love you, Danny—"

"I hear a *but* in there."

"I don't want to hurt you, but now isn't the time to push me for anything."

"I'm not pushing you." He ignored his father's voice in his head, warning him of this very thing. "I just asked a simple question."

"Simple?"

"You know what I mean." He cut his gaze toward her. Tears wet her cheeks as she pressed her hands against her eyes. "I didn't mean to make you cry."

"Well, you did." She opened her purse and pulled out a tissue. "Remember when we used to go to the maze out on Whitten Road? And how no matter which way we turned, we couldn't get out?"

"Yeah." A memory of her crying in the cornfield flashed through his mind. "Is that how you feel? That there's no way out of your situation?"

"Something like that. I feel like I'm butting my head against a wall. That I've wasted my whole life."

"No, don't feel that way. Look at what you've done for Maria. If it hadn't been for you, she would have been kidnapped."

She leaned her head back against the seat again. "There is that."

"And a whole lot more. Those kids at that school where you teach. I bet they all love you."

She smiled. "Maybe."

"No maybe about it. How could they not love you?"

She raised up. "Thanks."

"For what?"

"Making me feel better. Could we not talk about anything serious for the rest of the way home?"

"Your wish is my command, m'lady." Her mouth twitched as she stared straight ahead. He took a deep breath and said, "Remember that time we went skinny-dipping—"

"Danny Maxwell. I have never been skinny-dipping in my life."

"That must have been . . ." He shot a quick look again.

She was trying not to laugh but lost her battle. "You're something else, you know that?"

"Yeah. But I like hearing you laugh." He checked his mirror. Would he ever not watch behind him again? "Do you remember . . ."

They spent the rest of the trip reminiscing, and when they

reached the bed-and-breakfast, Bailey seemed to be in a better frame of mind.

"Why do you suppose Ben is here?" Bailey asked as they pulled past his car to the back of the house.

"Let's go see."

They went in through the back door and found everyone in the kitchen, except Maria and Charlie. "Well, I see all the usual suspects are here," Danny joked, only no one laughed. "What's going on?"

Angel folded his arms across his chest. "The guy we went to see yesterday is dead. Murdered."

■ ■ ■

Geoffrey Franks dead? Bailey covered her mouth with her hand as the greasy lunch threatened to come up. After what happened this week, she didn't know why violence surprised her anymore.

She closed her eyes, picturing him when he'd been a couple of years behind her in college. Skinny and wearing horn-rimmed glasses and a bow tie. A glance at Danny made her wince. The color had drained from his face.

"What do you mean, dead?" Danny shifted his gaze to Ben, and the sheriff nodded. "What happened?"

"Shot. At close range. The neighbors said you and another man"—Ben glanced toward Angel—"that I am assuming was you, were at his house yesterday."

"We were," Danny said. "I thought since he was going to walk anyway, he might talk to me."

"Did he?"

"He pulled a gun, ordered me off his property. And I left. Haven't been back."

Exasperation flew across Ben's face. "But I told you to stay away from him, and I know the DA told you the same thing. That I would handle this case. I didn't need you going off half-cocked." Ben took out a pencil and pad. "Where were you last night?"

Danny's eyes widened. "You think I might have had something to do with it?"

"You just admitted to going there. Did you take a gun with you?"

"Maybe."

Ben pressed his lips in a thin line. "What kind of gun do you have?"

"Nine millimeter Glock."

"Have you fired it recently?"

"Not in a month. Target practicing then." Danny's voice had gone flat.

"Then you won't mind getting it for me."

"Are you sure you didn't fire it when we were at the airport in Mexico?" Bailey said.

"No. Angel did all the shooting."

Ben shifted toward Angel. "How about you, do you have a gun?"

"Ben Logan!" Bailey fisted her hands on her hips. "I cannot believe you're questioning Danny and Angel about a murder."

"It's my job, Bailey."

Kate spoke up. "Not telling you how to do your business, Ben. But neither one of these boys killed anyone."

He nodded, looking uncomfortable. "Yes, ma'am."

"Next thing I know, you'll be asking me questions."

He shifted his gaze to Kate. "Actually, you're right. Can you tell me if either of these two left last night?"

Kate put her hands on her hips. "Do you seriously suspect them of killing that rat? And speaking of rats, have you questioned Gresham? He'd have the most to gain from Franks's death."

Bailey glanced toward Angel. Why didn't he tell Ben that he'd left in Danny's SUV last night?

Beside her, Danny stepped toward Ben. "Why not just ask us? I didn't leave the property last night."

"I can vouch they both were here when I went to bed," Kate said.

"And you didn't hear anyone go out?"

She shook her head.

"How about Charlie? Reckon he would know?"

"He might. He's keeping Maria occupied. Do you want me to go up and get him?" She wiped her hands with a towel.

"No, not just yet." He nodded to Danny and Angel. "You were getting your guns."

When Angel left to go upstairs and Danny to his SUV, Bailey turned to Ben. Should she tell him about Angel and Joel leaving last night? "Do you have any other suspects? You know Danny didn't do it."

"Come on, Bailey. You want me to do my job, don't you? And I don't mind telling you that Jonas Gresham is my primary suspect, but I have to look at everyone who might have a grudge against Franks. And Danny has made no bones about not liking the man after what he did."

"How will this affect Gresham's trial?" Kate asked.

"I don't know. I heard earlier this week that his lawyer has asked for a change of venue for both trials. Claims he can't get a fair trial here."

"What do you mean, both trials?" Bailey asked.

"Dogfighting and gunrunning. With a couple of his comrades turning on him, we have him dead to rights on dogfighting. With Franks dead, he might get a not guilty on the gunrunning."

She hadn't read about the dogfighting. For that one, he should be put *under* the jail.

She turned as Angel came into the kitchen and handed Ben his gun. "I don't know what caliber gun was used, but here's mine—it's a 9mm and hasn't been fired since Wednesday in Mexico."

Ben examined the automatic. "Do you have a permit to carry this in the States?"

Angel answered him with a curt nod. "Texas. And I believe Mississippi honors the Texas permit."

Ben handed the pistol back to him. "I don't know yet what

kind of gun was used, but if it turns out to be a 9mm, I'd like to compare a bullet fired from your gun to the slug taken out of Franks. Same for you, Danny," he said as Danny returned to the kitchen.

"What time was Franks killed?" Danny handed Ben his pistol.

"Hard to say. Heat was turned off and the back door left open. With the temperature dropping below freezing last night, I'm sure determining the time of death will be much harder." He sniffed the gun and handed it back to Danny. "Unfortunately, no one saw him after you two were there."

Bailey's heart sank. Ben actually viewed Danny as a suspect. And why didn't Angel speak up and tell Ben he went to see Chavez last night?

"Have you questioned Joel and my uncle?" Angel asked.

"Would they have a reason to want Franks dead?"

"That would depend on whether or not one of them was Franks's Mexico contact."

"You have a point. Where can I find them?"

"Joel is in Corning with his parents," Bailey said. "His father is having surgery tomorrow, so he probably won't be back before tomorrow afternoon."

"And Edward Montoya is probably still at Maxwell Industries," Danny said.

"There's one more person you might be interested in," Angel said. "Sergeant Chavez."

"Him I've talked to." Ben leveled his gaze at Angel. "He's staying at a motel here in Logan Point, said you came to see him last night."

Bailey swallowed hard. Ben knew all along Angel had left the house last night. Now it looked as if all of them were hiding something.

"I did, but I came right back here. I don't even know how to get back to Franks's house."

"So you say." Ben jotted something down in his notebook. "What motive do you think Chavez would have to kill Franks?"

Danny answered for him. "The same as anyone who might fear being exposed as the Mexico contact."

"Noted." Ben looked from Danny to Angel. "You two aren't planning on leaving Logan Point any time soon, are you?"

"No." They answered in unison.

"And the guns you showed me are the only ones you have?"

Angel nodded while Danny hesitated.

"Danny?" Ben said.

"I have another Glock. It's in my SUV."

"Would you—"

The door from the hallway flew open, and Charlie burst into the room. "This girl needs a doctor. She's burning up with fever."

A tremor shot through Bailey. Maria's pale body lay limp in Charlie's arms. She reached for the child, but Angel was faster and took her from Charlie. "She's so hot. How can she be sick? She was playing an hour ago."

"She just started throwing up and said her head hurt real bad," Charlie said.

"I'll call our family doctor," Kate said. She made the call, nodding as she talked with someone, then hung up. "The doctor just left for the day, and the nurse said to take her to the ER."

"I'll drive you," Danny said.

"And I'll provide an escort," Ben said.

Bailey grabbed her purse. "I'm coming too—you'll need the power of attorney Joel gave me in case something like this happened."

"I will stay here," Solana said. "Too many will be in the way."

■ ■ ■

Two hours later, the emergency room doctor asked permission to draw a small sample of spinal fluid. "There's a possibility it's meningitis, and the only way I can be sure is to draw the fluid and test it. If it is, and it's bacterial, we need to start treatment right away."

"Meningitis?" Danny said.

"How dangerous is the test?" Angel demanded.

"While there is a slight risk of complications, it's much more dangerous if we don't do it and she has bacterial meningitis. And it's not painful, merely uncomfortable."

"Could it be food poisoning?"

The doctor turned his attention to Bailey. "Have you all eaten the same food?"

She tried to think what they'd eaten in the past twenty-four hours. "Yes, except for lunch today. We ate at a diner, and Maria had a hot dog."

"Did anyone else eat a hot dog?"

"Solana did," Danny said. "And she's not sick."

"We're testing for food-borne diseases, but we'll lose precious time if we wait for the results and it's meningitis."

"Then do the test," Angel said. "I'm her father, and I'll sign the waiver."

Bailey exchanged looks with Danny. Angel might be her father, but he had no legal rights.

"Maybe Bailey should sign as well," Danny said.

"Yes," she echoed and shifted Maria's bag of clothes to her other hand. She still held the necklace she'd removed when they first arrived and tucked it in a side pocket in her purse.

After a hesitation, Angel lifted his shoulder. "As you wish."

After the waiver was signed and the doctor left, she pinned Angel with what she hoped was a determined look. "I'm going to give Joel a call."

"Why?"

"Because he's her legal guardian."

"But she's my daughter, and I owe Joel nothing. If he hadn't informed the wrong people, I would not have been shot and my wife would still be alive."

"You don't know that," Danny said. "What if he's not the one responsible for what happened that day in the warehouse?"

Bailey folded her arms across her chest. "He loves your daughter, and he's cared for her since Claire died. He didn't have to do that, you know."

Angel scrubbed the side of his face. Finally, he gave her a curt nod. "I know when I'm outnumbered. And now I need some coffee. Anybody else?"

The thought of coffee soured her stomach, and she shook her head as she found a chair to sit in and took out her phone. A list of incoming emails popped up when she turned it on, and she scanned through them. One was from Pastor Carlos. As soon as she talked to Joel, she'd see what he wanted.

Joel answered on the second ring. "Good evening, lovely lady."

"I don't feel very lovely," she replied. When did she get so tired? "Maria is running a fever and vomiting and I'm at the hospital with her. The doctor is doing a spinal tap right now. As soon as I know the outcome, I'll call you."

"What happened?"

"I don't know. How's your dad?"

"Holding his own. Look, I'm leaving and will be there as soon as I can."

Bailey felt better that he was coming. She didn't like being the one to make decisions, especially if something else came up. "Good. I'll let Angel know."

"Are you sure you're all right? You don't sound like yourself."

"I'm fine, just tired. I'll see you when you get here." She disconnected just as Angel returned with his coffee. "He's on his way," she said.

Angel nodded. "How is his father?"

"Like he was when we were there."

"Maria's doctor is coming now," Danny said, nodding toward the door.

A smile stretched across the ER doctor's face. "It's not meningitis. The fluid came back clear. I'm glad to be wrong, but when meningitis is suspected, you don't want to take any chances."

"What do you think it is?"

"With meningitis ruled out, I think it's probably the hot dog. I'd like to keep her overnight for observation."

Bailey's cell phone rang. It was her mom. "Hello?"

"We're bringing Solana to the ER. She's throwing up and looks as bad as Maria did."

"I'll tell Angel. We're still in the emergency room." She hung up and told the others.

"And you said she ate the same thing Maria did?" the doctor asked.

"Yes—hot dogs," Angel said.

"That pretty well confirms it's food poisoning." He turned to Bailey. "Call your mother back and have her bring your friend to the ambulance entry. That will get her treatment quicker."

20

A ngel followed Maria's bed as it rolled from the ER to the elevator. She looked so tiny in the bed, and her still form with an IV in her arm scared him—he'd much rather see her running and playing, but at least she was getting help from the antibiotic.

Solana looked awful when she came into the ER. He'd hated to leave her, but Bailey had stayed with her, and where Bailey was, so was Danny. Perhaps Solana would be put on the same floor as Maria when she left the emergency room.

Maria's blue eyes fluttered open. "Daddy?"

"I'm right here, baby."

"Are you going to stay with me?"

"I am. We'll go home in the morning." Home. Presently, he had no home. Joel had sold the small house where he and Claire lived after they married and when Maria was a baby. Just as well. It would be better to start over someplace where there weren't so many memories. If he was ever able to go back to Mexico, that is. Ben Logan had not been happy that he didn't tell him about leaving the bed-and-breakfast last night.

Once they moved off the elevator, the ER porter stopped at the nurses' station to hand over Maria's chart, then they proceeded down the hallway.

"Here we are," the attendant said when they arrived at the room.

"May I move her to the bed?"

The floor nurse came around to the front of the bed. "Sure, just be careful with the IV. We don't want it to come out."

No, Angel didn't want that. It had been hard enough hooking up the IV the first time, and he didn't want Maria to go through that again. The nurse held the IV bag while Angel picked her up and settled her in the bed. "Comfortable?"

She nodded. "I'm thirsty."

Angel shot the nurse a questioning look.

"How about ice chips, and then later we'll try a sip or two, and if she keeps that down, she can have more later." A page sounded on the nurse's phone. "I'll be back to go over her chart in a minute." She hurried from the room and almost collided with someone entering. "Excuse me."

"I'm sorry," a male voice answered.

Angel froze. He'd recognize that voice anywhere.

"Daddy." Maria's eyes lit up. "It's Tio."

A band tightened around his chest. He expected Maria to know Edward, but well enough to call him Uncle? He took in a breath and blew it out before turning around.

Edward Montoya stood at the foot of the bed. "Hello, Angel."

He nodded curtly. "Edward."

"You look well."

For a dead man. The unspoken words hung between them. Angel had seen his uncle from a distance since he'd recovered from the gunshot wounds, but nothing prepared him for being in the same room.

"How did this happen?" Edward waved his arm around the room.

"She got food poisoning. Maybe you would like to step outside in the hallway."

"No!" Maria cried softly. "I want him to stay."

"I'm not going anywhere, little one. If necessary, I would take a bullet for you."

Angel stared hard at Edward, but his uncle's gaze was on Maria, and it was evident he cared very much for her. For the first time, Angel noticed that Maria's eyes were almost the same color as Edward's. He'd always believed his daughter's cornflower blue eyes were inherited from Claire, but no, she'd gotten them from his grandmother, the same person Edward had gotten his from. His uncle turned to him.

"May I sit down?" He nodded to a chair on the other side of the bed.

That was a switch. Edward asking instead of telling. Angel nodded. For Maria, he told himself. Edward moved silently to the chair and took off the long overcoat and draped it across the back. How long did he plan to stay?

"How did you know?" Angel asked.

"Phillip Maxwell called his son to join us for dinner, and he told his father that Maria was in the hospital. I came immediately, and when I arrived, Danny was with someone who appeared quite ill."

"He was with a friend of ours." Angel glanced at the bed, where Maria had dozed off.

Edward cleared his throat. "Do you think it's possible that we can put the past behind us? For Maria's sake?"

His question ignited the fire smoldering in Angel's gut. It was all he could do to keep from reaching across the bed and throwing the man out. He counted to five, focusing on his breath with each number. "You killed my mother and father and then have the nerve to ask that?" Angel kept his voice low.

His uncle straightened in the chair and leaned forward. "I told you fifteen years ago I did not kill your parents. Your father was my brother. He was blood. Family."

"I didn't believe you then, and I don't believe you now."

"Why?"

Angel curled his lip. "My father left a letter accusing you of trying to take over the company. He told me if anything happened to him, to look no further than you."

"He was wrong. Because I criticized the way your father ran the business left us by *our* father, he thought I was trying to take over. All I wanted to do was make it profitable like it had been when our father ran it."

"You're lying," Angel said through his teeth. "My father was a good manager."

Edward heaved a sigh. "No, Angel, he was not. A good man, yes, but he let his employees slack off, he didn't pursue accounts aggressively, and he let the suppliers rip him off. I will be glad to show you the books from then and now, if you like."

Angel hated to admit that some of what his uncle said was true, but if Edward wasn't responsible for their deaths, who was? "Who do you think killed my parents?"

His uncle dropped his gaze to his tented fingers. "Your father refused to pay insurance money to a small cartel for their protection. I believe this drug cartel used their deaths to intimidate other factory owners in the area. To show what could happen if they refused to pay the insurance."

"Do you pay insurance?"

Edward looked up and stared into Angel's eyes. "Yes."

"To the same cartel?"

He nodded.

"Who is this cartel?"

"The Calatrava."

The same cartel that was after his daughter.

■ ■ ■

Joel took a deep breath and tapped on the door before pushing it open. He'd come up the back stairs and had been surprised to see Edward get on the elevator. Joel figured Edward would stay away from his nephew.

Angel turned from the window and held his finger to his lips. Joel glanced at the bed where Maria lay sleeping. "How is she?"

"Much better than earlier. Thank you for being concerned enough to return, but you really shouldn't have. Your father needs you."

His father had never needed him or wanted him around. Maria's illness had been a good excuse for leaving, although he did feel bad about leaving his mother alone at the hospital. The way he'd been pacing the waiting area, he thought she was glad for him to leave. Now if he could only get the necklace . . .

Maria opened her eyes and gave him a weak smile. "Uncle Joel, you came."

"Couldn't keep me away." Bailey had been right on the phone. This was one sick little girl. He gaze traveled to her throat. "Where's your necklace, sweetheart?"

Maria felt her neck, and her eyes grew large. "It's gone." Tears filled her eyes. "I didn't mean to lose it, Uncle Joel. I promise."

Joel swallowed the curse that almost ripped out of his mouth. He flexed his fingers. She couldn't have lost it. If she had, he was dead. He pressed his fingers against his temple, trying to work blood back into his face. "Think where you had it last."

Pain gripped him as Angel's hand clamped down on his shoulder. "Do not raise your voice. She is a child, a very sick child, and if this necklace is so expensive, you should not have given it to her."

If Angel only knew. "I'm sorry." He pressed his lips together and forced his body to relax. "I have another, less costly one I'll give her once I put Claire's photo in it. But if you find the other one, would you call me?"

Angel narrowed his eyes. "What's so special about this necklace?"

"It . . . it belonged to Claire," Joel said. He should have come up with that a long time ago. "I bought it for her when she first came to Mexico, and it cost quite a bit of money even then."

"I do not remember seeing it when we were married."

He searched for an answer. "She'd broken it, and I had it repaired. I don't think I ever returned it to her."

"You mean that was Mommy's necklace once?" Maria turned to Angel. "Daddy, we have to find it."

"It's not lost, baby. Bailey has it." He turned to Joel. "I'm pretty sure that's where it is, so you can quit your worrying."

Relief almost made his knees buckle.

"Can you go get it?" Maria said.

"I'll get it for you," Joel said. He couldn't believe he was this close to retrieving those numbers. "I need to talk with Bailey, anyway."

"Then hang around. She's downstairs with Solana and should be coming up to a room on this floor soon."

"Solana is sick as well?"

"Yes, she ate the hot dogs like Maria did."

Joel couldn't help but notice how Angel's voice changed when he spoke of Solana. Or how Maria seemed to like her as well. The future was plain. Once Angel had his parental rights restored, he would marry Solana, and they would live happily ever after with Maria. He flexed his fingers. His brother-in-law's life was coming together while Joel's was falling apart. Maybe he'd take Maria with him if he had to disappear. That would put a dent in Angel's happiness. But first he had to get that necklace. "I'll go and check the ER, see if they're still there."

Outside the room, his head cleared. What was wrong with him? There was no way he could take Maria if he left, at least not to the final destination—wherever that might be. But why not temporarily? He could hide her somewhere to divert Edward's attention. He knew his boss's single-minded focus. If Maria was missing, every brain cell he had would be focused on finding his great-niece.

Joel's step became lighter. He'd found the piece to his plan that had been missing. Now to get into that account.

■ ■ ■

Danny watched as Kate pressed a cold washcloth to Solana's face as she lay in the ER bed. The monitor indicated her fever was over 103. He'd never seen anyone so sick in his life. He looked up at the IV dripping into her arm, then at Kate. "Why isn't her fever coming down?"

"I don't know." She wrung out a washcloth and handed it to him. "They may have to give her an ice bath."

He didn't know what that was, but it didn't sound good. He turned as a nurse entered the room with a blanket.

"This should bring her temperature down." She spread the blanket over Solana and plugged it in. "It's a cooling blanket." She nodded at the overhead monitor. "We're monitoring her vitals at the desk, but press the call button if you need anything."

Danny lifted his eyebrows as Joel came into the room and looked around.

"Where's Bailey?" he asked.

"Gone to the house to get a few things. She's staying overnight with Solana," Kate said.

"Why aren't you in Corning?" Danny said.

"I was worried about Maria, and Angel told me Solana was sick as well and that Bailey was down here with her." He shifted back and forth on his feet and glanced around the small room. "Maybe I can catch Bailey at the house. Call me if you need me. I'll be there for a while, then I'll head back to Corning."

"Sure," Danny said. "How's your dad?"

"About the same." He edged toward the door. "Surgery is at nine in the morning."

"I'll keep him in my prayers," Kate said.

Prayers. As the door closed behind Joel, Danny glanced at the monitor again. Solana's fever hadn't changed, and he was certain Kate had been praying for her. It was like his mother all over again,

241

except he thought God would hear and answer Kate's prayers. If God didn't hear hers, just whose *did* God hear?

He stuffed his hands into his pockets. "I'm going after something with caffeine in it. Can I bring you something?"

"No, I'm good." Kate wiped Solana's face again.

He wandered down to the nurses' station and poured a cup of coffee. If there was anything to this prayer business, when he returned, Solana's fever would be down. When he returned to the room, he glanced at the monitor. No change. He set the coffee cup on the window ledge. "You really think prayer will do any good?"

"What?"

"Your prayers. You told Joel you'd keep his dad in your prayers, and I know you've been praying for Solana. I don't see that they've done any good."

The sadness in Kate's eyes reminded him of his mother.

"God hears our prayers, but that doesn't mean he always gives us the answer we want."

"Then why pray?"

"I don't know about anyone else, but I pray because it brings God close. It gives me comfort, and I know he'll answer my prayers in a way that's best."

He didn't see how his mother's death was best for anyone. *Unless heaven is real.* Sometimes he really wanted to believe that, especially since he'd been doing what Kate asked and was reading the Gospels.

Behind him, Bailey cleared her throat, then came into the small room and set an overnight bag on the floor. "How is she?"

He rubbed the back of his neck. "No change."

"These blankets are so heavy," Solana whispered in Spanish.

Kate bent over the bed as she struggled to throw the blanket off. "Leave it there. It's supposed to bring your fever down."

He checked the monitor: 102.5. Her fever was coming down. Because of prayer?

"How do you feel?" Bailey asked.

Solana opened her eyes. "Terrible. How's Maria?"

"Last I heard, she wasn't throwing up any longer and her fever was down."

Solana nodded, then drifted off to sleep.

An hour later, Kate had returned to the bed-and-breakfast, and Danny accompanied Bailey as Solana was moved from the ER to a room on the same floor as Maria. Once Solana was transferred to the bed and the nurse had taken her information, Bailey turned to him.

"There's no need for you to stay," she said. "There isn't any place for you to sleep."

"You mean you won't give me the daybed?" It didn't look that comfortable.

"We'll be fine. No one's going to bother us in a hospital, not with all the security guards around."

"We'll see," he said. True, he had seen several guards stationed in and around the building. He sat on the daybed. "You might as well sit down. The doctor said she'd probably sleep all night."

She sat beside him, slightly bouncing on the bed. "This won't be so bad."

He shifted his weight and raised his eyebrows. "If you say so."

She was quiet a minute, then sighed. "I heard you and Mom talking about prayer."

"You were eavesdropping?"

"Uh-huh." She glanced toward Solana. "I'm glad we didn't eat the hot dogs."

"Don't even go there," he said with a laugh. "Are you hungry? I can get us something to eat."

"Maybe a little later." She took his hand, and her eyes bored into his. "Keep searching, okay?"

"I will," he promised her. "But I want you to promise me something too."

"What's that?"

"That you won't go back to Mexico."

"Don't go there, Danny."

"I don't think you should." He sensed her bristling, but he plunged ahead anyway. "Why can't you do mission work in Logan Point?"

"Because that's not where God called me to work."

"How do you know? Have you asked him? Or are you just trying to find the most dangerous place to work, thinking it will earn you brownie points with him?"

Her jaw shot out. "I . . ."

He wanted to kick himself. Why couldn't he just be patient? This was not the time to push this, but he hadn't been able to stop himself. "Just think about what I said. Okay?"

21

For the hundredth time, Joel berated himself for using the necklace to hide the numbers. He should have hidden them somewhere else or memorized them. But that was why he'd engraved the numbers on the necklace—he couldn't memorize anything.

And now Bailey wasn't at the house and neither was the locket. He'd searched high and low for it and was returning to the hospital in hopes of finding Bailey by herself. He held up his hand to block his side mirror when lights from behind blinded him. When the vehicle pulled out to come around him, Joel slowed to let it pass.

Abruptly it swerved in front of him and stopped. He slammed on the brakes, stopping inches from the bumper. What was going on? A wreck maybe? Or a deer? The area was full of the four-legged creatures.

The driver of the car jumped out and ran his way, brandishing a gun.

Joel threw the car in reverse, and an alarm screamed. He jerked his gaze to his rearview mirror. A car blocked his escape.

"Get out!"

Ski masks. They were hijacking his car. Or they were going to kill him.

He pulled the keys out of the ignition and opened the door. "You can have it," he said, holding the keys out.

"I don't want your car. Get out."

Joel's blood froze at the Mexican accent. He swallowed the nausea that raced up his throat. It was over. He stumbled out of the car, and the man jerked his arm behind him, forcing Joel to face the car. "What . . . what do you want? Who are you?"

"Your worst nightmare."

That voice. It was the man he'd lost the hundred grand to—Enrico. Joel's legs threatened to buckle.

"Do you have the money?"

"N-no, but I will soon."

"Good. But now I want more. The Montoya girl and Bailey Adams."

"I . . . I can't. They're at the hospital. Someone is always with them."

"Figure out a way. You see how easy it was to get to you. You have twenty-four hours."

He licked his lips. "If I agree, what do I do with them?"

"Eagle's Nest. Room 106."

Suddenly pain ripped his head, and stars exploded in his brain.

When he came to, he was on the ground and the men were gone. He climbed back into his car and rested his head on the steering wheel until the dizziness passed. He felt the back of his head and cried out. There was a bump the size of a goose egg where they'd hit him.

How did they know where he was? They'd been following him. What made him think the calls had been coming from Mexico? If he didn't do as they said, they would kill him. He was as certain of that as he was that Edward or Angel would kill him if he helped kidnap Maria and Bailey.

He only had one option. Get into Edward's account and take enough money to disappear forever.

He massaged his temples. Why did they want Maria and Bailey? *Ransom.* What he owed these men was peanuts compared to what they would ask for Maria. But why Bailey? She had no money.

It didn't matter. If he didn't get the necklace, it would be their lives for his.

His cell phone rang, and he checked the caller ID and groaned. His mother. "Hello?"

"Where are you? Your father is asking for you."

"I'm in Logan Point. Maria is still in the hospital and . . ." What would be bad enough for her to not expect him? "She has a virus, and I think I'm catching it," he lied. "But if you want me to come back to Corning tonight, I will."

"No! Your father can't afford anything like that right now. You stay there until you're sure you don't have the bug."

"I will. And I hope Dad does okay tomorrow with the surgery."

"I'll tell him you wished you could be here."

You do that. "Thanks, Mom. I'll call you in the morning."

He tapped on his navigation app and typed in Eagle's Nest, Logan Point, Mississippi. Once he had the directions, he placed his phone in the cup holder and started the car. Fifteen minutes later, he pulled into the almost deserted parking lot of an aging motel located on Logan Lake. Bars covered the windows, and the parking lot was deserted except for a road grader and a dump truck. Must be the place that the road crew repaving the bypass was lodging.

If he were picking out a place to stash someone, this would be the place.

■ ■ ■

Angel stood at the side of the bed, watching the rise and fall of his daughter's chest as she lay sleeping. He'd missed too much of her life, the good and the bad. She'd been a month shy of her second birthday when he was shot, so he'd missed a lot. He smiled, remembering her first steps and how she'd said Dada before Mama. Claire had been so jealous and proud at the same time.

It especially rankled that Joel had been the one to replace Angel in Maria's life. And that Edward had become involved in his family. Certainly wouldn't have happened if he'd been there to stop it. He hoped his uncle didn't come back to the hospital tonight; he was unsure if he could stomach Edward another minute.

Edward was a fool if he thought Angel believed his story, although he'd have to admit Edward had been quite convincing earlier. Someone who didn't know what he was capable of would probably believe him. Angel wasn't ready to dismiss what he'd believed for fifteen years and what his father had believed before that.

But what if we were both wrong?

Angel turned as someone knocked at the door and pushed it open. Ben Logan. And he looked serious. "What can I do for you, Sheriff?"

"The ballistics came back on the bullet taken from Geoffrey Franks. Nine millimeter."

"It's not from my gun," Angel said. "Have you questioned my uncle?"

"Haven't been able to catch up with him."

"Stick around, he'll probably be back shortly."

Ben nodded. "I'd like to test your gun."

Angel shrugged. "Sure. I'm not worried. But can it wait until morning, after I take Maria home? I want to have a way to protect her here at the hospital."

"Leave protecting her to me. I need it tonight. Along with Danny's."

"Have you spoken to him?"

"Not yet, thought I'd see you first."

Angel pulled up his pants leg and unbuckled the gun strapped to his calf and handed it to Ben.

"You wore that into the hospital?"

Angel shrugged.

Before Ben could comment, Edward stepped into the room. "What's going on?"

Angel slid his pants leg down. "Nothing," he replied. "Sheriff, I'd like you to meet my uncle, Edward Montoya."

"Sheriff?" Edward queried Angel with his eyes.

"He's investigating the murder of Geoffrey Franks. You knew him, didn't you, Uncle?"

Edward removed his leather gloves, one finger at a time, before he answered. Then he removed his overcoat before shifting his gaze to Angel. "I did, but how did you know that?"

He hadn't known; it had been an educated guess. "Danny told me Franks was the purchasing agent for Maxwell Industries, and Montoya Cerámica produces their pottery, so it stood to reason."

Ben took out a pen and notebook. "Did you know him very well?"

Edward folded his arms across his chest. "He was a business acquaintance. My assistant, Joel McDermott, knew him much better than I."

"What do you know about the rifles he sold to someone in Mexico?"

"Nothing."

"How about a company by the name of Blue Dog?"

"Nothing at all."

Like his uncle would admit it if he did. "I'm sure my uncle carries a pistol. You might want to see what caliber."

Edward leveled a cool stare at him. "No businessman in Mexico goes without protection." He turned to Ben. "But since I am not in Mexico, I do not have a gun."

Ben looked up from his notepad. Angel thought he was going to challenge him, but the sheriff let it go. Angel would bet money his uncle had some type of gun on him.

"When was Franks killed?" Montoya asked.

"Sometime last night," Ben said. "Do you mind telling me where you were between 5:00 p.m. yesterday and 8:00 this morning?"

Edward rubbed the back of his neck. "I was with Phillip Maxwell until after eight, then I drove into Memphis to the Peabody."

"Anybody see you there?"

"Possibly. I went to the bar for a couple of hours, then returned to my room."

Like everyone else, his uncle didn't have an alibi.

"Franks was killed with a 9mm gun. You're certain you don't have one on you?"

"I'm certain, and I had no reason to shoot him, anyway. Do I need my lawyer?"

Ben looked up at him. "I don't know. Do you?"

The tenseness in the room was cut when the door swung open and the nurse came in. "Time for vitals." She halted. "I'm sorry, do I need to come back?"

"No, I think I'm finished here," Ben said. He eyed Edward. "I may want to talk with you again."

Angel turned to see his uncle's response. Edward's mouth pressed into a thin line, then he curtly nodded. "I'll be expecting it."

"How long do you plan to be in the area?"

"Several more days. Like I said, I'm staying at the Peabody in Memphis."

"Contact me before you leave." Ben nodded and walked out the door.

Angel turned to the nurse as she charted Maria's blood pressure and temperature. It worried him that she had barely roused and was now back asleep. "How is she?"

"Pressure is good, and her temperature is going down."

"Why is she sleeping so much?"

"More than likely the medication for nausea." She smiled reassuringly at him. "By morning she should be back to her old self."

"So you think she'll be able to go home tomorrow?"

The nurse smoothed Maria's sheet. "Probably. Let me see if the doctor wrote her discharge papers." The nurse looked over the chart. "I see he wants a chest x-ray before she leaves, and if it's clear, he'll release her within the hour. A porter will come get her first thing tomorrow and take her down to x-ray."

"Why has he scheduled this?"

"With all the vomiting, she could have aspirated."

"Aspirated?"

The nurse touched her chest. "Gotten particles into her lungs. He'll want to make sure that didn't happen."

"Excuse me, but the door was open."

Angel wheeled around.

"Chavez," Edward said. "What are you doing here?"

"I'm looking for Sheriff Logan. His deputy said he was here."

"Well, he's not," Angel said.

"I'm sorry about your daughter." The Mexican detective turned to leave, then halted. "Thank you for coming by the motel last night. I'd like to continue the discussion when your daughter is better."

251

22

ailey leaned against the door as the doctor unwrapped the blood pressure cuff from Solana's arm. It was almost eight— a long four hours since bringing Maria to the hospital. On top of being tired, now she had to deal with Danny's unreasonable request. Not return to Mexico, indeed. She had a contract to fulfill.

"You are sure I need to stay here overnight?" Solana directed the question to the doctor. "I have no money and no insurance."

"Don't worry about that," Bailey said. "It will be taken care of."

"But—"

"You need the IV antibiotic." A kind smile softened the older man's angular face. "Whatever you and Maria ate caused a particularly nasty bug, and it can wreak havoc for a day or so. The antibiotic helps to limit the time you're incapacitated." He smiled at her confused look. "Sorry. The antibiotic will help you get better faster."

Bailey turned to the doctor. "We ate at the same place, just different items on the menu, so does that mean if I'm not sick by now, I won't be?"

"Since no one else has gotten ill, I'm pretty sure it was the hot dogs," the doctor said. "So you're good to go."

After the doctor left, Solana sat up in bed. "What did he mean by that?"

"What?"

"Good to go. Are you going somewhere?"

Bailey chuckled. "No, it means I should be fine."

Her explanation didn't remove the puzzled look from Solana's face. "You Americans say funny things. Where did Danny go?"

"To check on Maria, then to get us something to eat." She winced at the shudder that crossed her friend's body. "I'm sorry. I wasn't thinking."

"At least I kept down a few spoons of broth," she said. "And now, I think I'll take a little nap."

"And I'll check my email."

Bailey walked softly to the small sitting area in Solana's room and made herself comfortable in the recliner. The hospital was full, and the only room available was an end room with the attached suite.

There was a rap at the door, and Joel stuck his head around it. "Okay to visit?"

Bailey put her finger to her mouth and then waved him in. "Solana is sleeping, but I'm glad you came by. I want to give you Maria's necklace."

"I'm not asleep," Solana said. "And you will not bother me."

Joel came inside the room as Bailey rummaged in her bag. "Where's Danny?" he asked.

"In the cafeteria. I put her necklace in this to keep it safe," she said, pulling out a coin purse. She held it out. "Joel, are you all right? You look awful."

His fingers shook as he took the necklace. "I have a humdinger of a headache, plus I've hardly slept with the roller coaster we've been on these last few days."

"Do you want to sit down?"

"Maybe for a second. I thought I'd catch you at the bed-and-breakfast, but Charlie said I'd just missed you."

"How's your dad doing?" Bailey asked.

"I talked to Mom, and she said he was still ornery." He gave her a wry grin. "So that means he's doing okay."

"Are you going to make it back in time for the surgery?"

"I'm not sure. It'll depend on how Maria is. I talked to Angel earlier, and he said she could go home tomorrow. I want to make sure she's okay before I go back." He put his hands on his knees. "Look, I know you're tired and Solana needs her rest, so I'm going."

"Sure."

Before she could get back to her email, Danny came in.

"Joel almost knocked me down. What was his hurry?"

"I don't know. He was totally weird." She frowned. "What did you bring us to eat?"

"Turkey sandwiches. It's all they had."

Another knock sounded at the door, and she exchanged looks with Danny. "What is this, Grand Central Station?" she muttered. "Come in."

Ben entered the room carrying a satchel, and the look on his face was anything but friendly, although his eyes softened when he spied Solana. "How is she?"

"A little better, but how did you know we were here?"

"I called Kate, looking for Danny."

"For?" Danny said.

Ben glanced toward the sitting room. "Let's talk in there. I don't want to disturb Solana."

They sat on the couch with Ben across from them. "The slug the coroner took out of Franks is a 9mm. I'd like to do a ballistics test on your gun. I've already talked with Angel, and he's given me his gun to test."

"You surely don't think either one of us killed him, do you?"

"I don't think anything, Danny. I have to check everything out, and since you and Angel were possibly the last ones to see him alive, I have to check your guns."

254

"Can it wait until morning? Bailey won't leave Solana, and I'm not leaving her by herself after what happened earlier this week."

She couldn't believe this was happening. "Ben, you know he didn't kill Franks."

Ben ignored her. "Where's your gun?"

"In my SUV," Danny said.

The sheriff rubbed his thumb along his jaw. "Tell you what; go get your gun, and I'll stay here with Bailey. And bring the other gun you mentioned at the house."

Danny started to argue with him, and Bailey shook her head. "Just do it. If Ben will stay here, I'll be fine."

"All right. I'll be right back." He shot a glance toward her. "I didn't shoot anyone."

She squeezed his hand. "I know you didn't, and this will settle it once and for all."

He kissed the top of her head. "I'll be back in five minutes."

After he left, she folded her arms across her chest. "Ben—"

"Bailey, you know I have to do my job. Just because Danny is a friend doesn't let me off the hook."

"I know," she said, her attitude softening. "I was going to check my email before you arrived."

"Go ahead. I'll just sit here until Danny gets back."

She took her phone out and opened the email account. Three emails from the pastor at the church in Valle Rojo. She opened the last one first.

Bailey,

I'm so sorry, but Elena's body was found this morning.

"No!" The room swirled as blood drained from her face. She blinked, trying to read the small print on the phone. "It can't be."

"What's wrong?" He was at her side in an instant.

Bailey tried to swallow the bile that rose up in her throat. "Read the emails from Carlos Mendoza."

He took the phone and scrolled through the emails. His eyes narrowed. "Who was Elena?"

"My best friend at the village when I first went to Mexico." Tears scalded her eyelids. Elena couldn't be dead. "I only read the last email. What do the others say?"

Ben hesitated. "Are you sure—"

"Yes." Surely Father Horatio didn't do this. *But he'd beaten another woman almost to death.* She sagged against the daybed. She should have discouraged Elena from going against him.

"The first email came in yesterday, and this Carlos was letting you know she was missing. Whoever took her burned her home down. He mentions a Father Horatio."

No. "Her children . . . did he say what happened to them?"

"Not in the first email, but in the second, he said they were safe. Evidently the husband had taken them to see his parents."

Did Elena's husband know what was going to happen? It wouldn't be the first time a man in that village failed to protect his wife against the priest and his cartel friends.

Ben handed her the phone back. "Do you know why she was killed?"

Images bombarded her. The swarthy priest mocking Bailey, yelling, swearing he would see her dead if she stayed in the village. "Elena told me she'd started a Bible class in the village, and Father Horatio was very upset about it."

"Do you think he killed her over these classes?"

"He was capable of it—he put three rattlesnakes under my car seat. I think he would kill anyone who threatened his power. And he has the backing of the drug cartel."

"What kind of priest would be in cahoots with a drug cartel?"

"He's not a real priest, just someone who goes around calling himself one. It's all about power with him. Not sure what his real name is, but after he gathered a following in the village, he started calling himself Father Horatio. What he teaches is a mixture of voodoo and animism with a dash of Christianity thrown in, and the drug cartel backs him because he controls the local farmers. One word from him and the farmers would quit growing marijuana and opium."

"Is there no one who will stand up to him?"

Bailey shook her head. Even the pastor at the church where she worked feared him, not that she blamed him anymore. "I think that's why Father Horatio thought he could scare me—no one opposed him until me and then Elena . . ."

Bailey bit her lip. She couldn't believe Elena was dead. Not vibrant, beautiful Elena who had two babies to live for.

■ ■ ■

Danny opened his SUV door and slid into the passenger side. He probably should listen to Bailey and Ian about keeping his vehicle locked. But this was Logan Point. Very few break-ins occurred unless you were in the wrong part of town, and when he was there, he locked his SUV.

He opened the glove compartment and searched without finding the gun. That would be rich—not being able to find it. Like Ben Logan would buy that.

It wasn't that he minded letting Ben test his gun; he minded being a suspect in the first place. He thought Ben knew him better than that. The console—now he remembered he'd had the gun in his hand when Maria became ill and had put it in the console when they left for the hospital. He flipped it open and found the 9mm gun on top. The sooner it was tested, the sooner Ben could look for the real killer. Now for the other gun that he usually kept in the backseat console. Danny reached over the backseat and searched the compartment. His chest tightened. Where was the gun? He climbed out of the SUV and opened the back door,

searching under the seats. No gun. Maybe it was at the office . . .
except he didn't remember taking it out of the car.

When he entered Bailey's room, he took one look at her face
and then Ben's. Something was wrong. "What happened? Are you
getting sick?"

She shook her head. "My friend Elena that I told you about.
She's been murdered."

"What? Why?"

She pressed her hand against her mouth. "Ben read the emails,
he can tell you."

He'd almost forgotten the gun and handed it to Ben. "I'd like
it back tonight."

"I'll return it as soon as I do the test. Where's the other gun
you mentioned?" Ben asked as he put the Glock in a paper bag
and placed it in the satchel he'd brought in.

"I'm not sure. It's either at the office or my cabin. I'll have Ian
bring it to you in the morning."

"I need it tonight."

Danny ground his teeth. "And I'm not leaving Bailey unless
you arrest me. You'll have it tomorrow." He returned Ben's steady
gaze.

The sheriff gave him a curt nod. "First thing in the morning,
then." Ben sighed. "I hope you know I'm just doing my job. If I
don't check out every lead, even when it involves someone I like,
the townsfolk will think I'm playing favorites."

"I understand. Now, who were the emails from and what was
in them?"

"They were from Bailey's pastor at the church where she worked
in Mexico. The first one was to let her know that her friend Elena
had disappeared. The last one said she'd been found dead."

"No." He took Bailey's hand. "I'm sorry."

"I should have talked her out of going against Father Horatio.
She might still be alive if I had."

"Do you think this Father Horatio killed her?"

"I don't know who else to suspect, but it's not something he'd do himself—he had the cartel for that." She pressed her hands into the side of her head. "Elena was trying to be brave and do what she thought God wanted her to do. And now she's dead."

Danny didn't know how to respond. He tried to think what Kate would say. "Bad things are always going to happen, Bailey. At least she died doing what she believed in." A thought sent a shiver down his back. "Do you think this priest could be responsible for what happened to you and Maria in Mexico? You said you saw him at the restaurant that day."

"I thought so at first, but if that was the case, why was Joel kidnapped?"

An alert sounded on Ben's phone, and he glanced at it. "Excuse me a minute." He read the text and looked up. "It's Sergeant Chavez. He's here at the hospital, just left Angel's room. Do you mind if he stops by here?"

Danny glanced at Bailey's pale face and said, "Can't you two talk somewhere else?"

"He might be able to get more information on her friend's death," Ben said.

"Then let him come," Bailey said.

Ben texted him and received an answer right away. "He'll be here in a minute."

Danny sat on the armrest of the couch next to Bailey. He felt they were missing something. "If—" He stopped as Sergeant Chavez entered the room.

Chavez nodded. "I'm sorry to bother you, but I need a word with Sheriff Logan."

"And we need your help," Bailey said.

Danny studied the Mexican policeman as he shifted his gaze from Ben to Bailey. The man had an agenda, and Danny wasn't sure he trusted him.

"What do you need my help for?"

"Bailey just received word that a friend was murdered in a village in Mexico," Danny said.

"Why was she murdered, and where is the village?"

"It's in the mountains two hours from Chihuahua—Valle Rojo." In a soft voice, Bailey explained what happened.

When she finished, Chavez tilted his head toward her. "Father Horatio," he said slowly. "He's been on our radar for a while now, but he's pretty well untouchable. And you think he killed her?"

"Or his friends in the Calatrava."

"You could be right—the man has no conscience." Chavez took out a small notebook. "Give me a couple of hours in the morning, and I'll see if there's anything new on him."

"Thank you." She leaned back against the couch.

Solana coughed. Bailey jumped up to check on her, and Danny followed.

"I'm thirsty," Solana whispered.

He poured a glass of water and handed it to Bailey. "You two need rest." He glanced at the other two men. "We need to clear out."

They agreed, and Danny followed them out into the hall. "Can you post a deputy here at the hospital? This priest has a vendetta against Bailey and he has cartel connections, so he's looking pretty good for the kidnapping attempt in Mexico. And if he'll kill someone in his village, he won't have second thoughts of tracking Bailey to Logan Point and killing her."

"Let me check. I'm stretched thin with two deputies out with the flu, but I know I can talk to the head of security in the hospital and have them move a guard to this floor."

That wasn't enough. It looked as though Danny would have to stand guard. "Do me a favor and get my gun back to me . . . or leave it now and test it in the morning. I don't want Bailey unprotected."

"I'll have it back to you in the morning before you leave." Ben chewed the inside of his cheek. "And I'll check with Wade, see if he'll give up his date tonight to sit outside the door."

He could tell by the muscle twitching in the sheriff's cheek, he wasn't changing his mind about the gun. Danny just hoped he wouldn't need it before they left the hospital.

23

After so many failed attempts to get the necklace, Joel couldn't believe he held it in his hands. That Bailey had just handed it to him. There had to be a catch. Maybe it was a trap. No. He was the only one who knew the locket contained the numbers to Edward's offshore account. Now he wouldn't have to turn Bailey over to those men. He'd wire the money as soon as he booted up his computer.

He stepped off the elevator and hurried to his car. He had to find a Wi-Fi spot. Maybe a McDonald's. No, not a public place. The bed-and-breakfast. He'd go there where no one could tap into his computer.

Ten minutes later, he parked and hurried into the house.

Kate was coming down the stairs. "How are our sick folks?"

"Better. I think Maria is coming home in the morning." He took off his overcoat and scarf. "I'll be in my room if anyone needs me."

He opened the locket and removed Claire's photo. Using a magnifying glass from his briefcase, he copied down the numbers etched in the white gold. He hadn't even been close.

Once he had the computer connected to the internet, he hesitated. This was it. Weeks ago he'd opened an account with a different Switzerland bank. All he had to do was tap into the account and transfer the money.

He licked his lips. How much did he want to take? If Edward

ever found out it was him, it wouldn't matter whether he took a half million or five million. His boss would kill him all the same. And five million had such a nice, even sound to it.

His fingers shook as he typed in the website, then filled in the user name. He made it past the first level of security. But he'd been here before. He sucked in a breath and held it as he typed in the account number then the password and hit enter.

ACCESS DENIED. ILLEGAL ATTEMPT. Red flashed across his screen, and a warning buzzer screamed from the speakers.

Joel's mouth gaped. A band tightened across his chest, cutting off his breath. What happened? He had the right numbers. And he typed it in right, he was certain of that. He slammed the computer shut, and the buzzer stopped. Carefully, he reopened it and stared at the screen. How could he be denied access? The numbers had worked before.

Edward changed the account number or password. Joel hadn't even considered he might do that. He slumped back in the chair, resting his head in his hand. Was it possible Edward discovered he'd tried to access the account?

No, otherwise Joel would be dead. It was probably normal procedure to change the numbers periodically. He beat his fist against the bed. If only he'd been able to get the necklace earlier.

What was he going to do now? Maybe he could ask Edward for a loan. His shoulders slumped. If he did that and his boss knew someone had tried to get into his offshore account, he would know it was Joel. Edward probably wouldn't loan him any money, anyway.

"But now I want more. The Montoya girl and Bailey Adams."

The man's demand rang in his ears. He had no choice now, but he still didn't understand why the man wanted Bailey. Because she knew something . . . or she'd crossed someone. It didn't matter. They wanted both of them, and delivering them was a way to get the cartel off his back.

Almost on cue, his cell phone rang. The same number as earlier flashed on the caller ID. With sudden clarity, he realized if he was coming out of this situation alive, he had to go on the offensive. *Don't answer it. Make them sweat a little.*

Finally it stopped, only to start again.

He punched the answer button. "Hello?"

"When do you plan on delivering the Adams woman to the Eagle's Nest?"

"I told you, she's never alone. If you want them, you're going to have to help me."

Silence stretched between them.

"And this has to go down in such a way that no one can ever suspect that I'm responsible for their disappearance."

"Getting a little cocky, aren't you? Don't forget you owe us money."

Anxiety inched into his spine. He squared his shoulders. He'd faced worse and won, he'd just momentarily forgotten it. "Do you want them or not?"

■ ■ ■

Angel thought Edward would never leave, but at last he had put on his long overcoat.

He stepped to the bed and leaned over, kissing the sleeping child on the cheek. "Good night, little one."

Maria blinked open her eyes. "Tio. Don't go. You didn't tell me a story yet."

"He can tell you one tomorrow when he comes," Angel said.

"No." She smiled at his uncle. "Tell me about the eagle and the chickens."

A slow smile spread across Edward's face. "You remembered." He turned to Angel. "You don't mind . . . ?"

Angel curbed his impatience. "No, tell her the story."

Edward took off his coat and sat on the side of the bed. "Many years ago, high on the mountain, there was an eagle's nest with four eggs in it. One day an earthquake shook one of the eggs out, and it rolled down the mountainside onto a chicken farm." He stopped and raised his eyebrows. "Now what do you think the chickens did?"

"They took care of the egg," she said softly.

"Yes, they did, and eventually a beautiful eagle was born. And, since the chickens were chickens, they raised the young eagle to be a chicken too. But as he got older, the eagle watched up in the sky as other birds soared high in the air. 'What is that?' the eaglet asked. 'Why, that's an eagle,' the hens answered. 'The king of birds. He belongs in the air, but we are chickens—'"

"And chickens belong on the ground," Maria said, lowering her voice.

"Yes," Edward said. "But what happened next?"

"The eagle decided he didn't want to be a chicken," she said, her eyes brighter than they'd been all day.

Edward laughed. "That's right. What happened next?"

"He tried to fly!"

"That's right," Edward said. "And after a while, he did, because he was really an eagle, and one day he flew off and never came back because he would never be happy being a chicken."

"But he came back to say thank you to the chickens who raised him," she finished proudly.

"Very good. And now I must go, but I'll be back tomorrow."

"Okay."

Angel didn't quite remember the story the way Edward told it, but he liked this ending better. He stared at his uncle, unable to connect the man he remembered from his youth to the one who had just told his daughter that story.

A light tap at the door drew Angel's attention, and he eased to the door as Edward bent over to hug Maria. Danny. "Come on in. How's Solana?"

"That's what I came over for—to give you a chance to check on her for yourself. And to tell you—oh, Mr. Montoya, I didn't know you were here."

"Just leaving." He held out his hand, and Danny shook it.

"Uncle Danny! Did you come to see me?"

A gentle smile tugged at Danny's lips. "Of course I did. Do you feel better?"

"Mm-huh."

He glanced at Angel.

"The doctor was by earlier. Evidently she had a fairly light case of food poisoning, and he's going to let her go home in the morning after a chest x-ray." His friend seemed antsy, more than he'd seen him since they'd arrived in Logan Point.

"Why don't you go see Solana, and then we'll talk?" Danny said. "I'll stay with our girl."

Edward frowned. "You could have gone while I was here."

"Then I wouldn't have heard that interesting take on the eagle." He wasn't ready to leave Maria with his uncle. "Tell me what's bothering you first," he said to Danny. "Is it the sheriff?"

"No. Well, that's bothering me, but it isn't what I want to discuss with you." Danny glanced at Edward.

His uncle cleared his throat. "Perhaps I should leave . . . unless this is about my great-niece. Those men who tried to take her—have they been seen here?"

"Perhaps we should step outside into the hallway?" Danny said, raising his eyebrows.

Angel glanced at his daughter, who seemed much too interested in what they were talking about. "The nurse said something about a bath. Let me see if they can do it now."

He pressed the call button and explained what he wanted when someone answered.

Out in the hall a few minutes later, Angel waited for Danny to explain.

"I don't think Maria was ever really in danger," Danny said. "I think it was Bailey all along."

"What are you talking about?" Angel said. To know his daughter wasn't the object of kidnappers . . . he couldn't wrap his mind around it.

Danny folded his arms across his chest. "The weekend before she was to return to the States, Bailey visited a friend in the small village where she was a missionary. She encouraged her friend to continue teaching these Bible classes—the same classes Bailey was forced to abandon because she crossed the local priest. Her mission board pulled her out after this priest put rattlesnakes in her car. Her friend is dead, probably at the hands of the priest."

Edward frowned. "Was he a real priest?"

"I don't think so. More shaman than anything else."

Angel had heard of men like Danny spoke of.

"Sometimes these priests have a lot of control over villagers, and they don't like their authority challenged," Edward said. Then he took a card from his coat and handed it to Angel. "I have things to attend to. Call me if Maria becomes ill again."

When Edward was out of hearing range, Danny gave him an apologetic shrug. "Sorry if telling my dad you were here at the hospital with Maria caused you grief."

"No. Perhaps I was wrong about him, and perhaps not, but I do see a different side of him when he is with Maria. Did the sheriff come to see you?"

Danny's face darkened. "He picked up my gun, said he'd have it back by morning."

Angel nodded toward Solana's room down the hall. "Who's the guy sitting outside by the door wearing a big gun?"

Danny's lip curled. "Wade Hatcher, Ben's chief deputy. He'll be here until our guns are returned."

"Good." Angel slapped Danny on the back. "You can go home and get a good night's sleep."

"Are you crazy? I'm not trusting anyone to guard Bailey except me. Now go see Solana so I can get back in there."

24

It was too early Saturday morning for Ben Logan to be babbling such nonsense. Bailey stared at him. The man had lost his mind. "What do you mean, you want Danny to go down to the jail to answer a few questions?"

The sheriff turned to her, his face drawn and unreadable. "Bailey, stay out of this."

Danny planted his feet wide. "I'm not leaving Bailey at this hospital by herself."

A slow flush crept up Ben's neck. "You don't understand—you don't have a choice. A 9mm Glock registered to you was found under a clump of leaves on Franks's property. It was the gun used to kill him. You'll either come voluntarily, or I'll handcuff you."

"Ben, if I'd killed Franks, I would not have left my gun there. Someone is framing me."

"You know Danny didn't kill Franks," Bailey said. She'd hoped morning would bring fewer problems, not more.

"I don't know anything right now." Ben ran his hand over his face. "If it were anyone else, I wouldn't be standing here arguing with you two." He eyed Danny. "Which is it going to be?"

"What about Bailey? Will you leave a deputy outside the door?"

"Tyrone Walker will replace Wade in an hour."

"Don't leave the room until I get back," Danny said. "It shouldn't take long to clear this up."

"I won't unless I'm accompanied by Wade." When the door closed behind them, Bailey rocked back on her heels. What if he couldn't clear it up? She didn't for a second believe Danny had killed Geoffrey.

Solana coughed, and she turned around.

"I'm so sorry," Solana said.

"Yeah, me too. Are you feeling better?"

"Yes. I'm ready to go home, but first a shower." She swung her legs over the side of the bed. "Thank you for staying with me last night. Were you able to sleep?"

"I'm just glad you're better, and yes, I slept after I convinced Danny we would be safe with a deputy outside the door." He'd gone home a little after midnight when he'd realized she wouldn't sleep if he didn't. But he'd returned at daybreak.

Her phone beeped a message. A text from Joel, saying he was on his way to their room. She noticed her battery was down to 20 percent and hoped it stayed up until she returned home. She texted Danny, explaining he might not be able to reach her by phone. She helped Solana to the bathroom, and a few minutes later Joel arrived.

"Solana is better?"

"Yes, but Ben's taken Danny in for questioning."

"Questioning for what?"

She wasn't ready to tell anyone that the bullet that killed Geoffrey came from a gun Danny owned. "Something about Geoffrey Franks."

"Is there anything I can do?"

"No."

"If he's not here, you need someone to take you home."

She hadn't even thought about that. And Danny didn't leave the keys to his SUV with her. "Surely he'll be back by then."

"Well, I'll hang around, just in case."

"How about your dad? Isn't the surgery this morning?"

"Mother's there, and that's all that matters to him."

"Have you seen Maria?"

"Yes," he said. "She looks much better too. If Solana doesn't need you, why don't you go see for yourself? I'll come with you."

Bailey did want to check on Maria, and Solana didn't need her. "I think I'll take you up on that."

After she explained to Solana where she would be, Bailey asked Wade to accompany her to room 235.

Just before they reached Maria's room, Joel stopped. "I need to call Edward. I'll be in shortly."

She nodded and knocked on the door before pushing it open. "How's our patient this morning?"

Angel turned from the window with Maria in his arms. "Much better. They've taken the IV out, and we've put on the overalls you brought yesterday, except a button is missing."

Maria laid her head on his shoulder, and the button-less strap dangled on her arm. The child still looked terribly pale.

"Let me see if I can find a safety pin," Bailey said. She rummaged in her purse and held one up. "Bingo!" Maria was still as she pinned the corduroy strap. "Are you ready to go home?"

She nodded. "Can we go now?"

Bailey pretended to think. "I think you have to go downstairs for a test first."

"Where's Wade?" Angel asked as he settled Maria on the bed.

"Outside the door."

He nodded approval. "Have you had word from Danny?"

"You know about that?"

"He called."

"You know he didn't do it."

"I agree, but why did the bullet match his gun?"

She'd been trying to figure that out herself. "Someone must have taken his gun."

"Who wanted this man dead?"

"I figure his Mexico contact . . . or Jonas Gresham, the man he's supposed to testify against."

The phone on the table rang, and Angel answered it. Bailey finger-brushed Maria's hair while he talked.

"Can it not wait?" he said into the phone.

"What's the problem?"

He held up his finger. "Yes, I understand, but—"

The door opened and a porter pushed a wheelchair into the room. He glanced at the chart in his hand. "I'm looking for a Miss Maria Montoya."

Angel hung up the phone. "Can this wait? I have to go to the business office." He turned to Bailey. "They won't discharge her or Solana until someone signs to pay."

"Why don't I go down with Maria?"

He frowned. "I don't think—"

"Wade will go with us."

"I'd really like to get out of here as soon as possible." Angel glanced from Bailey to the porter, then nodded. "As long as the deputy accompanies you. I'll be there as soon as I sign the papers."

A few minutes later, Bailey and Maria rode the elevator down with Wade. "I hope all this protection is overkill."

"So do I," the deputy replied.

The porter parked them outside x-ray next to the dressing room. "Someone will be with you—"

Three loud pops cut off his words. *Gunshots.*

Wade jerked out his gun and wheeled around.

A security guard ran past as hallway doors closed.

"What's going on?" Wade yelled.

"Some idiot is firing a gun in the parking lot."

Wade looked at her as more shots rang out. "Get into the dressing room and stay quiet until I come back."

With her heart slamming against her ribs, Bailey picked up

Maria and slipped inside the small cubicle, closing the door behind them.

"Are the bad guys after us again?" Maria whispered.

"I hope not, honey. I hope not."

"Bailey! Where are you?"

"Joel?" He wasn't Danny or Angel, but he was better than nothing.

The door jerked open. "Come on," he urged. "We need to get out of here."

"But the gunfire—"

"It's in the front parking lot. My car is in the back. This way." He pulled Maria from her arms and hurried to an exit door.

"But Angel will be here soon."

"You want to wait around and see? He may be the one they're shooting at. Now, come on!"

He had Maria—she had to follow him. She ran to catch up as he disappeared out the door.

Joel waited outside. "Over here."

When she reached his car, he'd already opened the door and put Maria in the back. "Get in and stay down."

Bailey climbed in behind her and held the crying girl tight as the car careened out of the parking lot. A few minutes later, she raised up. "Where are we?"

"Almost to where we turn off to go into town."

She looked out the back of the car. A van appeared in the distance.

"Get down," Joel said. "Someone is coming up fast."

She ducked down.

"I'm scared," Maria whimpered.

She wanted to soothe the child, tell her everything was going to be fine, but her mouth wouldn't work. Instead she pulled her closer.

An impact jerked the car to the right. Bailey screamed.

The van rammed their car again. She fell forward as Joel slammed on his brakes and the car shuddered to a stop. "Be very quiet," she whispered to Maria. She ran her hands over the carpet, looking for something, anything to help defend them. *Nothing.*

A man in a ski mask jerked the driver's side door open. "Get out!"

Bailey crouched on the floorboard, shielding Maria with her body. If they were after the child, they wouldn't get her without a fight. When the door opened, Bailey sprang at the man wearing a ski mask, knocking him down. He dropped his rifle, and she scrambled for it.

Arms jerked her backward. *"Estás un fierabrás."*

Two more seconds and he would have known just what a spit-fire she was.

"You," he said to Bailey. "Face to the ground."

"Don't hurt Maria," she pleaded.

■ ■ ■

Danny paced the sheriff's office.

"Let's go over this again," Ben said. "You're claiming someone took your gun from your SUV or your office and killed Franks. If you had guns in your vehicle, why didn't you keep it locked?"

"Because it's Logan Point and no one has ever stolen anything from me. I always figured if someone wanted something from my car, it wouldn't matter if it was locked or not."

After the fact, it sounded crazy even to him. "It's the only explanation I have. I didn't kill the man. And you didn't find any gunpowder residue on my hands." Ben had to believe him. "The gun wouldn't be that hard to steal whether it was in my SUV or office. Anyone could have taken it."

"Any particular person you can think of who would know that's where you kept the gun?"

He raked his hand through his hair. "Bailey, Solana. And Angel."

He rubbed his jaw, and his day-old beard prickled his fingers. "But no way Angel killed Franks. That's why I took him out there that afternoon—to see if he or Franks reacted at all."

"So you thought it might be him."

Danny shrugged the question off. "I wanted to make sure, but neither of them knew the other. But what if either Jonas Gresham or one of his boys saw me there with the gun? The oldest boy works at the plant, and he could have taken the gun."

Ben leaned back in his chair. "That's pretty far-fetched. Who else knows you keep the gun in your car?"

"My dad . . ." Danny searched his memory. "Charlie, probably Kate, Joel, Edward Montoya—"

The sheriff sat up straight. "Why would Joel and Montoya know?"

"Ian told me he mentioned my habit of carrying a gun in the SUV in one of our meetings with them."

Ben's cell phone rang and he answered it. A second later he said, "I'm on my way."

"What's wrong?"

"There's a sniper in the hospital parking lot."

Bailey. "I'm going with you."

Ben eyed him, then nodded curtly. "Stay out of the way."

As they sped to the hospital, Danny called Angel. "What's going on there?"

"There's a shooter in the parking lot. I'm looking for Maria and Bailey now."

"Call Bailey's cell!"

"I did, and it goes to voicemail. I should never have left them."

Ice water raced through his veins. "You left them?"

"It was a trick. But Wade was with them—I thought they'd be safe."

"Is the shooter still there?"

The phone went dead. He pressed his foot to the floor mat as if that would make Ben's car go faster.

Ben's radio squawked. "The shooter is gone."

"Are you sure, Wade?"

Wade? He was supposed to be with Bailey. "They've taken her!"

The sheriff jerked his head toward him. "Bailey?"

"Wade is supposed to be with her, and he's not."

Ben spoke into the radio. "What's the 10-20 on Bailey?"

"I thought we had a sniper, and I hid her in a dressing room next to x-ray."

"Find her!"

Danny held on to the handgrip as Ben wheeled his pickup into the hospital parking lot littered with police cars. Danny jumped out before it stopped and ran to the front door. "It won't open," he yelled.

"The hospital is in lockdown. Only the ER entrance is open."

Danny took off running. X-ray was next to the ER.

25

Maria!" Frantically, Angel searched the hallway near the x-ray
room. Where were they?

Footsteps ran toward him, and he whirled around. The
deputy, Wade Hatcher. "Where's Bailey and the girl?"

"I told Bailey to stay in the dressing room. Isn't she there?"

"No. Why did you leave them?"

"We had a sniper—I had no choice."

Angel scanned the hallway. "The shooter, where is he?"

"Gone. One minute he's shooting, and the next he's disappeared, like a ghost." Hatcher jerked his cell phone off his belt
and dialed. "Ben, Bailey and the girl are gone." He listened, then
hung up. "He's on his way from the parking lot."

"How do you know the shooter isn't inside the hospital? He
could be on any floor."

"The hospital went into lockdown while he was still shooting.
All entrances except the emergency room are closed—and it was
guarded. No one could get in—only out."

Angel's heart sank. An accomplice had been inside the hospital.
And now they were gone. He searched the dressing rooms. "Where
is everyone?"

"In hiding. It's protocol."

He turned as footsteps stomped down the hallway. Danny.

"Did you find them?" Anger flashed in Danny's eyes.

Angel shook his head. "Someone has them. I'm sure of it."

"What happened?"

"We were getting ready for Maria to go to x-ray and a man called. Said he was from the business office and I needed to make arrangements for Maria and Solana's bill. Bailey said she would take Maria to x-ray—that Wade would go with her." Angel shot the deputy a dark look. "I was anxious to get home, so I agreed."

"And there was no man in the business office," Danny said.

"No. And when I heard the gunshots, I knew what had happened. They're gone, and I don't know where to start looking." He turned in a circle. People gathered in small pockets in the hallway.

"Maybe someone who works here saw them leave," Ben said. "Wade, you take the offices, and I'll interview the people in the hall."

Danny went with Wade, and Angel accompanied the sheriff. Time ticked away as, one after another, no one remembered seeing Bailey and Maria, until finally a janitor nodded.

"I saw a woman and small girl leave with this redheaded dude."

Hope sparked in Angel's chest. He looked at Ben. "It has to be Joel." He scrolled to his brother-in-law's number and called. The call went to voicemail. Next he dialed Danny's number. "They left with Joel."

"I'll be right there."

"What kind of car is he driving?" Ben took out his phone and dialed.

"Some kind of small SUV. White. It's a rental." Angel nodded as Danny approached. "What kind of car was Joel driving?"

"Toyota 4Runner."

"Did you get that, Maggie?" Ben asked. A frown creased his brow. "What?"

Angel exchanged glances with Danny. What was going on?

"We'll be waiting for the ambulance." He ended the call. "One of my deputies responded to a call about an abandoned car on Malone Road, near here. Only it wasn't abandoned. The driver was found beside it, unconscious. Driver's license identified him as Joel McDermott."

Angel swayed as blood drained from his face.

■ ■ ■

Maria sniffed, and Bailey slipped her bound hands over the child's shoulders, pulling her closer as the van hit a pothole. She wished she could see her, but the men had tied a blindfold around her head. "It's going to be all right."

Now if she could just believe what she said. *Where are you, God?*

Maria's small hands patted her cheek. "I know, Miss Bailey," she whispered.

"Can you see where we're going?"

"No talking!"

The man's gruff voice sent a shiver down Bailey's spine. She'd kept her voice down, so he must be closer than she'd thought. Maybe her suggestion would be enough for Maria to pay attention to the countryside. At least the men had not tied Maria's hands, nor had they blindfolded her.

The implication of that slammed her so hard she lost her breath. If the men weren't concerned that Maria could identify them, it meant once she was of no use to them, they planned to kill her . . . and Bailey as well.

Thoughts swirled in her head. Jumbled thoughts. There were two kidnappers, and at least one of them spoke Spanish. Probably the same men who had chased them in Chihuahua. If the men were after *her*, why hadn't they left Maria with Joel? The last thing Bailey had seen before being blindfolded was his body crumpled to the ground.

The van hit another pothole and lurched, throwing her against the side. Second bad hole they'd hit on an already rough and winding road. Bailey believed they were still in Bradford County since they hadn't been driving long, but she had no inkling of the direction they traveled. She took a deep breath, smelling the air. It had a moist, earthy smell.

They slowed, and she tried to balance as the van turned again but lost it as they went down a steep incline. She should be able to put the pieces together and figure out where the kidnappers were taking them. The vehicle was creeping now. It stopped, and light seeped through the blindfold as the back doors opened. Rough hands pulled her out into the cold air.

"No! I want Miss Bailey!"

"You will have her, so be quiet, little one."

A kind kidnapper? No, he probably didn't want a hysterical child on his hands. Bailey stumbled as someone pushed her forward, and once again rough hands caught her. A door scraped open, and a blast of heat wrapped around her. At least they wouldn't freeze to death. One of the men guided her as she counted nineteen steps before he stopped, and she heard another door open.

"Keep walking."

"What are you going to do with us?"

"No talking. Sit."

"Can you take this blindfold off?"

"Shut up and sit."

She felt in front of her and touched a nubby but soft surface. It creaked when she put her weight on it. A bed. So, they were in a cabin. She sniffed the air again. Not a cabin, since she didn't smell a fireplace. Maybe a small house or . . . a motel? If only she could see. She reached toward her eyes.

"Leave the blindfold on."

The bed moved as Maria burrowed in her lap.

"I'm thirsty."

"Oh, honey, I'm sorry." She lifted her head. "Can she have a drink of water? She's been sick."

"*Un momento.*"

"Maybe something to eat as well." This last was met with silence. She bent her head until Maria's hair tickled her chin. "Are you hungry?"

"No," Maria said, her voice small. "I want to go home."

"Soon, honey. Soon." She hoped and prayed it would be soon.

Bailey jumped as the door slammed, shaking the windows. If both of the men had left, she could take off the blindfold. "Is anyone here?"

"Quiet!"

■ ■ ■

El Jefe stared at the number flashing on his cell phone. The insolence of the men infuriated him. Who did they think they were, calling *him*? He made the calls, not them. Finally the phone ceased ringing. Seconds later, a message dinged.

"*We have both the girl and the woman, but the plan has changed. Answer your phone.*"

The phone rang again. El Jefe's hands curled into fists as anger swelled his chest. On the fourth ring, he answered. "Yes?"

"It is foolish to let an opportunity pass. We're asking ten million for the Montoya girl."

"Who authorized this?" he asked through clenched teeth.

"The board."

"I see." And he did. A chill shivered through him. He pictured each member of the board, trying to decide which one was his Judas. Maybe they all were.

"This is a mistake. Get rid of the Adams woman."

"The mistake would be in not taking advantage of the situation, and we will dispose of the woman when we no longer need her to care for the girl."

The line went dead.

26

anny drew a slow, steady breath as the paramedics opened the bay doors on the ambulance and unloaded a dazed-looking Joel. Probably wouldn't do to pound sense into him at this point. But what was he thinking, taking Maria and Bailey out of the hospital? Judging by the look on his face, Angel felt the same way. Angel took a step toward the ambulance, and Danny grabbed his arm. "Let Ben talk to him first. He can probably get more out of him."

"I don't know . . ."

They followed as the glass doors slid open, and the medics pushed the gurney into the ER. Ben turned around, stopping them. "They won't let us back there until he's been assessed. And afterward probably only two will be allowed, so you need to decide which one of you is going back."

"Maybe you need to talk to someone about making an exception. I can't speak for Angel, but *I'm* getting answers from Joel."

"Same here," Angel said, planting his feet wide.

"I'll see what I can do." He turned and walked to the receptionist desk. "I'd like to talk to Dr. Somerall."

"Sheriff Logan!" The receptionist smiled at him. "I'll see if I can find your wife." She talked with someone on the phone, then motioned Ben through the doors to the patients' rooms.

Danny exchanged glances with Angel. "You're Joel's brother-in-law. See if family can see him."

A tight smile formed on Angel's lips, and they approached the desk. "May I see Joel McDermott? He's my wife's brother."

She glanced at the monitor. "Not yet. He's being assessed. I'll let you know as soon as you can go back."

"Thank you." He gave Danny an "I tried" shrug.

Danny's cell phone rang, and his heart sank. Kate. He answered.

"What's going on? I heard on the scanner there was a shooter at the hospital. And Solana called to see if Bailey and Maria were home."

"The shooter is gone . . ." He took a breath.

"What are you not telling me?"

"Maria and Bailey are too."

"What do you mean?"

"They're missing." The metal doors to the ER opened, and Ben hurried through them. "Let me call you back."

"Leigh is the ER doctor on duty today. She said all three of us can talk to him as long as everything stays stable."

They followed Ben back through the doors. "Is he hurt?" Angel asked.

"Concussion where the men hit him over the head. He said there were two of them." They turned a corner, and Joel was in the room at the end of the corridor.

They entered the room, and Danny spoke to Ben's wife as she wrote on Joel's chart. She nodded and said, "Five minutes, gentlemen."

"Why did you take them out of the hospital?" Angel leaned toward Joel, his voice rising with each word.

Danny pulled him back as the heart monitor jumped over a hundred. "Not now. Let Ben question him, then we can ask anything he misses."

Angel shook his hand off. "I want to know where my girl is."

Joel rolled his lips in. "I don't know. I'd tell you if I did."

"Tell me again what happened," Ben said. "Why *did* you leave with them?"

Joel refused to look at either Danny or Angel but kept his eyes on Ben. "I heard the gunshots and thought the gunman might be after Bailey or Maria, and when I found them in hiding, it . . . it just seemed like the thing to do. Get them away from the danger. I didn't know the gunmen would come after us."

"Can you describe them? Or their vehicle?"

"Shorter than me. They wore ski masks, and the only skin I saw was around their eyes. Almost black eyes, tanned skin, and they spoke with a Mexican accent. They were in a blue van."

Danny's hands curled into fists. "What did they say?"

Joel dropped his gaze to the bed.

Angel grabbed him by the shirt. "Answer him!"

"They want ten million dollars for Maria." He spat the words out, then sank into the bed.

"Ten million?" Angel's mouth slackened.

Danny's breath hitched. "What about Bailey?"

Joel refused to look at him. Finally he spoke. "I'm pretty sure they'll keep her alive to take care of Maria."

Danny's knees almost buckled. Then he'd have to find her before the ransom was paid. "Where do they expect you to come up with that kind of money?"

"I . . . I have an insurance policy on Maria that will pay in case of kidnapping." Joel licked his lips. "Anyone with money in Mexico has a policy. I even have one on me. But we have to pay the money up front."

"Did they indicate how they'll contact you?" Ben asked.

"I had to give them my cell phone number. They said they would call tonight."

Leigh stuck her head in the doorway. "Time's up. He's going

to have an MRI to make sure there are no blood clots. You can go with him, Ben." She eyed Danny and Angel. "But not you two."

"Can we wait here in his room?" Angel asked. "He is my brother-in-law."

"All right, just don't get in the way."

Angel paced the small room after they left. "I don't have the ten million dollars up front."

"Why does Joel have insurance on Maria?"

He paused in his pacing. "Because kidnapping is so prevalent in the world, particularly Mexico and South America. I've even heard of a family who was express kidnapped."

"What do you mean, express kidnapped?"

"This family was held in their home while the father was driven to an ATM and forced to withdraw money. He was left unconscious on the side of the road, but his family was all right. He survived. Others are not so lucky, even if the ransom is paid." He took out his wallet and extracted a card.

"What are you doing?"

Angel sighed. "Calling my uncle. I don't know anyone else who might have five million dollars lying around."

"But I thought it was ten million."

"The cartel always asks for more than they get. Then the negotiations begin." Angel dialed the number on the card. "Edward, Maria has been kidnapped and the asking price is ten million." He listened, then spoke again. "At the hospital. In the emergency room with Joel. Call me when you get here, and I'll come out and get you."

Danny leaned against the wall. Angel and Joel were talking about ransom for Maria. Why didn't the cartel want a ransom for Bailey?

■ ■ ■

Angel checked his watch for the hundredth time. Three hours after leaving the hospital with Joel, and the kidnappers had not contacted his brother-in-law. What were they waiting for?

Inactivity grew the dread filling Angel's mind as he leaned against the wall in Kate's living room. The sheriff had decided they would wait for the call at the bed-and-breakfast. Angel glanced at Joel, who sat in a wingback chair with his eyes closed. Solana rested upstairs. He hoped Maria was not as weak as Solana—that would be something else to worry about.

Behind him, a tech monitored the machine that everyone hoped would locate where the call originated from when it came in. Ben had called in his friend, FBI agent Eric Raines, and the living room looked like a command center. Angel almost welcomed the call that was sure to come.

But what if it didn't? What if the kidnappers knew the FBI had been called in and . . . He couldn't go there.

"What's taking so long for them to call?" Danny said.

It was obvious he felt the same pressure Angel did.

"They are stretching your nerves," Edward replied. "They want to make you more willing to pay their asking price."

Danny stopped pacing. "I don't understand what you mean by 'asking price.'"

"The kidnappers expect to negotiate," Eric said. The FBI agent shook his head. "In Mexico it's become nothing more than a business transaction with negotiators who are trained in mediating these situations."

"No one goes to the police?"

Angel snorted. "Very often the police are in on the kidnapping."

"And even if they're not, families fear the Federals might bungle the rescue effort," Joel said, speaking for the first time.

Not something Angel wanted to consider. The room froze as Joel's phone rang.

"Be sure to tell the person you're not paying until you talk to both of them," Ben said.

Joel waited until the tech indicated he should answer. "Hello?"

"I see you brought in the FBI. That will cost you." A man's voice, slightly accented, filled the quiet room. Angel leaned forward. He'd hoped he might recognize the voice, but he should have known better.

"What did you expect," Joel said. The tech held up a note. *Not a cell phone.* Then he made a rolling motion with his finger for Joel to keep the conversation going. "You left me on the side of the road, and someone called the cops."

"Fifteen million now. In hundreds. I'll call back with the drop-off location."

"It takes time to get that much money together."

"You have until eight o'clock in the morning. Be ready then."

"Wait! I'm not paying anything until I know Maria and Bailey are safe. I want to talk to them."

Silence filled the room, broken only by the clock chiming in the hallway.

The tech swore. "He hung up."

"Did you get the location of the call?" Eric demanded.

"Can you get it that fast?" Danny asked.

"In the digital age, it's almost immediate unless it's a throwaway cell phone." Eric turned to the tech. "Location?"

"Yeah, he used a public phone. I'm getting the location now. It's at a Walmart here in Logan Point."

"Aw, great. There's at least five hundred people there right now," Ben said as he dialed his phone. "Maggie, dispatch deputies to the pay phone at Walmart. I'll be there in five minutes." He listened. "I don't know—didn't even know there was one there. Tell whoever gets there first to ask the manager the location of the phone."

Danny turned to the FBI agent. "Do you think he'll call back?"

"I'm sure he will. We have to hold out to talk to the hostages." He looked at Joel and Edward. "Did either of you recognize the voice?"

Edward shook his head. "It did not seem disguised, either."

"It wasn't the man who hit me," Joel said. "He had a stronger accent."

"How about the money," Angel said. "When will it be delivered?"

Joel shifted his eyes away from him. Angel turned to Edward. "It *is* being delivered?"

■■■

Why, God? Bailey moved from her cramped position on the bed. In the pitch-dark it was hard to judge time passing, but she'd spent what seemed like hours asking God to help them.

Ask and it will be given to you.

How many times did she have to ask? What had her prayers gotten her so far? Guilt swept over her. The men had removed the blindfold. And she had one hand free. Yeah, but the other one was handcuffed to the head of the metal frame, and the room was pitch-black. She peered into the blackness, not even able to see her free hand.

It was impossible to tell what kind of room they were in. She'd heard cars coming and going, so they weren't out in the middle of nowhere. The room smelled musty, like old cigarette smoke, but there was another scent . . . not exactly fishy, but . . . *damp* was the only word that came to mind.

Where are you, God?

Never will I leave you . . .

Between what happened to Elena and the situation she and Maria were in, Bailey was having a little trouble with that verse right now. She sucked in a deep breath. Time to do something.

Beside her Maria stirred. The child had slept for a couple of hours at least. "I'm thirsty," she murmured.

With her free hand, she smoothed Maria's hair. "I know."

"Can I have a drink of water?"

Surely the men would give her that. "Hey!" she yelled, trying to get their attention.

Bailey didn't know anyplace could be so dark. There must be blackout curtains on the windows. Or they were in the middle of the woods where there was no light. No, she hadn't walked that far from the car. And the surface had been rocky, like gravel. Why didn't they answer? "Hey!" she called again.

Silence.

"Anybody here?" Had they gone off and left them? She nudged Maria. "I'm going to move, so don't be scared. Maybe there's a light I can turn on." She felt the air beside her and bumped her hand on a corner of something. A table, maybe? She moved her hand over the top. Nothing there. She tried standing up, and the handcuffs cut into her wrist. "Ow!"

"Miss Bailey, I'm scared."

"It's okay," she said. "I pinched my arm." At least the handcuffs allowed for some slack. "Do you think you can get off the bed?"

"Huh-uh. I mean, no, ma'am."

"What if I hold your hand?" Bailey bent over the bed, searching for Maria. A slight rustling, then they connected. Maria's small fingers were warm in her palm. *Please don't let her fever come back.* She had to find a way out of this room. "Come on, Maria."

The bed creaked, and she felt Maria slide down beside her to the floor. "Listen to me, honey. It's dark, but we're going to see if we can find a lamp in here. Okay?"

"Yes, ma'am."

"You're so brave." *Please, God, help us here.* "Hold on to my hand and walk around. See if you can feel a table or a lamp."

Bailey stretched as far as the handcuffs would allow as Maria inched away from her.

"I'm scared. What if those men come back?"

Then we deal with it. But she couldn't tell Maria that. "God's going to help us."

"Will he really?"

"Yes." She willed herself to believe her words. She repeated it with more conviction.

Maria moved again, stretching Bailey's arm. Suddenly, the child dropped her hand. "Where are you?" Bailey asked. "What are you doing?"

"God whispered and told me to go farther."

Bailey held her breath. The child had more faith than she did.

"Miss Bailey, I found—"

Light flooded the area, and Bailey blinked against the brightness until she could see Maria standing in the corner of the room, a wide grin on her face. "Good job, sweetheart."

"I did it!"

"Yes, you did. I'm proud of you." She swept her gaze around the small room. A metal door near Maria. Another door on the other side of the bed. Wood paneling. Built-in dresser. Rustic and very dated. She'd been right—they were in a motel room, but which motel? "Can you look out the window and tell me what you see?"

Maria moved the curtain, and Bailey's heart sank. They'd been blacked out.

"I can't see anything."

"That's okay. Look around for a notepad or something with writing on it." She didn't know why it was so important to her to know where they were. Who would she tell? She scanned the room, looking for anything that would help them escape. A bathroom. The dresser. The bed and lamp. That was it.

A motor purred to a stop, and doors slammed.

"Turn the lamp off, and come to the bed. Quickly." At least with the windows blacked out, the men couldn't tell they had a light on.

Bailey swept her gaze around the room once more before the room went dark. She squinted at a small photo on the wall before the picture disappeared in the dark. Seconds later Maria wrapped her arms around Bailey's legs, and she helped the child onto the bed. "Let's pretend we're asleep."

A lock clicked, and a sliver of light slid into the room when the door opened.

"Here are hamburgers and fries for you to eat."

The odor of onions and meat turned Bailey's stomach. She raised up, peering at the dark figure. "Maria had food poisoning. A hamburger will make her throw up."

"Then she will do without."

"Please, can you get her chicken noodle soup or gelatin? The child needs something in her stomach. And she needs water."

With a grunt, he closed the door behind him, then in a minute it opened again. He gave Maria the water, then disappeared back into the other room.

"Are you thirsty?" Bailey asked Maria.

"Mm-huh."

"Can you get the bottle cap off?" She feared Maria becoming dehydrated.

"You do it."

She thrust the bottle in Bailey's hand.

She broke the seal and let Maria drink first. When Maria finished, Bailey took a sip.

Maria climbed back into bed. "Would you tell me a story?"

Bailey stroked her back. "What story would you like for me to tell you?"

"The one about the eagle and the chickens."

"I don't believe I know that one. Why don't you tell it to me."

"Okay. Then you'll tell me one?"

"Yes."

"Once upon a time, there was an eagle's nest high in the—"

"What did you say, Maria?"

"I said there was an eagle's nest. Is something wrong?"

"No. I'm sorry I interrupted you. Tell me your story." Her mind whirled as it all came together . . . *Eagle's nest*. The photo had been of an eagle. The dated furniture, the wood paneling, the dampness . . . they were at the Eagle's Nest Motel.

27

O w!" Bailey groaned as the handcuffs dug into her wrist.

"Miss Bailey, what's wrong?" Maria's voice sounded weak.

"Everything is fine," she said, trying to comfort Maria. Like anything would ever be fine again. She really needed to get some food in the child. Bailey sucked her finger where she'd pricked it with the safety pin from Maria's overalls. With darkness their constant companion, she had to do something or fall prey to despair. Her attempts to pick the lock on the handcuffs had netted her nothing but sore fingers from missing the keyhole and sticking herself.

"Can we go home?"

"Not yet, honey. But they're going to let us go soon."

Her knowledge of kidnapping was limited to television shows, but wasn't that what usually happened? The families paid the ransom, and the victims were released. She refused to let her mind go to the stories she'd heard about the victim being killed . . . or the fact that Maria could give a general description of the men.

What were the odds of two sisters being the victims of kidnappers almost three years apart, anyway? Even two totally different types of kidnapping. Robyn's kidnapper had been crazy and didn't demand a ransom, unlike the men who held her and Maria. She felt for the keyhole in the cuffs again, hating the dark.

The only time she'd experienced dark like this was on a moonless night on the lake, and she'd been safe with Danny. Her heart ached for him. He must be going crazy, probably blaming himself. And her mother and daddy. What were they going through?

She had to get her thoughts away from home. Think about those TV programs. Sometimes the victims escaped . . . Wait. She pulled her bottom lip through her teeth. Didn't the families of the person kidnapped always demand to talk to the victim? To make sure they were still alive before they paid the ransom?

Bailey had lain awake all night, trying to come up with some way to let Danny know where they were, and now she had it. Danny and Angel would insist on talking to her before they paid any ransom money. When that happened, she wanted to be ready.

The door flew open. She blinked against the bright light that flooded the room and caught a glimpse of the man keeping them captive. An old man? No, he wore some sort of mask and cowboy outfit. Even so, he couldn't hide how tall he was.

"Hold this and look up." He thrust a newspaper into her hands.

She stared at the paper. The kidnappers were going to use it to prove they were still alive. There would be no phone call. She tried to push the paper away, and he stepped closer, towering over them. "Do as I say, or the child will suffer."

"No! Don't hurt her." She tried to shield Maria with her body. "I'll do what you say, just leave her alone."

With a sinking heart, she held the paper up, and a flash of light blinded her as he took their picture. Seconds later, he was gone and they were plunged into darkness again. She yanked on the handcuff, and pain shot up her arm. They were stuck here, and it'd take a miracle to get them out.

■ ■ ■

Danny stepped out on the front porch as the first rays of the sunrise streaked across the sky like red welts. He breathed deeply, but other than filling his lungs, the cold air did nothing to clear the fog brought on by a sleepless night. What he wouldn't give for a run right now. But he couldn't leave. The kidnappers might call again.

Tires crunched on the drive, and he turned as a sixties-model Ford pickup eased past the house. Charlie. Bailey's dad was taking this hard. The door opened, and Kate joined him. "Where's Charlie going?"

She held out a steaming cup of coffee. "He had to get out, said if he stayed around here all day, he'd go crazy. I told him to go, otherwise it'd be us he drove crazy."

Danny knew how he felt. "Thanks," he said and took the mug. "How's Solana this morning?"

"Weak. I can't get her to eat. Angel is upstairs now trying to get cream of wheat down her."

They stood quietly facing the sun until Kate sighed. "It's a beautiful Sunday morning for so many things to be wrong."

He grunted. Nothing would be beautiful until Bailey and Maria returned safe and sound.

The sun broke over the horizon, scattering the earlier red and purple streaks. "How can you stand here so calmly? Aren't you worried about her?"

"Of course I'm worried, but I know God is in control. He loves my daughter even more than I do, and that gives me peace."

"So you think we'll save them?"

"I didn't say that. I pray we do, but God's the only one with that answer." She shivered and rubbed her arms. "I better get breakfast started."

After Kate left, Danny sipped his coffee. It was hard to understand how Kate could trust God so much. It seemed like she was just letting God off the hook—even if this turned out bad, God didn't get the blame.

■ ■ ■

At 7:55, eight pairs of eyes stared at Joel's phone on the coffee table as though that would make it ring. Edward had arrived not long after Ben. Raines and the tech had spent the night in Kate's living room in case another call came in. Danny flexed his fingers. What if the man didn't call back? He certainly hadn't called and let them talk to Maria or Bailey. He flinched as an alert sounded on the phone. "What's that?"

"An email." Joel picked up the phone and tapped the message. His eyes widened. "It's a picture of Bailey and Maria with today's paper."

"He's not going to let us talk to them," the FBI agent said. "But maybe this will buy more time."

Danny didn't see how that helped. "What do you mean?"

The room stilled as Joel's phone rang.

"Answer it and tell him the picture looks like it's been photoshopped. Insist on talking to Maria and Bailey."

Joel nodded and pressed the answer button. "Hello."

"Do you have the money?"

"I haven't talked to Bailey and Maria. No money until I do."

"I emailed you a photograph."

"Yeah, a picture that's been doctored. If you want me to pay, I have to talk with them first."

"In two hours I will call back, and you can talk. Then the money. Do not think you can negotiate this business transaction—I expect the full amount at that time."

Joel looked at the phone. "Did he hang up?"

"Yeah."

"Where was he?" Ben asked.

"Another pay phone at the corner of Polk and Linden."

Ben relayed the location to his deputies, then shook his head. "Not that he'll still be there. And it'll probably be just like Walmart and no security camera anywhere near."

Eric spread a city map out on the coffee table. "Bradford County has twenty pay phones in Logan Point and ten in the county. I've marked all their locations—the city in red and the county in blue. How many deputies do you have available?"

"Ten, eleven counting me."

"We need you here. Show me which of these locations would be the best place for him to make the call."

Ben leaned over the map while Angel and Danny looked over his shoulder. Danny tried to picture the area around each circle. Most of the phones were in congested areas that the kidnapper would avoid for fear Bailey would be recognized. The best location was the one he'd just called from, and he wouldn't use it again. "He's called twice and both times from a public city phone. Why do you suppose he hasn't used one out in the county?"

"Not as many people, and perhaps he feared he'd stand out," Angel said. He shifted his attention to his uncle. "When will the money arrive?"

"By noon. It's coming from a bank in Memphis." Edward stood and rolled his shoulders. "But I hope we find them first. Even the bank in Memphis didn't have a million dollars in cash available."

"How much did you get?" Danny said.

"Half a mil," Joel said.

Danny tapped his foot on the floor. Something was different about Joel this morning. "How's your dad?" he asked.

Joel startled, and the look on his face made Danny think it was the first time the man had thought about his father.

"I talked to Mom last night when he was still on a ventilator. He was stable. I haven't called today."

That was understandable, but Danny doubted he could be so disconnected if it was his dad. But then, he'd never seen Joel excited about much of anything. Still, something nagged at the back of his mind . . . but maybe it wasn't Joel that was bothering him.

Perhaps something about the call . . . He'd have to think about it. "Did you get a fix on where the photo came from?"

"Yeah," the tech replied. "The McDonald's here in Logan Point. All he had to do was boot up his computer in the parking lot and send it. Then it's about a five-minute drive to the pay phone."

"And once again," Ben said, "no one saw anything."

"Any fingerprints on the phone at Walmart?" Danny asked.

"Only about a hundred on yesterday's. Evidently, no one cleans those phones. Ever," Ben said.

"I wonder why he doesn't use a throwaway phone," Angel said.

"I don't know." Ben looked to Raines. "Any thoughts on that?"

"Who knows what's going on in his mind. Could've figured pay phones would catch us by surprise."

Angel nodded but didn't seem satisfied. Danny caught Angel's eye and barely lifted an eyebrow before grabbing his coat. "I need some fresh air. I'm going out to the barn to see if Charlie has come back."

"I can use some exercise. I'll come with you," Angel said.

Outside, the wind cut through his jacket, and he pulled it closer. "You wanted to talk?"

"Yeah." They reached the barn, and Danny looked around for Charlie's pickup. "I wonder why Charlie hasn't come back?"

"Do you know where he went?"

"No. I'm sure he'll be back soon." He turned to Angel. "Does anything seem odd to you about the ransom demand?"

"The whole thing has been odd. What's bothering you about it?"

"I don't know. Something's off, but I don't know what. My mind keeps going back to the phone call. Like I should be catching something." He replayed the call in his mind. "That's it!"

"What?"

"The caller said something about not negotiating a business transaction and expecting the full amount. Does that sound familiar?"

"I'm not sure."

"Raines said almost the same thing yesterday. It's like the kidnappers can hear what we're saying. Maybe there's a bug at the house."

"Or someone's feeding them information."

■ ■ ■

Bailey tried not to disturb Maria as she slept. The child's fever had returned, and if they didn't get out of this damp room . . . She didn't want to think about what might happen. At least they'd brought in some oatmeal and left the light on, and she'd fed her a few bites.

While the constant light wasn't as bad as the darkness, she still couldn't tell what time of the day or night it was or how long they'd been captive. Sometime between the taking of the photo and when she realized Maria's fever had returned, Bailey had given up asking God to send someone to rescue them. She couldn't control whether help came or not. That was up to God. It surprised her how freeing that realization was.

It had taken coming to the end of her rope to understand that she wasn't in control. He was. And she didn't believe that God had sent Danny to rescue them last week only to let them die today.

Another thing she believed—Danny would not let Joel or Edward hand over any amount of money without hearing her voice or Maria's. She would get the opportunity to talk to her family, so she had to be ready to send them a message.

The sound of a scuffle outside the motel jerked her straight up. Hope soared until the door opened and one of the men entered, carrying something over his shoulder. Without ceremony, he dumped her father on the floor. Maria grabbed Bailey and clung to her.

"Daddy!" Bailey stared at blood oozing down the back of his head. "What did you do to him?"

"The fool was snooping around outside. He's lucky I didn't shoot him."

She scrambled off the bed and stretched as far as the cuffs would let her, but she couldn't reach him. "Please unlock these so I can help him."

"No."

This wasn't the same man who took the picture. This one wore a full gray beard and sunglasses. She widened her eyes, pleading. "Then take them off so I can go to the bathroom."

The sunglasses obscured his eyes, so she couldn't tell if he was softening or not. Then he motioned her to move to the other side of the bed. "I will unlock them for now. When the old man comes to, you better convince him to cooperate unless you want to see him dead."

"I will. He won't bother you, I promise."

He pulled a key from his pocket and unlocked the cuffs. "I'll be back in five minutes. Don't get any bright ideas of trying to escape—I'll be right outside the room."

As soon as the door closed behind him, Bailey ran to her father. He was breathing. Then she checked on Maria. The child was burning up. "Stay here and rest," she said softly.

"Is Uncle Charlie going to be okay?"

"Yes. I'm going into the bathroom, and I'll be right back. Okay?"

Bailey took care of business, then found three washcloths and soaked them in cold water and wrung them out. She put the first one on Maria. "This should make you feel better." She checked the front door. Nailed shut. No surprise there, but she'd had to see. She kneeled beside her dad and cradled his head in her lap and wiped the blood from his hair. She laid the other cloth across his forehead. Slowly, he began to come around.

He groaned. "What hit me?"

"I don't know. Probably the butt of a gun. Does anyone know you're here?"

He blinked open his eyes. "No. I was just following a hunch."

"If you can sit up, I'll help you get to the bed."

He raised up and pressed his hand against his eyes. "The room is moving."

"Sit there a minute. Do you have your cell phone with you?"

He felt his pocket. "Whoever coldcocked me must have taken it." He winced. "Along with my .38."

She squeezed his shoulder. Her hero. She'd rarely seen him when she was a small child since he'd spent so much time at sea as a merchant seaman. But he was here for her now. "Let's see if you can make it to the bed."

He stood on shaky legs, then took a deep breath. "I can do it."

She turned as the side door opened and both men came into the room wearing the same disguises as earlier.

"You." The man in the old geezer mask pointed at her. "Over here."

When she hesitated, he shifted his gaze to Maria. "Right now or I'll take the girl."

Bailey moved to where he pointed.

The one with whiskers clamped one end of the cuffs on her wrist and the other on his. "We're going to take a little trip."

"Maria?"

"She stays here with the old man." He turned to her dad. "And if you try to escape, I'll kill this one," he said, jerking his head toward Bailey. "Got it?"

"Yeah," Charlie growled.

"Good." Whiskers handed her a black sleep mask. "Put this on."

"But I won't be able to see."

"That's the point."

Once she had the sleep mask in place, he jerked her arm. "This way."

Half stumbling, she went where he led. The sleep mask slipped as they stepped outside the motel, allowing Bailey to see peripheral objects. Her heart sank. Bars covered all the windows. A car door creaked opened, and Whiskers put his hand on her head. "Get in the car."

Bailey felt for the seat, then half climbed and half fell into what she decided was the backseat. The car lurched forward, jerking her back, then made a sharp turn. She didn't know how long they were driving before the car made another turn and stopped.

One of the kidnappers spoke to her. "In a minute, I will hand you a phone. Tell the person on the other end you and the girl are all right. Tell them to pay the money. That's all you say. Got it?"

She nodded and heard the sound of numbers being pressed.

"Hello?"

Bailey recognized Joel's voice through the speaker on the phone. "I have the woman." Whiskers nudged her. "Speak."

"Joel?" she said. "Maria has a fever."

Whiskers nudged her again.

"Pay them the money."

"I don't know what kind of trick you're trying to pull, but this isn't Bailey," he said.

"It is the woman," Geezer insisted.

There was a pause, then Joel said, "If this is Bailey, tell me who Danny is."

"Go ahead," Geezer said.

"Danny is my fiancé. Tell him not to stop reading his Bible, and if this goes bad, Job 39 will comfort him."

"That's enough. I will call you in two hours with instructions on the exchange."

Bailey sank back against the seat. Now it was up to Danny.

28

"Will the money be here in two hours?" Danny had not seen any activity that indicated money would be delivered to the house.

Joel shook his head. "We don't need it yet and don't even know how much we'll need. When he calls back, I'll offer $250,000."

"Are you trying to get them killed?" Angel demanded. "That amount will just make them mad."

Edward stood from where he'd been sitting on the couch. "They will expect a low counter offer."

"Not that low. And what about Maria—Bailey said she was running a fever again. We need to speed this up."

"We can only go as fast as they allow," Joel retorted.

"Arguing will get us nowhere," Ben said. He turned to the tech. "Did the call come from a pay phone again?"

"Cell phone. I'm triangulating the coordinates now." He looked up. "Got it." He walked to the map. "It pinged off this cell tower."

Ben examined the map. "He drove over the state line it looks like. Have you pinged it again?"

"Yeah. It hasn't moved."

"Probably decided to use a throwaway this time. I'll call the sheriff over there and have his deputies search for it." He turned to Danny. "What do you think Bailey meant by the reference to Job 39?"

"I assume she was trying to tell us where she's being held," Danny said. He grabbed the Bible on the end table. "Where's Job?" he asked Kate.

She took the Bible and flipped almost to the middle. "I told her to read Job earlier this week," she said to Danny.

"I have it up on my computer screen," the tech said. "There are thirty verses here."

Eric Raines and Ben gathered around the computer. "I wish she'd pinpointed it with a verse, but that probably would have gotten her killed."

"Do you have another Bible, Kate?" Joel asked.

"Every bedroom has one," she replied. "I'll take this one into the kitchen and see if I can understand what she's trying to tell us."

For the next few minutes, the house grew quiet as everyone pored over Bibles. Danny motioned for Angel to follow him into the kitchen. He sat down beside Kate. "Have you found anything yet?"

"I've scanned the verses, and nothing jumps out. The message was to you, so it's probably something only you will put together."

Danny glanced at Angel, then back to Kate.

"What's going on?" she said.

He lowered his voice. "I don't trust everyone in the house. If you think you get the message Bailey is trying to send, tell me first."

She held his gaze. "I assume it's Joel and Edward you don't trust."

He nodded.

"Something about this whole deal is wrong," Angel said.

Danny worried the watch on his arm. "Our first priority is getting our girls—"

"But if possible, we'd like to get whoever is responsible for taking them too." Angel's hands curled into fists. "And those men who took them are only acting under orders from someone else."

Kate frowned. "Surely it isn't Maria's uncles."

"I hope not," Danny said.

Angel folded his arms over his chest. "Me too. I'd hate to have to kill one of them."

Danny stiffened as he realized Ben hadn't returned his gun. He turned to Angel. "Do you have your gun?"

He patted his ankle. "Yes, Logan returned it to me."

"He still has mine. Do you have another?"

"Not with me."

Kate stood. "Charlie has a .38 revolver. I'll get it."

While she was gone, Danny read Job 39. He grabbed a notepad Kate had on the table and scribbled notes as he read. *Wild animals, wilderness, city, pasture* . . . He looked up when Kate returned, her face pale. "What's wrong?"

"His gun is gone." She glanced toward the door. "And he always tells me where he's going, but he didn't this morning . . . I thought he'd be back by now or at least called."

"Do you think he went looking for Bailey and Maria?" Danny hoped not.

She rubbed her hands together. Suddenly, her eyes widened. "He said something last night before we went to bed about there being only a few places in Logan Point where you could hide someone."

"He didn't mention any of the places?"

"No." She picked up her phone and dialed it. After half a minute, she hung up. "He doesn't answer. I should have realized he'd go looking for them. I need to tell Ben."

He and Angel followed her into the living room.

"Charlie went looking for them, and he hasn't come back," Kate told Ben.

"What do you mean, he went looking for them? Why didn't you tell me?" Ben said.

"I just put it together when I realized he'd been gone all morning. His gun is gone too."

"Oh, great." Ben groaned. "Have you called him?"

"Yes, and he doesn't—" Kate turned as the doorbell rang. "Maybe he forgot his key and that's him."

Danny followed her to the door. No, it was Sergeant Chavez. Kate's shoulders slumped as she opened the door. "Come in, everyone is in the living room."

"Good morning, " Chavez said as he scanned the room. "I heard about the abduction."

"Any word on who killed Bailey's friend?"

A frown turned the corners of the sergeant's mouth down. "The Calatrava, on orders from the priest. He's disappeared. Have you had a ransom demand?"

"Started out at ten million, and they got mad and raised it to fifteen," Joel said. "Maria is insured for five against kidnapping."

Chavez whistled. "Either one is a lot of money. Have you countered?"

"That's next."

Danny couldn't believe how casually the men talked about the situation.

"I've had experience back in Mexico with negotiations, if you would like my help."

Ben looked at Raines, then Joel and Edward. "I, for one, would like the sergeant's help."

Raines stuck out his hand. "Eric Raines, FBI."

Chavez shook hands with him. "It's been my experience that they will counter your offer with another one, usually half of what they asked for first before settling for about a quarter." He shifted his gaze to Angel. "In the cases I've handled, the victims have been returned unharmed."

"Good."

Danny leaned forward. "So you think Maria is the focus of the kidnappers and not Bailey?"

"Have they asked for a ransom for Bailey?"

"No," Danny said.

"If she was the focus, they would have simply killed her. She's alive because they need her to take care of Maria."

Danny would like to believe that, but his gut warned him there was more to the kidnapping than what was on the surface. But why did he feel that way? Pinning that down was a lot like squeezing Jell-O. Just when he thought he had a lead, it slipped away. "I'm going back to the kitchen to read Job 39 again."

When Angel started to follow, Chavez asked to have a word with him. Angel glanced at Danny.

"I'll let you know if I discover anything," Danny said.

In the kitchen, Danny looked at his notes, and nothing jumped out at him. He picked up the Bible and a pencil and started reading, jotting down the key words of each verse. *Wild ox, bind with ropes.* He paused at that one. He hoped and prayed Bailey wasn't bound with ropes. *Ostrich, wisdom, horse and rider, valley, strength, sword, hawk, south, eagle, nest, prey—*

Kate stuck her head in the doorway. "They've called again!"

■ ■ ■

"Through here." The guttural voice guided Bailey.

She shuffled her feet, trying not to trip over anything. *Please don't let them cuff me again.* She lifted up the silent prayer. If her hands were free, she and her dad could surely figure how to get out of the room without getting caught. When the side door closed behind her, Bailey removed the sunglasses and sleep mask and searched for Maria and her dad.

Maria ran to her. "Miss Bailey! You came back."

She bent over and wrapped her arms around the girl. Still hot. "How do you feel?"

"Sleepy. Uncle Charlie has been telling me stories about little girls everywhere in the world."

Bailey remembered some of those stories. "Thanks, Daddy."

"For what? Getting myself caught?"

She hugged him. "No, for being so special. For keeping Maria from being worried."

"Were you able—"

She put her finger to her lips. For all she knew, bugs were hidden in the room. "Yes, I was able to tell them Maria had a fever."

"The poor little tyke needs some medicine."

"I know." She picked Maria up and settled her in bed. "Why don't we rest awhile?"

"But I didn't tell you what else we've been doing."

"You did other things?" She looked at her dad, and a pleased smile spread across his face. "What have you two been up to?"

Maria hunched her shoulders and concentrated. "Alk-ing-tay inway ig—" She looked at Charlie. "You tell her."

"I've eenbay eachingtay erhay igpay atinlay."

Pig latin? She threw her arms around his neck. "That's awesome! But how? She's only four."

"Maria is one smart cookie. So, you remember?"

"Yes." At least now they could talk without worrying that they were being bugged. She seriously doubted that the men in the other room had *ever* learned pig latin or even knew what it was.

"Can Uncle Charlie teach me some more ig-pay at—" She frowned and looked to Charlie.

"Atin-lay," he finished for her.

"How about if he tells you a story, and when we get home, he can do the other? Does that sound good?" When Maria nodded, she moved so her dad could sit on the bed. In the bathroom, she ran cold water over Maria's washcloth and wrung it out, then placed it on the child's forehead. "What day is it?" she asked her dad.

"Sunday."

"Just Sunday?" Only one day since they'd been taken? It seemed a week since Saturday morning. Maria's eyes drooped, and Bailey nudged her dad, then in pig latin said, "We'll talk as soon as Maria goes to sleep."

Once Maria was asleep, Bailey kept her voice low and, continuing in pig latin, asked her dad if he'd found a way out of the room.

He answered her in the same way. "If they leave us alone again, we can take the bed apart and use the rails as weapons."

She shook her head. "Too dangerous—they have guns. And we can't break out through the windows."

"Yeah, I saw the bars. There has to be a way out of here."

Suddenly the door opened, and Whiskers entered the room. "I don't want to hear any more talking. You got that?"

Bailey nodded. So there *were* bugs in the room.

■■■

Joel paced the room. This thing was spiraling out of control. No one ever mentioned he would be the one to drop the money. That had been the last demand. Joel was to bring a hundred grand —they called it good faith money—to Walmart and wait at the pay phone for further instructions. If anyone followed him, Bailey and Maria would be killed.

"The courier is here," Angel said.

Joel hurried to the door and signed for the box. Edward had decided to withdraw two hundred and fifty thousand in case more was needed. He examined the package, surprised it was such a small box.

"Okay, here's the plan," the FBI agent said as he handed him a small transmitter the size of a dime. "This is in case something goes wrong, and we lose you. Put—"

"What could go wrong? You'll keep me in your line of vision, right?"

"Yes, but I don't take chances. Put the transmitter in your shoe so we'll know where you are at all times."

He slipped his shoe off and put it under the insole. He could barely feel it.

Ben Logan opened the container and removed ten bundles of hundred dollar bills and placed them in a briefcase. "The bills are in sequential order. I'm glad they didn't want it in twenties."

Joel didn't know why that was important. The money wouldn't be spent here. He nodded his agreement anyway.

Raines stuck a pen in his shirt pocket. "Hold the phone where this will pick up your conversation."

"Got it." Joel scanned the room and caught Edward's eye. His boss's gaze bore through him. "We'll get her back."

The FBI agent nodded. "We'll follow at a distance."

"Make sure no one sees you. I don't want to end up dead."

"Nor do we want you to," Ben said.

Ten minutes later Joel set the briefcase beside his feet as he waited by the phone located in the entrance to the grocery section. A steady stream of people went in and out of Walmart. Suddenly, the phone rang, and he answered it. "Hello?"

"Do you have the money?"

"Yes."

"Drive to the park. There's a pay phone located at the west entrance. Wait for my call."

The line went dead. "I hope you heard that," Joel said into the microphone. They hadn't given him an earpiece, fearing it would be seen. "I'm headed to the park."

He turned and almost ran over an older man. "Excuse me," he said, steadying the old guy.

"Watch where you're going," he snapped.

Next time he wouldn't bother apologizing. He hurried to his car and drove across town to the next rendezvous. At the park he drove through the west entrance and looked around. A pavilion was to his right. Probably a pay phone there. Just as he reached the phone, it rang, and he answered it. "Get back in your car and drive to the courthouse and park beside the statue of Stonewall Jackson. Then get out. And take your shoe off and remove the transmitter."

The line went dead.

"I hope you heard that." He glanced down at his pocket for the pen. It was gone. *The old man*. He'd picked his pocket. He was on his own.

Joel drove to the courthouse and parked in front of the statute like he'd been instructed. He scanned the area. There weren't even any walkers out and about. He climbed out of his car, and before he could get to the statue, a blue Buick pulled behind his car and the old man who had been at Walmart got out, an overcoat draped over his shoulders.

"Take your shoes off and get in."

"Why? This isn't the way we planned it."

"Plans change. Now get in." He moved the coat to reveal a gun pointed at Joel.

29

D anny stared at Ben and Eric. He and Angel had been sitting around the kitchen table while Kate made coffee when the sheriff and FBI agent and Chavez came in the back door. "What do you mean, you lost Joel?"

"First we lost the microphone signal, then at the park, the transmitter. We found his car, the briefcase with a transmitter in a pocket—all at the courthouse. The transmitter in his shoe indicated he was still at the courthouse. It's probably in a drain. The money was gone, and so was Joel."

"They knew he was wired?"

"Why would they kidnap him?"

Danny and Angel asked questions on top of each other.

Ben held up his hand. "To answer Danny—either they knew or Joel removed them. And I have no idea why they took him, if they did. My money says he's in collusion with the kidnappers." Ben looked around the room. "Where's Edward?"

"Ian called him," Danny said. "Dad's leaving later tonight, and the contract needed Edward's signature. Edward offered to go over and sign it—I think he needed to get out of the house. Said he'd be back by the time Joel returned."

"Have you checked the house for bugs?" Chavez asked.

Eric ran his hand over his head. "Gordon checked both mornings. Nothing."

Chavez shifted from one foot to the other. "Then how did the kidnappers know about the transmitters?"

Danny drummed his fingers on the table. "Like Ben said, Joel is in on the kidnappings and decided to take the hundred thousand and skip."

"Maybe," Angel said. "He could be part of the kidnapping, but if he is, would he settle for a hundred grand when a million is a good possibility?"

The Mexican sergeant nodded.

Kate set sugar and creamer on the table, then sat beside Ben while the coffee finished percolating. "Have you asked your deputies if they've seen Charlie or his pickup?"

Danny squeezed her hand. "They're looking for him, Kate. And you didn't have to make coffee. I'm sure you're worried to death."

"Making coffee is what I do. And feed people, but I don't figure anyone's hungry. I know I'm not." When the coffeepot gurgled, she filled five mugs. "Do you think the tech would like a cup?"

"Pour it," Eric said. "And I'll take it to him. He's running all the facts of this case through some software program to see if it fits any other kidnappings."

Ben stirred creamer in his coffee. "I'll go with you. I want to see how that program works."

When they were alone in the kitchen, Danny tilted his head toward Angel. "You never told me what Chavez wanted to discuss with you."

"He wanted to apologize. Some of his men arrested a couple of drug dealers with the cartel. After their interrogation, the drug dealers told him the tip about the warehouse meeting where I was shot came from a crooked cop."

"Do you believe him? I've wondered if he was the one leaking information here."

"I learned a long time ago not to make rash judgments. Time will tell exactly who Chavez is, and in the meantime, I'll watch my back."

"Good idea." Danny picked up the Bible again. He'd tried reading the thirty-ninth chapter of Job after Joel left, but he couldn't concentrate. "Kate, have you been able to figure out anything?"

"I've read it over and over. Nothing. I've even looked through every chapter that had thirty-nine verses to see if that's what she meant."

Danny picked up his notes from earlier and started to scan them when the doorbell rang. "Maybe that's Joel."

All three of them hurried to the front door, but Ben had already opened it and let Edward in.

"Not here?" he was saying. "What happened?"

"Come into the living room, and I'll fill you in."

Danny and Angel returned to the kitchen while Kate checked to see if Edward wanted coffee. Danny picked up the notepad he'd dropped and read over what he'd written—*strength*, *sword*, *hawk*, *south*, *eagle*, *nest*, *prey*. His heart jumped into his throat. *Eagle's nest*. "Angel, I think I have it!"

Angel looked up from the Bible. "What?"

Danny held the notepad where he could see it. "See—eagle, nest—Eagle's Nest. There's an old motel near the lake by the name of the Eagle's Nest. Mostly itinerant workers stay there. Haven't thought of that place in years."

"Should we tell Ben?"

"Not yet. If it pans out, we'll call him. Someone is tipping off the kidnappers, and if it isn't Joel, it can only be Edward or Chavez. Let's take a ride out there instead. After we go by the Maxwell Industries office and pick up some firepower."

■■■

Just when Bailey thought she'd scream if her dad didn't quit pacing the room like a caged lion, he stopped in front of the windows. Using his thumbnail, he scratched the paint on the window. Then he made the scratch longer. And another. What was he doing? When he connected the two, she realized he'd made an *H*.

"No!" The word came out before she could stop it. If the kidnappers saw what he'd done, they would move them and Danny would never find them.

He walked closer and whispered, "We have to do something to let the world know we're here."

He had a point. "But what if they see it?" she mouthed.

Her dad lifted his shoulders and hands, then he walked back to the window and scratched an *E*.

The lock in the joining door clicked. "Dad!" Bailey hissed.

Nodding, he pulled the flimsy drape back in place and walked away from the window.

The door swung open, and Whiskers entered the room with a package. "Something for the fever. And chicken noodle soup."

"Thank you." Bailey chewed her lip. Whiskers seemed almost human. Perhaps if she could make a connection with him, she could reason with him. "You've been kind."

His gaze bore through her. "No, I have not been kind. You are a commodity, and I must keep you in good shape. Don't read more into my actions than what they are." Without another word, he turned and returned to the other room.

Her hopes deflated. He was as cold and heartless as the other one.

She turned to awaken Maria. Where was Danny? He was coming. She knew he was. God would not abandon them.

■ ■ ■

Joel wiggled his hands, trying to work feeling back into them. He didn't know how long he'd been in the straight-back chair, blindfolded with his hands tied behind his back. Long enough for them to be numb. "Hey! Can't you at least take the blindfold off? I already know what you look like, so what's the point? Is it the money? I gave you Maria and the Adams woman. And you already have a hundred grand. We're even."

"Our orders said blindfold, so that's the way it'll be." The voice came from behind him.

"Who's giving the orders?"

"That does not concern you."

"Is he coming here?"

Silence answered. They didn't know. They were simply waiting for more orders. "How about the kid? When are you going to turn her loose? She needs to see a doctor."

"We gave her medicine for the fever."

Joel strained against the plastic zip tie that bound his hands. It didn't give at all. "Come on, guys. I helped you. You can at least loosen my hands. I don't have any feeling in them anymore."

A slight movement on his left. Someone was beside him, kneeling. Breathing garlic breath on him.

"Do you know what this is?"

Something flat and cold lay against his neck. Adrenaline pumped into his body.

"I asked you a question."

"Yes."

"Yes, what?"

"I know what it is. A knife."

"If you don't quit talking, I'm going to use it to shut you up."

30

"Where are you going?" Ben stood at the foot of the stairs, his arms crossed.

"To look for Charlie. Kate's worried about him. We won't be gone long." Danny forced himself to not look away from the sheriff's curious gaze.

Finally, he nodded. "Any idea where to look?"

"We thought we'd check out some of the places he hangs out. We'll call if we find him."

"Good deal."

Danny let out a slow breath as Ben let him pass. Angel met him at the SUV.

"Did Ben ask where you were going?" Danny asked.

Angel nodded. "Told him we needed to get out of the house."

At least they hadn't contradicted each other.

"What's the plan?" Angel asked.

"I have a 270 rifle at the office. Thought we'd swing by there, pick it up, and then go out to the motel. I know a place we can leave the SUV about a mile from it. Check and see if my binoculars are in the console."

"Yep," Angel said, holding them up.

Danny hoped to get into the plant and out without seeing anyone, but Ian caught him before he reached his office.

"What are you doing here? With Bailey, you know . . . I thought you'd be at the house where the action is."

"Yeah. We were getting claustrophobic." Danny tilted his head toward Angel. "This is Edward's nephew, Angel. My cousin Ian."

Ian held out his hand. "You've got a great uncle. Excellent businessman."

"Thank you." Angel shook Ian's hand.

Yeah, Ian would appreciate Edward's attention to detail, but Danny knew Angel's reply cost him something.

"You never said why you're here."

"I wanted to show Angel the Maxwell 270. He's never seen one of our guns."

"You'll like the 270," Ian said to Angel. "It's the company's flagship model. You won't find a better hunting rifle anywhere."

Danny nodded at Ian's long overcoat. "You look like you're on your way out, so we won't hinder you."

"I was leaving, but I'm glad I got to meet Edward's nephew. Are you returning to Mexico with your uncle and Joel?"

"No."

The terse answer subdued Ian, and after another long look at Angel, he nodded. "Well, I won't keep you boys. Good night."

When Ian was out of sight, Angel turned to Danny. "Your cousin, does he usually work on weekends?"

"My cousin works all the time. He likes money more than I do." Danny unlocked his office and flipped on the light switch. The rifle was mounted on the wall behind his desk, and he took it down.

Angel weighed it in his hands, then handed it back. "Good feel. Do you have another one?"

"Dad has one in his office. I'll be right back." He ran up the stairs to his dad's office and unlocked it, then took one of the 270s from the gun case in the corner. When he returned, he handed Angel the rifle.

Again, he weighed it then lifted it up in a firing position. "Nice balance. Is that the gun that Franks was selling to the cartel?"

"No. That was an AR15 type gun. Just as nice, though." He handed Angel a box of shells, then squared his shoulders. "Are you ready?"

Angel stood straighter. "Let's do it."

"If, ah, this doesn't turn out like we hope . . ."

"It will."

Danny walked to the door. "Then let's go."

Half an hour later, Danny parked his SUV on a dirt road near the lake. A cold-looking moon gave just enough light to shadow the trees in ghostly light. "We'll have to walk through the woods to another road, but I don't want to take a chance on them seeing our vehicle."

After ten minutes of tramping through the woods as quietly as they could, they found the other dirt road.

After another five minutes of walking, Angel pointed to a dark object off the road. "What's that?"

Danny pointed the flashlight on his phone at it. "Charlie's pickup."

"Do you think he's in it?"

Danny hoped not—the only way he'd be there was if he was dead. He shined the light inside. No Charlie. "Stuck way off the main road like this, it's no wonder none of Ben's deputies found his truck."

"You think they have him?"

"Yep." Danny pressed his lips in a grim line. Why hadn't Charlie told someone what he was thinking?

Angel glanced down the road. "Maybe it's time to call the sheriff."

"Not yet. Let's check out the motel first."

After a half mile down the dirt road, Danny veered off into the woods. "The motel is over this ridge. Once we get there, we can see the back side."

Hiking with the rifle was harder than he'd expected, and the thick undergrowth and briers snagging his clothes didn't help matters. Behind him, Angel pulled off his coat, and Danny did the same as sweat rolled off his face. At least the bare limbs allowed in enough of the light of the moon to see where they were going. At the top of the ridge, the motel came into view.

Danny counted the vehicles, most of them work trucks. An asphalt roller sat near the entrance to the motel—most of the men staying there were probably part of the highway paving crew that had been repaving the bypass around town. "If you were using that motel for a hideout, where would you be?" he asked.

"On the end," Angel answered.

He trained the binoculars on the last room. No vehicle in front of it, but maybe that was because a blue van sat parked in the middle of the last space and the next one. "Didn't Joel say the men were in a van?"

"Yeah."

Then he handed the glasses to Angel. "Tell me what else you see."

Angel scanned the lot. "Why are the windows all dark?"

"Shades, maybe?"

"No, I see light under a door or two, but absolutely nothing from the windows."

"Let me look." He peered down at the windows. Angel was right. Every window was dark. "Maybe they have them painted black?" He studied the end window. "There's a thin light coming from the last room. Looks like . . . it couldn't be writing, could it?" He handed the glasses to Angel once more.

"I think it is. Maybe an *H* . . . and an *E*." Excitement crept into his voice.

"Help," Danny said. He exchanged glances with Angel. "I think it's time to call in Ben."

"So do I." As he took out his phone, the second door from the end opened and a man stepped out.

"Do you see him?" Angel asked. "It looks like he's talking on a phone."

"Let me have the binoculars." He lifted them to his eyes in time to catch a glimpse of him before he ducked back into the room. "I've never seen him before. Did he look Hispanic?"

"Could've been. Do you think he's getting orders to do something—like kill them?"

Danny couldn't find Ben's number fast enough.

■ ■ ■

A phone rang, then a door opened, and cold air hit the right side of Joel's face before it shut. He wasn't that far from the door. The feeling had returned to his hands, and he'd been working to loosen the zip ties that bound them on a nail that protruded from one of the spindles in the back of the chair.

No more than a minute later whoever left returned. So far he'd only heard two voices—presumably the two men who'd taken Maria and Bailey.

He strained to hear the low words being spoken between the two men.

"Kill them all." His blood chilled. He'd tried to convince himself he would make it out of this alive. He didn't have much time. There had to be something he could do. Bargain, maybe?

■ ■ ■

Danny gripped the phone, waiting for Ben to answer.

"Where are you, Danny?"

"Who's there at the house?"

"What?"

Danny repeated his question. "Someone is leaking information to the kidnappers, and while it could have been Joel, I don't trust Edward or Chavez, either. Are they there?"

"As far as I know. At least they were fifteen minutes ago when I left. Now, what are you talking about?"

"You're not at the house?"

"No."

"We've found where they're keeping Bailey and Maria. We think Charlie's with them."

"What!"

"They're at the Eagle's Nest Motel. Bailey's clue refers to the twenty-seventh verse in that chapter of Job—it mentions eagles and nests. Then we found Charlie's pickup parked nearby. We think they're holding them in the end room."

"Why do you think they're at the end?"

"There's a blue van parked in front of it, and all the windows are blacked out. Looks like with paint, but someone has scratched a big *H* and an *E* on the end window."

"How do you know that hasn't been there for weeks?"

"The blue van is enough, Ben."

"You're right. Hold on a minute while I call Maggie and have her contact each deputy," Ben said. "I don't want this to go over the scanner."

Angel nudged him. "They're preparing to leave."

Danny lifted the binoculars to his eyes. Angel was right. The man who had come out earlier loaded two suitcases into the back of a blue Buick parked two spaces away from the van.

"I'm back. What's your exact location?"

Danny focused the glasses on the license plate, but it was too dark.

"Are you still there?" Ben said.

"Sorry. Yeah, I'm here. One of the men just loaded suitcases into a car. How fast can you get here?"

"I'm on my way to the motel now. Meet me at the entrance."

"I'll be there." He hung up and turned to Angel. "Stay here until you see Ben arrive and let me know if *anything* changes."

"I will."

Danny nodded. "We're going to get them."

Hiking down the ridge was faster than going up, and he reached the entrance to the motel just as Ben and eight patrol cars pulled in. Looked like he'd called in his whole department. "Where's Raines?"

"At the house, chomping to join us, but we decided he should stay with Chavez and Montoya in case Joel's not the mole. He's keeping this operation under wraps until it's over as well as a close eye on them both."

So the lawman agreed with them. Danny's phone buzzed. Angel. "What's going on?"

"You won't believe this, but there's another letter. An *L*."

Yes! His whole body responded. He'd been right. "Someone is sending us a message," he said and repeated what Angel said.

"I don't think we have a lot of time," Ben said. "I'm afraid they're going to take the hundred thousand and run."

Danny agreed, and if that's what they planned to do, they wouldn't leave anyone behind to testify. He scanned the group of men who had assembled. Wade Hatcher and a deputy Danny didn't recognize wore padded armor and carried large shields. He quizzed Ben with his eyes.

"Wade and Smitty are taking care of the door." Ben turned to his second in command. "Ty, I'll give you five men and five minutes to evacuate the rooms directly above and adjoining the two end rooms. Then we're coming in."

"There aren't any cars parked within three doors of those rooms," Danny said.

"Good. We still need to make sure. Don't want any civilians hurt." He assigned two of the deputies to stay in the office. "Tell the manager we suspect drug dealers are holed up in his motel. Don't let him use the telephone. I don't think he's part of the kidnappers, but no need to take a chance."

Ben glanced around the circle of officers, then nodded. "Let's move in place."

The men silently quick-stepped to the back of the motel. Angel was waiting for them and shook his head when Danny asked if anything new had happened.

Ben checked his watch, then motioned Wade forward. "Plant the explosive, and then move out of the way." He turned to the other deputy. "Be ready with the flash-bangs. As soon as the door blows, throw them in." He cut a hard look to Danny and Angel. "And you two stay here until it's over."

"But—"

"We have vests and you don't."

31

ook, I don't know what you're being paid, but I can double it,"
Joel said. He'd worked his brow, loosening the blindfold until
it slid down barely enough to see that he faced a black window.
He'd continued to rub the ropes against the head of the nail, and
they had loosened slightly. But not enough to slip his hands free.

A hollow laugh echoed in the room. "You cannot even pay your
gambling debts."

"I have money in an offshore bank account." He tried to keep
the desperation out of his voice.

"Then why didn't you use that money to pay your debt?"

"Because I'm not a good person. I was going to take the money
and disappear."

"Why didn't you?"

"I . . . I had to find my niece."

"An honorable thief."

"You don't have to be sarcastic. The money is yours, just let
me go." Silence greeted his plea. It was no use. These men were
going to kill him.

He had to do something. He ducked his head so he could see
more of the room. A shadowy figure moved in the dim light.

"Is it time?"

Time for what? What were they talking about?

"Not quite." The other voice came from across the room.

"Come on, let me go and I'll make it worth your while."

Garlic breath leaned in close to him. "Okay, I'm setting you free."

His heart jumped as cold steel touched his temple.

"No!" The word roared from his mouth as he jerked his head away. They might kill him but not without a fight.

He leaped forward, dragging the chair with him as he hit the floor. A bullet whizzed past his head. He kicked free of the chair and staggered to his feet. Another shot fired, and white-hot pain exploded in his chest.

■ ■ ■

Bailey finger-combed Maria's hair while her dad scratched yet another letter on the window. "Dad, you're wasting your time." With them listening, she had to be careful with her words.

"I don't think so."

"I'm hungry, Miss Bailey. Can we go home now?"

"Not yet." Maria's fever was down, thanks to the medicine. How much longer were the kidnappers going to keep them? She bolted upright as a crash came from the other room.

A gun fired, then another shot.

She froze as a bullet pierced the wall.

Charlie ran toward her. "Get into the bathroom!"

Bailey grabbed Maria and ran.

■ ■ ■

From a hundred feet away, Danny tensed as Wade moved to the door. Once the plastic explosive was on the door, Wade backed off and ran behind the shield. Behind his own shield, Smitty waited to throw in the flash-bang grenades.

Ben counted. "Five, four, three, two—"

Gunfire sounded from the room.

They were shooting the hostages! Danny took off running for the motel. Ben grabbed him just as a puff of smoke appeared on the door, followed by a boom as the door blew in. The shock wave rocked Danny back.

Smitty ran forward and threw in his grenades. Immediately there were flashes and booms almost as loud as the explosive. Ben and his deputies stormed the room. "Police! On the floor," they yelled.

More gunfire erupted. Vest or no vest, Danny was going in. Just as he reached the door, a man raced past him. Danny dropped his rifle and made a flying tackle. A solid blow hit him in the stomach. He grunted, then managed a counterpunch before Angel pulled the man off him. A deputy took over, cuffing his assailant.

Danny climbed to his feet and stepped into the smoky room. His eyes burned, and he blinked to clear them. Two men lay on the floor, and deputies were giving CPR to one of them. The other man lay facedown, handcuffed. With all the gunshots, he feared what was in the next room. He looked closer at the man they were working on. Joel. "Is he—"

One of the deputies looked up. "It doesn't look good. He took a bullet in the chest."

"There's an ambulance on the way," Ben said as he came into the room from the connecting door.

"Bailey and Maria?" Danny's heart almost stopped waiting for the answer.

Ben nodded toward the connecting door as a grin took over his face. "In there. Alive, along with Charlie."

At the door, Danny stopped and Angel bumped into him. An ambulance with its siren blaring rolled into the parking lot.

"What are you waiting for?" Angel pushed Danny aside and entered the room. "Maria!"

"Daddeeeee!"

Tears burned Danny's eyes, and this time it wasn't from the

smoke. He couldn't let himself believe they were alive until he heard Maria's squeal. He rounded the corner. "Bailey!"

She almost tackled him as she threw her arms around his neck. "I knew you'd figure it out!"

He wrapped his arms around her. "It's over, and you'll never get away from me again." Her body shook against him. "Are you cold?"

She nodded, and he slipped his coat on her, then he looked around as Ben held up a .38 Smith & Wesson. "Charlie, is this yours?"

Red crept into the older man's face. "Yeah. I lost it outside in the scuffle."

Ben handed it to him. "Well, don't shoot yourself with it."

"I think I'll take care of it until we get home," Bailey said, intercepting the gun and slipping it in the coat pocket.

"Can we go home?" Danny asked.

"I want to see Uncle Joel," Maria said. "And Tio."

Danny exchanged glances with Angel. "Tio is at Kate's." He turned to Ben. "Does everyone know Maria and Bailey are safe?"

"Not yet," Ben replied. "Thought we'd let them tell everyone in person."

"Good," Bailey said. "I can thank Mr. Montoya personally for helping us."

■ ■ ■

It was over. Finally over. Bailey leaned back in the passenger seat of Danny's SUV. "Thanks for—"

"It wasn't just me. A lot of people helped. Ben, Eric Raines—he's an FBI agent and he brought a tech, and Edward furnished the money for the ransom, but it was your clue that did it."

He glanced toward her, and the love in his eyes warmed her from the inside out.

Danny took one hand off the steering wheel and wrapped it over hers. "I'm glad the others rode back with Ben."

His touch sent tingles up her arm. Tomorrow she would have to deal with her feelings for Danny, but tonight, she would just enjoy them. "Have either of the men talked?"

Danny shook his head. "They haven't said a word. But their fingerprints came back and both belong to the Calatrava cartel in Mexico. I figure the cartel bought the guns from Franks, and killed him as well."

"We may never know the whole truth," Bailey said. "But at least it's over."

She leaned forward as he followed Ben's SUV into her parents' drive.

The inviting glow from the bed and breakfast sent a sweet tremor through her heart. God's grace was the only reason she had lived to see it again. She didn't know what her future held, but for once, that didn't matter.

Danny parked in front of the house.

"Looks like Mom's going to see Dad first." Bailey laughed as Ben's car emptied of its passengers. Angel carried Maria up the steps and into the house. To look at her now, no one would think she'd been sick or through such a trauma. Children were so resilient.

Her dad's .38 bumped her side as she and Danny climbed the steps and entered the house just in time to hear Maria squeal.

"Tio!"

Bailey heard the child's feet tap across the floor and could imagine her throwing herself into her great-uncle's arms. At least Maria still had him. Maybe Bailey would finally get to see the elusive Edward Montoya. She sniffed the air. Brownies. When her mother was worried, she baked.

"Your mom is in the kitchen with Charlie," Angel said. "Everyone else is in the living room."

Her mother and dad needed a few minutes alone. She blinked

back tears and pressed her lips together, then she took a breath. "I'd like to thank everyone for helping."

In the living room, Ben introduced her to Eric and the technician, and she thanked them. A man stood looking out the window with Maria—Edward Montoya, she supposed. He turned around, and his right hand slid into the pocket of his coat.

Her world stopped. Milliseconds became minutes. Everything receded except the man she and Elena had seen in the poppy field.

In this room.

Now.

32

Bailey's heart jackhammered in her chest, in her throat, in her ears. She could not let him know she recognized him. Without missing a beat, she summoned a smile from deep in her gut and held out her hand, praying it wouldn't tremble. "Thank you so much for being willing to provide your money." How her voice could sound normal was beyond her.

His blue eyes bored through her, and she mentally pictured a soothing beach and held his gaze. One wrong move on her part, and he'd pull out the gun that was more than likely in his pocket. *Keep it together.*

What seemed like an hour passed, then a subtle relaxing of his shoulders, and he slipped his empty hand from his pocket and clasped hers. "It was the least I could do for my Maria."

"She's a sweetheart, but I'm sure she's starving." Bailey reached for Maria, feeling the .38 again. She stilled, hoping he didn't notice the bulge in Danny's jacket that she wore. But could she use it? *Breathe.* If Edward sensed her fear . . .

"Can you smell the brownies, Maria?" She willed the girl to come to her. "Don't you want one?" For half a second Bailey wasn't sure he'd release her, then Maria wiggled loose and went into Bailey's waiting arms.

"I want a brownie."

"Angel, why don't you take her to the kitchen?" She handed Maria to him.

Maria looked over her daddy's shoulder. "Tio, come with me?"

Her nerves screamed *Run*, but instead, she turned back to Edward. *Normal. Keep it normal.* "Yes, why don't you? My mother makes great brownies."

Bailey didn't know what she'd do if he agreed. She couldn't say or do anything to alert Ben that Edward was a murderer with Maria around him.

"No, I think I'll return to the hotel now that everyone is safe."

"Okay." The child slid out of Angel's arms and ran out the door.

Bailey waited until Maria's footsteps reached the kitchen before she slipped her hand in the coat pocket. Her insides still screamed for her to run and not stop. *Please give me courage.*

"I don't think you'll be going anywhere, Mr. Montoya," she said, pulling the gun out.

His eyes narrowed, and his lips thinned.

The gun wavered, and she forced it to be still.

"Bailey, what are you doing?" Ben cried.

"You won't use that." Edward rammed his hand in his pocket.

Her hand froze on the gun. This wasn't target practice. She couldn't shoot him.

His hand came out of his pocket, the gun aimed at her.

Everything in the room faded except the gun. *He'll kill everyone here.* A dose of adrenaline shot through her veins.

"He has a gun!" she yelled and pulled the trigger. The gunshot rang in her ears as blood spurted from above his knee.

Danny dove toward him.

Too late.

He fired just as Danny kicked the gun out of his hands. The bullet whizzed by her ear and embedded in the wall.

Eric and Ben grabbed Edward and handcuffed him. Then Ben

stood and looked at Bailey. "I don't suppose you want to tell me what's going on, do you?"

"I—ah—man. Poppy field . . ." The room swam, and her knees buckled.

■ ■ ■

When Bailey came to, her mother held a cold cloth to her head. "What happened?"

"I'm afraid you fainted," her mom said.

Fainted? She wasn't the fainting kind. She raised slowly—no need to faint again. Someone had carried her to the library.

"That was a good knee shot." Her dad's smile stretched across his leathery face.

"Thanks to you." She swallowed. "Where's Edward? I didn't kill him, did I?"

"They're working on him, trying to staunch the blood. The bullet severed the artery above the knee."

"Is . . . is he going to make it?"

Her mother avoided her gaze. "Like I said, they're working on him. But if he doesn't, don't blame yourself. He would have killed you . . . and no telling who else."

Bailey leaned her head back on the couch. "He was the man in the poppy field."

"Yeah," Danny said. "Ben figured out that's what you were trying to say when you fainted."

Bailey turned as Danny sat beside her. Angel and a pale Solana came in behind him. "Where's Maria?" She didn't want the girl to see her tio on the floor, bleeding.

Angel helped Solana to a chair. "We took her to your sister's house."

"Good. I still don't understand why he wanted to kill me."

Danny put his arm around her. "Angel thinks he's El Jefe."

Angel nodded. "There's never been any indication my uncle was involved in the Calatrava drug cartel—he hid it well."

"Until I saw him in that poppy field. He knew if I identified him, the game was over." She shook her head. Edward Montoya was the head of the Calatrava drug cartel? She rubbed her forehead. "What about Joel? What's his part in it?"

"We don't know yet," Angel said.

"Do you think Edward ever loved Maria? Or was it all an act?" Danny asked.

"My uncle is not capable of loving anyone," Angel said.

Danny squeezed her hand. "How did you know Edward had a gun?"

"The way he first looked at me. He had his hand in his pocket, and it was like he was waiting for something. When I realized who he was, I was afraid he'd use Maria as a hostage, so I pretended I didn't know him."

"I doubt he would ever have felt safe as long as you were alive and might eventually remember who he was."

"Poor Elena." Tears scalded her eyes as a siren wailed from the road. Would it have made a difference if she'd reported seeing the poppy field? With the Calatrava in so many pockets, probably not. But it was something she'd have to live with.

Ben appeared at the doorway, and from the look on his face, she knew Edward was dead before he spoke.

33

A mockingbird trilled his song as Bailey and Danny walked toward the barn. Bailey inhaled deeply, taking in the scent of fresh-turned dirt from where her dad had used his tractor to break up the garden. What a difference a week made. It was still windy, but the cold weather had receded northward.

Once Joel was able to talk, he confessed his part in the kidnapping, confirming that the two men captured were the masterminds. Ben was able to pit the two against each other, and the facts began to emerge. Edward was indeed El Jefe and had told the one named Enrico where to find Danny's gun. According to the other man, Enrico killed Franks, and it had been Enrico who coerced Joel into helping them.

Danny took her hand, sending a delicious shiver up her arm. She was going to miss him when she returned to Mexico. But return she must. Besides the contract with the school, there were things she'd left undone. "I love spring in Mississippi," she said. "I'll miss our walks when I leave."

"Stay here, then."

"You know I can't."

He stopped and she stopped with him and turned so she could see his face.

Danny's face was impassive, and he'd folded his arms across his chest. "I wish you would reconsider going back to Mexico."

Bailey ignored the shiver of anxiety that crawled down her back. "I have a contract to fulfill. Besides, we need time to sort out our feelings."

"I don't. I want you to marry me." He took a small box from his pocket and opened it. "I want us to live the rest of our lives together."

Bailey pressed her lips together as she stared at the square-cut diamond. It wasn't the same ring he'd given her before. She lifted her gaze to Danny. Hope, love, fear—all were reflected in his eyes.

"It was my mother's."

Four simple words. But she knew what they cost him. He'd come to terms with his mother's death. She loved him. More than anything on this earth, she loved him. Bailey struggled to find words.

"Don't give me an answer yet," Danny said before she could speak. "Take this ring to Mexico with you. It will remind you how much I love you." He held the box out to her.

She swallowed. He knew it would be harder for her to give the ring back than to simply tell him no, she couldn't marry him. In spite of that, she took it from his hand. "I'm not making any promises, but I'll think about it."

His grin lit up his face.

Bailey held up her hand. "There's something you have to think about as well. What if God wants me to stay in Mexico? Will you still want to marry me?"

He started to speak, and she shook her head. "I'm coming back to Logan Point for a couple of weeks at the end of the school year. Let's take these next two months to think about it—and pray about it."

Slowly he nodded. "Deal."

■ ■ ■

"Come on, Daddy!" Maria yelled over her shoulder.

"We have to wait on Solana," he called back. He turned to the dark-haired woman beside him. It had been a week since she and Maria had food poisoning, and while his daughter had bounced back, Solana was just recovering her strength. "You sure you feel up to walking to the swings? You can stay at the picnic table."

"It's too beautiful and warm to just sit."

He admired her spirit and laughed, agreeing. The weather was strange in Mississippi. Freezing cold one week and 75 degrees the next, although the March wind still blew.

When they reached the swings, Maria had already climbed in one. "Push me, Daddy!"

He would never get tired of hearing her call him Daddy. He pulled her back and let go.

"Higher!"

"You sure?"

For an answer, she pumped her legs, trying to get the swing higher.

He glanced at Solana, and his heart thudded in his chest as he caught her watching them, yearning blazing in her dark eyes. Her beauty radiated from the inside out, and like a thunderbolt, the desire to know this woman who had hidden his daughter from the drug cartel almost knocked him to the ground. He held his hand out to her. "Want me to help you into the swing?"

Color tinged her cheeks. She nodded, shyness suddenly evident in her eyes.

Their hands touched, sending an electric shock up his arm, and he held her gaze. "I never thanked you properly for what you did for Maria."

She shook her head, her black hair shining in the sunlight. "I didn't do anything special."

"But you did. It took a brave person to hide Bailey and Maria."

Sadness flashed in her eyes, and she turned away from him to sit in the swing.

"Did I say something wrong?" he asked as he bent to put his hands on her shoulders. She didn't answer, only shook her head.

"Push me again, Daddy."

"Okay, baby." He gave her a gentle shove and then turned his attention back to Solana. She'd stopped the swing, and when she turned around, her cheeks were wet.

"What's the matter?"

Solana ducked her head. "Nothing. I will wait for you at the bench." She hurried to the wooden bench behind them.

He slowed the swing. "Maria, I'm going to sit with Solana for a few minutes. Okay?"

Maria nodded solemnly. "She's been sad today. Make her laugh, Daddy."

"I'll try." Not quite sure how he'd accomplish that, Angel walked to the bench and sat down.

"I'm okay," Solana told him. "You didn't have to come babysit me."

"Babysit you? I'm not that much older than you."

"What?"

"To babysit implies one person is much older than the other, like a father to a child. You do not look at me like a father, do you?"

A tiny smile tugged at her lips. She ducked her head. "No."

"Good. Now, do you want to tell me what's wrong?"

She traced an outline in the dirt with her foot. "Thinking of that day when I hid them reminds me of Juan. And the restaurant."

"Oh." Everything had changed for her, plus she'd lost a good friend. "You have had a lot of casualties lately."

"I think I must decide if I will stay in Chihuahua or go live with my sister in Arizona."

His heart sank. He had no idea she was considering leaving Mexico for good.

"I don't want to leave, but I have no job now."

"I'll give you a job." The words jumped out of his mouth.

She shook her head and lifted her tennis-shoe-clad feet. "You have already done too much for me."

"A pair of shoes and some clothes are nothing." He lifted her chin. "Would you consider being Maria's nanny?"

A mixture of emotions crossed her face. Hope, questioning, and briefly something else. Disappointment? He swallowed. "Solana, I don't know what the future holds right now. I don't know how you feel about me, but I want you to know I care very much for you."

She started to speak, but he placed his finger on her lips. "Hear me out. The past few days have been very intense, and we both need time to sort out what we feel. In the meantime, I will be going back to Chihuahua. Do you want to come with us?"

Her dark eyes never left his face. Slowly she nodded. "I would like that. Do you think Maria will be pleased if I become her nanny?"

"We'll ask her, but I'm sure she'll love it."

A grin stretched across her face. "I hope so. What will you do when you return?"

"I'm taking over Montoya Cerámica. Legally, I'm the owner, anyway. And I'm moving back into my parents' house—the one Edward kicked me out of. If you come and live there, it would be completely proper—there is a cook and a housekeeper."

"What about the drug cartel? Do you think they will allow you to operate?"

"With my uncle out of the picture, and the information from the men who were captured, we can break the back of the cartel. While they are unorganized, the merchants and factories must band together and stand up to them."

Maria hopped out of the swing and ran to the bench. "Daddy! Come go down the slide!"

"In a minute. First, I want to ask if you would like for Solana to come and live with us at Tio's house."

Her mouth formed a small O. "Is she going to be my new mommy?"

Solana had a coughing fit while Angel struggled for an answer. His daughter was much more observant than he imagined. "I, ah, I don't know. Would you like that?"

Without hesitation, Maria bobbed her head. "I like her." Her smile faded. "But I miss Tio. And Uncle Joel."

"I know, baby." Angel had told her that Tio had died and that Joel was in the hospital, but nothing of the circumstances. He would have to someday, but not today.

"Can we go see Nana Sue and Papa Joe before we leave?"

"Maybe when we come back for a visit. But for now, you can make them cards, and we'll mail them. Okay?" Joel's father had come through the surgery and was on the mend, but he was still too ill for visitors. And Angel wasn't sure how Joel's mother would handle a visit from them right now.

Maria tilted her head. "When are we going home?"

"Tomorrow."

She lifted her shoulders and let out an exaggerated sigh. "Good. I miss my friends at kindergarten." She grabbed his hand. "Come on, let's go down the slide. You too, Solana."

Angel glanced down at Solana and took her hand. "Game for it?"

With shining eyes, she nodded. "I think I can handle anything you two throw at me."

Laughing, he pulled her up. He wasn't sure where their relationship was headed, but he knew it would be an adventure.

34

Candlelight flickered on the table as Bailey held up her glass to touch Angel's and Solana's. A diamond sparkled on Solana's left hand. "I'm so happy for both of you."

"Wait, I want to do it too!" Maria lifted her water glass up, and they all lowered theirs to touch hers. "To my new mommy."

Their glasses clinked, and Bailey smiled at the glowing couple. She'd enjoyed watching their relationship grow over the past two months, but seeing their love made her ache for Danny. At least she would be seeing him by the end of the week when she returned to Mississippi for a visit. A tremor went through her as she thought of the decision she'd made to remain in Mexico.

But first, she had a trip to make to Valle Rojo. She looked up as she realized Solana had asked her something.

"When do you leave for Mississippi?" Solana repeated.

"Friday."

Maria climbed up in Bailey's lap and put her hands on either side of her face. "Don't go back to Mississippi."

"I have to, but I'll be back."

"Soon?"

"Soon."

Satisfied, Maria returned to her seat. "Is Uncle Danny coming back with you?"

"I don't know."

■ ■ ■

The next morning, Bailey arranged for a driver to take her to Valle Rojo. Miguel, her usual driver, was no longer in Chihuahua, and she wondered if he'd been part of the cartel. Her new driver was Arturo. She felt bad that he didn't have family in the area as Miguel had—it would probably be a boring day for him. After a few unsuccessful attempts to draw her into conversation, he'd given up.

She wanted to use the two-hour drive to rehearse what she'd say to the pastor at the church. The board in Mexico had made it plain that he had to approve before they could reassign her to the village. But first, she wanted to visit Elena's grave.

It should not have taken her two months to go to the village. She'd been busy, for sure, but busyness had only been an excuse for not facing Elena's mother . . . and Father Horatio.

Just thinking about him dried her throat, but she knew she had to confront him if she was to get on with her life. He had to know he couldn't run her off again. Scratch that. *She* had to know. They rounded a bend in the road, and Valle Rojo came into sight. It was a small village with scattered wooden structures, many that would be condemned in the States. But some of the houses, like the one Elena's mother lived in, were adequate. The church was at the end of the road, and she pointed it out. "I'll get out there," Bailey said.

"Is that where you want me to pick you up?"

"Yes. I'll call you."

Bailey walked inside the church, surprised to hear the chattering of women coming from the back room. Curious, she walked that way, passing the pastor's office. It was empty. When she opened the door to where they held church services, the sight of at least ten women with open Bibles and the pastor at the lectern dropped her mouth open. They had continued the Bible classes, even after Elena was killed. One of the women—Gabriela—spied her. "Bailey!" she squealed. Then in rapid Spanish, she cried, "Look who's here. She's come back!"

Pastor Carlos grinned when he saw her and motioned her in. "Bailey, it is good to see you!"

The women gathered around her, but Bailey had eyes for only one of them. Claudia, Elena's mother. The women parted and allowed Bailey to walk to where Claudia waited.

She swallowed down the lump that threatened to choke her and took the older woman's hands. "I'm so sorry about Elena."

Tears filled Claudia's eyes and ran down her cheeks. "She was so brave."

Bailey drew her in an embrace, and they both stood, weeping in each other's arms.

"She was a good daughter and mother," Claudia said as she took a tissue from one of the other women.

"She was a good friend. Can you take me to where she's buried?"

At first, Bailey thought she might refuse, then she nodded. "It's not far. Then we come back here and talk."

"Yes, I would like that."

They walked to the edge of town to the small cemetery. From Elena's grave, Bailey could see the mountains in every direction. Her friend would approve of the site. She stared at the simple tombstone, her anger building. "Is Father Horatio in jail?"

"No. There is no proof he killed her. The local authorities are saying it was the Calatrava."

"Where is he?"

"Gone."

He couldn't be. She wanted to confront him, tell him she was returning to the village, and this time he was not running her off. "What do you mean, gone?"

"Word went through the village that he was responsible for my Elena's death, and that night someone burned his house down."

Bailey turned so she could see Claudia's face. "Do you know who did it?"

She shrugged. "No, and I don't want to."

"Do you think he's dead?"

"No. He left with some of his thug friends. And he will not be back."

Bailey didn't know whether to be disappointed or relieved. She brushed dust from the headstone. She would come back tomorrow before she returned to Chihuahua. "How is the church? The women who came to the tea parties?"

Claudia smiled. "Very good. Gabriela stepped into Elena's shoes after . . ."

"The pottery classes—how about them?"

"Gabriela again. She has grown up." Claudia lowered her voice. "I think she has her sights set on Pastor Carlos."

"No!"

She nodded, her lips pursed. "They will make a good team."

A team that would not need Bailey. Was God closing a door? She walked back to the church, her footsteps heavy.

Claudia grabbed her hand. "Come in—the women are anxious to show you what we've been studying and some of the clay pots we've made."

Bailey allowed the older woman to pull her inside the plank building and down the hall where the women waited. She listened as Gabriela explained in her soft voice how they were studying the letters Paul wrote to Timothy. Excitement lit the young woman's eyes.

"Come see the pots we have made."

Bailey followed her to a small building. She caught her breath at rows and rows of brightly colored pots of all sizes. "They're beautiful."

"Some are coils and some are pinch pots, and these"—she pointed to several tall cylindrical vases—"are made using the kick wheel. But now we don't know what to do with them."

Bailey stared at the work the women had turned out. In the right hands—Danny's hands—the women could make some real money. "I think I might be able to help. But it will take a couple of weeks before I'll know."

"That would be wonderful."

■ ■ ■

Danny scanned the skies as he crossed the border into Mexico. He couldn't wait to get on the ground and find Bailey. He smiled, imagining the look on her face when he showed up at her apartment. She was coming home in five days, but he hadn't been able to wait another day to see her.

And he was anxious to see Angel. His friend had emailed him last night that he'd asked Solana to marry him and she'd accepted. Maybe they could have a double wedding. No, Bailey would probably want to get married in Logan Point.

But what if she wanted to live in Mexico? He'd prayed like she asked, and he'd kept reading the Bible that Kate gave him. And it had changed his heart. But was he willing to give up everything he knew to serve God in . . . wherever? It was one of the reasons he'd jumped in his plane and flown to Mexico.

Maybe once he was there, he could see what made Bailey want to be there. And that was the vibe he'd gotten lately. That she wanted to return to Valle Rojo. Did the small village even have electricity and running water?

Two hours later, he parked the rental car outside Bailey's apartment building and bounded up the steps to the second floor and her apartment on the end. He knocked on the door and then smiled in anticipation of her opening the door. Except she didn't open the door. Two doors down, a young Mexican woman came out of her apartment with a basket of clothes, and he called out to her.

"Uh, do you know where Miss Adams is?" he asked in Spanish.

The woman set her basket down and approached him. Her wary expression gave way to a smile. "You are Danny!"

He stepped back. "Um, yeah, but how did you know?"

"She has your photo on the table. And she talks about you."

Good, he hoped. "Do you know where I can find her?"

"She went to somewhere in the mountains—the village where she used to teach. I don't remember the name."

"Valle Rojo?"

"Yes. That is it."

"Do you know how long she was going to be there?"

"A day or two."

Air whooshed from his lungs. He should have let her know he was coming. "Thank you."

He trudged back to his car and climbed in. Maybe Angel knew where the village was. He fished his cell phone from his pocket and dialed his number.

"Hello?" Angel's voice was guarded.

"It's me, Danny. How are you, my friend?"

"Danny! Where are you?"

"In front of Bailey's apartment, unfortunately."

"But she's in Valle Rojo."

"I know that now. Do you know how to get there?"

"Yes, but it is a two-hour drive."

"Could I land my plane there?"

Angel laughed. "Only if you are ready to die. Come to the plant and we will discuss how to get you there."

■ ■ ■

Later that evening, Bailey walked through the village, enjoying the peace and tranquility that had not been there before. Even the men seemed more friendly. Too bad it was a good-bye walk.

With deliberate steps, she made her way out of town and to the cemetery, where she stood at Elena's grave again. She wished she had a bouquet of flowers to leave.

Bailey knelt beside the grave marker. "I feel I failed you," she whispered. "I hope you can see what you started and how it's grown. Your friends are doing so well, I don't think I'm needed here. So I guess this is good-bye."

She slipped the ring box from her pocket and opened it. The diamond glittered against the velvet, and she took it out of the box. Peace filled her heart. She took a deep breath and slipped the ring on her finger. No doubts plagued her. She sat quietly for a while longer, then stood and brushed the dirt from her knees.

She turned and gasped. "Danny?"

She must be seeing things. She blinked to clear her eyes, but he was still there, walking toward her. She ran to him, and he opened his arms.

"I hope you're not upset, but I couldn't wait another day to see you."

She lifted her face. "I would never be upset with you. I'm so glad you're here."

Danny's gaze slid to her hand, and his breath hitched. He looked into her eyes. "Are you sure?"

Bailey bit her lip and nodded. "I love you, and I would be honored to be your wife."

His lips captured hers, and she slid her arms around his neck, kissing him back with all her heart.

Acknowledgments

As always, to God, who gives me the words.

To my family and friends, who believe in me.

To my editors at Revell, Lonnie Hull DuPont and Kristin Kornoelje, thank you for making my stories so much better. To the art, editorial, marketing, and sales team at Revell, thank you for your hard work. You are the best!

To my agent, Mary Sue Seymour, thank you for believing in me.

To my readers, thank you for taking a chance on a new writer and then coming back for my other stories.

Patricia Bradley is a published short story writer and is cofounder of Aiming for Healthy Families, Inc. Her manuscript for *Shadows of the Past* was a finalist for the 2012 Genesis Award, winner of a 2012 Daphne du Maurier Award (first place, Inspirational), and winner of a 2012 Touched by Love Award (first place, Contemporary). When she's not writing or speaking, she can be found making beautiful clay pots and jewelry. She is a member of American Christian Fiction Writers and Romance Writers of America and makes her home in Corinth, Mississippi.

Meet
Patricia
BRADLEY
www.ptbradley.com

 @PTBradley1